A Kendall O'Dell Mystery

FORBIDDEN
ENTRY

CONTINUE TO FOLLOW THE
SUSPENSE-FILLED ADVENTURES OF
FEISTY, FLAME-HAIRED REPORTER
KENDALL O'DELL

#1 Deadly Sanctuary

NOW A FEATURE FILM!

#2 The Devil's Cradle

#3 Dark Moon Crossing

#4 Seeds of Vengeance

ALSO BY SYLVIA NOBEL
Chasing Rayna
A Scent of Jasmine

Published by
Nite Owl Books
Phoenix, Arizona

Visit Our Website:
WWW.NITEOWLBOOKS.COM
to Read the First Chapter of each Book and for
Updates on Book Signing Appearances or
New Releases by the Author.

Print Books and eBooks are available through
most retail book outlets and online bookstores.

A Kendall O'Dell Mystery

FORBIDDEN ENTRY

SYLVIA NOBEL

Nite Owl Books

Phoenix,
Arizona

Phoenix, Arizona

This is a work of fiction. The characters, incidents, and dialogues are products of the author's imagination and are not to be construed as real. Any resemblance to actual events or persons, living or dead, is entirely coincidental.

For information, contact Nite Owl Books
2850 E. Camelback Road, #185
Phoenix, Arizona 85016-4311
Phone: 602-840-0132
Fax: 602-277-9491
E-mail: Niteowlbooks@cox.net
www.niteowlbooks.com

ISBN 978-0-9839702-4-8

Original Cover Photo – Patrick Lange

Cover Design by
Christy A. Moeller, *ATG Productions*
Phoenix, Arizona

Library of Congress Control Number: 2014954997

ACKNOWLEDGMENTS

Linda Jackson, *Prescott National Forest, District Ranger*
Cynthia Barrett, *Law Enforcement Ranger, BLM*
Dr. Laura C. Fulginiti, PhD, D-ABFA,
Forensic Anthropologist, Phoenix, AZ
Harold Linder, *Exploration Geologist*
Tina Williams, *Editorial Services*
Donna Jandro, *Editorial Services*
Jon Young, *State Chief Ranger, BLM*
Kevin Weldon, *Geologist, Prescott National Forest*
Toby Cook,
Assistant Fire Mgt. Officer, Prescott National Forest
Jerry Elian,
Fire Prevention Tech, Prescott National Forest
Cathy Cordes
Miner Bob
Kelly Powell, *Manager, Bumble Bee Ranch*
Tom & Lynn Miller, *G & S Gravel, Inc. Mayer, AZ*
Bradshaw Mountain Guest Ranch, *Crown King, AZ*
Gary Mackey, *Dobson Plant Manager, Mesa, AZ*
Manny Mungaray, *Plant Manager, Arizona Metro Mix*
Patrick Lange, *Cover Photo*
Taryn Holman
Teah Anders
Lee Ann Sharpe
Kelly Scott-Olson and Christy A. Moeller,
ATG Productions, Phoenix, AZ

**My husband, Jerry C. Williams, for his patience,
support and countless hours spent accompanying me on
my research trips around the beautiful state of Arizona.**

To my Loving Family,
Cherished Friends
and
Devoted Fans

Thank you for your continuing
encouragement, patience
and support

Dedicated to the memory of:
Elizabeth Bruening Lewis

Mentor,
treasured friend,
#1 cheerleader

CHAPTER

1

Energetic music thumped from the speakers, fueling my already upbeat mood. I pressed the accelerator of my spanking-new, lime green Jeep a little harder, relishing the instantaneous response. Oh yeah. Sweet. Cruising along the two-lane road that sliced through the cactus-strewn landscape, I sipped hot vanilla-laced coffee and marveled at the sight of the vast desert panorama enveloped in a thick layer of ground fog—a rare occurrence that added an interesting dimension to the ordinarily parched Arizona topography. A shadowy platoon of moisture-plumped saguaro cactus stood at attention alongside the road, accentuating the eerie scene. Awesome.

But I knew it wouldn't last long. According to the local weather forecast, it was slated to be another picture-perfect day with afternoon temperatures climbing to the low-seventies. Having spent the first twenty-eight winters of my life in damp, chilly Pennsylvania, I was still getting accustomed to flowers blooming, green grass and the luxury of sunbathing outdoors in the middle of December. Hard to believe nine months had already passed since I'd been flattened by acute asthma, dumped by my fiancé, then made the agonizing decision to quit my job at the *Philadelphia Inquirer* and head west to the small town of Castle Valley. To say there had been a lot of changes in my life would be the understatement of the century. But happily I had a new job, a new love, and the scorching Arizona heat had apparently baked away the majority of my debilitating symptoms, although extreme stress or a preponderance of cigarette smoke would sometimes set me off again.

I cracked the window slightly and inhaled the rain-cleansed air saturated with the rich aroma of damp earth, creosote and greasewood. How great was this? The epic storm that had pounded Arizona for six days had finally blown away during the night. Even though I'd enjoyed the welcome rainfall and even a few snow flurries, my prayers for clear weather had been answered. At least for the next few days. The ten-day forecast called for another Pacific storm to move in, but I consoled myself with the fact that there was a chance it could be wrong. I'd been looking forward to this particular day for months. I wanted it to be absolutely perfect. So far, so good.

I glanced eastward at the snow-covered ridgeline and drew in a breath of sheer delight. Pastel pink clouds, crisscrossed by brilliant streaks of magenta jet contrails, stood out in sharp relief against the pale turquoise light of dawn. Mesmerizing! With difficulty, I dragged my gaze away to refocus on the road, accelerating past a slow-moving cattle truck, one of the few vehicles I'd encountered since leaving home. But then, how much traffic would there be on a Thursday morning? I'd checked road conditions several times online and made the decision to avoid what seemed to be perpetual road construction on the I-17 freeway. No sense getting caught in that annoying snarl of congestion if I could avoid it. No. Not today. My schedule was too full to risk even the slightest delay. I'd be smart and take surface streets. At this rate I'd easily make it to Phoenix by nine o'clock, have a couple of hours to complete my 'to-do' list from Ginger, meet my friend Fritzy for lunch and still make it to the airport in plenty of time to pick up my parents and younger brother, Sean. Things were finally going my way and I was determined that, for once, everything would go according to plan.

My pulse ramped up again at the thought of actually seeing my family in the flesh, instead of merely Internet FaceTime. What would they think of my new home? I could hardly wait to show off the majestic beauty of Arizona's deserts, mountains and red-rock canyons. But, best of all would be having them and all my newfound friends gathered to celebrate my engagement to Tally. Or, as Ginger constantly reminded me, *'Dumplin' you've nabbed yourself the finest lookin' stud in the whole dang state!'* And she was right. Envisioning Tally's sharply-chiseled features, serious brown eyes and the impressive picture he presented sitting tall and lean in the saddle as he galloped across the countryside on one of his prize Appaloosa horses, sparked a pleasurable tingle. But there was a flip side to my euphoria. What would my family think of this steadfast, pragmatic rancher who, at times, seemed to personify my polar opposite? I felt sure Tally and my dad would hit it off famously, but doubted my mother's reaction would be as enthusiastic. From day one she'd been critical of my choice to remain in Arizona and marry, as she often derisively remarked, 'a backwoods middle-aged cowboy.' Never mind that he owned the Starfire Ranch, one of the largest cattle and horse ranches in the state. No, she still had her heart set on me returning to cosmopolitan Philadelphia to reconcile with my former boss, mentor and fiancé, Grant Jamerson, who also happened to be the son of her new best friend, Phyllis. To my mother's credit, she had devoted a significant amount of time and energy planning a grand wedding for us only to see her dreams go down the tubes. I felt confident that once she'd met Tally, he would win her over, but my stomach shrank when I visualized my family's first encounter with his aggravating mother. Oh boy. What would they think of Ruth Talverson, a ditsy, pill-popping, chain-smoking emotional and mental basket case if there ever was one? Not wishing to add fuel to the fires of my mother's long list of objections to Tally, I had not shared with them just how off-the-wall she could be sometimes, but in retrospect, perhaps I should have. With luck, maybe she'd be in a mellow frame of mind while they were here. One could only hope.

My cell and car phone rang simultaneously and I glanced at the screen on the dashboard. Curious. Why would Ginger be calling me at the crack of dawn? I pressed the TALK button on the steering wheel. "Yes, ma'am, what can I do for you?"

"That you, Sugar?"

"Yep."

"Yep? I swear, the longer you hang around Tally, the more you're gittin' to sound like him."

Tally was known as a man of few words, unlike me,

and most certainly a galaxy removed from Ginger's ultra-chatterbox persona. "What's up, girlfriend?"

"Oh, I just wanted to add one or two things to the list." Odd. Her voice sounded lackluster, totally devoid of its usual vitality.

"What are you doing at the office so early?" I asked, banking into a series of gentle hairpin turns.

"Gittin' a jump on the day." She exhaled a long, vocal yawn. "Mercy me, I'm as tired as an ol' yeller dog on a hot summer day."

I loved her colorful Texas idioms. "How come? It's pretty early for that."

"Couldn't sleep. Finally gave up tryin' and figured I might as well get my butt in here and catch up on some of this here filing I been putting off for the past couple of months."

More like a year, I thought, considering the sizeable tower of folders piled on the credenza behind her desk. I slowed and splashed through a mud puddle spanning the dip in the road. A lot of good it had done to wash the Jeep. "So, why couldn't you sleep?"

"Because Aunt Marcelene phoned me kinda late last night and I..."

I cut in, "Speaking of your lovely and generous aunt, I owe her big time for arranging such a super deal on the rooms for my family." Recently remodeled, the Desert Sky Motel reflected the true charm of the Old West. I loved the heavy, rough-hewn furniture, cowboy art and colorful patchwork quilts complementing each four-poster bed.

"Yeah, she's a peach, ain't she?"

"She sure is." I had to admire the woman's tenacity.

5

She'd had a rough year after losing her husband to cancer. She had busied herself restoring the formerly shabby motel as well as the cottage next door where she lived with her daughter, Jenessa, a talented young pianist who was scheduled to play at our engagement party.

Silence. And more silence. Very un-Ginger like. "Okay. So, why'd Marcelene call you so late?"

"She's worried sick about Jenessa. She was bawlin' her head off and she got me so riled up I got to bawlin' with her."

"What about Jenessa?"

"She and Nathan, that new boyfriend of hers, they took off on a campin' trip ten or eleven days ago and shoulda been back day before yesterday. They ain't showed up yet and no one's heard word one from them."

"Well...the weather has been pretty awful. Did she call the sheriff's office to report them missing?"

"I think so. But...they're both real experienced hikers and they had plenty of supplies. There's just no good reason they ain't home yet." Ginger's voice quavered slightly and I grew uneasy. Her account sounded uncannily similar to the story I'd unearthed less than a month ago regarding a local judge. He'd disappeared while hunting in the midst of the biggest November snowstorm the state had experienced in a decade. The subsequent discovery of his mutilated body had horrified the community. But even more bizarre was the judge's unexpected connection to Tally's family and the tragic consequences that followed. I reassured myself with the knowledge that hikers were constantly getting lost in the Arizona wilderness for a host of reasons, so I refrained from voicing my misgivings. "If they're seasoned hikers, they're probably fine. But, I hope they weren't camping above the six-thousand-foot-level or they might be stranded in the snow."

"I know," she answered, her tone hollow, despondent. "Aunt Marcelene said Jenessa told her they was headin' out into the boonies to camp someplace way back yonder in the mountains for a couple of days and then they planned to rent quads in Crown King and go exploring."

During one of our statewide sightseeing trips, Tally had driven me to the old mining town situated high in the Bradshaw Mountains. The sometimes deeply rutted dirt road, fashioned from the remains of the old railroad bed, zigzagged its way straight up the mountainside. It had been a rather harrowing journey along a road replete with dizzying switchbacks tracking above sheer cliffs, along with stomach- dropping views and few guardrails. I remember feeling a huge rush of relief when we finally arrived at the Crown King Saloon located in the center of the isolated forest community. "Well," I said with forced cheerfulness, "looks like it's going to be a beautiful, clear day. Hopefully they'll be searching for them by air, so try to stay optimistic."

"I'll try." Before hanging up, she added two additional items to my list of things to pick up at the party store. Sad. I'd never heard Ginger sound so grim, her usual effervescent personality and infectious giggle glaringly absent.

Her obvious distress dampened my spirits, but then I thought of how blessed I was to have found a jewel of a friend like Ginger King. Not more than two minutes had elapsed from the first time she'd heard the news that Tally kissed me until my fun-loving friend, who had become like the sister I never had, began planning our nuptials. She'd enthusiastically made it her mission in life to make sure my engagement party and subsequent wedding would be the biggest social events in the history of Castle Valley. Good thing. Having survived a first brief, ill-fated marriage, I'd have just as soon skipped all the fuss and eloped to Las Vegas. But she wouldn't hear of it and insisted on handling all of the details.

When the first fiery rays of the rising sun streamed over the rough spine of the mountain range, I grabbed for my sunglasses. Arizona's dramatic sunrises and sunsets never ceased to evoke within me a feeling of awe. Within minutes the landscape was awash in shimmering light, transforming the ghostly silhouettes of saguaro cactus into glorious golden pillars. Ever so slowly, the radiant glow slid across the rolling hills, banishing the mist and chasing the shadows from the rocky crevices.

Forty minutes later, I zoomed across the freeway overpass, joining the cavalcade of cars heading towards metropolitan Phoenix. Even though traffic slowed at times, it was nothing compared to the miles long backup choking the Interstate construction zone. I congratulated myself on the decision to avoid it, only to have my triumphant mood squashed a mere three miles further. My heart dropped at the sight of the orange and white highway markers. Not today, please! I slowed to a crawl and then a complete stop. Crap. I gripped the steering wheel. "Un-friggin'-believable!" Go. Stop. Move a few feet. Stop. I drummed my fingers and strained to see beyond the seemingly endless procession of vehicles. Feeling trapped and helpless, I forced myself to breathe deeply. *Temper, hold your temper, O'Dell.*

Hopefully, it was just a temporary delay. Okay! We were moving! I edged forward a few feet, then several more, but traveled no faster than five miles an hour. The irony of the situation hit me as I drifted past a sign indicating the recommended speed limit of 55. "I wish!" I glanced at the clock again and did some swift mental calculations. If I continued the rate of five to ten miles per hour, it would take me...what, five or six more hours to reach Phoenix? That would ruin the entire day—no shopping, no lunch with Fritzy and my family would be left stranded at the airport.

Fidgeting restlessly in my seat, I checked out the traffic alert apps on my phone, but none confirmed the backup. After watching several bicyclists in brightly colored gear glide past, I growled, "Damn it!" and opened the door. I stood on the running board and peered into the distance, trying to make out what could possibly have traffic tied up to this degree but couldn't see anything but a sea of cars and trucks ahead. Several other people had exited their vehicles and were milling about pointing, talking, walking their dogs. With a loud groan, I slumped into the driver's seat and reached for my phone to dial Fritzy's work number. I'd been looking forward to our meeting for two weeks and hated to disappoint her, but unless a miracle happened, lunch looked like a wash at this point. Oh wait. We were moving again. Perhaps there was still hope. I waited to hit the call button and reached the thrilling speed of fifteen miles per hour before I had to slam on the brakes again. Craning my neck, I spotted a signalman ahead with one of those SLOW/STOP signs in hand. A dump truck was backed into the middle of the road where half a dozen workmen stood leaning on their shovels. How long was this going to take? It appeared that my well-laid plans for the day were going up in smoke. "Oh, come on!" I finally shouted. "Fix the stupid road tomorrow!"

Should I make a U-turn and head back towards the

freeway? Would I be trading one traffic backup for another? I spotted a second group of bicyclists heading towards me, this time from the opposite direction. I shouted out the open window as they approached. "Hey! Got any idea what's going on up ahead?"

One of the riders slowed, thumbed behind him and shouted, "Rollover crash! Cave Creek Road intersection… medical chopper on the way."

Oh. So it wasn't just road construction. So much for the phone app. "Thanks!" I watched wistfully as the bikers raced on by, free as the flock of birds flying overhead. I hit the call button on my phone. No response. What? Then I noticed *No Service* blinking back at me. Groaning, I laid my forehead against the steering wheel. I waited another interminable amount of time and had just made the decision to make the U-turn and deal with the freeway, when I heard the thumping whir of helicopter blades. The chopper flew in low and descended to the ground a mile or so ahead. At that moment it struck me that someone or perhaps more than one person must be gravely injured or worse. And as that realization sunk in my agitation diminished. So I was going to be a little late. How lucky was I not to be lying on the ground or trapped in the crushed, twisted remains of my vehicle? So I might not get the place card holders Ginger wanted, or the three-dozen bud vases. So I might miss lunch. I was fine. As I sat there, engine idling, I savored the warmth of the sun on my face and the fragrant breeze shepherding fluffy white clouds across the sapphire sky. All a matter of perception, I guess. A half hour later when the chopper rose into the air, speeding southeast towards Phoenix, traffic began inching forward again. All right! I might just make it after all.

The voice message alert on my phone chimed. I tapped the screen and listened to Fritzy's husky voice, smiling at the nickname she'd given me in third grade. "Hey, Stick, call me when you get this message."

Was I imagining the somber undertone in her voice? That didn't sound promising. I dialed her number. "You have reached the office of forensic anthropologist Dr. Nora Fitzgerald Bartoli. Please leave a message and I'll return your call."

Dang it. I tapped her number. Two rings later I heard, "Hey there, Stick, how you doing?"

"I've been stuck in traffic for over an hour so I'm going to be late for lunch."

"Don't sweat it. Turns out I have to cancel anyway."

My perfect day was swiftly vanishing. "Oh, don't tell me that! Why?"

"Sorry to back out on such short notice, but I just got a call from the Yavapai County Sheriff's Office. They've got a couple of bodies they need me to take a look at and I'm already on the road."

I tried to stifle my extreme disappointment. "That's not good news. Where are you headed?"

"Working my way north on I-17 going about ten miles an hour. Traffic is a bitch."

"Tell me about it. I took the Carefree Highway thinking it would be faster but I ran into road construction plus a bad accident. Smart, huh?"

"I'd have probably done the same thing. Guess we'll have to hook up at your party. So...what time does your family get in today?"

I looked at the digital clock. "Two-fifteen, but

11

judging how the day has gone so far, I'd better check and see if the flight is on time."

"You might want to do that. I heard there's some pretty nasty weather back east."

"I know. I sure hope it's nice while they're here."

"How long are they staying?" she asked.

"Two weeks."

"Cool. And you're going to get that whole time off work?"

"That's my plan. I've got their sightseeing itinerary all mapped out. Saturday we're going to Prescott for breakfast, lunch in Jerome, Sunday we'll stop in Flagstaff and then we'll be on to the Grand Canyon. Tuesday we take a Jeep tour in Monument Valley, Wednesday, Canyon de Chelly, then lunch and sightseeing in Sedona on our way back home on Thursday. After the party, we'll head to southern Arizona for a few days with the rest of the family."

"Wow! Ambitious schedule. Sounds like a blast. I'm jealous. I've been so darn busy working, there are still a ton of places in Arizona I've yet to see. Oh well, someday. Hey, I'm looking forward to reconnecting with your family at the party. It's been ages."

"They're excited about seeing you too."

"Good." She paused and added, "Hey, Stick, I'm sorry about cancelling on you."

"I understand. Where did you say you were going?"

"Northwest of Black Canyon City to a place called Bumble Bee. I'm meeting the sheriff there."

Bumble Bee. I vaguely remembered passing through the tiny community during the sightseeing trip with Tally. "Can you share any details?"

"Not yet."

"Off the record?"

A short pause. "I can tell you this much. Early this morning a BLM ranger or a Forest Service ranger, or both, I can't remember exactly, reported that one of the locals had discovered the bodies of two people somewhere in the Bradshaw Mountains, but I can't divulge any other details until family has been notified."

Two people. In the Bradshaws. A pang of uneasiness nudged my gut. Why would the authorities call Fritzy in unless there was something out of the ordinary? "Ah…it wouldn't happen to be a young man and woman?"

Her ultra-long hesitation was more revealing than her eventual answer. "I…I can't answer your question at this point."

"Fritzy," I asked, unable to subdue my rising sense of urgency, "can you tell me where the bodies were discovered?"

"The sheriff said about a mile from a place called Raven Creek."

"Where's that?"

"Don't know for sure…wait a sec. We're at a dead stop. Let me look at the map on my navigation system."

I listened to silence for a least a minute before she murmured, "Um…okay, it looks like Raven Creek is out in the middle of nowhere northwest of Cleator and about ten miles northeast of Crown King."

As the full significance of her words sunk in, I felt like someone had jammed a fist into my belly. Oh no! My mind and heart did not want to go there but my instincts told me otherwise. What were the odds that the two dead people could be anyone other than Jenessa and Nathan?

CHAPTER
2

The traffic jam finally broke free as I snaked my way into Phoenix along with the thousands of other people who'd been stalled on the road for almost three hours. So far, the day was turning out to be far different than I'd imagined and I had to fight a sensation of gloom. Fritzy's revelation was too much of a coincidence to ignore. My finger was poised over Ginger's number, but I hesitated. Don't put the cart before the horse, my wise grandmother used to tell me. Why upset her and Marcelene needlessly? I had nothing to go on but a hunch, but the uncomfortable feeling persisted. Against my nature, I urged myself to be patient, wait for more information and verification of identity.

Twenty minutes later, I pulled into the shopping center, found what I needed at the party store, made a quick lunch stop and then checked the plane's arrival time on my phone. Fortunately for me, bad weather had delayed the flight from Pittsburgh, so I had a little breathing room. As usual, Sky Harbor International Airport was an annoying zoo of traffic. I circled the parking garage several times until I eventually snagged a space on the 4th floor. Then, it took me another fifteen minutes to get to the terminal where the "arrived" sign for their flight number blinked. I sighed with relief. Even with the three-hour traffic delay, I'd made it.

As the passengers flooded into the terminal, I searched faces until I finally spotted my mother holding a carry-on bag in one hand, her purse and heavy winter coat in the other. I could tell by her sour expression as she emerged from the gate area that something was bugging her. The corresponding smirk on my brother's face conveyed the initial impression that he'd most likely been the cause of her aggravation. But knowing how hard-headed they both were—we all were for that matter—and knowing how hypercritical my mother could sometimes be, I felt instant sympathy for my younger brother. Apparently the old adage, 'absence makes the heart grow fonder' is true, because I was genuinely happy to see them. I loved them all fiercely, even with their numerous imperfections, of which I certainly was not exempt. My mother turned to my brother, Sean, mouthed something I could not hear and his expression turned sullen. What in the world was going on? My initial curiosity as to the cause of their disagreement faded at the first glimpse of my father's ruddy face and a wave of elation washed over me. But, my joyful anticipation turned to dismay when I noticed the crutches and the black boot on his right foot. I rushed towards him.

"Kendall!" My mother intercepted and enfolded me in one of her not overly effusive embraces. "It's been such a long time!"

"I know!" I said, hugging her back before she

suddenly pushed me to arm's length.

"Look at you!" she marveled with a concerned frown. "You are so tan. And you have freckles on your nose. You're getting way too much sun. That is not good for your skin. Aren't you wearing any sunscreen?" Before I could respond, she concluded with, "You must take better care of your skin or your face will wrinkle like an old prune."

I bit back a testy rejoinder. How typical of her to greet me with a disapproving remark. "I'm fine, Mom. Really." In direct contrast, my family looked pale. My dad always joked that her blue-blooded English ancestry was the basis for her cool façade and the older I got, the more merit his theory seemed to hold. She had always been less approachable than my dad and definitely lacked the fiery Irish disposition that I inherited from the O'Dell side of the family.

"Let me see the ring." She grabbed my left hand, her immediate expression of disenchantment predictable and mildly amusing. "Oh my. It looked so much bigger in the photos you sent." A raised brow accompanied her thin-lipped smile and it was hard to miss the trace of sarcasm in her critique.

I knew she was comparing it to the enormous and pretentious ring Grant had bought for me. "Mom, it's two-carats. What do you want?"

"Oh, it's fine. It's fine. And as long as you're not disappointed, I guess that's all that counts," she responded airily. Her calculated barb made me feel right at home and I cautioned myself against giving it right back to her. "So, I'm assuming you've set the wedding date?" she inquired, still scrutinizing my ring.

"Not yet. Let's all get through this engagement party

first, okay? But, just so you know, it will probably be within a year."

"Hey, Kenny." Sean intervened, flashing me a conspiratorial grin before wrapping me in a bear hug, which I returned whole-heartedly. In the nine months since I'd seen him last, he looked more mature, seemed leaner and his once lush strawberry blond hair was cropped close to his head. It was also hard to miss the new skull and crossbones tattoo on his neck. By the time we pulled apart, my dad had hobbled up beside us.

"There's my pretty Pumpkin!" His familiar sunny smile seemed to light up the entire waiting area and as I slid my arms around his waist he crushed me to his chest with one arm. It was a bit awkward with the crutches clattering in my ears. Sudden tears blurred my vision as I realized just how much I had missed my family, and particularly my dad these past nine months. I squeezed him hard and drew back, meeting his sea-green eyes. "Okay, Dad, what happened to your foot and why didn't someone tell me?"

He exchanged a meaningful glance with my mother who answered for him with a sniff of disdain. "Your father didn't want to worry you. Two days ago he decided to be a hero and chase after that silly old dog. I thought we were going to have to cancel our trip."

My brother chimed in, "Dad took one hell of a header on a patch of ice trying to keep Bozwell from getting flattened by the garbage truck."

"Quit talking about me like I'm not here. I can speak for myself," my dad griped, eyeing them both with irritation. "I fractured my ankle not my mouth." Wow. They all seemed a bit grouchy today. Sean's reaction to my dad's outburst was to give him an indifferent shrug and insert his ear buds, effectively tuning him out while my mother fussed needlessly with her coat. Turning back to me, my dad explained, "Poor old thing is almost deaf and blind now. I wasn't going to just stand there and do nothing."

Nope, that was not his style. I leveled him a look of sheer adoration. "Way to go, Dad!" Laughing, we exchanged a high five and then I asked, "How long do you have to wear that thing?" I nodded at his booted foot while linking my elbow through his, feeling grateful to once again be included in the give and take banter of my much-missed family circle. "It looks uncomfortable."

"It is. Doctor said another six weeks or so, but I wasn't about to let this stop me from seeing you."

"Oh, boy. I'm guessing the walking tours and the trail ride I had planned for you are out of the question."

"Not at all," he firmly insisted. "It's just a fracture. I'm up for just about anything unless you have hiking the Grand Canyon as part of our itinerary."

I matched his conspiratorial grin, but caught his grimace when he put weight on his foot. "Dad, are you in a lot of pain? Do you want me to get a wheelchair for you? It might make it easier to get to the car. It's a pretty long walk to baggage claim."

He shook his head. "I don't want to be babied. I'm not going to let this get me down. Lead the way." He clomped along faster, but couldn't quite hide the look of discomfort in his eyes. Yep. He was just as stubborn as me and I knew he'd tough it out even if he was in screaming agony.

I caught my mother's glance of resignation and gave my brother a wink. Nothing much had changed. At least that's what I thought at that moment.

By the time we reached the baggage claim area, my dad's face was brick red and beads of sweat glistened on his forehead. I didn't want to hurt his pride, but insisted that he sit down and rest while I went to get the Jeep and drive it to the closest exit. It kind of worried me that he didn't protest too much and I experienced a twinge of guilt knowing he'd just flown 3000 miles to see me when he probably should have stayed at home to recuperate. My heart also ached a little to notice that both my parents seemed to have suddenly aged. The lines on my mother's oval face appeared deeper, my dad's red hair looked thinner and a touch more faded than I remembered.

I pulled the car keys from my purse and turned to leave when my brother stepped to my side. "Wait up. I'll go with you."

"What?" My mother slid him a withering glare. "You're going to leave me here to handle all this luggage by myself? That's so typical of your selfish, irresponsible behavior."

His lips hardened and I could tell he was stifling a rude retort. "I'll be back to get it. Just lay off me for a few minutes, will you?"

Whoa. What the hell was going on between these two? Puzzled, my gaze flitted between them until my mother turned her back to him. "Let's go." Sean's tone was clipped.

I hesitated in the ensuing silence. Neither of them offered an explanation for their ultra-touchy exchange. I was tempted to demand an explanation right then and there, but decided against escalating the argument inside the terminal. "I'll be back in a few minutes," I said, unable to miss the look of weary forbearance shadowing my dad's face.

As we weaved our way through the throngs of travelers crowding the terminal, Sean was furiously texting someone on his phone. "Everything okay?" I asked after he jammed the phone into his jeans pocket.

A simultaneous scowl and shrug. "Not really. My girlfriend's turned into a real bitch."

I frowned. "You mean Robin? I heard she's really sweet."

"Used to be. But, I'm tired of her bullshit and I'm gonna dump her when I get back home."

His pronouncement puzzled me. According to my mother, the young woman was pleasant, attractive and serious about her college career. I waited a few seconds to see if he'd elaborate, but he didn't. "Oh. Well, I'm sorry to hear that."

"I'm not."

He fell silent and several minutes passed before I caught his eye. "Let me guess. It's not so much that you wanted to visit with me as you wanted to get away from Mom, right?"

His faint smile looked a tad sheepish. "That obvious, huh?"

"Yeah." I said nothing else until we reached the elevators. I punched the button and then turned to meet my brother's hazel eyes. "So, do you want to tell me what's going on between you two? You could have cut the tension with a really dull butter knife."

He looked away for a few seconds and then stared at the floor, fidgeting. "Oh, you know how she is. Always on my ass about something."

"Something? Like what?" Considering their hostile behavior towards one another, his vague answer didn't fly with me.

The elevator chimed its arrival and when several other people crowded in with us, our conversation ended. Everyone rode in the usual strained elevator silence, but when we stepped into the parking garage, I put a restraining hand on his arm. "Sean, level with me. What's going on?"

He hesitated for extended seconds, his gaze guarded. "Okay, well…I guess I messed up a little."

"What do you mean, 'messed up a little'?"

He sighed and rubbed the back of his neck. "I kind of got busted last week for selling pot to an undercover cop. No biggie." A defensive grin accompanied his protracted shrug.

"No biggie?" I gawked at him. "What the hell were you thinking? You should know better than to pull a stupid stunt like that!"

A dramatic eye roll. "Oh, man! You sound just like Mom and Dad. I know what you're thinking. Here he goes again. Sean is always a disappointment, such a loser. It really pisses me off to hear them constantly comparing me to you and Pat." His voice dripped with resentment. "Patrick's got a great-paying job, Patrick's got a big, honkin' house, Patrick's married with two perfect kids, look how smart, ambitious and successful Kendall is, blah, blah, blah. Why can't you be more like them? Why can't you make something of yourself? I'm sick of hearing it!"

I drew back, stunned by his bitter sarcasm. "Sean, you're twenty-five years old, not sixteen. You do understand what you did was wrong?" When he didn't answer, I continued with, "Last time I checked, dealing drugs was

against the law, so don't try to lay this off on me and Pat."
I wanted to add that he should also be ashamed of himself
for what had to be hugely embarrassing to our parents. I
was quite familiar with how lightning-quick news travels in
small towns.

He scrunched his face unattractively. "Well, it's a
dumb law. And I don't need a third lecture from you. Just
chill out, okay?"

"Chill out? Seriously? You knowingly commit
a felony and I'm supposed to be fine with it? Well, I'm
not." I struggled to control my rising temper. "Frankly, I'm
surprised at you. Have you forgotten all the misery Aunt
Alyce caused the family?" I asked, referring to my mother's
younger sister. "Have you forgotten the devastating results
of her constant drinking and pill popping? Her marriage
breaking up, all of her trips in and out of rehab? How
screwed up our cousins are now because of her? I haven't
forgotten the trail of carnage she left behind and vowed I'd
never be like her."

"Well, aren't you a Miss Goody-Two-Shoes."

My anger flared hotter. "I'd rather be known as that
than a low-life drug dealer."

"I'm not a drug dealer!" he responded with a snarl.
"I was in a bind and needed a little quick cash, that's all."

"Whatever."

"You know what your problem is?"

I flashed him a look of disbelief. "What *my* problem
is?"

"You're still living in the Dark Ages. Look, Mom
and Dad are old school. I get that, but I thought you'd be
more enlightened," he griped, poking my shoulder painfully

22

with one finger. "Smoking a little dope isn't the same thing as getting hammered. It's not harmful and it's not addictive."

More irritated than ever, I shoved his hand away. "I'm hardly in the Dark Ages, little brother. I've read enough about this subject to know that we're not dealing with your grandmother's pot. The stuff being grown now is way stronger and it *can* become addictive…"

"Too bad we can't all be as smart as you think you are," he cut in, looking genuinely peeved. "Sorry, but you don't have a clue as to what you're talking about."

The much-anticipated visit was off to a poor start. I forced myself to calm down. "Okay. Truce. So, what's going to happen to you now?"

"I dunno. Dad posted my bail and got me a lawyer. I guess I'll go to court and probably just get probation 'cause it's my first offense." His dismissive, unremorseful attitude conveyed that his arrest for dealing drugs was on par with jaywalking. "Me personally? I don't think smoking a little bud is any worse than sucking on a cigarette or having a couple of brewskis. You're all making way too big of a deal out of this. All my friends get high."

I pressed the remote and unlocked the car. "Maybe you should get some new friends."

He stared at me, his expression cynical. "Come on, Kenny, get with it. Are you telling me that you never tried a little weed? Not even once?"

The way he said it made me feel like I was fifty years older than him instead of five. "Apparently I'm not as cool and hip as you are or you think you are, but no, I never really felt the need to get into the drug scene, cover myself with tattoos, pierce my tongue or wear a nose ring for that matter."

He stared at me like I'd just landed from another galaxy and I stared back at him as if he had. "I got news for you, Sis. I've seen you throw back a few drinks in your time and I'll tell you what, booze can have far worse consequences than getting high. I've been helping out a buddy who owns a bar and believe me, I've seen some pretty nasty shit go down there."

"I can't argue with that. I'm not defending any kind of substance abuse. If someone gets tanked and starts a knife fight, beats their kids or drives drunk and injures or kills someone, I'm with you, but the last I heard it wasn't against the law to have a glass of wine." I reached for the door handle.

"Oooh, check out these wheels," he crooned with an approving nod at my iridescent, lime green Jeep. "Makes a statement. It's a given nobody is going to miss seeing you in this color. Cool choice."

"Thanks."

"Four-wheel drive?"

"Of course. It makes it a lot easier to maneuver the rough back roads I have to travel sometimes."

He nodded. "It looks like something an Arizona girl would own."

"Thanks. I love her."

"Her?" he asked, cracking an impish smile.

"Yeah, I call her Peppy, because she really is compared to my old Volvo."

We slid into the seats and he inhaled deeply. "Mmmmm. New car smell. Sweet!"

Shifting into reverse, I backed out of the space and could feel his gaze boring into me. I eased down the ramp and turned to meet his questioning eyes. "What?"

"So, you're not bullshitting me? You got through college and never got high even once? No weed, no coke, no…"

"Yeah, that's exactly what I'm telling you."

Again, the look of disbelief. "Seriously?"

"Seriously."

"Unreal." He stretched and yawned. "You don't know what you're missing. There's some really outstanding product out there now. Know what I think?"

"What?"

"It should be legal to smoke everywhere like it is in Colorado, Washington and a bunch of other progressive states. I think the whole country is heading in that direction."

His self-righteous smirk increased my irritation further. "Look, Sean, I guess you're entitled to your opinion, but I have a different view. I mean, look at what's going on right here, for heaven's sake. Illegal drug trafficking is no joke. Arizona is a major smuggling corridor. Hell, they just discovered another elaborate tunnel near Nogales the other day and seized drugs with a street value of more than a million dollars."

His expression turned smug. "My point exactly. Make all drugs legal, problem solved." He dusted his hands together. "The government can tax the shit out of it and make a bundle of money. Everybody's happy."

"I doubt it would be that simple."

"There are tons of people who think like me. What's your solution?"

I shook my head. "I honestly don't have the answer, but I do know we've got serious issues here with the criminal drug cartels operating right across the border and spilling into Arizona complete with kidnappings, murders and ruined families as a result."

He didn't respond immediately, but then said, "Well, on the bright side, I read that the good citizens of Arizona are actually more open-minded than I thought."

"What do you mean?"

"You know. The medical marijuana law that passed here."

"That's true."

"So, what do you think of it?" Before I could answer he tacked on, "Wait, don't tell me. I'm guessing you're against people with cancer and glaucoma, anxiety and chronic pain being able to get a little pot to help make them feel better."

He was obviously trying to bait me. "You can drop the snarky attitude. Did I say that? Evidently you didn't read the articles I've written on this subject where I present both sides. They're online, you know."

"Sorry. Missed 'em. Been kinda busy."

"Apparently," I answered him dryly. "Anyway, my point is, the medical community is miles apart on how effective the program is and the jury is still out on how workable it's actually going to be. In fact, problems have already developed. Over sixty thousand medical marijuana cards have been issued and they've discovered that a fair number of these card holders are getting their prescribed ounces from the dispensaries and then selling it for profit on the street, not to mention that the Feds are raiding dispensaries in other states as we speak because it's contradictory to the Controlled Substances Act. And on top of that, now small children are getting ahold of it and ending up in the emergency room, so there's a movement on to have the law repealed."

"Well then, those people have their heads up their asses. It's just a plant for crissake! It should be legal the same as booze and cigarettes, only at least cannabis has proven medical benefits. Lots of other countries realize this and are now growing it for profit."

I felt like I was talking to the wall. "Sean, the majority of medical practitioners I quoted in my piece question that assertion and also suggest that marijuana is considered a gateway drug to the more dangerous ones like heroin, cocaine, meth and…"

He cut me off with a harsh, "That is so totally bogus!"

His defensive stance roused my suspicions. "Is it?"

Red-faced, he glared at me for several seconds, then declared earnestly, "Here's the deal. I don't think government belongs in the business of regulating drugs or regulating me or you in any way, shape, matter or form." He folded his arms and added matter-of-factly, "I guess if you want to stick a label on me, you could call me a Libertarian."

That didn't surprise me. He'd always been a free spirit. "Reality check, Sean. Until drugs *are* legalized, keep in mind that right now, today, it's still against Federal law in most states to be in possession, use and certainly to be dealing drugs. Got it?"

"Oh, cut me a freakin' break, will you? I totally thought you'd be more cool about this." His petulant expression reminded me of how he'd been as a kid: rebellious, adventurous, determined to always have his own way. A problem child. A difficult child. He'd gotten into minor scrapes as far back as I could remember, but his pranks and bad behavior escalated as he got older. My parents had been heartsick when he'd been expelled for two weeks his junior year in high school for verbally challenging one of his teachers and then being accused of shoplifting along with some of his buddies. He'd often been defiant when it came to following rules and he and my parents repeatedly clashed. I remember several times my mother stating with great drama that someday he'd be the death of her.

I circled down the ramp and drove around the terminal to the entrance I calculated was the closet to where my parents were waiting. Turning to Sean, I placed a hand on his left arm as he reached for the door handle. "Maybe we can continue this discussion later when we have more alone time, okay?"

He sighed deeply, staring straight ahead. "Why bother? We're never going to agree."

His churlish behavior made it difficult for me to keep my hair-trigger temper at bay. "Hey, don't take it out on me just because *you* screwed up. I'm willing to listen to your viewpoint and conversely, maybe you could open up your stubborn-as-a-donkey ears and take a little advice from your older sister."

He turned back to me. "You guys are so mired in your close-minded opinions you don't give a shit about mine. You know what? If Mom hadn't gone through my bag and flushed my weed before we left, I'd be feeling nice and mellow now instead of being stressed out from this shit storm coming down on me."

"You mean the shit storm you brought on yourself?"

Ignoring me, he said, "Don't sweat it, Ken. Everything's cool. Really. You guys are making way too much out of this." He pushed the door open, slammed it shut and sauntered towards the terminal.

As I watched him step through the sliding door, I had to admit to myself just how uncomfortable I felt about the whole situation as it hit home that a close member of my family was not only a pothead, but had been arrested for selling it. I could only imagine how angry and mortified my parents must be. It disturbed me greatly that Sean seemed so self-absorbed and nonchalant about getting busted. From what I remembered from Pennsylvania law, they were pretty hard on drug dealers and Sean could possibly go to jail. He'd better have a really good lawyer. I leaned my head back against the headrest and closed my eyes, a slight headache tapping at my temples. My well-laid plans for a perfect day continued to unravel.

CHAPTER

3

In light of the bulky cast on his foot, I decided it would be more comfortable for my dad to sit up front with me, but that meant sequestering my brother and mother together in the back seat. Not a great combination with the family dynamics already strained, but what could I do? After we reshuffled my bags from the party store, got the luggage and crutches crammed into the back of my Jeep and everyone was seated, I noted the time. There were only three hours of daylight remaining at best and I was already running behind my carefully calculated sightseeing schedule. I made an executive decision. The tour of the greater Phoenix area would have to wait if I was going to fulfill my promise to Morton Tuggs, my co-editor and longtime friend of my father. He'd insisted that I bring the family by for a quick visit to the newspaper office and meet the staff before everyone left. It would be the first time the two men would meet in person for almost twenty years and I suspected it would be an emotional reunion, considering their history of working together as photojournalists during several past military conflicts.

The time had arrived to show off some of Arizona's breathtaking scenery on the road to Castle Valley. The slanting rays of the late afternoon sun would provide the ideal combination of soft lighting and long shadows necessary to showcase the beauty of the lush Sonoran landscape. As we merged onto the freeway, I pointed west to the impressive cluster of glass-paneled office towers dominating the downtown area and then identified some of the landmark mountain ranges surrounding the Valley of the Sun.

"That one sort of looks like a kneeling camel," my brother muttered, pointing towards the ridged coral-colored rock formation rising majestically from the desert floor.

I flashed him a grin in the rearview mirror. "Good call. That's Camelback Mountain. Over there to the right of it are the Papago Buttes, and out there in the distance you can see the McDowell Mountains and Pinnacle Peak."

"I took an online tour of Phoenix last week, but I gotta say, it's like night and day being here in person," Sean remarked with an appreciative nod. "And, hey, I'm lovin' this weather."

I couldn't agree more. Since moving here, I'd grown accustomed to blue sunny skies and found that if it was overcast for more than a day or two, I'd feel mildly depressed.

"I don't think I'm gonna need this any longer." Sean tossed his jacket behind him and pressed the button to lower his window. "Whoo hooo! It was snowing like hell when we left Pittsburgh this morning and now look at this! Short sleeves in December!"

31

Thrilled that he mirrored my sentiments exactly, I darted a hopeful look at my mother to see if she concurred, only to feel a stab of disappointment. I sensed by her distracted, slightly agitated expression that she'd rather not be listening to us chitchat about the weather, but would prefer to finish whatever argument she and Sean had been engaged in on the plane. Even if she was on the losing end of a dispute, she was famous for always getting in the last word and apparently that had not yet happened. Ah yes. Family. Again, I wondered what Tally's take would be on these opinionated, squabbling people who would soon become part of his family. Lord have mercy.

"Be happy your introduction to Arizona is in December," I advised Sean, braking for heavy traffic. "Believe me, trying to get accustomed to living in 100-degree-plus temperatures for months on end was no fun. There were a couple of days last summer when I thought I would actually burst into flames!" My announcement brought a roar of laughter from everyone and my stiff shoulders began to relax a little. I'd spent untold hours planning what I hoped would be an interesting, educational and enjoyable visit with them. But it remained to be seen if my hotheaded family, myself included, would be able to maintain a modicum of civility with one another considering all the unresolved issues.

It took another forty minutes to leave behind the mixture of new housing developments, apartment buildings, office parks, strip shopping centers and the ever-present traffic congestion. I breathed a sigh of relief as I took the freeway exit. Within a few miles, traffic thinned and the striking panorama of wide-open desert spread out before us. My dad, who'd said little since we'd left the airport, blew out an appreciative whistle. "Man, this is really something," he murmured, his admiring gaze traveling back and forth, taking in the eye-catching scenery. "Phoenix has sure grown by leaps and bounds since I was here 25 years ago, but this," he said, gesturing with his hands, "this is still undeveloped. It's pristine!"

My chest swelled with pride. "I was hoping you'd love it as much as I do."

He was right. The combination of infinite blue sky dotted with clouds, rugged, snow-dusted mountain peaks, along with the sprawling tapestry of cactus and native vegetation painted a stunning desert mosaic worthy of an award-winning photo spread.

My dad waved his hand back and forth. "Is this all ranchlands out here?"

"No. Believe it or not, only twelve percent of Arizona is private land."

"You're kidding!"

"I'm not. What you see out there is a hodgepodge of state trust land, private ranches, BLM land and the rest is national forest. Tally leases thousands of acres from BLM for grazing."

"What does BLM stand for again?" Sean asked. "I'm blanking on that."

"Bureau of Land Management," I answered, accelerating past several motor homes.

My dad nodded. "Interesting. Okay, so I know the tall cactus with the arms is called saguaro, but what are the short ones with all the pads?" he said gesturing out the open window.

"Prickly pear." I took great pride in pointing out

other native flora and fauna to them as we rose in elevation. It was fun playing tour guide as I identified hedgehog and barrel cactus, along with acres of golden teddy bear cholla fields, brittlebush, ocotillo and mesquite, creosote, ironwood and palo verde trees. "Palo verde means green stick in Spanish," I informed them, savoring the feel of the fragrant desert wind on my face. "Well, Mom," I asked, glancing at her in the rearview mirror, "what do you think? Isn't it gorgeous? Can you believe how green everything looks after all the rain we've had?"

She arched a thin blond brow. "Really? You think so?" A delicate shoulder hitch followed. "It looks...I don't know, sort of brown and dry to me. Not my cup of tea, I'm afraid." Our eyes locked for a second in the mirror. "I prefer rolling hills and leafy green trees. But," she tacked on hastily, "if you think it looks pretty, that's all that matters since you're the one who has to live in this...desolate looking place."

True to her contrary nature, she was applying her expert bubble bursting techniques, but I was determined not to let her get under my skin. She'd made no bones about her displeasure regarding my decision to remain in Arizona, so why should I be surprised? And if I were to be honest with myself, hadn't my first impression of the stark desert landscape been less than enthusiastic?

I flicked a sidelong glance at my dad and caught his perceptive wink. "Come on, Alana," he said to her over his shoulder, "lighten up. Kendall's an Arizona girl now so don't give her a hard time. I'd appreciate it if we could just try to be civil with one another for a little while. After all, we're here to have a good time with Kendall, meet our new family members and party our socks off!"

"Well, I think the scenery is awesome!" Sean remarked from behind me, pointing eastward towards the serrated, snow-dusted backbone of the imposing Bradshaw range. "There's certainly nothing like this back home in good ol' Pennsylvania. Nope. Not even close."

I noted Sean's mischievous expression. His deliberately worded remark was obviously designed to reignite mom's frayed fuse, so I quickly jumped in to diffuse any further escalation of family bickering. "And speaking of that," I said, tossing a grin back at my mom, "Right now, we're headed straight to the *Castle Valley Sun* newspaper office so you can see where I work and meet the gang. After that, I'll take you to the motel so you can freshen up and then we'll all go and have dinner at Angelina's." My stomach rumbled at the thought of a savory Mexican food meal. My hastily eaten lunch seemed like a distant memory. "And tomorrow Tally is throwing a welcoming barbeque at the Starfire Ranch where you'll get to meet everybody. Sound like fun?"

"Yes!" my parents answered in unison, while Sean's "Cool," sounded distracted. A quick look behind me confirmed that he was busily engaged in texting again.

"Oh, and Mom," I continued, "Ginger and I are looking forward to hearing your ideas on the engagement party. I'm afraid I haven't had time to be much help to her, so she's anxious for your input."

My final statement appeared to placate her. Almost immediately her pinched facial features relaxed and I was treated to one of her luminous smiles that my dad said had broken many a male heart prior to his arrival on the scene, 'stealing her away' from a bevy of suitors, as he liked to tell it. Indeed, photos of their wedding day thirty-five years ago featured a stunningly beautiful couple. Having them all gathered around me, warts and all, made my heart lighter, as if it were pumped full of helium. As soon as my brother Pat arrived with his wife and kids, along with my aunts, uncles and two cousins from Ireland, the family circle would be complete. I could hardly wait.

"And speaking of the party," my dad said, "didn't you say that your old friend Nora Fitzgerald will be attending?"

"That's right. Fritzy, her husband and their little boy."

"How about that! How's she doing anyway? It will be great to see her again after what? Fifteen years?"

The mention of her name reawakened my earlier apprehension. I couldn't help it. The reporter in me was dying to know more. I was itching to call her to see if I could find out something definitive. But, right now, that was impossible. "Yep. We were supposed to have lunch today, but two bodies were discovered this morning on the east side of the Bradshaw Mountains and she got called to the scene," I said, pointing to the undulating ridgeline to my right.

My dad, ever the curious reporter, cocked his head to one side. "Oh? Tell me more."

I thought about sharing Ginger's worst fears, but decided to say nothing until I had confirmation of my suspicions. "She wouldn't say much."

"How terrible," my mother murmured, staring off into the distance.

She was right. No matter who they were, it was a tragedy. But if one of them did turn out to be Marcelene's daughter it would be nothing short of horrific. Both she and Ginger would be devastated and the fact that my gut instincts were not often wrong was doubly depressing.

As we entered Castle Valley and drove along the quiet streets, the late day sunshine bathed the tiny business district in a peachy glow, masking the reality of how run-down and sorely in need of restoration some of the flaking stucco structures appeared. Since the highway bypass had been completed, more than a dozen downtown businesses had closed. A quick peek at my mother confirmed that this fact was not lost on her, but to her credit, she said nothing. I remembered vividly my first impression after arriving from Philadelphia. I thought Castle Valley was the dumpiest little town I'd ever seen in my life. And now I loved it with all my heart. Funny how things change.

"Wow! Look at that!" my dad cried, pointing to the eye-catching gold and salmon-colored monolith of Castle Rock looming large in the distance. "That is simply magnificent in every sense of the word! Isn't that where your house is located?"

Infused with territorial pride, I answered, "Yep. That's Castle Rock and I get to enjoy watching that tower of sandstone change color everyday all day long. It's really something at sunset. Get your phones out or your cameras ready!"

I'd hoped that the dilapidated exterior of the *Castle Valley Sun* would be painted by now, but the severe fall off in ad revenues and print circulation had put that project on hold indefinitely. Oh well. At least the interior renovation had been mostly completed.

My dad winced as he slid out onto the hard-packed dirt of the parking area and my mother frowned at her watch. "Bill, you're overdue for your pain pills. Do you want them now?"

"No," he groused, accepting the crutches from Sean, "I'll take them before bed. They make me feel loopy and I don't want to miss anything."

"Suit yourself."

The door emitted its familiar squeak as I pushed inside the shallow lobby area. Ginger's head snapped up and her golden eyes widened with expectation. She leaped to her feet and came around her desk. "Well, howdy there y'all! We was all just chewin' the fat wonderin' when you'd get here!" I chuckled to myself. Ginger always enjoyed playing up her Texas colloquialisms for general entertainment purposes. Her freckle-dusted face appeared flushed as introductions flew all around. "I've heard so much about y'all, I feel like I know everybody already."

"And we've heard nothing but wonderful things about you, my dear," said my dad graciously, giving her hand a hearty shake.

Ginger's face glowed a brighter pink. "Aw, flapdoodle. Ain't you sweet."

Sean murmured, "Hey, how's it going?" and my mother brushed Ginger's cheek with an air kiss.

"Well, well, you old goat, it's about time you decided to grace us with your presence," came a booming voice from the doorway. We all swung around to see Morton Tuggs, hands on hips, his round face beaming with pleasure.

"Who are you calling an old goat, you ornery old bastard?" my dad challenged, grinning ear to ear.

Tugg's eyes twinkled. "Ornery debatable, bastard for sure! What the hell did you do to yourself?" he barked, pointing to my dad's black boot.

"Fell on my ass, that's what."

"Humph. Got the cast in the wrong place then, don't ya?"

My dad was laughing along with everyone else as Tugg crossed the room with his hands outstretched, a hint of moisture shining in his eyes. As the two men embraced, slapping each other on the back, their affection for each other was palpable. My heart warmed witnessing the emotional scene, cognizant of the magnitude of the event that connected them. The fact that Morton Tuggs had saved my father's life during the Gulf War where they'd both served as photojournalists had sealed a bond between them forever and added a significant dimension to their reunion.

"Bill, come and see the remodeled office I share with your daughter," Tugg commanded. "I'll tell you what, she's whipped me and this place into shape. I can actually see the top of my desk now." He winked at me. "Oh, and she's one hell of a good reporter to boot."

"Thanks, Tugg." I gave him a grateful smile before turning to my dad. "Why don't you two go ahead? I'm going to show Mom and Sean around while you guys visit for awhile." Nine months ago, I'd have been embarrassed for anyone who'd known me before to see the dismal place I worked, but now with the fresh paint, new tile, carpeting, furniture, upgraded computers and printing equipment, I was proud to show it off.

Thinking back, it was nothing short of amazing how much my life had changed since I'd started out doing odd jobs at my dad's small newspaper in my hometown of Spring Hill, Pennsylvania. Reporting got in my blood and soon I became obsessed with being not just any old reporter, but the best reporter. When I'd accepted a job at the prestigious

Philadelphia Inquirer I'd worked like a maniac to make a name for myself, only to end up at the dreary little *Castle Valley Sun.* It had been quite a comedown, but it had also given me the opportunity to scoop four of the most bizarre and dangerous assignments of my career.

Tugg slid his arm around my dad's shoulder and I could hear bits and pieces of their sobering conversation as they commiserated about the decline of print media as we followed them along the narrow hallway. "Did you know that no one under thirty even reads the print version of the paper anymore?" my dad remarked, moving gingerly with his crutches. "These kids get most of their news from social media sites, so you've probably experienced the same drop off in ad revenue as we have."

"Down more than fifty percent from ten years ago. Hell, technology is changing so damn fast we've become dinosaurs," Tugg opined gruffly as they rounded the corner into the office he and I now shared.

They were right. Print journalism was in deep trouble—the dead tree industry. The next generation would most likely never know the pleasure of holding a newspaper, hearing the crackle of the pages, finding some obscure little article or juicy tidbit of information, savor the unique aroma of newsprint. *What would people line their bird cages with?* I wondered wryly, and had to admit seeing my pieces published digitally didn't give me the same satisfaction as seeing them on the printed page. It was also evident that even holding the job title of "journalist" was changing by the minute, what with the fluid 24/7 news cycle that sent stories whizzing around the globe via cell phones, web newscasts, conventional news websites, social media sites and blog posts by citizen journalists. Working for days or even weeks to develop a big story was becoming harder and harder as news outlets and private individuals scrambled to be the first to break a sensational story or post a photo or video. And it was disturbing that in some cases the facts be damned. It was all about being first. The industry was changing so fast I wondered if I was to become a dinosaur as well before I'd even hit my 30th birthday.

I ushered my mother and Sean into the room where three of us had been crammed last spring, where I'd worked on my first phenomenal story, where Tally and I had first fallen in love. The irregular-shaped room now seemed much less crowded, containing only two desks and three filing cabinets. "This is Walter Zipp," I said, introducing our jovial new reporter who'd been with us almost two months and had thankfully taken over covering the mundane stories that I been assigned as the 'newbie'. "Meet my mother, Alana O'Dell, and my brother, Sean."

A wide grin lighting up his face, he shifted his substantial bulk and rose to shake hands with everyone. "Welcome to Arizona, folks! I hear you've got a ton of sightseeing planned."

"Yeah, I think my sister's got that all covered," Sean answered, stuffing his hands in his pockets as his gaze roamed around the room.

"We've got a lot to see in a short amount of time," I concurred.

"Good, good! Well, you folks have fun! We'll hold down the fort here."

I turned to introduce Jim, who'd just hung up the phone. "Meet Jim Sykes. He's..."

"Well, well, well," he cut in, swiping a handful of limp blonde hair from his forehead, "so this is the infamous O'Dell clan. I hope the rest of you aren't as big a pain in the butt as this woman." He pointed in my direction, the humorous twinkle in his eyes contradicting his deadly serious expression.

My family looked predictably taken aback and I had to stifle a laugh. They had no way of knowing that he was renowned for his acerbic wit. I shook my head and lightly admonished him. "Try to behave yourself," then explained, "Jim is taking over the sports desk from Tally full-time starting in January."

"And not a moment too soon, I might add!" His ice-blue eyes sparkled with pure devilment. "It's time that cowpoke was put out to pasture with the rest of his cattle and horses. Out with the old, in with the new."

I knew he was referring to Tally's stubborn resistance to changes in the industry. He didn't like computers and balked at having to file his stories online. Jim teased him mercilessly about being behind the times and he was right. I'd run out of patience trying to convince him to get a cell phone and had finally bought him one as a gift. But half the time he didn't remember to take it with him and if he did, he didn't have it powered on. I'd often grouse at him, 'Why can't you at least turn it on? How am I supposed to reach you?' He'd level me with that crooked grin of his, push the brim of his Stetson up and say, 'Maybe I don't want to be reached.' Yes, the man could be exasperating, but then I was far from perfect and yet he patiently endured, so it was hard to complain.

While everyone was chitchatting, I took Ginger aside

and whispered, "Have you heard anything concrete about Jenessa and her boyfriend?"

Her eyes clouded. "Not yet. Marcelene is about to go out of her mind. The not knowing is killin' us."

My spirits took a nosedive. There was little doubt in my mind that the news they awaited was not going to be good. Not good at all. "I'm so sorry. I hope you hear something soon."

She somberly agreed. "It's past closing time. I'm gonna scoot over yonder to the motel and let her know y'all are checkin' in real soon."

"Thanks, Ginger. Keep your chin up." It pained me to see her down and I gave her a comforting hug before continuing the tour. Swiveling around, I noticed that Jim and Sean appeared to have hit it off, but then, why not? They were about the same age.

We moved on to the production area and I introduced them to Harry, our longtime print operator, then Rick, who now handled online layouts and computer issues, and lastly, Al in advertising. A glance at the wall clock confirmed that we were running short on time. Last stop was my office, where it proved difficult to separate Tugg and my dad, who were busy comparing cell phone features and exchanging numbers, but I finally got everyone herded towards the door amid a series of goodbyes and promises to see everyone the next day at the barbeque. It was closing in on five-thirty as we stepped outside, where we were greeted with a sunset that literally took my breath away.

"Man, you weren't kidding!" my dad exclaimed, staring transfixed at the deep persimmon-hued horizon overlaid with an assortment of gold-rimmed black clouds backlit by fiery flares of scarlet orange rays shooting skyward. The dark silhouettes of saguaros framing the foreground completed the picturesque scene.

"Awesome!" Sean dug out his phone and took a series of shots while my mother snapped away with her camera. The sun slid behind the distant mountains, pulling the heat of the day down with it, and everyone grabbed for their coats. "It does get pretty chilly at night," I advised them as we cruised along the twilight streets until the bright green neon DESERT SKY sign appeared ahead.

"Suddenly I'm starving and yet I could totally crash at the same time," Sean announced, yawning audibly. "My body is telling me it's really more like eight o'clock."

I parked in front of the motel office. "Let's get you settled in and then we'll drive over to the restaurant as soon as you're ready."

My dad clomped ahead of us into the lobby and was greeted by Squirt, Marcelene's adorable, fawn-colored Pug, while we followed with the luggage. Their heads bowed close together in muted conversation behind the counter, Marcelene and Ginger both looked up as we entered. I'm sure only I noticed the almost imperceptible shake of Ginger's strawberry blonde curls, indicating there was still no news. Damn! What was taking so long? As I had many times, I fervently wished it were possible to be in two places at once. If I could, I'd be at the scene right now asking questions and waiting for information from Fritzy.

"Welcome to the Desert Sky, folks! I'm so pleased to finally meet all of you!" Marcelene's brave smile contradicted the sheen of anxiety reflected in her caramel-colored eyes as introductions flew all around, and my parents raved about the vintage furnishings. Not only had she done a superb job of retaining the 1950's charm of the old motel, she'd staunchly refused to abandon the old-fashioned paper registration system, claiming that she was too old and set in her ways to undertake the challenge of learning to operate a computer, even though Ginger's brother Brian, who was the town's only IT guy, constantly bugged her to get with it and go digital. She laughingly called herself a 'tech-tard' and Ginger was always grumbling about the fact that she didn't even want to learn how to use a smart phone. I could certainly sympathize with her since I'd had to practically drag Tally into the digital age as well.

After all the paperwork was completed, everyone marveled that she issued an actual door key to their rooms rather than the usual coded card. With the luggage unloaded and deposited in each room, we finally headed out into the bracing night air, and by the time we arrived at Angelina's it was close to seven o'clock.

The mouth-watering aroma of chilies and spices along with the cheerful strains of Mexican music greeted us as we stepped inside the squat stucco building. Angelina, the rotund owner, bestowed on us her signature full-toothed grin and lead us through the half-filled restaurant to a large red vinyl booth.

"Order Angelina's homemade green corn tamales," I urged as menus were passed around. "They are the best in the state!"

My mother, of course, complained that eating spicy food would give her indigestion, but nonetheless, joined us in consuming several saucers of cilantro-seasoned salsa piled onto crisp tortilla chips and washed down with a frosty pitcher of margaritas. As the steaming platters of enchiladas, tamales and tacos arrived, I typed a quick text to Tally reiterating again that I wished he had joined us. He'd politely declined my invitation, saying he'd be too busy getting ready for the barbeque, and he wanted me to enjoy some alone time with my family. His thoughtfulness was another reason I loved him, and that he put up with what he impishly labeled my pigheaded personality.

By the time we finished eating, it was after eight o'clock and everyone was quickly fading. My dad's face was etched with his increasing discomfort and my mom insisted that he take one of his pain pills.

"Shit, it's friggin' cold out here!" Sean announced, pulling up the collar of his coat against the wind as we stepped outside.

"Told ya," I responded, unlocking the car. "It's still better than August."

My mother paused and stared up at the star-studded sky. "I've never seen so many stars before in my life. It looks like I could reach up and touch them. Beautiful." I was encouraged to actually hear her utter some positive words about Arizona for a change.

Having thoroughly enjoyed every bite of my Mexican dinner, I basked in the contented cocoon of being with my family again and joined in the lively banter flying around the car. As we approached the motel, my mellow mood evaporated at the sight of the sheriff's patrol car parked near the front door. "Oh, no." I thought I'd whispered the words to myself, but my dad turned to me sharply, asking, "What's going on, Pumpkin?"

I opened my mouth to tell him, but then shut it again.

Wait. Don't jump to conclusions. Perhaps this wasn't what I feared. "I'll be right back." I sprang from the car and was inside the door before the rest of the family knew what was happening. The lobby was empty, but I could hear voices coming from the adjacent office. I hurried to the doorway and stopped dead when I caught sight of Sheriff Turnbull perched stiffly on a chair, his expression so glum even his white handlebar mustache seemed to droop.

Slumped on the couch opposite him, Marcelene wept softly, her head bowed, tissues pressed to her nose. Ginger was seated next to her with a comforting arm wrapped around her shoulders. Apparently she heard my whispered, "Oh, Lord, no," and looked over at me, eyes glistening, mascara smudging her cheeks. When our gaze connected, my stomach clenched and the tamales I'd just eaten rose to my throat. Her slight nod and grief-stricken expression confirmed the worst.

CHAPTER
4

Tears stinging the back of my eyes, I mouthed the words, 'I'm so sorry,' which seemed incredibly inadequate considering the circumstances. Not wishing to intrude any longer on this very tragic, very private moment, I backed away from the door even though the reporter in me was eager to find out what happened. I heard the squeak of hinges behind me and swung around to see Deputy Duane Potts saunter in the main entrance, clipboard and file folder in hand.

"Kendall O'Dell," he said, his lips breaking into an ingratiating smile. "Now why am I not surprised to see you here? If there's trouble around, you're bound to be front and center."

I sighed inwardly. "Hello, Duane."

"Yes, sirree, I'd recognize that curly red hair anyplace." As expected, his insolent stare swept over me and it irritated the hell out of me, knowing he had a wife and four kids at home. Smarmy jerk. And that was unfortunate, because he always proved to be a solid contact when I needed information. He was decidedly more forthcoming with confidential details than Sheriff Turnbull. Somehow I managed to conjure up a synthetic smile. "Are you going to be here for a few minutes? I'd like to talk to you about this situation."

He clicked his tongue and pointed a finger at me. "Where you are concerned, I'm always available."

My skin crawled. He seemed to be a competent lawman, but as a 'decent' human being, not so much. "Great. I'll be back in a flash."

I hotfooted it outside knowing my family must be puzzled as to why I'd bolted from the car. "Sorry about that," I said, starting the engine again. "I'll drive you around to your rooms."

My dad, ever the seasoned reporter, eyed me curiously. "So, are you going to tell us what's going on or not?"

It wasn't very well lit at the back of the motel and I peered into the gloom, searching for their room numbers. "Do you remember the bodies I was telling you about earlier that were found dead in a remote area of the Bradshaw Mountains? You know, where Fritzy was called to investigate today?"

"Yes."

"Well, it appears that the girl was Marcelene's daughter, along with her boyfriend."

My mother gasped. "You mean the nice lady we just met?"

"Yes."

"How tragic."

Sean piped up from behind. "Bummer."

49

"I'm going to go back inside and see if I can get more information."

Dad opened the car door and turned to me, a perceptive glint lighting his eyes. "So, you're going to follow up on this story, right? I know I would."

"I'll get enough to file the initial story tomorrow, but I can't right now. I'm going to be tied up with you guys all next week so I'll have to assign it to Walter." It absolutely killed me to say it aloud. But what could I do? I couldn't just abandon my family, scrap all of my carefully thought-out sightseeing plans and then rush off to cover this story, could I? "I'll come by in the morning and take you to the Iron Skillet for breakfast," I said, sliding out of the car to give everyone a goodbye hug. "You'll love the food and there's lots of it. Afterwards, we'll take a tour around town and then I'll drive you out to see my house. After that, we'll head to the Starfire Ranch, so wear jeans and comfortable shoes." I grinned at my dad. "Or in your case, shoe."

"Yeah, don't think I'll be doing all the walking I'd planned." He edged me a wistful smile and gathered up his crutches.

"Don't make it too early," Sean said with a wide yawn, slipping the key into the door lock. "I don't plan to be up much before nine."

"I'll call first." I embraced everyone, then drove to the front of the motel feeling a strange mixture of joy and trepidation. I'd been dreaming about my family's visit for weeks and the timing of this tragedy couldn't be worse. I could only imagine how devastated Marcelene and Ginger must be and my mind whirled with possibilities. What could have happened to the young couple? Had they been victims of the unexpected snowstorm and died of exposure? Or, I thought grimly, could it have been the work of a psychopathic killer? My urgent need to find out compelled me to hurry inside, only to feel a twinge of disappointment. The lobby was empty. Damn it. My opportunity to grill Duane appeared to be gone for now. I crossed to the office doorway where I could hear his muffled voice emanating from inside. At that exact instant, I came face to face with Marshall Turnbull, who emitted a startled grunt.

"Good grief, Kendall." He planted his worn Stetson hat firmly on his head and brushed past me. "Don't you ever sleep?"

"If I did, I might miss something."

He flicked a shrewd glance over his shoulder. "That might not be a bad thing. Maybe you could actually stay out of trouble for a few hours," he said, keeping his voice low. Motioning for me to accompany him, I fell into step beside him as he strode towards the front door. His ruddy complexion appeared ashen and the customary twinkle in his light blue eyes was noticeably absent.

"Knowing you, you're primed to ask me a thousand questions, so let's step outside." When the frigid night wind grabbed my hair and slapped it across my eyes, he grimaced and held onto his hat. "Man oh man, it's too cold to stand out here and talk. Let's go sit in my patrol car." I gladly agreed and slid into the passenger seat as he laid his hat aside and slumped behind the wheel, huffing out a protracted sigh. "Having to deliver this kind of news to folks is one part of my job that I truly hate."

I didn't envy him. As it was, I was dreading my forthcoming encounter with Marcelene and Ginger, well

51

aware of how deeply emotional it would be. "So, you're positive it's them?"

"Unfortunately, yes," he replied, looking more somber than ever. "We did a look see before the medical examiner arrived. The boy had ID and…well, I was real sure about Jenessa. Even though there had been some decomposition, she was still recognizable and we also picked up her dental records this morning."

I sat in mournful silence for a few seconds, picturing the sweet-faced, honey-blonde young woman, my heart aching for my cherished friend and her aunt. Solemnly, I pulled my notepad from my purse. "I'm assuming you guys have checked their social media pages to see what they may have posted?"

"Oh, yeah. I had Duane doing that most of the day and the last time either of them posted photos and comments was the day Jenessa met the boy near Bumble Bee. Someone took a photo of them posing beside the camper, but there's nothing posted anyplace he could find after that. But then, that's not too surprising. We know that there are a lot of places back in those mountains where cell service is nonexistent."

I made a note to check out their social media pages and other Internet sites as well. "What else have you got?"

He rubbed the back of his neck. "We probably won't have a final report from the medical examiner's office until next week and even later for forensics, but it appears they've been dead for about a week." He turned the ignition key and dialed up the heat before reaching up to snap on the dome lights.

"What was the cause of death?" I braced for the worst.

He shook his head sadly as he flipped through pages

on his clipboard. "Dumb kids. From what we can tell they were using a charcoal grill to cook or possibly for heat and it appears they died from carbon monoxide poisoning."

"Oh my God," I murmured, penning notes on my pad. "Any thoughts about possible suicide?"

"We didn't find a note, but again, we don't really know yet. I asked Marcelene if Jenessa had given any indication that she'd been despondent about anything. She told us that at times she was still depressed about her father's recent death, but no more than what she would consider normal. In fact, she said Jenessa was really upbeat about the trip and appeared to be crazy about the Taylor kid."

"What do you know about him?"

"Not a lot yet."

"Ginger told me they had gone camping. Where exactly were they found?"

"As the crow flies, about half way between Bumble Bee and Crown King and about two miles northwest of Raven Creek."

I nodded. "Yeah, I searched online earlier and I can't seem to locate a town by that name. "

"It's not really a town per se. More like a little unincorporated cluster of shacks and mobile homes on an island of private land tucked back in the Prescott National Forest. Used to be an apple orchard there many years ago."

"That's interesting."

"Yep. But, it's a strange little place. And you sure don't want to be caught nosing around or you're liable to get a load of buckshot in your hind end. Nobody in law enforcement is crazy about having to answer calls there." His mouth twisted in a sheepish grin. "In fact, we have nicknames for it, Felon

Creek and Spooksville to name a couple."

My interest level ticked up. "Why's that?"

"Because it's populated with a bunch of ex-cons, people with mental disorders, drug addicts, people who flat don't want anybody knowing what they're up to, like hoarders, survivalists, some disabled ex-military along with other ne'er-do-wells and weirdos of all stripes who just don't want to be bothered. Off the grid, so to speak."

"What do these people live on?"

"Government checks, gold panning, gold mining, odd jobs. There's also a sand and gravel operation nearby that employs a few of them and," he tacked on, lifting his bushy brows, "I suspect half the town is cooking meth, which is not unusual in these out-of-the-way places. We just busted two guys and a woman in Black Canyon City a couple of weeks ago for running a meth lab out of their garage."

"I remember reading about that. Well, Raven Creek sounds like an intriguing place to me."

"Humph! Maybe to you, but I'm serious, Kendall. It's a place spooks go to hide away from the general population for whatever reason." He eyed me severely. "So take heed, if you plan to go poking around over there."

"Gotcha." I paused. "Could you give me the correct spelling of their names for my article? I know…knew Jenessa, of course, but who was her boyfriend?"

He glanced at the page in front of him. "The full names of the deceased are Jenessa Ann Wooten, age 22 and Nathan Brice Taylor, age 25. We found her car in a staging area near Bumble Bee."

"What do you mean staging area?"

"You know, where folks park their motor homes

and trailers while they're out in the boonies riding off-road vehicles or horses."

"I see. Go on."

"Marcelene told us Jenessa planned to meet up with the Taylor boy there and then take his pickup with the camper shell. We recovered driver's licenses for both of them and the pickup is registered to Stuart Taylor, the young fellow's father, whom we have notified. His parents are recently separated and we're trying to locate the mother. She moved to the Seattle area and is now apparently off at some out-of-the-way retreat in Alaska with her new boyfriend."

As I jotted down names and details, the sick feeling returned to my stomach full force. It was only a slight relief to know the young couple had not met a violent death at the hands of a psychopath, but had passed away in their sleep. But even that fact would be of little consolation to Marcelene and Ginger. "And who found the bodies?"

He flipped the page over. "Guy named Harvel Brickhouse."

"Odd name."

"Yeah, well, he's kind of an odd bird. I had Julie check him out and he served time for involuntary manslaughter."

"Really. How recently?"

"Twenty years ago and I don't know any details yet."

I continued writing. "Where does he live?"

"He's got a cabin outside of Raven Creek, where he's working a couple of mining claims. He's also the caretaker at the old McCracken Ranch."

I looked up from my notes. "Why would the owners be employing an ex-con?"

A shrug. "Maybe he didn't tell them, or maybe they

don't care. It was a while ago and it's probably hard to find people to stay out there. Who knows? He may have been the only game in town." He studied his report momentarily and then continued. "Anyway, according to Brickhouse, he was out riding his snowmobile, checking on his mining equipment, when he noticed the sun reflecting off something. He went to check it out and came across the camper half buried in the snow on a closed Forest Service road. He called out, banged on the door and when no one answered he yanked it open to see if anybody was there. That's when he found the bodies. He said it smelled so putrid he lost his breakfast."

The mental picture made me cringe inwardly. "No doubt," I remarked dryly. "So, he's the one who called you?"

"Nope. He doesn't have a phone. Told us he didn't want to be bothered and there's no service out there in the sticks where he's mining, so he made his way out to the main road where he flagged down..." pausing, he ran his forefinger across the sheet of paper, "a fellow by the name of Burton Carr. He said Carr couldn't get a good signal on his cell phone, so he drove down the hill and met up with a gal named Linda Tressick somewhere around Cleator."

"And who is she?"

"Law Enforcement Ranger with the BLM. She notified us."

"And what do you know about Burton Carr?"

"Not much. Just that he works as a forest ranger and he lives in... let's see..." he glanced at his paperwork again. "Mayer."

"Okay." Puzzled, I tapped my pen against my lips before asking, "What do you suppose Jenessa and Nathan were doing on a road that was closed to the public?"

"Don't know. According to Carr, that particular one had been abandoned for years. It's unmaintained and in pretty rough shape, I can tell you that. Them getting stuck out there in the middle of a snowstorm was a recipe for disaster. But then, I guess that's something you'd know all about."

With a grim smile I acknowledged his reference to my recent ordeal while investigating my last disturbing story. "Yeah, all too well. Anyway, I'm wondering about something. Was this road clearly marked as closed?"

He glanced again at his notes. "Uh, huh. Carr says it is and also gated and locked."

I drew back, surprised. "Well then, how do you suppose they wound up there?"

Marshall wet his thumb and turned to another page. "We can only guess at this point. Assuming that visibility was probably poor, most likely they drove off the main road, somehow ended up getting stuck there and well, you know the rest."

"Can you share details of where exactly they were found inside the camper?"

He didn't answer directly, but drummed his fingers on the clipboard, apparently deep in thought. His obvious hesitation spiked my interest level further and when he finally turned his skeptical gaze on me, he cautioned, "We don't know yet if any of this is relevant, so what I'm going to tell you is off the record for now because we still haven't notified the young man's mother. Agreed?"

"Agreed."

He consulted his report once again. "It appears that at least the Taylor kid may have realized they were in trouble because his body was found facing the door of the camper where he had collapsed. Jenessa was found inside a sleeping bag in the back. We can theorize that he woke up, made an attempt to get the door open, but it was either frozen shut or perhaps he was too disoriented to know where he was or what he was doing at that point. We'll probably never know for certain."

Something about his explanation wasn't gelling. "So, you're saying that these two supposedly experienced campers may have been burning charcoal for heat? They didn't have another heat source?"

"We found a propane heater with extra canisters that appeared to be full."

I blinked my confusion. "That doesn't make sense. Why wouldn't they just use the propane heater?"

"We don't know. Evidence shows that the grill had been used at some point for cooking."

"And they didn't have a window cracked open or anything?"

"That's correct."

His troubling answer fueled my curiosity even further. "Where was the grill located?"

"Just inside the door. We found the lid on the floor nearby so, again, we can only speculate that it was either already off or perhaps he knocked it off when he fell."

I threw him a sharp look. "So, if they were using the grill for heat, would it have been covered or not?"

Marshall met my questioning gaze. "We don't know that either. Again, we can only speculate. Whatever, at some point the coals re-kindled."

I sat in silence for a few seconds before asking, "Did Nathan try to call for help?"

"We didn't find any cell phones at the scene."

"You're kidding! What are the odds of two young people not having their cell phones with them?"

A pensive nod. "I agree. We're still searching for them."

"Shouldn't you be able to track them through their providers? When was their last communication with the cell tower?"

"We're working on it." He consulted his notes again. "Marcelene told me that they intended to rent an ATV in Crown King and also had planned a nighttime hike and rock climbing. It's possible their phones were lost prior to them getting stranded."

I frowned disbelief at him. "That doesn't sound plausible that they'd both lose their phones."

He hitched one shoulder. "As it turns out, they wouldn't have been of much use. There's no cell service in that particular spot anyway."

My discomfort level increased markedly. "Marshall, why wouldn't they hike out to the main road? Why would they just stay there and freeze to death? It doesn't make sense."

"Dr. Garcia told us that Jenessa had multiple cuts and bruises on her body and he is almost certain her left ankle was broken. If he confirms that, it would offer an explanation as to why she was unable to hike out of there. And remember, the snowdrifts in that area were over four feet deep at one point." His weary sigh filled the space between us. "Anything else?"

"One more thing. If it was simply an accident, why did you call in Dr. Bartoli?"

His expression turned guarded. "Just covering all

the bases."

"In other words, you're not going to say."

"Look here, Kendall, I know you're looking for a headline, but I can't comment any further until we know all the facts. What I can tell you is that there have been two other deaths reported within a few miles of that general location during the past year, so I wanted to make sure our investigation is thorough."

"Well now, that's intriguing."

"Normally, we wouldn't call her in on this type of case, but since the bodies were in a state of decomposition and Dr. Bartoli is the best forensic anthropologist in the business, it seemed like the right thing to do. If this case is anything other than what it appears to be, she'll know."

Pride for my old friend Fritzy welled up inside, but in the same instant the sheriff's quiet revelation stoked the flames of my seemingly insatiable curiosity, as Tally was always quick to remind me. "Can you fill me in on the other two cases?"

"I can't give you too many particulars off the top of my head, but I believe one guy was filming stuff for a documentary and the second one was a Department of Transportation surveyor. Call or stop by the office tomorrow and I'll be able to give you more information."

"Were they homicides?"

He blinked and stared into space, searching his memory. "I seem to recall that both cases were eventually ruled as accidental death or maybe one of them was a suspected suicide, but again, I have to review the records. I'll have Julie pull 'em for you." He focused on the digital clock. "Look, it's getting pretty late…"

"Right. Thanks, Marshall." I stuffed my notepad into my purse and stepped out of the patrol car into the brisk night air before turning to lean back inside. "I'm going to file what I've got in the morning, but I'm going to be out of the office all next week with my family here, so if anything new develops, can you follow up with Walter?"

He gave me a two-fingered salute. "Will do." I was in the process of closing the door when he added, "And, Kendall?"

"Yes?"

"If by any chance you find anything of interest, you'll be sure to let me know, right?" Even though the light was low, I didn't miss the unmistakable gleam of skepticism reflected in his steady gaze.

I grinned. "What makes you say that? I told you I'm not going to be working this story."

Humor sparkled in his eyes. "Just asking."

It was no secret that I thrived on breaking a provocative story, and this one was packed full of more questions than answers, but as much as I yearned to follow up on my mounting suspicion that there might be more to the situation than met the eye, it wasn't going to happen this time. Tally's sage words, 'You can't have them all,' rang in my ears. "Night, Marshall."

When I returned to the motel lobby, Duane Potts was crossing to the front door. "Sorry about that, Kendall. Sometimes duty calls," he said, shoving some papers into a folder. "I have a few minutes now."

"No worries. I think I got what I need from Marshall for the moment, but as you get more details, I'd appreciate you keeping me in the loop."

He stopped close enough for me to get a whiff of his cloying aftershave. "I'm always happy to help you out with anything you might need." His intimate, insinuating smile was combined with his signature tongue click. "And you know where to find me."

Good grief. It took all my willpower to bite back a cutting remark. "Thanks, Duane."

When the door closed behind him, it suddenly seemed deathly quiet standing there alone in the small lobby listening to the solitary ticking of the clock behind the desk. Mentally bracing myself, I crossed to the office and rapped gently on the doorframe. "Okay if I come in for a minute?"

Both women looked up, their red-rimmed eyes moist with tears, the tips of their noses bright pink, piles of used tissues scattered on the couch and floor beside them. Heavy-hearted, I bent down to embrace Marcelene. I could only wonder at the sheer enormity of her grief, having lost first her husband and now her only daughter within a year's time. "I don't know what to say except I am so terribly sorry," I whispered, patting her bony shoulders.

"Thank you, Kendall." She grabbed for more tissues.

I took a seat beside Ginger and folded her hand in mine. "Are you going to be okay?" Her face was so pale the maze of freckles sprinkled across her nose and cheeks stood out in sharp relief. I had never seen her look so distraught, so utterly crestfallen.

"What can I say?" she sniffed. "I'm alive and kickin' an' Jenessa ain't."

Marcelene dabbed the corners of her eyes. "All I want is my baby girl back. I can't believe she's gone, that I'll never see her again, never hold her, never hear her laugh…"

Choking with anguish, her voice cracked and, when I tried to swallow, it felt like a cold, sharp-edged rock was lodged in my throat. Realizing there was really nothing I could do or say to soften such a horrendous loss left me with an overwhelming sense of helplessness.

Ginger honked loudly into a wad of tissues. "I just can't reconcile them two kids being so dang stupid. What were they thinkin'?" She stared at me blankly as if I had the answer. With both of them in shock, I had no intention of pressing for additional information, but Ginger's remark appeared to have caught Marcelene's attention and she leveled me a curious look.

"She's right. Jenessa of all people would know better." With that she burst into heaving sobs again and I knew it was time for me to go.

Rising, I murmured to Ginger, "I'm going to leave you two alone now," and then added, "Marcelene, if there is anything at all that I can do to help, just name it."

Ginger pinned me with a meaningful look that left me perplexed. She jumped up and then bent down to kiss her aunt's cheek. "I'll be right back, darlin'."

She practically pushed me out the door into the lobby. Closing it behind her, she whispered fiercely, "Sugar, I need to talk to you for a minute."

"Sure. What's up?"

She grabbed my elbow and steered me towards the big, potted fern in the far corner of the lobby. "Okay, here's the deal." She drew in a deep breath. "Maybe I'm full of it up to my ever lovin' eyeballs, but…did you ever get one of those tickly feelings that kinda roll around inside your belly? The kinda feeling that tells you something just ain't quite right?"

"Sure. All the time. What's going on, Ginger?"

She shook her head slowly. "I don't really know how to put it into words except…well…something's not right."

The fact that she was echoing my exact thoughts bothered me. "What do you mean?"

"It wasn't these kids' first rodeo. I remember Aunt Marcelene and Uncle Arnold taking Jen along on camping trips from the time she was an itty, bitty toddler. As for Nathan, well, Jenessa told me that he's…he was a real super jock. Besides hiking, mountain climbing, zip lining and riding his quad all over creation, she said he was into extreme sports like base jumping, skydiving, rappelling off cliffs an' flying around in one o' them wing suits like a danged bat. I went online and watched a couple of videos he'd posted. He did some crazy stunts." She folded her arms and locked eyes with me. "So, don't you think he'd know better than to do something so boneheaded?"

"Ginger, you know I'm always looking for a good story angle, but I just finished talking with Marshall. Even though there are a couple of things that seem questionable, right now the initial assumption is accidental death, so that's what I'm dealing with unless something else comes to light. And remember, nothing is definitive until the investigation is complete but, just for the sake of argument, how about I play devil's advocate, okay?"

She frowned skepticism, but said, "Okay."

I filled her in on everything Marshall had told me with the exception of what he'd asked me to keep confidential. "So, the question is, considering what must have been dire circumstances, does it sound plausible that they opted to use the charcoal grill for heat rather than freeze to death?"

"I suppose it's possible," she said grudgingly.

"And if, as you say, they were seasoned outdoors people, they would already know the dangers of using it in an enclosed area, right?"

"I'm thinking yes."

I palmed my hands skyward. "So, it stands to reason that they obviously didn't plan to fall asleep, but did and were overcome by the fumes. Given what we know now, what other explanation is there?"

She pursed her lips appearing uncertain. "Well, I guess that all sounds real logical, but..."

"But what?"

Her golden eyes signaled doubt. "You know what? Maybe I've been hanging around you too long or watching too many crime shows on TV, whatever, but something about this don't pass the smell test and I can't tell you why."

As the significance of her assertion slowly sunk in, another wave of uneasiness settled over me. "Ginger, are you suggesting that it was not an accident?" If I combined Marshall's refusal to provide his confidential information with the vague reference to two other deaths in the same area, the missing cell phones and then added in Fritzy's involvement, her allegation gained merit. Or not. Intriguing as it all sounded, I cautioned myself not to jump to conclusions. We both stood silent for several seconds before I ventured, "Ginger, what did Marcelene mean when she said Jenessa of all people would know better? Know better than what?"

The faint lines on her forehead deepened as her gaze turned blank. "I think she might've been referring to some kind of accident that happened to her way back before I moved out here…but I can't say as I remember the details clearly." Her shoulders slumped and her eyes welled up with tears again. "I'm sorry, sometimes things just go in one ear and out the other. Or maybe I'm just not thinkin' straight right now."

"Don't worry about it now. If you think it's significant, call me later."

"Thanks for listening to me ramble on."

I laid a comforting hand on her arm. "Hey, you're my best friend. You can ramble anytime. And, considering the circumstances, it's perfectly understandable."

"It's just so doggone hard to accept. Them being so young and, like Nona always says, full of piss and vinegar."

I nodded, concurring with the archaic phrase borrowed from her wise but colorful grandmother. "Listen. Don't worry about coming into work tomorrow. I'll text Tugg and see if Louise can sub for you and maybe a few days next week, if necessary. Marcelene is going to need your help. Please don't feel obligated to come to the barbeque tomorrow night either. Everyone will understand."

"Oh no, I want to! I was really lookin' forward to that! Doug is going to be bartending so maybe I'll just drop by for a short spell."

"Whatever works." I embraced her again, and when I finally climbed into my Jeep and started the engine, only then did I realize how profoundly exhausted I felt. I rummaged around in my purse and pulled out my phone. My quick text to Tugg contained minimal details and suggested that his daughter man the reception desk for a few days. I hit the send button, lamenting that since my very first day at the

Castle Valley Sun we had been perpetually understaffed. I glanced at the digital clock and was surprised to see it was after eleven. No wonder I was so fried.

I wished I could inform Tally of today's turn of events, but it was far too late to call or even leave a message. I always teased him that he went to bed with the chickens but woke early enough to personally wake the rooster. Instead, I sent him a text briefly explaining the day's events and that I'd call him in the morning with additional details.

It was kind of eerie driving alone along the deserted streets, now dark except for a smattering of Christmas lights. I was anxious to get home to the cozy ranch house I'd been renting and would continue to rent until after the wedding. I'd made it clear that I could not live in the same house with his chain-smoking, screwball mother. Happily, the plans for the new house Tally was having built for us were being finalized next week. It would be great fun showing everyone the building site and plans.

Once on the main highway, I headed into the open desert, as always marveling at the striking beauty of the radiant starlit sky. Fifteen minutes later, I swung onto Lost Canyon Road and stared ahead at the moonlit silhouette of Castle Rock sporting a ragged crown of silver-rimmed clouds. Spellbinding! The solitude of the desert provided a soothing balm to the conflagration of emotions engulfing me as the disturbing events of the day looped endlessly in my mind. What irony. This perfect day I had built up in my mind for so long had turned out to be possibly the most imperfect day I could have ever imagined.

CHAPTER
5

The insistent rumbling purr and gentle kneading on my chest woke me from deep slumber. So much for my plan to sleep in. Being a recent and first-time cat owner, I was still getting accustomed to the unique personality and subtle demands of my ginger-colored kitten, Marmalade, and I wryly acknowledged what long-time cat owners already knew—that cats rule and are benevolent enough to allow humans to live in their house. When I didn't respond immediately, she gently nipped the end of my nose. "Okay, okay, I'll get up and feed you."

The second my eyes locked with her luminous turquoise ones, she let out a plaintive meow, stretched to her feet, circled around a few times and then vaulted off the bed. She raced to the doorway, stopped and turned see if I was following. Laughing aloud, I threw off the covers and padded after her to the kitchen where she sashayed back and forth, eyes aglow with anxious anticipation, her tail curled into a fluffy question mark. "Here you go, baby,"

I murmured, spooning the canned food into her bowl. As she ate, I stroked her soft fur, lamenting the fact that I could have had my family stay here if my mother wasn't so deathly allergic to cats. But then, considering the prickly relationship that currently existed between her and Sean, perhaps it was best they had not.

The dawn sky, pearl grey and cloaked with wispy clouds, slowly brightened to a soft buttery yellow as I sipped hot coffee and tried to fight off the clutch of melancholy as memories from yesterday flooded into my mind. So many unanswered questions. A call to Fritzy might be in order after I finished filing my story at the office. Would she tell me if she'd found anything unusual at the scene or would that, too, be confidential? Considering the volume of material I needed to review, it was just as well I'd been awakened early.

After a quick shower, I dressed in my favorite Western outfit—jeans, blue and white checkered shirt, leather boots—and then slid the tooled leather belt around my waist, cinching it snugly. The impressive silver and turquoise belt buckle Tally had given me for a birthday gift last August completed the look I was going for. Marmalade, demanding more attention, brushed against my ankles as I surveyed the results in my full-length mirror with satisfaction. Like my dad had said, I was an Arizona girl now and I intended to look the part.

I pulled my felt cream-colored western hat from the closet and murmured, "Come here, sweetie." Scooping my ball of fluff onto one shoulder, I returned to the kitchen to check my emails. Junk and nothing else that couldn't wait. For a few minutes, I scanned my favorite site for local news and came across a story regarding the horrific car accident that resulted in the traffic backup where I'd been stranded yesterday. There had been four fatalities, a young mother and her two small children along with the driver of a pickup that had crossed the centerline and plowed into them. Authorities suspected the pickup truck driver was under the influence of a controlled substance and had ordered an autopsy. Awful! Struggling to erase the mental image, I pulled my phone off the charger, surprised to find a return text from Tally sent at 4:30 am. Wow. He'd actually turned his phone on for a change. Yes! Progress. Not one to waste a single word, his succinct message read: CALL THE HOME PHONE.

I dialed the number wondering if he felt the same level of apprehension that I did regarding a potential meltdown by Ruth. We'd had more than one heated discussion and when I'd voiced my concerns about his unstable mother, he'd attempted to allay my doubts by asking, 'What's the worst that could happen?' Of course, he was accustomed to her erratic behavior patterns, and perhaps he was right. But then he was pretty laid back, where I tended to overreact. Or as Tally liked to point out, especially during an argument, that while he appreciated my admirable qualities, my sizable list of shortcomings, which included being overly impulsive, short tempered, impatient and mulishly stubborn at times, tended to annoy the hell out of him.

Tally's sister Ronda answered on the second ring. "Hey, Kendall. What's up?"

"Oh, this and that. Is Tally around?" His younger sister, also not one to mince words, had never really warmed up to me. While she wasn't as brooding and withdrawn as their mother, she didn't go out of her way to be sociable towards me either.

"Hold on." I heard her set the phone down and shout, "It's Kendall!" Less than a minute passed before he came on the line. "Good morning, pretty lady."

"Hey there, cowboy. Marmalade and I sure missed you last night."

"Same here." He lowered his voice to a husky whisper. "What would you think about sneaking away to the barn for a while during the barbeque?"

His suggestive tone sent a delicious heat coursing through my body. "You are so naughty!" I answered, unable to suppress a chuckle. "That's a very tempting invitation and I will definitely keep it in mind."

"You do that."

I hated to terminate our playful exchange, but I was running short on time. "How are preparations going for the big bash?"

"Good."

"You are a sweetheart to go to all this trouble for my family."

He laughed. "Well, thanks, but I couldn't do it without Ronda's help."

"And I will tell her how much I appreciate it when I see her. Oh, by the way, did you book Buzzy and his band?"

"They weren't available."

"Oh no! So…we're not going to have any live music tonight?" Damn! I'd had my heart set on having a live western band to create just the right ambiance for my family.

"Well now, hold on before you get yourself all worked up into a tizzy," Tally advised calmly. "I did arrange for Randall Clay and his guys to come."

"Randall? How on earth did you manage to get him away from the Hitching Post on a Friday night?" The newly remodeled Hitching Post was a favorite hangout among the town's genteel citizens and tourists alike, famous for western fare served up on tin plates and served on rows of long picnic tables.

I wondered why he hesitated a fraction of a second before answering matter-of-factly, "Let's just say a friend pulled a few strings."

His cryptic answer puzzled me but I didn't press the issue. "Okay, well, I'm impressed. What about the food?"

"Gloria's two sisters are here and they're whipping up a feast right now. Miguel's got the ribs and steaks marinating and I've got George, Juan and a couple of neighbors helping too, so I think we're covered."

I said a silent prayer of thanks that his housekeeper, Gloria, had returned from Mexico in time to spare us all the horror of having to endure any more of his mother's wretched cooking, which I had to pretend I enjoyed. "Yum! I can hardly wait!" At the mention of food, my stomach rumbled and I knew there was no way I could wait until after nine to eat something.

"Ah…sorry to hear about your dad. I'm guessing the trail ride is off the table."

"Well, I think my mother and Sean could still ride out to the building site with me. I really wanted to show off Starlight Sky," I mused wistfully, referring to my new Appaloosa mare Tally had recently bought for me. "Maybe he could go with Jake in the truck."

"Do you think he's even up to that?"

"Knowing my dad, he'll insist on participating

somehow. If not, we'll figure something out. And speaking of my family, get prepared for the invasion of the fighting Irish. And I mean that literally."

"What's going on?"

I gave him a brief overview of the situation with my brother and he whistled softly. "Are you bothered because he's a pothead or because he was dealing drugs?"

"Both. My folks are royally pissed off and I'm guessing he and I will get into it again before the trip is over. He's got pretty strong opinions on the subject."

"And unsurprisingly, so apparently do you," came his quiet reply. "This is a subject we've never talked about."

I put the phone on speaker and rummaged around in the cupboard, pulling out a pre-breakfast snack of peanut butter and crackers. "I guess we haven't. Well, just so you know, I've never had the inclination to do any kind of drugs." Jokingly, I added, "Have you?" The absence of his immediate response stopped me cold. Tally was about as straight-laced a guy as I'd ever met in my life.

"I…uh…tried pot a few times in college."

His answer stunned me. "You're kidding! You never struck me as the kind of person…"

"Hey, don't make this out to be more than it is," he interjected. "I was young, I was stupid, I didn't like it and I never tried anything else, end of story." His dismissive tone signaled that the subject, at least as far as he was concerned, was closed.

"Okay, well, I can't say that I haven't done some stupid things in my life." I spread peanut butter on a cracker, hoping my super-calm tone had concealed my shock. Tally and drugs didn't go together in my mind.

He chuckled softly. "And I can certainly attest to that Miss Daredevil." I knew he was referring to the chances I was willing to take in order to snag an important story.

"Point well taken," I answered lightly, mindful that I could no longer postpone the pressing question that weighed on my mind. There was no diplomatic way to ask him about his obstinate, irritating mother and I hated to tick him off, so instead of blurting out how I really felt about her, I attempted to be diplomatic. "By the way, how is Ruth feeling on her new medication? Do you think her ah...mental state has improved any?"

A hesitation. "I think so."

"You think?" What a lame answer.

"I can't really tell if the new pills are working yet, but I did ask that she try to be civil to everyone."

"And?"

"We can only hope."

That didn't sound encouraging. Part of me would just as soon not have my family meet her at all, but if there were going to be any issues, I preferred to face them tonight where she could escape to the sanctuary of her room if things got dicey, rather than risk having her make a scene at our party.

"All she has to do is be cordial for a couple of hours. Do you think that's too much to ask of her?"

Tally's exasperated sigh hissed in my ear. "Ronda and I have lived with her mood swings our entire lives. Maybe we'll get lucky and she'll be in a good place tonight."

"And if she's not?"

"I don't know, Kendall. What would you suggest? That we put her to sleep?"

I'd become somewhat accustomed to her mercurial

mood swings and understood that, being her son, Tally was far more forgiving of her squirrely behavior. The peanut butter caught in my throat as I imagined how Ruth might react to meeting my family, especially my mother, whose critical, sometimes cutting observations could slice a person to the bone. It would be a toss up as to whether the visit would go well or be a complete disaster.

"I wasn't thinking of going quite that far," I joked, hoping to lighten our exchange. "I just don't know if I'll ever have the patience to tolerate it like you do."

"That's understandable since you don't possess one ounce of patience."

He was right, I didn't. "Tell me something. Do you think she's still pissed off at me about how things turned out with…you know, my story on the judge?"

"What do you want me to say?" he groused in my ear. "That she's finally forgiven you for humiliating her by forcing her to disclose the secret she kept from me all these years?"

Okay, he sounded officially ticked off now and I wondered if deep in his heart, he'd actually forgiven me. "Hey, I didn't force her to…well, maybe I did, but it was her idea to get me involved in his murder, remember?"

"Yes, I do. So, we'll just hope for the best," he said, sounding brusque.

"Okay. Just asking. I don't need any more bad news on top of everything else."

"Oh, right. You mentioned in your text that you'd share details," he said, his attitude moderating somewhat. "Sounds like yesterday was no picnic for anybody."

"That's putting it mildly."

"Want to tell me about it?"

A quick calculation told me that I had another ten minutes before I absolutely had to leave so I quickly filled him in on what I'd learned about the young couple, where they were found and apparent cause of death.

"That's a damn shame," Tally said gruffly. "I know that area. It's near the McCracken Ranch. How's Marcelene holding up?"

"She's devastated."

"That's understandable. How about Ginger?"

"Predictably stressed. But get this. She's not buying that it was an accident."

"Carbon monoxide poisoning? How could it be anything else?"

I took another bite of peanut butter-laden cracker and replied, "She swears they were both too savvy to use a charcoal grill in an enclosed space, even if they were freezing."

Tally, who volunteered for Search and Rescue with the sheriff's department, sighed heavily. "I've seen this sort of thing happen before. People don't intentionally set out to kill themselves, it just happens. What did Marshall say?"

"He agrees with you, but with the caveat that nothing is definitive until he gets the reports from the medical examiner's office and forensics."

A few seconds of silence. "Okay, so what is your take?"

"I don't know. Apparently Marshall is sitting on some evidence he wants to keep confidential for now, so naturally I want to know what it is. It's possible Ginger may be onto something." He didn't respond so I tacked on, "I told her to take today off and maybe a few days next week. They'll need time to plan the funeral."

"No doubt." His morose tone matched my flagging spirits. I didn't mention it because it seemed too selfish to even think about, but what was I going to do if Ginger could not continue in the role of our party maven? The engagement celebration had been her brainchild and she had insisted on handling almost every detail. Suddenly I was faced with the daunting task of assuming the reins at the last minute with little knowledge of her preparations. Ruefully, I reminded myself again that compared to her problems, mine were miniscule. "Hey, I've really got to go. I'm stopping by the office to file this piece before picking everyone up for breakfast." He was silent so long I wondered if we'd been disconnected. "Hello?"

"I thought you were taking some time off?"

"I am."

"Doesn't sound like it. In fact, this incident is made to order for you, isn't it?"

Was I imagining a whisper of censure in his tone? "What are you talking about?"

"Just admit it. It's past time for your adrenalin fix."

The pilot light on my fiery temper kicked on. As much as I loved this man, sometimes he could be utterly exasperating. "Why are you being so snarky? Are you trying to pick a fight with me?"

"Are we fighting?"

Ginger often compared our volatile relationship to two bucks clashing antlers and if I objected she would fire back with a wicked laugh, 'Oh, flapdoodle! I know you two enjoy snappin' at each other. It keeps the sparks flyin' in the bedroom, don't it?' She was right. Makeup sex was pretty hot. Nevertheless, it was really early in the morning for one of our spats. "I'm not taking the bait," I said, striving to keep my voice placid. "I'm simply filing the initial story. Walter is covering for me next week."

"Come on, Kendall, I know you too well. If there's a story here, you're going to move heaven and earth to find it. You can't help yourself."

His droll cynicism rankled me to the point of choking on the last bite of cracker. Why should I give him the satisfaction of knowing that his assessment of me was right on target? In my secret heart, I would like nothing better than to jump on this story, but I snapped back, "You really think I'd abandon my family to go prowling around the Bradshaw Mountains hunting for trouble?"

"Yes, I do."

I could not think of a suitable comeback and contemplated hanging up on him but instead, sweetened my tone. "I'm going to prove you wrong this time, cowboy. Care to make a sizeable wager?"

His burst of laugher irritated me even further. "Recent history has the odds on my side, so sure, I'll be happy to take your money."

I let out a groan of frustration. "Tally! How did we get from planning a rendezvous in the barn to here?"

"You started it," he replied, his teasing response only serving to fan the flames.

"I did not!"

"Face it. You love being argumentative. It's part of your adorable personality."

"That is not true!"

More laughter. "Are you listening to yourself? You've just proved my point."

Oh my God. I did sound contentious. Best defuse this before I said something I'd regret. "Well, we'll see who's right this time."

"That we will. Catch you later."

CHAPTER
6

The sky had brightened to a soothing powder blue patterned with white waffle-shaped clouds as I slammed out the front door. Damn! Tally was a master at pushing my buttons. I zipped up my coat and marched towards my car. While the bracing dawn air chilled my hot cheeks, the peanut butter snack had become an elephant-sized lump in my stomach.

I jumped into my Jeep and tore out of the driveway. Still teed off, I flew along Lost Canyon Road, leaving a swirling rooster tail of dust behind me. It had certainly not been in my plans to start the day squabbling with Tally and I vowed to put it behind me. Why should I allow our disagreement to color the rest of my day, especially when I would be seeing him in just a few short hours? One second after I filed my article and hopefully spoke with Fritzy, I would be officially off duty for ten days. A whirlwind of fun and sightseeing with my family awaited me and I was determined not to miss a moment of it. In an effort to dispel my blue funk, I tuned in soft music and concentrated on the ever-changing beauty of the desert landscape. The promise of another spectacular day emerged as I watched the pleasing interplay of light and shadow crisscrossing the landscape and rugged mountain ranges.

By the time I pulled into the *Castle Valley Sun* parking lot, my agitation had lessened considerably. "Okay, O'Dell," I admonished myself, hurrying towards the door, "get over yourself and get busy."

A sharp pang of sympathy hit me as I passed Ginger's empty desk and I reminded myself how petty my problems were compared to hers and Marcelene's. I would call soon to see how she and her aunt were coping. As I entered the newly renovated office, I stopped short. It was barely seven-thirty and Tugg was already busy at his desk. "Good morning!" I called, shedding my coat. "You're early, so I gather you got my text."

Tugg glanced away from his computer screen, looking glum. "Yeah, I got it. Hell of a shock," he muttered, with a sad shake of his head. "How are the girls doing?"

"As well as can be expected, " I answered, switching on my computer. I took a few minutes to fill him in on the details. When I finished, he leaned back in his chair, the speculative gleam in his eyes matching my thoughts. "I'm assuming that you are going to follow up with Marshall?"

"You know I can't right now, but I'll make sure Walter does. And by the way, is Louise going to be able to cover the reception desk?"

His grimace answered my question. "She's in Chicago with the kids until Wednesday. Didn't I tell you that already?"

My heart dropped. "No, you didn't." I tapped my fingers on the desk. "It's going to be tough going around here with both Ginger and me gone next week, but there's really nothing I can do about it." Well aware that Tugg was not in the best of health, I added sheepishly, "Sorry. I know your doctor doesn't want you stressing out. I'm sure Al and Jim can handle the phones."

"Don't concern yourself. We'll hold down the fort." He edged me a conspiratorial grin. "I'll be just fine as long as Mary doesn't give me a load of grief about putting in too many hours."

His doting wife kept pretty close tabs on him since his last medical emergency, and even though I knew he was imminently capable of running the show without me, I couldn't suppress a tiny twinge of guilt as I began writing my article.

By the time I finished and tapped the send button, shafts of bright sunlight streamed through the blinds, enhancing the effect of the lemon yellow paint I'd chosen. The drab, scarred furniture had been replaced, along with the ancient computer equipment, creating an updated working environment that had improved productivity and morale, but we still struggled with the aggravation of being constantly understaffed. Why work out in the sticks when the bustling metropolis of Phoenix offered a seasoned reporter far more challenges?

"Okay, Tugg," I said, gathering my things, "I'm out of here."

"Have a great time with your folks! We'll see you later at the Starfire."

I stepped into the hallway and paused to dial Fritzy's number. I wasn't surprised to get her voice mail and left a message for her to call or text me. When I entered my old office, Jim was at his desk working, but Walter's chair was empty. "Hi, Jim, where's Walter?"

He cocked his head in my direction. "Apparently he's taken up residence in the shitter," he announced with a devilish smirk. "He's having himself a royal crapathon this morning."

"Charming."

"I'm not kidding. He's got a serious case of the squirts!"

"Whoa, whoa! That's more information than I need, but thanks for the visual." I was poised to leave when Walter shuffled into the room, tucking his shirt into his pants, his thinning brown hair slightly disheveled. "Are you okay?" I asked, concerned by his pallid complexion. "Jim says you're...uh...feeling a little under the weather today?"

"I'm fine," he insisted with an impatient gesture, easing his corpulent frame into the chair. "Probably that chili I ate for lunch yesterday at the bowling alley." As if to affirm that, he let out a loud belch. "Excuse me. Sorry."

"Dude!" Jim admonished him, feigning disgust. "Get it together. You're a festival of bodily noises today."

"Stuff it, Sykes," he retorted with good humor, obviously enjoying their customary banter before returning his attention to me. "No worries here."

I hoped not. "Got a few minutes?"

One hand strayed to his abdomen and he winced, "Sure thing."

I filled him in on the situation, suggested that he read my article and then contact Sheriff Turnbull or Duane Potts later for more information on the two previous deaths. As I talked, I couldn't help but notice beads of sweat glistening on his forehead and tiny alarm bells clanged in my head.

Was he really just suffering from indigestion or something more serious?

"Will do!" Walter concurred with a strained smile. "Now you get out of here and go enjoy yourself. Lavelle and I will catch up with you later at the cookout."

"See you both there." I only got about six steps along the hallway when I heard running footsteps from behind. I glanced around just as Walter pounded past me and disappeared into the men's room. Not an encouraging sign. As I slid into my car, I had to counsel myself against giving in to my natural pessimism. Walter was going to be fine, nothing was going to mar my plans and that was that. Clinging to that thought, I dialed my brother's cell number and drove towards the motel. After five rings, I heard his sleepy response. "Wassup, sis?"

"Sean! Don't tell me you're not out of bed yet?"

A loud yawn. "I'm getting there. Wait for me in mom and dad's room while I grab a quick shower."

"Well, hurry up, bro. It's after nine and I'm starving!"

"When aren't you starving?" he said with a droll laugh. "Give me fifteen."

It was a pleasant surprise to find my parents sitting on the stone bench in the cactus garden fronting the motel. They waved and smiled as I parked. Even though I imagined the temperature was still in the high fifties, the sunshine felt warm on my back as I walked up to them and exchanged hugs. While we stood beneath a dome of flawless blue sky, my parents once again celebrated the beautiful weather, praised their accommodations and complimented me on my outfit. My picky mother proclaimed that she had slept well, but my dad admitted he'd had a long night after refusing another pain pill. As we made our way to the car, he grilled me for details concerning Marcelene's daughter and expressed surprise that I'd passed on pursuing the story further.

"It may have just been an unfortunate accident," I reminded him, holding the crutches as he eased into the front seat.

He turned and pinned me with a quizzical look. "Always remember to follow your gut, Pumpkin."

"I do, Dad, believe me."

Good to his word, Sean strolled up, joking, "Hey, people, what's the hold up? Are we going to eat today or not?"

I felt a measure of relief that everyone appeared to be in good spirits. Following the short drive to the Iron Skillet, we piled out of the car and were greeted by the mouth-watering aroma of frying bacon as we pushed through the heavy glass doors. It was encouraging to note that the breakfast crowd had mostly thinned out as we entered. Good thing. I was in no mood to wait. Even though I'd hoped to avoid it, well-meaning residents, eager to meet my parents, buttonholed us as we weaved our way among the tables. Another ten stomach-growling minutes passed until we were finally seated at a corner table where my dad could comfortably stretch out his booted foot.

While I adored the café's scrumptious food, the predictable zing of irritation surged through me as Lucinda Johns approached our table, menus in hand, wearing her usual skintight jeans. Sean caught my eye and winked. I'd already told them all about my nemesis—the busty, dark-haired woman who had unsuccessfully pursued Tally for thirty years. I'm positive she'd intended to ensconce herself at the ranch after the death of his wife, but then I'd unexpectedly entered the picture and thwarted her plans. However, I had to give her credit for being tenacious. She'd cleverly befriended Ronda and even gone so far as to board her horse at the Starfire thereby giving her a ready excuse to hang around. More recently, she'd hooked up with one of the new ranch hands, but I wondered if their relationship was genuine or merely a smokescreen so she could continue stalking Tally.

She issued us what I recognized as a synthetic smile and insisted that I introduce her to each family member. I did so reluctantly. "Well, folks, we're mighty glad to have you join us for breakfast at the Iron Skillet!" Leaning over, she provocatively flaunted ample cleavage while passing menus all around. "We got the best food in town and I highly recommend our award-winning biscuits and gravy."

Dad made a monumental effort to stay focused on her face as he laid his menu down on the red vinyl tablecloth. "Sounds good. I'll take you up on that."

Her attempt to ingratiate herself with my family really pissed me off and I glared daggers at her when she crooned, "Kendall, it's always so great to see you!" The glint of malice in her dark eyes negated her syrupy demeanor. Redirecting her attention to the others she asked sweetly, "Coffee, anyone?"

I knew her too well. She could go from zero to bitch in five seconds. Fuming inwardly, I forced a congenial tone. "Coffee for everyone, thanks."

"Oh, and I'll have a double…I mean, a big glass of orange juice, please," Sean murmured, his mesmerized gaze zeroed in on her enormous breasts. I could just picture her in the kitchen gathering those puppies together, pushing them up and then pulling her top down for maximum effect.

Insufferable cow. As she slinked away from the table, waving her substantial behind at us, I turned and caught my mother's narrowed look of disapproval and my dad's expression of suppressed amusement.

"Oh man!" Sean whispered, mischief dancing in his eyes. "She is just like you described her...only better! Please tell me those Winnebagos are real."

"Apparently they are," I answered dryly. "Try to maintain, okay? And for your information, baby brother, she's a good ten years older than you are."

"Whatever. For a cougar, she's smokin' hot."

I made a face at him. "Shut up."

My mother glowered at him. "Sean, really? Is this any kind of conversation to be having at the breakfast table?"

"Just asking," he replied, feigning innocence. "You gotta admit they were hard to ignore."

"Well, you shouldn't have been staring," she snapped, her lips pinched white with irritation. "Can't you see that's very demeaning to women?"

Sean eyed her with incredulity. "If she didn't want me to notice her ginormous boobs she wouldn't have put 'em right out there."

"Ginormous?" she repeated sarcastically. "What kind of stupid language is that anyway? Is it even a proper word?"

Being a language arts professor, she'd always been a stickler for correct grammar usage, and it was obvious Sean was deliberately baiting her. Ever the peacemaker, my dad intervened with a soft sigh of exasperation. "Enough. Sean, stop goading your mother and Alana, we're all aware of how important the women's rights baloney is among your fellow professors on campus, so can you two please knock it off?"

Hiding her annoyance, my mother fluffed her ash blonde hair looking chastened, but Sean's eyes still twinkled with mirth. If there was to be a truce, I feared it would be only temporary.

While waiting for our food, we chatted about safe subjects like the weather, scenery, the engagement party and how my dad wanted to handle the tour of the ranch. When breakfast arrived everyone dug in with gusto, myself included. The western omelet stuffed with ham, cheese and green peppers, topped with a generous portion of spicy salsa went perfectly with three homemade biscuits slathered with butter and jelly. Sheer heaven.

Not wishing to give her the opportunity to flash my brother several more times, I had my credit card ready when Lucinda dropped the bill on the table. She scooped it up and when she returned moments later I could have gladly choked her when she airily informed us, "See you all later at the Starfire."

What? Who the hell invited her? Dumbfounded, I said, "I…uh…wasn't aware that you were coming."

Her cheesy grin was nothing short of sanctimonious. "Well, of course I'm going to be there! You and your intended need to work on communication skills, girl! My goodness, doesn't he tell you anything?" Her expression switched from patronizing to dreamy. "What was I supposed to do when Tally called and begged for my help? I couldn't very well say no, now could I?"

Really? Begged? If that actually happened, why would he not tell me? Smug bitch! Her deliberate attempt to belittle me in front of my family sent my blood pressure rocketing to the boiling point as I struggled to keep the impressive list of expletives whirling in my head from exiting my mouth.

Defusing what could have escalated into an ugly scene, my easygoing dad flicked me an insightful look and quickly interjected with a benign, "We're all looking forward to the barbeque."

"You have yourselves a real fun day now!" Throwing me one last spiteful glance, she beamed an angelic smile at Sean and my dad before she disappeared through the swinging kitchen door.

Her voice filled with wonder, my mom shook her head slowly. "My goodness! You were spot-on, Kendall. That is one obnoxious young woman."

I hadn't realized how tense my shoulders were until that moment. "Obnoxious isn't a strong enough word."

"Gotta give you credit for holding your temper, Pumpkin," my dad said with a chuckle, grabbing for his crutches. "I don't know which is redder, your face or this tablecloth."

"If I had to bet, I'm going to go with her face," Sean teased as we all rose and moved towards the door.

The remainder of the morning went smoothly—a vast improvement over the rocky beginning. It was a kick chauffeuring them around Castle Valley, showing them the various points of interest and stopping often for photo opportunities. And it was enlightening to view the town through the prism of new eyes, remembering how foreign the desert had looked to me and how difficult it had been adjusting to the harsh environment. At the same time, however, I was bothered by the notion that Tally had invited Lucinda to the barbeque and neglected to tell me. I consoled myself with the thought that there had to be a good explanation, or she was lying through her teeth just to get a rise out of me. Either way, it was irritating.

It was close to one o'clock when we finally headed out into the open desert—a spectacular sight all dressed out in cheerful afternoon sunlight, complemented by an unblemished sky of pure sapphire. Windows down, brisk air blowing my hair, I pointed out the names of more desert foliage and several nearby mountains as we bounced along Lost Canyon Road, finally pulling up in front of the rustic ranch house. "This is it!" We all got out and I helped my dad with his crutches.

"Awesome," breathed Sean, staring up at the mammoth sandstone pillar of Castle Rock towering above the desert floor.

My mother stepped out and turned in a slow circle. "It's quite...desolate. Aren't you afraid to live out here by yourself?" she remarked to me, appearing apprehensive.

"Not really. I feel pretty safe," I answered, digging my .38 caliber handgun from my purse. "Because I've got this now."

Sean gave me a thumbs-up. "Way to go, Kenny!"

My mother's eyes widened in horror and she stepped back. "Good God! Is that real?"

"Don't panic, Mom, and yes, it's real." She'd always been terrified of guns and refused to allow any in the house. "Tally bought it for me last month. We've been target shooting several times and I'm getting to be a pretty decent shot." Actually he had insisted that I learn how to use a weapon because of what he termed, my propensity for getting myself into life-threatening situations.

"Well, good for you, honey," my dad said with an approving nod, while my mom kept staring at me as if I'd lost my mind before requesting that I please put it away. Oh, dear. She already harbored the notion that Tally was a corrupting influence on me. Had I just added to the list of negatives she'd already built up in her mind? Would meeting him in person finally dispel some of her reservations? I sure hoped so.

I unlocked the front door and waved them inside. Dad and Sean were immediately taken by Marmalade, who responded to the unexpected attention by purring, rolling around on the floor and then racing madly through the house. Because of her allergies, my mother kept her distance and held a tissue against her nose. But everyone liked the house, and my dad could not stop talking about how much he loved the wide-open spaces of Arizona. "I could definitely get used to this," he announced, turning his head in all directions as we all trooped out to the car. "This is about as far from city life as you could get."

I smiled at him. "Wait until you see the Starfire." Twenty minutes later, we turned onto Quail Crossing and cruised along the freshly graded dirt road flanked by miles of range fencing. Off in the distance a herd of cattle grazed on winter grass.

Sean let out a long whistle. "Man, how many acres does this dude have?"

"I'm not exactly sure, but a couple of thousand at least and he leases thousands more from the BLM for grazing the cattle." I noticed the thoughtful expression on my mother's face in the rearview mirror. "Well, my dear, it appears you are poised to become quite the landowner," she murmured, staring off into the distance.

Her judicious choice of words was her way of pointing out that I was about to marry into a well-heeled family, which I still couldn't quite believe. Of course, she had no idea of the cost of running such a large cattle and horse ranch.

"It's going to be a very different life for me," I admitted. Moments after driving beneath the Starfire ranch entrance sign, Tally's two-story, white house jumped into view along with the three cottages occupied by the hired help. To our right stood the two imposing horse barns along with a half a dozen horse trailers parked close to the maze of corrals. A small herd of Appaloosa horses grazed behind the white piped fencing that surrounded the property. In the clearing between the house and barns, several ranch hands were erecting the large white tent Tally had borrowed from the Whispering Winds Resort. Adjacent to it were stacks of tables and chairs, at least two dozen outdoor patio heaters, a portable dance floor, bar and risers for the band. Wow. Tally had really gone all out.

As I parked beside Tally's extended cab pickup near the house, my dad roared with laughter as he read the prominent bumper stickers: WELCOME TO ARIZONA. NOW GO HOME! A second one read: EAT MORE BEEF! THE WEST WASN'T WON ON SALADS. "That's a little insight into Tally's character," I informed them with a grin.

"Pretty clever," my dad remarked as everyone else joined in the merriment. "I think I'm gonna like this guy!"

I glanced back at the still doubtful gleam in my mother's eyes and held fast to the belief that Tally would eventually win her over. And then I thought about Ruth's unpredictable nature. That was going to be a tough sell indeed.

CHAPTER

7

The slamming car doors ignited a chorus of barking as all four dogs raced around the corner of the yard towards us. It was a pretty intimidating sight, so I dropped to one knee. "Come say hello to everybody, boys!" One by one they sniffed and circled, greeting each family member with thrashing tails and joyous whimpering. Always vying for extra attention, Atilla, the black Doberman, licked me in the face so hard, I almost fell over backwards.

The noisy excitement came to an abrupt halt when Ronda whistled and called sharply, "Leave it!" The dogs immediately fell silent, pivoted and ran towards the porch. Tally's dark-haired sister lifted a welcoming hand and issued a halfhearted smile. She had a real knack for communicating with animals, but people, not so much. She and her mother shared that particular trait. I introduced her to everyone and then she herded the dogs behind the house just as Tally stepped outside, raising one hand in a friendly greeting. "Howdy, folks. Welcome to the Starfire!"

Howdy? He was pouring on the Arizona rancher persona a bit thick, wasn't he? Nevertheless, my heart quickened as he ambled down the steps and strode towards us. Damn, he looked good. So good that I momentarily forgot I had a bone to pick with him. Wearing a soft blue shirt, slim jeans, well-worn boots and Stetson hat, he looked every bit the part of the quintessential American cowboy. When he flashed me his signature crooked grin, I was reminded again of how much I loved this ruggedly handsome man with his keen intellect, calm temperament and steadfast disposition. I glanced towards the house to see if there was any sign that his mother planned to make an appearance as well. Nope. So far so good. If she waited until later that was fine with me. The less my family had to be exposed to her, the better.

As I'd predicted, Tally and my dad hit it off from the first handshake. "Bradley Talverson, sir. Pleasure to meet you, Mr. O'Dell."

"Bill, just call me Bill," my dad replied, his face beaming. He pointed to the big tent. "Thank you for inviting us here today and going to the trouble of having this shindig for us."

"No trouble at all and call me Tally."

My brother extended his hand exclaiming, "This is a really cool place."

Pride glistening in his deep brown eyes, Tally replied with a winning smile, "Thanks, but there's still a whole lot more to see."

His attempts to charm my mother didn't appear to be as successful. She assumed a polite smile, but still seemed detached as we toured the barns and corrals to show off his line of prize-winning Appaloosa horses. Dad and Sean asked a million questions so I waited patiently while Tally recited a brief history of how they'd been originally bred by the Nez Perce tribe in Idaho, explained the selective breeding process to maintain the genetic purity and pointed out the unique coloration—the various spotting patterns overlaid on top of the recognized base colors including splashes of contrasting color on the hindquarters of each horse known as the 'blanket.'

Tally introduced everyone to Jake, his long-time, craggy-faced foreman, and several of the other ranch hands, one being the new hire, Vernon Holmes, chunky, blonde and current squeeze of the dreadful Lucinda. If I had to guess, I'd say he was at least ten years her junior, definitely placing her in the cougar category. Tally had given him high marks, citing his expertise with horses, but he didn't rate very high in my book because of their relationship.

It seemed to take forever, but we finally made our way towards the main barn where my horse was stabled. Itching to show her off, I dug in my pocket for the sugar cubes she'd be expecting. As I approached her stall she nickered softly. "Hey, you cutie!" I crooned, reaching out to stroke her mottled black muzzle. "Well, here she is! Meet Starlight Sky, the prettiest little mare in Arizona."

Sean, who had learned to ride horses bareback at his best friend's farm and was a far more accomplished rider than me, stepped forward to stroke her neck. "Didn't you luck out getting your own horse?"

I couldn't keep from grinning. "I did, didn't I?"

While Starlight Sky munched the sugar cubes, I grabbed her halter off the hook and secured it before leading her out into the sunlit corral so everyone could get a better look at her stunning 'white splotches over black' color pattern. Acting as if she was aware of all the attention, she put on quite a performance by tossing her head, swishing her tail and prancing around in circles showing off her striped hooves.

There was additional oohing and aahing as Tally led his stallion Geronimo, a spirited bay boasting a distinctive white snowflake pattern, into the arena. He discussed the more unique features of the breed, which made them popular for riding, cutting, reining and roping. Even my mother appeared more interested. "Well, what did you folks decide about seeing the building site for our new house?" Tally inquired, casting a doubtful glance at my dad's booted foot before pointing to the northeast. "That's Sidewinder Hill. It's about a mile and a half or so from here. I can have my men saddle up the horses for a short ride or Jake can drive you over there in my truck."

Sean grinned at me. "I know how much Kenny is dying to show off her riding skills, so I'm down for that."

I could tell by my dad's frustrated expression that he was struggling with his decision and was surprised when he boldly announced, "You know what? I didn't come three thousand miles to miss out on this adventure." He winked at me and turned to Tally. "Young man, if you can get me on the horse, I think I can handle the ride."

Genuine concern crossed my mother's face. "Are you sure about this, dear? I don't really think it's a good idea considering your condition."

He eyed her with a look of stubborn determination that invited no argument. "I'm sure. What about you? Would you be more comfortable riding in the truck?"

She hesitated and I felt kind of sorry for her being put

on the spot, considering that he knew how nervous she was around horses. "I...I guess if you feel up to it, I can give it a try." I could tell she didn't want to be left out.

Tally and I exchanged a perceptive glance. "The horses will be ready in about twenty minutes," he said, leading Geronimo towards the gate before turning around to address my mother. "I'll make sure you get Sheba. She's even-tempered, very gentle and in fact, she's the one Kendall rode on her first ride with me last spring."

"Thank you," she said with an indulgent smile. "That's very kind of you."

We followed Tally from the corral and I waved to two of his experienced stable hands. Juan and George returned my greeting with wide grins and as we neared the barn, Vernon appeared near the entrance. "Want me to saddle her up for you, Miss O'Dell?"

"No thanks, I'll do it."

"You can help with the others," Tally instructed him, pointing towards the second corral where Jake was leading three of my favorite horses.

"Yes, sir."

While Big Blue, Apache, and Sheba were being readied, I saddled Starlight Sky and then led her back to the corral. When I mounted her smoothly and began to trot her around the corral, a tingle of pride rippled over me as Sean hollered "Yee Haa" and my dad clapped enthusiastically.

But it was even more gratifying to see the look of reluctant admiration on my mother's face. Hopefully she would accept the fact that I wasn't a city girl any longer. If someone had told me a year ago that I would be living in the Arizona desert and engaged to marry a wealthy rancher I wouldn't have believed it.

To make things super easy for my father, Tally had provided a couple of wooden pallets for him to stand on. He and Jake helped him up, then laced their fingers together and gently eased him into the saddle, adjusting the one stirrup he could use. Sean bantered with Vernon as I reassured my mother, who was clearly uneasy straddling Sheba. In a surprise move, Tally gifted each of them with a beautiful new Stetson hat, which brought gracious smiles and words of gratitude from each family member. It was heartening to see the shadow of uncertainty in my mother's hazel eyes finally recede as everyone posed for a photo.

By the time we rode out single file with Tally in the lead and Jake pulling up to the rear, it was closing in on three o'clock. A feeling of euphoria overcame me as we rode across the cactus-covered desert. Now this was perfect—bright sunshine in my face, a light breeze and my loved ones gathered together to share a memorable experience and a little slice of my new lifestyle.

"You doing okay, Dad?" I inquired, loping up beside his blue roan while Starlight Sky tugged at the bit in her attempt to break into a gallop.

"So far so good," he responded, his face beaming with pleasure as he adjusted his hat to shade his eyes.

"Is your foot okay? Does it hurt?"

"Yeah, but I can deal with it."

"You're a trooper, Dad," I said, grinning.

"No big deal." Lowering his voice, his nodded towards Tally riding ahead of Sean. "You made a good choice, kiddo."

"Yeah, I think so too." He'd said it loud enough for

my mother to overhear behind us. I glanced back and caught her faint smile. While not exactly a ringing endorsement, her expression conveyed gradual acceptance. Progress! As we rode on past imposing rock formations, saguaro and barrel cactus plumped up from the rain, Tally turned and warned everyone to stay away from the jumping cactus, called cholla. The golden field of teddy bear cholla that appeared soft and inviting from a distance, was anything but. My dad rode up beside Tally and continued to grill him for details on running a ranch. When we neared Sidewinder Hill, it struck me that I had been so preoccupied all day, I'd completely forgotten to call and check on Ginger. Stung with guilt, I vowed to contact her before the festivities got under way later. It also dawned on me that Fritzy had never returned my call or sent me a text. But that wasn't unexpected. She was either busy or, more likely, it was too early in her investigation to have any concrete news.

Long afternoon shadows had begun to creep across the landscape as we advanced up the slope towards the building site, and when we finally arrived at the top, everyone looked suitably impressed. I dismounted, tied Starlight Sky to a tree, then helped my mother down before pulling the building plans from Tally's saddlebag while he and Jake got my dad comfortably seated on flat rock. He was visibly uncomfortable, but I knew he'd never complain about it.

Aware that we had a finite amount of time before dusk, I spread out the plans on the ground and then Tally and I fielded questions. "That's going to be some house," my dad remarked with an approving nod before his gaze traveled to the valley below and beyond to the distant purple mountains. "And you're gonna have one hell of a view!"

Anxious for my mother's endorsement, I made eye contact with her. "Well, Mom, what do you think?"

She chewed her lower lip for a few seconds before answering. "Well, I love the layout, but four thousand square feet is going to be a lot to take care of and…do you think you'll be happy living here on this isolated hilltop so far from the main house and…everything?"

I traded a knowing look with Tally. She had no idea how ecstatic I would be to have more than a mile separating me from Ruth.

"She'll have house help," Tally interjected with a benevolent smile, sliding his arm around my waist. "And she won't be alone." His intimate suggestion brought a blush to my mom's face and she quickly looked away, clutching her coat tighter. "It's getting chilly. Shouldn't we be starting back?"

"Not before I find a place to take a dump," Sean announced impishly. I could tell he was deliberately needling her.

"Sean, really. Must you be so crude?" She skewered him with a contemptuous glare while the rest of us stifled laughter.

Tally directed him to go behind some boulders while he and Jake helped my father remount Big Blue and then gave my mother a leg up. I glanced at my watch, calculating that we should get back just about sunset, which would give everyone a half an hour to freshen up before the barbeque got underway. We trekked back down the hill, Tally in the lead followed by my parents, Jake, and Sean behind me. When the ground leveled out, Sean trotted up beside me. "How about you and me have a little race?" His eyes sparkled with challenge. "Just plodding along at this pace is putting me and this awesome animal to sleep."

Starlight Sky, who'd been champing at her bit to cut loose the entire ride, apparently agreed by yanking the reins insistently and blowing softly. "You sure you're up for it?"

"Try me."

When we pulled even with Tally I told him we were going to give the horses their head and he nodded with instructions to first walk our horses in the opposite direction from the ranch. "We don't want to get the others all wound up," he cautioned, looking back to check on my folks.

"We'll be back shortly," I informed my parents before turning the horses westward into the waning afternoon sunlight. The animals seemed to instinctively know what was in store and we had trouble keeping them contained until I determined we were far enough away. When I finally relaxed the reins, Starlight Sky took off and Sean hollered, "Ride 'em, cowgirl!" as he urged Apache into a full gallop. It was exhilarating to race side by side through the desert on the sure-footed horses and we were both laughing breathlessly by the time we'd guided them in a wide arc and finally spotted the other riders ahead. As we approached, I reined Starlight Sky to a slow trot, but Sean ignored Tally's warning about exciting the other horses and, in an apparent effort to impress our parents, loped the powerful chestnut in circles around them, waving his hat in one hand and yelling, "Yeeee Haaaaw!"

Tally's eyes flashed with annoyance and Jake intervened with a stern, "Best simmer down now, young fella."

Looking sheepish, Sean immediately slowed to a walk behind my mother. "Son-of-a-bitch that was fun," he crowed, jamming the hat back on his head.

I teased him for being a show-off as Jake eased up enough to allow Sean to cut in behind me. We rode on in companionable silence watching the sun's slow journey towards the molten amber horizon. We were only about ten minutes from the ranch when Sheba, usually gentle and mellow, suddenly kicked up her heels and lunged sideways, almost unseating my mother, who lost her hat, panicked and dropped the reins. Before any of us could react, the palomino neighed loudly and bolted across the desert with my mother hanging onto the pommel for dear life and my dad shouting, "Alana! Hold on!"

Icy fear stabbed my heart like a knife as her horrified screams filled the air.

CHAPTER
8

We all sat frozen in open-mouthed indecision for what seemed like hours, but in reality it was mere seconds before Tally sprang into action. Spurring Geronimo hard, he thundered after Sheba, swiftly closing the distance between them. And then, in a move reminiscent of countless old western movies, he reached out, wrapped one arm around my mother's waist and scooped her onto his saddle while he simultaneously slid off it onto the horse's rear. Sheba kept kicking and bucking as Jake rode up beside her and somehow managed to grab the reins.

"Holy shit!" Sean gasped, goggle-eyed. "That was epic!"

Released from my fear-induced paralysis, I kneed Starlight Sky towards Tally, my adrenalin-charged heart pounding furiously. "Mom, are you all right?" I shouted, riding along side him, both relieved and grateful.

Shaken and disoriented, she replied, "I think so," then turned to look up at Tally with newfound admiration shining in her eyes. "Thank you so much," she added in a tremulous voice.

"Yes, thank you," I chimed in, beaming him an affectionate smile and wondering if he had any idea how much I loved him at this moment. "That was nothing short of miraculous."

"All in a day's work," he said, keeping his tone light. But when we locked eyes, the intense light in his told the true story of how grave the situation could have been. My heart contracted painfully at the thought of her being thrown from a runaway horse and badly hurt or killed. "What's the story with Sheba?" I asked. "She's never done anything like this before."

"Don't know," he answered in a distracted tone, watching Jake dismount and attempt to soothe the agitated animal just as my dad and Sean rode up beside us.

"Alana, are you hurt?" my dad inquired in an anxious tone as Sean echoed his concerns. Once they were convinced that she was okay, Dad exclaimed to Tally, "Young man, that was an outstanding feat of horsemanship."

Tally tapped the brim of his hat just as Jake whistled and beckoned him to come. We all rode the short distance together and found Sheba standing still, calmly swishing her tail as if nothing had happened. Jake held up his pocket comb with something in it. "She had a couple cholla balls wedged under the blanket."

"Ouch. No wonder she went ape shit," Sean muttered. He darted me a strange look that I interpreted as guilt as I dismounted to retrieve my mother's hat and return it to her. Was he blaming himself for the horse's odd behavior? I had to admit that it was possible. Apache may have kicked up the offending spikey cactus balls during his little rodeo act earlier. Just to be safe, Tally decided against putting my mother back on Sheba and as we all rode into the corral, the postcard skyline glowed like a halo of fire—quickly fading from brilliant shades of iridescent copper to fiery scarlet-orange as the sun winked out behind the darkened mountains.

Jake insisted on tending to the horses himself and assured us he'd join us all later. My mother fretted that she should have brought a change of clothing so she wouldn't smell like 'horse.' Looking amused, Tally assured her that since everything around us smelled like horses no one would notice. Then he grabbed my hand, and when we rounded the corner of the barn, I gaped in surprise at the sight of the big tent blazing with light and packed with rows of tables and chairs. Several ranch hands scurried here and there, taking instructions from Ronda who stood in the soft reddish glow of a tall propane heater. The fiddle and guitar players were warming up on the bandstand and the pungent odor of burning mesquite wood permeated the air. Sparkling string lights draped over the palo verde trees and cactus gave the usually empty clearing a carnival-like ambiance. "Tally!" I exclaimed, squeezing his hand, "What an amazing transformation! You guys have really outdone yourselves!" It was obvious he'd spared no expense and my throat tightened with appreciation.

When everyone chimed in, echoing my sentiments, Tally grinned with pleasure, then said, "Let's head over to the house so everybody can wash up and then we'll get this party started."

My parents were still marveling at the idea that an outdoor party was even possible during the month of

December when the first guests began to arrive. When we reached the front door, Tally and I paused to trade an anxious look. I knew we were thinking the same thing. "Might as well get it over with," he whispered in my ear as we entered the warm kitchen, which bustled with activity. Gloria, the family's treasured Hispanic housekeeper, and her younger sisters, Moya and Brisa, greeted us with genial smiles. Stomach clenched nervously, I looked around for Ruth, but she was nowhere to be seen. I couldn't decide whether I was disappointed or relieved.

"Oh, my goodness! Will you look at this!" my mother marveled, staring in disbelief at the long kitchen table overflowing with plates of appetizers, bowls of tossed greens, potato and macaroni salads, cowboy beans, huge trays of marinating ribs, steaks and chicken plus an impressive variety of pies, sheet cakes and several platters of cookies.

Overcome by the divine aroma and array of mouth-watering dishes spread out before me, I couldn't resist sampling a few bites as Tally made the round of introductions and then escorted my family to the back of the house to freshen up. He returned moments later, gave me a quick kiss and headed for the door, saying he'd see me later. I was washing my hands in the kitchen sink when Ronda breezed in moments later, looking more dressed up than I'd ever seen her, all decked out in black jeans, gold-fringed shirt and black vest. When I complimented her on the outfit and praised her organizational skills her normally sullen expression brightened perceptibly. After she had given instructions to the staff on where to transport the food, I ventured, "So, ah, where is your mother?"

She wrinkled her nose and shrugged. "Probably still

holed up in her room. She's been sort of belligerent all day."

"About what?"

"The barbeque. She's been bitching about all the commotion and stuff. I guess it's stressing her out."

My jaw tightened. "So, I gather the new medication isn't working."

"It might if she'd take it once in a while."

Great. Was it really too much to ask that just this one time she come out of her room, or smoking lair, as I called it, and act like a normal human being for a few hours? Spiteful old bitch.

Ronda's cell phone rang and she put it to her ear, listened intently, then said, "Okay, be right out," shoved it in her back pocket, grabbed up a covered dish and called over her shoulder smiling, "Lucy's here with her yummy biscuits," before rushing outside.

Lucinda was bringing biscuits? That frosted me.

"All this fresh air has fired up my appetite!" my dad announced with a winning smile, clomping back into the kitchen with my mom and Sean close behind. "I'm so hungry, I could eat an entire cow right now."

With effort, I suppressed my aggravation and put on a happy face. "I think that can be arranged."

Outside in the cold night air once more, we were caught up in the festive atmosphere, listening to foot-stomping country music and lively conversations as we threaded our way through the crowd of guests. It seemed as though I'd introduced them to half the townspeople and a fair number of neighboring ranch owners by the time we got to the bar and ordered margaritas from Ginger's boyfriend, Doug, who was bartending. I wanted to ask him how she was doing, but could tell he was too busy to talk. Sudden guilt grabbed me. Damn! I still hadn't had time to call her. Instead, I sent her a quick text telling her I was thinking about her and would talk to her soon.

Sean opted for beer and within minutes, had hooked up with Jim Sykes and his girlfriend Sheryl, plus several other men and a couple of young women I didn't recognize. As I helped myself to chicken wings, I noticed that the Hinkle twins, well known in the community as troublemakers, had also joined Sean's group. Meanwhile, Morton Tuggs and his wife Mary arrived and were soon engaged in an animated discussion with my parents regarding all the sightseeing destinations we planned to visit.

The smoky air was thick with the delicious aroma of grilling steaks by the time I finished my second drink and had a nice buzz going. My earlier irritation had all but vanished when I heard a familiar throaty laugh behind me. Turning my head, I spotted Lucinda talking with Tally and standing waaaay too close. Her hot pink western shirt, unbuttoned practically to her waist, blazed with what looked like a gazillion rhinestones and her cream-colored jeans were so tight they looked like they'd been sprayed on. In fact, they were so snug no one could possibly question her gender. Her blatantly flirtatious behavior spawned a sudden rush of jealousy. What a total slut!

The tap on my shoulder made me flinch. "Kendall, how are you, my dear?" Still fuming, I dragged my gaze away and swung around to see Walter Zipp's hefty wife smiling at me with her great, big rabbit teeth. "Oh hi, Lavelle. I'm…just…perfect."

"Well, that's good. Listen, Walter wanted me to give

you his apology for not being here tonight," she announced, gripping a platter of food piled in a dangerously high pyramid. "He was feeling so rotten he came home from work an hour early and he's been either in bed or in the bathroom ever since." That didn't sound promising. "Sorry to hear that. Did you call Dr. Garcia?"

She popped a cherry tomato into her mouth and chewed. "Yes, he phoned something in to the drug store, but I can't get it until they open tomorrow morning."

My spirits wilted. "I see. Well, tell him I hope he feels better soon." And what if he didn't? Tugg was going to be in one a hell of a mess next week. Could the timing possibly be worse? "Thanks for coming, Lavelle. I hope you enjoy yourself anyway."

"Oh, I intend to. This is quite a party! Oh, hey there, Mavis!" she shouted over the music to an elderly, white-haired woman waving to her. She excused herself, waddled away, miraculously balancing the tower of food, and left me standing there wondering if I should mention her news to Tugg, who was engaged in lively conversation with my parents and two other couples. No. I'd wait. Walter might be fine by Monday. Why worry him unnecessarily?

I looked around again and Tally was no longer there. Relief flowed through me at the sight of Vernon leading Lucinda onto the dance floor where her suggestive moves captured the attention of every man, while the women glared daggers at her. I had to smile. At least I wasn't the only one who found her conduct thoroughly distasteful.

I went in search of Tally and bumped into Ronda carrying a tray of biscuits. "I got Ma to come out," she informed me, inclining her head towards the big canopy.

"She's in there having supper with Dot."

I pulled a blank. "Dot?"

"You know her," she explained with an impatient sigh. "You met her right here at the barbeque last summer." I must have still looked blank because she added, "She brought all those great apple pies everyone raved about, remember? I think you ate three pieces."

"Oh, yes!" I remembered the melt-in-your mouth pies and also that the woman's face was so incredibly sun-weathered it looked like a wrinkled old work glove. "Thanks, Ronda."

She started to walk away and then swiveled around. "If you still want her to meet your family, I'd suggest getting over there before she has any more to drink."

I frowned at her. "Really? Should she be mixing booze with prescription drugs?"

"Hey, I don't have time to babysit her tonight. I'm just telling it like it is." With that, she hurried away as I pulled out my cell phone to dial Tally's number. It was vital that he be present to act as a referee should any problems arise. His number rang and rang and went to voicemail. Why wasn't he answering? Did he even have his phone turned on?

I left him a terse message asking him to please be there for the long-awaited, long-dreaded introduction to Ruth and then went looking for my folks. It took me several minutes to locate them and they had no idea where Sean was, so I sent him a text as well. After promising Tugg and Mary that we'd catch up with them later, I escorted my parents towards the big tent. Once inside, we worked our way between the tables crowded with families eating, drinking and generally having a great time. We had to stop repeatedly for more introductions. Another ten minutes passed before I noticed Ruth seated at a small table in the furthest corner, deep in conversation with Dot Mullen. I took a measured breath. Show time! The closer we got, the more my agitation increased. Apparently meeting my family was so unimportant that not only had Ruth declined to dress for the occasion, she had not even bothered to comb her stringy, oily-looking salt and pepper hair. In fact, she looked like she'd just crawled out of a dumpster. Dressed in her usual ratty, old sheepskin coat, faded jeans and scuffed boots, she had a cigarette going and a drink in her hand. She was facing away from me and I was poised to call her name when she stated in a loud voice, "All I can say is I hope my son has better luck with this redhead than the last one. That dumb bitch was a huge pain in the ass and this one isn't much of an improvement."

"What do you mean by that?" Dot asked, just seconds before she spotted me.

"I asked her to do me one tiny favor and what does she do? Runs around all over town spilling the family secrets and spreading vicious lies to try and ruin my good reputation."

Her face red with embarrassment, Dot lowered her eyes and the look of stunned disbelief on my parent's faces was classic. Me? I felt like the top of my head was going to blow off. I could not think of a polite response and wondered if it was even worth the effort to rebut her lies. I had a sneaking suspicion that she'd seen us coming and planned that we would overhear her disparaging remarks. Oh, how I would love to wring her scrawny neck. But, in an attempt to maintain peace, I decided to ignore her. Summoning what little patience I possessed, I forced a cordial tone. "Hello, Ruth. I'd like you to meet my parents, Bill and Alana O'Dell."

She sat perfectly still for a few seconds before slowly turning her head in our direction. Her mouth pursed tightly shut, she gave my parents a cursory glance, then fastened her fathomless dark eyes on me and said nothing. My dad finally broke the silence. Clearing his throat uncomfortably, he said, "Mrs. Talverson, we've...ah...been looking forward to meeting you for a long time."

"Have you now?" She took another long sip of her drink and sucked deeply on her cigarette before adding gruffly, "I hope you're enjoying...all of this," she said waving her hand in a wide arc. "My children have gone to a great deal of trouble and expense to impress you people." Her gaunt face turned crafty. "So tell me, are you impressed?"

You people? Could the old bat be more insulting? Their faces frozen in shock, my folks leveled a questioning look at me as if to ask, 'What do you want us to say?' which only increased my sense of regret that I had not told them the truth about her condition.

"Actually, we are very impressed," my mother answered coldly, her eyes hard with dislike, "and doubly so that your son had the good sense to choose this very talented, exceptionally beautiful redhead to be his bride. Aren't you?"

Way to go, Mom! I tossed her an appreciative glance and absorbed my dad's disconcerted stare. Not one to be outfoxed, Ruth casually stubbed out her cigarette. "Oh, I can hardly wait." Her cynical half-smile disturbed me, but I reminded myself that her hostility was indicative of her ongoing mental and emotional issues. And alcohol could also be a contributing factor.

Refusing to be drawn into a heated verbal exchange she was so obviously spoiling for, I clapped my hands together in mock glee. "Well, hasn't this been fun?" I almost laughed out loud at Ruth's startled expression. "Mom, Dad, what do you say we go get some of those super-expensive steaks that have been provided to impress you?"

They both stared at me as if I'd lost my mind before realization dawned in my dad's eyes. "Great idea, Pumpkin! I'm hungry enough to eat two or three at least. Let's go, Alana." He positioned his crutches firmly, nodded curtly to Ruth, and as we walked away, I turned back and fired her a challenging look. "We both know the truth, don't we? You and I will talk later." The nasty old bitch had better get used to the idea that the new Mrs. Talverson wasn't going to put up with her shit.

Once we were out of earshot, my mother grabbed my arm and gave me a penetrating look. "What a thoroughly obnoxious woman. What's her problem anyway?"

"No wonder you want to live a mile away from her," my dad chimed in, shaking his head with obvious concern. "In fact, I don't think that's nearly far enough."

I broke eye contact for a few seconds then looked back at them. "I should have told you sooner, but...here's the deal. Ruth is bipolar and God knows what else. She's on quite a few medications, when she chooses to take them. She can be bearable at times and unpleasant and hard to live with at others, as you saw. Unfortunately, she's part of the family package."

Worry lines creased my mother's forehead. "Honey, this is going to be really rough on you. Why didn't you tell us?"

I stared up at the stars for several seconds before answering. "Because I know you haven't been happy about my decision to stay here in Arizona and marry Tally and, well, I didn't want to add one more reason for you to be critical of him."

Looking contrite, she said, "I'm sorry. I should have known better than to rush to judgment. Now that I've met him, he seems…like a truly fine man." She paused as if searching for the right words. "I honestly didn't think this would be a way of life that you would…I mean I didn't think you'd want to stay here forever and live on a ranch in the middle of nowhere. I thought you'd want to come home again…" her voice trailed off when Tally suddenly pushed through the crowd and strode to my side, holding his cell phone. I noticed the odd expression on his face and he no doubt saw the look of exasperation on mine. Even though I was glad to see him, I couldn't help but be a little ticked off that he'd left me hanging out to dry with his mother.

"Yes, I got your message. Sorry about the delay. I've been tied up with a rather ticklish problem—"

"Yeah," I interrupted him, "and speaking of ticklish, your mother was in rare form tonight. I would say rude was the operative word."

He glanced at my parents. "I apologize. I had planned to be here but ah…listen, would you excuse us for a few minutes?" He took my hand. "We'll be right back."

I stared at him, unable to decipher the strange message in his eyes.

"Sure thing," my dad said quickly, both of them casting me a curious look. "We were just about to get some dinner." As they moved towards the grill, Tally steered me into the shadows away from the noisy crowd of people. There was just enough ambient light playing across his rugged features to reveal his serious expression. "Tally, what's going on?"

"I need to talk to you."

"I'll say. First, you owe me an apology for leaving me in such a bind tonight. Your mother was just awful! It was unbelievably embarrassing! And secondly, why the hell did you invite Lucinda here tonight? You know very well that I cannot stand her!"

"What? Why are we talking about Lucinda?"

"Because, she told me you begged her to come here. Really? You begged her to bring biscuits?"

"Biscuits? I didn't beg her to bring biscuits." He sounded incredulous.

"Ah ha! I knew she was lying! And I saw her flaunting her giant—"

He broke in harshly, "Kendall, calm down! This is not important—"

I cut in, "It is to me."

His growl of frustration sounded like one of the dogs. "Damn it! What do I have to do? Arrange a duel for you two or maybe you ladies would rather duke it out?"

"Only one of us is a lady and yes, that sounds agreeable to me. I'd love to punch her lights out." Only after the words escaped my mouth did I realize how ridiculously childish I sounded.

He grabbed my shoulders, his face only inches from mine. "Listen to me, my incredibly adorable, but exceedingly pig-headed lady. You're going to have to get over Lucinda. In fact, instead of badmouthing her, you ought to be thanking her."

I was so incensed, I could hardly breathe. "Thank her! For what?"

"We'd have no live music tonight if it wasn't for her."

"What do you mean?"

"Apparently she's buds with Randall and somehow sweet-talked him into playing here tonight. Now will you please shut up and let me speak?"

His explanation left me feeling foolish and deflated. I was glad the light was low enough that he couldn't see my flushed cheeks. "Sure. What's up?"

He lifted his hat, combed his fingers through his thick hair and replaced it before answering. "I didn't want to say anything in front of your folks because I knew it would get them all riled up, but Jake caught Sean with Danny and Daryl Hinkle, plus a couple of girls I don't know, all smoking pot behind the barn."

"I had a bad feeling when I saw him with them earlier. Why did you invite those boys anyway?" I called them boys but they were actually only two years younger than me. I'd yet to meet them in person, but learned their history of school bullying and scrapes with the law as juveniles while writing a piece on Daryl's arrest for a DUI last summer. The record also showed they had been arrested two years earlier for disorderly conduct and assault after their alleged involvement in a nightclub brawl in Scottsdale. The charges had subsequently been dropped due to lack of evidence and witnesses refusing to come forward.

"I didn't," Tally informed me crisply. "Apparently, they piggybacked on our invitation to Elizabeth. She's had a pretty rough year since John died. It would have been cruel not to invite her, don't you think?"

"I suppose so. I just don't like the idea of Sean being influenced by those guys." Because Elizabeth Hinkle lived on the neighboring ranch from me, I'd always waved at her when we passed each other on the road and had talked briefly with her several times at various town functions. I'd always wondered why she wore such a sad, harried expression and felt sorry for her. After questioning Tally, he'd filled me in on a few salient details about her background. Being the only not-terribly-attractive daughter of rancher Buster McCracken, she'd remained single until the age of 38, when she'd married widower John Hinkle and taken on the thankless task of raising his two out-of-control ten-year-old sons who had been running wild since their mother's death four years earlier. According to Ginger, whom I affectionately referred to as the Castle Valley Gossip Queen, Elizabeth had finally ordered the two aggressive young men off the Hinkle ranch earlier in the year, but had recently allowed them to return and stay in the bunkhouse, even though they continually harassed her for money, claiming their father's ranch rightfully belonged to them.

Tally nodded sagely. "No question they are a couple of certified misfits. But how do you know it was them?" he asked, folding his arms over his chest. "Suppose it was your brother who provided the dope?"

Good point. Fuming, I groused, "Apparently my brother learned nothing from getting busted and spending the night in jail."

"I wasn't as concerned about them drinking and smoking a joint as I was about the white powder being passed around."

Intense dread knotted my stomach. That confirmed my fear that he was experimenting with other, possibly more lethal drugs. "Did you say anything to them?"

"I told them I wouldn't tolerate that kind of behavior on my property and to take it someplace else."

I shook my head sadly. "I ought to slap the crap out of him for being so stupid and irresponsible! Where is that little shit anyway?"

Tally expelled a long breath. "I hate to tell you this, but I don't know."

CHAPTER
9

My grandmother would have pronounced this a fine kettle of fish. I fought to corral the mixture of emotions roiling in my empty stomach. Think. What to do? I'd had so many ups and downs the past two days I could not wrap my brain around this new problem or what to do about it. "What do you mean, you don't know?"

"I mean, I saw him leave with them and I don't know where they went."

For a few seconds, I really felt like I was going to lose it. "I don't believe this." I pulled out my cell phone and dialed Sean's number, only to be disappointed when it went to voicemail. "The brat is not answering." I fired off a quick text demanding that he get his butt back to the ranch pronto. "Oh, my God," I moaned, resting my forehead in one hand. "I cannot seem to catch a break." Sighing heavily, I looked up into Tally's sympathetic eyes. "Having them all here was supposed to be fun and some of it has been, but it's also been kind of stressful. I mean, if you start with my dad's fractured foot, then proceed to learning about Sean's arrest," I said, counting on my fingers, "factor in Ginger's cousin's death, then consider the rotten scene with your mother and finally add in Walter getting sick and probably being absent from work while I'm gone..." my voice faltered as I tried to conceal the tremor in my voice.

Without saying a word, Tally stepped forward and enfolded me in his arms. I leaned into his muscular frame, slid my arms around his waist and immediately felt more at peace than I had for days. I wished I could stay there forever. Listening to the lilting strains of a slow country ballad in the background, we were soon moving gently to the beat of the music. Locked in a tight embrace, it wasn't long before he tipped my chin up and locked his sensuous lips against mine, igniting all my senses. It was a blissfully romantic moment and I was enjoying myself so much I lost track of time. When we eventually pulled apart, he said softly, "Listen to me, Kendall. There's no use worrying yourself about things you have no control over. Most of this stuff will work itself out. I'm sorry as hell about Ma's behavior and I will make damn sure she apologizes to you and your folks."

"What if she refuses?"

"Then she won't be coming to our engagement party."

My breath caught in my throat. "And you'd be okay with that?"

"I'd be okay with that."

His selfless offer sent a powerful surge of love and admiration coursing through me. "Thank you for that," I said, caressing his cheek then kissing him again passionately, deeply gratified to have this pragmatic man as the love of my life. When we finally came up for air, I added, "And thank you, thank you, thank you for that super-amazing rescue of my mom. That was some kind of riding, cowboy."

He chuckled. "Think she likes me a little better now?"

"I'm thinking…mmmmm… yes."

"Good. So, what about you," he said, pushing a stray curl away from one eye. "Has your mood improved any?"

I hesitated before saying, "For the most part."

He fixed me with a perceptive look. "I know. You're worried about your brother. Look, he's a big boy and I'm guessing that group all went someplace to party the way young people do nowadays."

"That's what worries me. I'm really bothered by his juvenile behavior. He acts like he's fifteen, not twenty-five."

"Let's face it, if your brother is a stoner, you may just have to accept it."

"I get that, but considering what he's just put my folks through, wouldn't you think he'd cool it on the drug use at least while he's here with all of us? What am I going to tell them? When they find out he's not here, they'll have an atomic cow."

"Maybe, but I'll tell you what. First, we're going to get you something to eat," he said, his tone soothing. "Then we'll deal with it. Okay?"

I agreed and when we returned to the festivities, I was heartened to see my parents seated at a table with Tugg, Mary and two other couples laughing and engaged in lively conversation. They looked so happy and relaxed I decided to postpone telling them anything at least until after I had eaten. Maybe I'd luck out and Sean would return soon, sparing me the task of having to explain his absence.

While Tally and I stood in line waiting for grilled steaks, baked potatoes and corn on the cob, scores of friends and acquaintances congratulated us on our engagement and when we finally got to eat, I must admit my temperament did improve. I was still sampling various desserts when Tally excused himself to go find Ronda. I kept checking my phone to see if Sean had returned my call or text, but he had not. There was, however, a text from Ginger asking me to stop by Marcelene's house later. She'd talked with her aunt and had information regarding Jenessa that might be significant. That got my imagination cooking. I could hardly wait to find out what it was and yet, I knew myself well enough to realize it would be better for me if I didn't know. Whatever it was would no doubt drive me crazy because I couldn't do a damn thing about it.

It was closing in on ten o'clock, getting cold enough to see your breath, and guests were saying their goodnights when I spotted Jim Sykes talking with Tally some distance away. Wait a minute! He'd been with Sean earlier. Maybe he knew something. I sprang off the chair. He and his girlfriend were almost to his truck when I intercepted them. "Hey, Jim, got a second?"

They both turned and he asked, "Sure, what's up?"

"A couple of quick questions."

"Okay, well, let me turn on the heat for Sheryl, she's freezing."

"Hi, Sheryl," I said, waving to his tall, blonde companion. "Did you have fun?"

"I sure did! Thanks for inviting us, Kendall." She wrapped her scarf around her neck and climbed into the truck. Jim started the engine, then stepped out and shut the door, rubbing his hands together before buttoning his coat. "What's going on?"

"Earlier tonight, I saw you talking with my brother Sean and the Hinkle brothers. Do you know where they went?"

His expression turned crafty. "I gather you already know Tally ran 'em off the ranch."

"Yes and I'm assuming you know why."

He hitched his shoulders. "I don't know all the details, but I'm thinking they might've gone to their ranch, or I overheard Danny say something about maybe going over to the Rattlesnake to play pool."

The Rattlesnake Saloon was well-known as a hangout for the rougher element of Castle Valley. "Thanks, Jim. Oh, and I heard Walter went home sick. Do you know if he talked to Duane or stopped over at the sheriff's office? He was supposed to check out some things for me."

He shook his head. "Unless he met up with Duane in the can, I don't think he did. He was in there most of the day."

My spirits sank. "Man, I sure hope it's just food poisoning."

"Me too," Jim concurred, jamming his hands in his pockets, "because he looked like he was at death's door when he left. I mean it. His face looked sort of green. If he's got some kind of creeping crud, I definitely don't want it."

"You'd better not get sick. I'm counting on you guys to hold down the fort until I get back."

He gave me a thumbs-up. "That's the plan!" He jumped into his truck and as he roared off into the night, the sinking sensation in my gut intensified. There was no way out of it. I could not put off telling my parents any longer, but decided that I didn't have to tell them the circumstances just yet. Tally was right. He was not a kid and I had to believe that at some point someone would drive him back to the motel.

Keeping that optimistic thought in mind, I met up with Tally and we went to find my parents, who were still visiting with Tugg and Mary. They both looked so cute sitting there wearing their new western hats. After we all said our goodnights and waved goodbye, I reminded them of my plan to pick everyone up at seven-thirty for our drive to Prescott for breakfast at one of my favorite restaurants. From there we would travel the scenic, winding road up Mingus Mountain to visit the former ghost town of Jerome, now turned artist colony. Later, we'd join Tally for dinner at the new Crab Shack for dinner.

"Where's Sean?" my mother asked, pulling her coat closer as she shouldered her purse. "I haven't seen him for hours."

I didn't miss the observant gleam in Tally's eyes when I explained that he'd been invited to join some of the other younger people at another party and that I expected they'd drop him back at the motel later on. My mother gave me a long, searching look before exchanging a suspicious glance with my dad who then transferred it to me.

"You'd think he could be considerate enough to at least let us know he was going someplace, but no, he only ever thinks of himself," my mother fussed, her mouth fixed in a straight line.

It seemed to be an evening of regrets. I should really tell them the whole truth, even though it would absolutely ruin the evening and perhaps the entire visit. Wasn't I only postponing their eventual pain by giving Sean the benefit of the doubt? What was I going to do if he didn't return tonight?

As we sailed through the pitch-black landscape, illuminated solely by the bright haze of starlight, I tried to quell my apprehension and enjoy the scenery, but failed. Why wasn't Sean answering my phone or text messages? What if he wasn't at the Rattlesnake? He was in new surroundings, mingling with strangers well-known locally for their corrupting influences. What if he did something stupid and got himself into more serious trouble? I was driving myself crazy with 'what ifs.'

"You're awfully quiet," my dad remarked softly. "You must be pooped, I know I am." He absently rubbed his leg above the ankle boot and I could tell by his drawn face that he was in pain again.

"Yeah, it's been a pretty active day. How about you, Mom? Are you feeling okay after your wild ride? I'm really sorry about that."

"My shoulders and neck are a little sore, but in an odd way, I'm kind of glad it happened."

I glanced in the rearview mirror, but it was too dark to see her face clearly. "Why?"

"Because, it was…kind of a revelation of how wrong I've been about Tally all this time. I think you've chosen a good man, a brave man, and I couldn't be happier for the two of you."

After so many months of listening to her constant criticisms and engaging in heated exchanges on the phone, her unexpected answer triggered a rush of euphoria. "Thanks, Mom. I think I'll keep him."

"I'm with her one hundred percent, Pumpkin," my dad interjected, reaching over to pat my shoulder. "But, I certainly don't envy you having to put up with his mother. She is something else again and I know you're kind of light in the patience department."

"It's been a real struggle," I admitted, turning into the motel parking lot. I walked them to their room and hugged them both while they thanked me profusely for what my dad called 'a one-of-a-kind day and a first class party.' As we waved goodbye, I noticed the agitated look in my mother's eyes when she glanced next door at the darkened window in Sean's room. Sharing her sentiments, I drove around the front of the building, parked beside Ginger's car and hurried along the rose-flanked walkway that lead to the small cottage tucked behind the motel office. As I walked up the shallow steps onto the well-lit front porch, I decided the manicured honeysuckle vines crawling along the railing added just the right amount of character and assisted in making the place look more like a big dollhouse.

My light knock on the door was answered within seconds. Illuminated in the bright rectangle of golden light, Ginger waved me inside. "Get in here, Sugar! It's colder 'n a frosted frog out there tonight."

"It's not too bad." It was hard not to smile when Marcelene's pug, Squirt, rushed to greet me. He emitted friendly snuffling noises and showed his pleasure by whirling around in circles. I knelt down to pet him and was rewarded by squealing grunts. "You are so darn cute!" I said with a laugh, petting his taut, little body.

"Sorry about missin' the cookout," she lamented with a sigh. "I was yakkin' with Doug a minute ago and he said it was a real big success."

"It was. I'm sorry you both missed it, but I

understand." Having become accustomed to being out in the cold night air for so many hours, it seemed stuffy inside so I immediately shed my coat.

"Just toss it over the back of the couch and come on into the kitchen," Ginger said. "Marcelene's got a story you need to hear."

"Okay." Super curious to hear what she had to say, I followed Ginger and Squirt towards an arched doorway, noting that the place was just as cozy inside as I'd imagined. The small living room was tastefully furnished in a country decor—lots of bric-a-brac on the tables and shelves, an upright piano, colorful throw pillows brightened beige overstuffed furniture and a highly polished parquet floor with scattered area rugs. When we entered the little kitchen, Marcelene sat slump-shouldered at a round maple table pouring steaming water from a flowered teapot. Behind her, the cheerful blue and white gingham curtains adorning the windows, along with the animated chirp of a cuckoo clock, belied her downcast expression.

"Hi, Kendall," she said, looking up at me with a forlorn smile, "I'm glad you came by. Would you like a cup of raspberry tea? I have some freshly baked cookies too."

"Thank you. How are you holding up?"

Her shrug and wordless grimace said it all. Once she'd set out more cups and we were seated, Ginger urged, "Okay now, tell Kendall what you just told me."

Marcelene took a sip of her tea and at the same time, slipped a piece of cookie to Squirt, who gulped it down and then sat on the floor gazing up at her with bulbous, adoring eyes. Her hand trembling slightly, she set the cup down with a despondent sigh. "It was July, fourteen years ago. Jenessa was seven years old. Arnold and I had rented a houseboat on Lake Powell along with Jack Dugan, a family friend, and his son, Eric, who was eleven, I think. Jenessa had begged us for weeks to allow her best friend Kailey to come along and after some hesitation and consulting with her parents, we finally said yes."

"Why were you hesitating?" I asked.

"Because she was not a well child. We debated taking responsibility for her, but Jenessa was insistent that she be allowed to come, so...we eventually gave in."

"What was wrong with her?"

"She suffered from a congenital heart issue called ASD. She was small, kind of skinny, tired easily and didn't have many friends, so Jenessa being the kind of person she is..." she swallowed hard and drew in a controlling breath, "was...befriended this child when few else would." Tears shimmered in her eyes. "That's who Jenessa was—compassionate, loving, always there to lend a helping hand. You remember?"

"I do." Even though I'd only met her a few times, she struck me as a gentle soul and goodness seemed to radiate from her.

"Kailey's parents balked at first, because she was scheduled for a second heart surgery the following month," Marcelene continued, "but we convinced them that she would be fine and that we would keep a close eye on her. They finally agreed, so we packed up our van planning to spend the week there." She stared blankly into space for a few seconds as if she were remembering something and then resumed. "Anyway, the first three days were a lot of fun, but on the evening of the fourth, Arnold started the boat generator so he could watch TV and cool the interior before we went to bed. All three children were having a grand old time swimming and playing in the shallow water near the shore. I can still hear their peals of laughter…" While Marcelene cleared her throat and drank more tea, I wondered where she was going with this seemingly innocuous story. I didn't have to wait long to find out.

"I remember going below deck to cook dinner," she said, her voice falling almost to a whisper, "and the next thing I knew Arnold was shouting for me to come up on deck. I could hear the panic in his voice and my heart just froze." Her voice quavered and as she fought for control, dark apprehension wrapped around my heart. I traded an inquisitive look with Ginger before turning back to Marcelene.

"I got topside just as he and our friend Jack were jumping into the water." The look of horror reflected in her eyes made my stomach constrict with dread. Part of me really didn't want to know what happened next. "While Arnold wasn't paying attention," she went on, "the kids swam into the airspace beneath the swim deck where the exhaust from the generator was directed. It…it only took two or three minutes before…" In obvious distress, she paused, inhaling a shaky breath before continuing, "before the children were overcome by carbon monoxide fumes trapped under the swim platform."

Uh-oh. Tension expanded inside my chest. I murmured, "Oh my God."

Marcelene swallowed hard. "Once I stopped screaming hysterically, I got on the marine radio and called the National Park Service for help. They got there pretty fast and were able to revive Jenessa and Eric, but we could not find Kailey even though Arnold and Jack searched until they were both exhausted." Closing her eyes momentarily, she gripped her throat as if the words burned. "The authorities didn't find her body until the next day," she sobbed, tears snaking down her cheeks, "I can still see her little face in my mind. I swear not a minute has gone by that I have not been haunted by that poor child's death."

Her eyes shining like liquid amber, Ginger placed her hand over Marcelene's. "I know this is awful hard for you to talk about," she said kindly, "but she had to hear it."

"I know, I know." Marcelene swiped away tears and trained her troubled gaze on me. "There's no getting around the truth. It was our fault! We should have been more watchful. Needless to say, the Higglebottoms never forgave us, and who can blame them?"

"That's a name you don't hear everyday."

A tremulous smile hovered around her lips. "Jenessa used to jokingly call her Kailey Gigglebottom." She stood up, crossed to the baker's rack and brought back a framed photo. "They were like sisters. Inseparable. That's Kailey on the right."

It was impossible not to feel a rush of sorrow as I studied the laughing faces of the two young blonde girls entwined in each other's arms, their cheeks pressed together, their eyes brimming with love. "And how did Jenessa react to this...horrific situation?" I inquired, glancing at her stricken face.

Fresh tears sprang to her eyes and my own misted up when she broke down again. "Dear Lord," she wailed. "I wish it had been me instead of her." Ginger and I exchanged morose looks as her heart-rending sobs filled the room.

Several minutes passed before she regained control. "I'm sorry, I'm sorry. My daughter, my darling daughter…she was devastated. I don't think she truly ever got over losing her friend." She pressed a wad of napkins to her nose. "She suffered terrible nightmares for a long time afterwards. We put her through years of counseling." She paused, inhaled a ragged breath and narrowed her eyes at me. "Now can you understand why I'm having a hard time accepting that Jenessa's death was an accident?"

The heavy silence that fell upon the room wasn't broken until the little bird popped out and cuckooed eleven times. I hated to bring it up, but felt it necessary to ask. "Marcelene," I began tentatively, "can you think of any reason she would have taken her own life?"

A vehement head shake. "Marshall asked me that same question and the answer is no! Sure, she was sometimes sad because of her father's recent death, but…she had a lot to live for. She loved her music. She loved her job at the dress shop. She loved her church work. She loved helping animals and people in need. She loved Nathan. She loved…life."

"And what about him? How were things going in his life?"

Her frown accentuated the lines on her gaunt face. "Well, he was pretty unhappy about his parents breaking up and I got the feeling that his wild antics and risk taking was his way of dealing with it, but I would never in a million years believe that he would harm himself or her. In fact, he confided to me just a few weeks ago that he'd been looking at engagement rings. No, I reject the idea of suicide completely."

That left only one plausible explanation. I stared at her hard. "Are you saying that you think they may have been murdered? How?"

"I don't know. But, in here," she whispered, pointing to her heart, "something tells me there is more to this than meets the eye."

Overwhelmed with compassion for her loss, I said softly, "I totally sympathize with your situation and understand where you are coming from, but as of right now, today, there doesn't appear to be any evidence to support your suspicions. Are you prepared to accept that Jenessa and Nathan just made a...a disastrous mistake?"

"No." Her mouth tightened in a stubborn line. "Call it a hunch, call it mother's intuition, whatever, I'll never believe it."

Ginger leaned towards me, chiming in with a breathless, "If you lost your best friend and almost died yourself from carbon monoxide poisoning, would you be puttin' yourself in that same position twice?"

"No, I wouldn't."

"I didn't think so." Her golden eyes glittered with triumph. "So don't tell me you ain't got that hollow feelin' rollin' round deep in your gut," she said, rubbing her hand expressively around her middle. "Anybody who believes those kids died accidentally don't know shit from apple butter! So, Sugar, it's time to cowgirl up."

I gave her a curious stare. "Meaning what exactly?"

"Meaning you'd best be gettin' your butt in gear and find out what really happened to them."

"But..."

"Ginger says your track record is better than most detectives," Marcelene cut in, her face brightening with a look of such hopeful expectancy that a heavy cloak of responsibility settled on my shoulders at the same instant my heart quickened at the prospect of pursuing what might prove to be a tantalizing story. But I had to restrain my natural impulse to jump on it as I normally would. How could I? What about my family obligations and all the carefully laid plans? "Listen, I appreciate the vote of confidence and wish I could help you guys out, but this next week is not good for me..."

"I know you got a real full plate right now," Ginger interjected with an imploring gaze that made my insides twist with guilt, "but this can't wait!"

"Ginger, I just can't. Look, Walter will follow up with Marshall and then after everyone leaves maybe I can..."

"Walter ain't you!" she fired back, her face flushed with emotion. "Not that he's lazy or nothin'," she tacked on apologetically, "but he don't have that pit bull disposition like you do. Nope. If anybody can get to the bottom of this, it's you, Missy."

Marcelene reached out and grabbed my hands, imploring tearfully, "Please, Kendall! This is of utmost importance. I will never know another moment's peace again in my entire life if you don't help me. Please, I'm begging you."

I sat there wrestling with myself, fidgeting uncomfortably beneath two pairs of beseeching eyes, yearning to act on what I had instinctively suspected from the very beginning. I don't know if it was the intense pressure or being overcome by the emotion of the moment, but before I could stop myself, I blurted out, "Okay, I'll think about it." The moment the words left my mouth, I regretted them. What was I doing? Just how did I intend to be in two places at once?

CHAPTER
10

Moments later, after insisting that Marcelene take time to review every detail she'd told the sheriff and try to remember if there were any pertinent facts that she may have omitted, I slid into my Jeep. Tired beyond belief and feeling emotionally drawn and quartered, my mind whirled in different directions like a monsoon wind. Why, even though I'd vowed to myself and to Tally that I would work on my weak points, did it not seem possible for me to quit making these impulsive decisions that consistently got me into trouble? Why hadn't I kept my big mouth shut? You'd think I'd have learned my lesson by now, but no, I had to go and get myself mired in yet another impossible bind. What I should have done was kick my own ass with the pointed toe of my boot. What was that old Pennsylvania Dutch saying my grandmother had frequently used—We Get Too Soon Old and Too Late Smart? "That would definitely be you," I muttered to myself, driving around the back of the motel once again.

Hoping against hope that Sean had returned, I knocked on his motel room door repeatedly. No answer. "Where the hell are you?" I whispered between clenched teeth. I dug out my phone noting the time with dismay. 11:17 pm.

I returned to my car and for the first time since he'd left the Starfire, felt a twinge of trepidation as I turned onto the highway, heading towards home. No matter how I tried, I could not seem to shake the uneasy feeling. The fact that he'd ignored my text really agitated me. What if he had not returned by morning? I could only imagine the disastrous scene with my parents. I sighed heavily. Could my life possibly get more complicated? As the lights of town disappeared behind me, I was gripped by a sudden realization. Even though I was totally exhausted, I wasn't going to get one single wink of sleep unless I made an attempt to find Sean, even though he was a grown man and didn't need his big sister chasing after him. But, as I drove further into the desert another thought kept bugging me. Considering his recent arrest and lifelong propensity for irresponsible behavior, how smart was it to ignore the fact that he was in the company of the Hinkle brothers? What if he got into serious trouble?

"Shit!" I wrenched the wheel in a U-turn and headed back towards town, winding my way along darkened streets towards the southwestern part of Castle Valley where I would not normally venture this time of night. As I cruised past a series of boarded up businesses and crumbling homes with overgrown front yards crammed with junk and abandoned vehicles, I began to doubt myself. What was I doing? What if he wasn't even here?

The commotion from the Rattlesnake Saloon reached

my ears before the garish neon beer signs plastered all over the front of the rambling structure jumped into view. I lowered the window and listened to the lively strains of country rock music mingled with hooting, hollering and bursts of raucous laughter. Tally would be furious if he knew I was planning to enter the place alone, as it was notorious as a hangout for druggies, lowlifes, troublemakers and biker gangs. It was not unusual to have the sheriff summoned at least once or twice a month to break up fights.

I drove around the packed, dimly lit parking area searching in vain for a spot among the assortment of Jeeps, SUVs, pickups, rattletrap old cars and a half dozen Harleys. Nothing. "Oh, come on," I moaned, circling once again. The second run through I spied the Hinkles' jacked up black pickup, complete with oversized tires and the words BAD BOY printed on the back window. Like the Hinkle brothers themselves, it looked large and intimidating. So, Jim's hunch had been correct. Craning my neck in both directions, I maneuvered past several groups of people drinking and talking, but could not find a single open space. The fact that I even had to be here looking for my brother at this time of night irritated the crap out of me. Damn him. Tomorrow would be a long day of driving and I desperately needed to get a good night's sleep.

After a third swing around, I gave up and headed towards the far end of the dirt lot designated for overflow parking. It was going to be quite a hike back to the saloon. Slowly approaching the murky corner of the lot, thick with towering, untended oleander bushes and shaggy, neglected date palms, the sound of raised voices caught my attention. Deep in the shadows to my left sat two vehicles parked side by side. Suddenly, I heard a male voice shout, "You don't have a choice! You do what I tell you, or face the consequences. Now take this and get the hell out of my face, you pussy!"

In the dim light, I was able to make out a man, attired in what appeared to be a white dress shirt and tie, throw something into the driver's side of a darkish-colored pickup. "Keep your damn blood money!" another masculine voice hollered back. Laughing manically, the man jumped into a low-slung sports car. The engine roared, the lights flashed on and the guy accelerated in front of me so fast, gravel sprayed at my pristine new Jeep. "Watch out, you moron!" I screamed, hearing the sharp pop of rocks hitting my grill and windshield. Hot with fury, I pounded the horn and watched the expensive-looking, silver car race through the lot at breakneck speed and squeal onto the pavement. In a matter of seconds, the taillights vanished around the corner.

More than curious about the altercation, I pulled into the newly vacant space just as the pickup's engine started. I wanted to get a look at the driver, and in the low light could just barely make out the silhouette of a man wearing glasses and a ball cap. The truck had an emblem or something written on the driver side door, but it was too dark to read it. As he tore out of the parking spot, I thought it seemed odd that he had raised his left hand as if to shield his face from me. I sat there in the ensuing silence pondering what I'd just witnessed—a drug deal gone sour or something else? I would probably never know, but their brief conversation had intrigued me. Shouldering my purse, I stepped out of my car and marched purposefully towards the saloon, wondering why an apparently well-heeled guy driving a sports car would be hanging around a rowdy place like this. What was the meaning of his obvious threat to the other man and the puzzling rejoinder about blood money? Momentarily distracted from the task at hand, I had to force my mind to refocus as I approached the entrance. Oh no. I'd have to pass through the cluster of men loitering outside smoking, laughing and shooting the breeze to get to the front door. I braced for the anticipated personal remarks likely to be thrown my way. There were a couple of wolf whistles to start and then one burly guy with a leather vest who wore a bandana wrapped around his forehead remarked, "Well, now, ain't you somethin' to look at!" Leering, he raised his beer bottle in my direction while his dark eyes swept over me. "I've always been real partial to tall, beautiful redheads. Buy you a drink, sweet lady?"

I suppressed a shiver. "No, thanks." I hurried through the noxious cloud of smoke, ignoring several other lewd invitations shouted out behind me. Classy bunch.

Deafening music along with the strong odor of sweat and alcohol greeted me as I stepped inside the jam-packed cowboy bar. I jostled my way through the mass of chattering men and women hunting for Sean among those perched at the bar on stools and gathered around small tables, drinking. No luck. Having been inside the building only once before during the daylight hours on one of my assignments, I knew there was a labyrinth of other rooms to explore, plus several outdoor patios.

I squeezed my way through the crush of patrons into the next room, also crammed with boisterous people laughing, drinking and conversing in loud voices. The sizeable dance floor was filled with couples hoofing it to the beat of a popular country song. Quite a lively place. Watching everyone having such a good time, I momentarily lamented the fact that I'd not had the chance to dance with Tally at the barbeque. I watched the dancers for a few more minutes and then canvassed the entire room with no results. With a growing sense of frustration, I continued my search through the adjacent cavernous room only to feel another rush of disappointment. He wasn't at any of the six pool tables, nor was he playing any of the blinking, dinging video games or slot machines. Was it possible he wasn't here at all? And if not, where was he?

The only places left to search were two outdoor patios—the spacious, well-lit one with rows of long picnic tables and also a smaller, more private one at the rear of the building. I had my hand on the door leading to the large patio when I heard shrill laughter behind me. Turning, I saw two young women, both on their cell phones, lurch out of the ladies room. I immediately recognized them as having been with Sean at the Starfire earlier. Well, well. Finally some progress. I followed them along the wood-paneled hallway leading towards the small patio. Judging by their goofy behavior— staggering, giggling, almost falling, it appeared they were either drunk or high on drugs. Or both.

A refreshing gust of wind hit me in the face when I stepped outside into the dimly lit enclosure bordered by tall oleander bushes. I searched for Sean, but except for a few couples huddled around tables tucked away in secluded corners, the area appeared deserted. Odd. I turned back in time to see the girls careen around the building and disappear. Where could they be going? I broke into a run and rounded the back of the saloon in time to see them stumbling into the open desert heading towards a roaring bonfire. Employing stealth, I quietly sneaked after them. Drawing closer, I ducked behind a conveniently placed saguaro cactus. There appeared to be at least a dozen young people gathered around the flickering firelight listening to the mellow strains of guitar music. Immediate concern gripped me when I spotted my brother sitting next to one of the Hinkle brothers. Wearing a silly half grin and apparently stoned, Sean stared at the flames with a sort of glassy-eyed fascination.

It was disconcerting to witness a young guy with shoulder length blonde hair crawling around on the ground mumbling gibberish while another kid sat nearby on the ground cross-legged, rocking back and forth gazing into space as if in a trance, his hands cupping the air periodically as if he were trying to catch a really slow-moving bug.

The girls I'd been following playfully pulled one of the Hinkle twins to his feet and began dancing suggestively with him. Seated a little further from the fire were two other young men lounging against some boulders, smoking what I assumed to be pot while three dark-haired young women, their eyes outlined in charcoal and wearing black lipstick, performed strange undulating movements to the mystical-sounding music within a Pentagram someone had spray-painted on the ground.

Alarm bells sounded in my ears when I glanced back and noticed one of the Hinkle brothers holding the flame of a cigarette lighter beneath a small square of foil. He inserted a small tube in one nostril, positioned it against the foil and inhaled sharply. Then he threw his head back and pinched his nose momentarily before shouting, "Whoo hoo! Feel the burn!" He then extended the tube to Sean, who sat munching on potato chips. A skanky-looking girl with purple hair, a star tattooed on one cheek and enough studs and rings on her face and ears to open a jewelry store, knelt at his feet with her head leaning against his knees. Sean handed the bag of chips to her and eagerly accepted the offering. He ducked his head, took a hit and then looked up in watery-eyed surprise, his face contorted in pain. "Shit, man! That burns like hell!"

"Give it a minute, " advised the Hinkle boy. "You're gonna like it."

At that instant the sickening truth hit me. My brother was far more than a pothead. For extended seconds, I debated what to do. Before I could even formulate a plan, instinct took over. I rushed forward out of the darkness, scaring the hallucinating kids so much, they both screamed like banshees, then rounded the bonfire and knocked the tube from Sean's hand. It hit a nearby rock and bounced out of sight.

"Hey, bitch! What the hell are you doing?" snarled Danny or Daryl, staring at me looking dazed. I had trouble telling them apart. Built like tanks, they both looked equally menacing with their thick necks, wide bulldog jowls, blunt upturned noses with flared pig-like nostrils and deep-set hooded eyes of ice blue. Hair buzzed short, they each sported a limp, blonde goatee. This one had a spike stuck through his left earlobe. In any other situation I might have felt endangered, but these doofuses appeared to be so out of it they probably posed no real threat. But it did give me a small measure of comfort to have the .38 tucked in my purse. Okay. Now that I had injected myself into this situation, I wasn't really sure how to proceed. Ignoring the plethora of expletives directed at me, I put my hand on Sean's shoulder and got right in his face. "Come on, it's time to go."

He blinked up at me looking stupefied. "Whoa! Kenny! Where'd you come from? Hey, I'm super-happy to see you! You...wow! Look at that! Your hair...it looks amazing in the firelight. It's like...a million rainbow sparks shooting out of your head. And it's like I can see each single strand of red hair! It's awesome." He shook his head in wonder. "I wish I had a mirror so you could see how red your hair is! It's...I mean...like scarlet and like...bright as the sun!" He paused, looking confused, and then murmured, "Did I say it looks really, really red?"

My concern intensified. "Sean, are you all right? What are you on anyway?"

"Mmm...not sure," he said, grinning foolishly. "But, this is good shit. Super-good."

I stared at him, astounded. "So you don't even know what you just...sniffed up your nose?"

His pupils looked dilated. "No, but it's totally awesome." He tried to wink at me and failed. "We're so not done partying. I'm not going yet."

"Yeah, you are. Someone has to be the adult here."

"Leave the dude alone," growled the same Hinkle brother, squinting at me through the smoke and flames. "He don't need no babysitter. We'll drive him back later."

I stood up tall and glared back at him. "Which one are you? Danny or Daryl?"

Rapid eye blinking. "Daryl. Do I know you, Bitch?"

Still confident that I held the upper hand, since it appeared I was the only sober person present, I contained my mounting anger and kept my voice deliberately calm. "Here's the deal, Daryl. Since none of you have any business being behind the wheel of any kind of vehicle considering the shape you're in, I'm calling the shots. So, I'm going to take my brother and we're leaving now. Got it?"

Apparently whatever Daryl had just ingested had begun to take hold because his aggressive attitude suddenly mellowed. "Whatever."

At that point, his nasty-faced brother Danny, who looked the least drug-addled of the group, turned away from his two dance partners and eyed me with suspicion. "So, you're this guy's sister? Well, be cool and keep your mouth shut."

Did I see a hint of angst reflected in his eyes? "Are you threatening me?"

He must have sensed that I wasn't cowed in the least and backed off. "Nooooo. Everything is cool here. Just a little private party. We're just having a little fun, okay?"

No sooner had he finished speaking than the longhaired kid struggled to his feet and announced in slurred tones, "I'm seeing some scary shit here! Everything is like upside down and backwards...there's some big flying bugs comin' at me with people faces..." He stumbled towards Danny. "Help me, man, I feel sick. I think I'm gonna hurl." And he did. Right into the fire. My stomach tightened as he retched violently. It was a miracle his hair didn't catch on fire.

"Dude! Don't be puking here, ruining the party," Danny snarled at him, his flinty gaze completely devoid of sympathy. "Take your sorry ass someplace else."

The kid's eyes rolled back in his head as he slid to the ground and began inching his way along like a caterpillar towards the open desert. Much to my dismay, Daryl, Danny and both girls burst out laughing. Nothing about this situation seemed the least bit funny to me. In fact, the whole scene was nightmarish. When the hapless young man finally managed to push himself up to his hands and knees, I stared in amazement as one of the girls jumped on his back, slapped his butt and began to squeal, "Giddy up, horsey! Come on, baby!"

That was it. I'd had enough. "You people are sick," I announced with disgust, reaching down to pull Sean to his feet. "Let's go."

He didn't protest, but as I led him past the fire, he stopped and stared dreamily at the embers blowing past him in the wind.

"Can you see those butterflies?" he murmured, dreamy-eyed. "Their wings are on fire and they're flying all the way up to the stars! Awesome!"

Flaming butterflies? Oh my God! What kind of psychotropic drug had he ingested?

CHAPTER
11

By the time we reached the car, my mind was on overload trying to process the sheer magnitude of the day's unexpected events, and my patience level finally reached rock bottom. I'd been busy lecturing Sean about his irresponsible, self-destructive behavior, haranguing him about cutting out on the barbeque, not returning my texts or caring that I'd repeatedly been called a bitch by Daryl Hinkle, and just generally chewing him out while he was waxing poetic about being able to see every individual star in the Milky Way. It finally struck me that in his present muddled state of mind he probably didn't even understand what I was saying and it was doubtful he'd remember the conversation when he came down off of whatever hallucinogenic drug he'd inhaled. "You'd better not barf in my new car," I warned him severely, opening the passenger side door. "Now get in."

"Don't worry. I'm cool." He dropped onto the seat and stared enthralled at absolutely nothing.

"No, you really aren't." Did I dare leave him alone

in his motel room in this spacey condition? "You know what? You're coming home with me tonight so I can keep an eye on you." I shut his door, thinking that at least this way I would make sure he didn't wander off somewhere. The now frigid midnight night air felt good against my flushed cheeks and I was pretty sure my explosive headache was due to a combination of fatigue and repressed anger. My brother was headed down a dangerous path, and since I had no experience dealing with people tripping out on drugs, I wasn't sure what to expect. Sure, I'd dealt with intoxicated friends who got loud and silly, or sometimes aggressive, but nothing compared to the scene I had just witnessed. Sean's bizarre behavior, as well as that of the other attendees at the impromptu party, had really shaken me.

I started the engine and we'd only been traveling about ten minutes when Sean, who'd been sitting motionless staring out the window, suddenly began to wave his right hand as if in greeting.

Startled, I asked, "What are you doing?"

"Waving back at them."

I pulled my attention from the road for a few seconds and cast a quick glance into the dark desert landscape. "Waving back at whom?"

"Them."

An uncomfortable pang shot through me. "What are you talking about?"

"Don't you see all the shadow people standing out there waving at me?"

I followed his gaze and when I realized what he was referring to, my heart faltered. "Oh, Sean. Are you talking about the saguaro cactus?"

"Huh? Looks like people to me."

"Trust me, they're not moving." What kind of a concoction had he consumed to cause such a weird illusion? He appeared skeptical, but then must have accepted my explanation and fell silent again. Fifteen minutes later, I swung off the pavement onto Lost Canyon Road, overcome with fatigue, my stomach growling. Dinner seemed like years ago. What a long, long day. As we bounced along the washboard dirt road I turned to Sean. "Tell me something. How much stuff have you been into this evening?"

"Mmmmm... a couple of beers, a little pot.... mmmm...whatever the dude gave me."

I gripped the wheel tighter and counted to ten. "Sean, are you trying to kill yourself? Why would you take some unknown drug from someone you don't even know? That's just stupid! Honestly, I'm at a loss as to why you would make the deliberate choice to put yourself in such a state of unreality."

"You would if you could feel like...like...as good as me. I mean...you should see the moon the way I'm seeing it."

I glanced up at the bright crescent moon. It looked perfectly normal to me. "Okay, how are you seeing it?"

"It looks like..." he paused, apparently searching for words, then murmured in awe, "like a pearly-white cashew nut just floating there among a gazillion shining stars. It's almost like...like 3D."

I slid him a bewildered look. A pearly-white cashew nut? He really was in another world. "We're going to talk about this tomorrow when your brain isn't the consistency of a scrambled egg. And I think it's time you took a good look at what you're doing to your life and how it's affecting other people. I could kick Daryl's ass for introducing you to whatever you're on and yours for taking it."

Wearing a really silly grin, Sean gave me two thumbs-up. "This stuff is definitely primo. Darren's the main man."

"Daryl," I corrected him, turning into my driveway.

He blinked in confusion. "I thought he said his name was Darren?" He paused. "Or maybe it was Darwin."

"You're confused about everything," I muttered, as we exited the car. "Your charming benefactor's name is Daryl Hinkle." I put my hand on his shoulder. "Pay attention to what I'm saying to you. Those two guys are bad news. Do us all a favor and stay away from them." I unlocked the front door and felt a stab of guilt when I heard Marmalade's plaintive yowl. Poor baby! I'd been gone much longer than originally planned and she was probably starving and lonesome as well. "I'm so sorry, little one," I crooned, scooping her into my arms and stroking her soft fur. "You deserve a special treat tonight."

"And I need to crash," Sean mumbled.

I pointed to the hallway. "Bathroom is second door on the left and you'll be sleeping in the spare room, third door on the left. Can you comprehend that?"

"Uh-huh."

"Good. I'll wake you early in the morning and drive you to the motel so you can shower and change clothes before we leave for Jerome." I could tell that the drug was wearing off because he actually made eye contact with me.

"So…are you going to rat me out to Mom and Dad?"

Hmmm. A little leverage perhaps? "I don't know yet. I guess that depends on you."

He nodded and without another word ambled towards the hallway as I went to the kitchen to check Marmalade's food bowl, which was empty. Her purr grew louder and she bumped against my leg as I poured a saucer of cream and piled her bowl high with tuna. Then I joined her on the floor, eating the remaining tuna straight out of the can, still ruminating about the evening's disturbing events. Cheese, crackers, an apple and half a dozen cookies completed my post-midnight snack. At this rate, I'd barely get five hours of sleep. With Marmalade following at my heels, I stopped to peek in on Sean sprawled out on the bed fully dressed, lying motionless. What was to become of my little brother? With a despondent sigh, I pulled two blankets from the linen closet and gently laid them over him. My anger now cooled, I studied his peaceful face, unable to slough off the sensation of hopelessness I felt. Incorrigible since birth, he'd always trod a rocky path, but the one he was headed down now seemed destined to have tragic consequences. Was there any way to reverse it? I wanted to help him change his destructive ways, but what could I actually do?

Even with all his faults, and the fact that we were as different in our approaches to life as two people could be, I still loved him, but had to admit that this new and different Sean was not very likable. Perhaps tomorrow, in the light of day when he was sober, I'd be able to talk some sense into him.

The sudden buzz of his phone vibrating on the nightstand startled me. I looked down at the screen and noticed an incoming text from his girlfriend, Robin. Under normal circumstances I would have never considered reading his private messages, but this one gave me one of those little gut twinges. DON'T COME BACK HERE

AGAIN. I MEAN IT! DON'T CALL ME AGAIN. EVER. PUTTING YOUR STUFF IN STORAGE. COPS R STILL WATCHING MY APT, U SELFISH ASSHOLE!

Well, well, so much for Sean's tall tale about breaking up with Robin. Stung that he had so easily and glibly lied to me, I picked up his phone and swiped through the previous messages. When I'd finished reading, my initial surprise had turned to disenchanted irritation. What else had he lied about? According to the texts, Robin's father, who was paying for her college tuition and living expenses, found out about Sean's arrest and threatened to cut her off if she did not throw him out. Sean had begged her not to listen to him. Robin expressed her deep feelings for him, but was 'freaked out' because the undercover detectives were also watching her. After his arrest she could not afford to have him stay with her any longer. Sean begged her to take him back but she refused. There was an earlier exchange of texts regarding his increasing drug use, having strangers come to her apartment at all hours and another big surprise. Sean had been fired from his job months ago and had been unable to pay his share of the rent and other expenses. I set the phone down, swallowing hard. Had desperation lured him into the drug trade? This situation was much more serious than he'd led me to believe. Closing the door softly, I headed for bed, wondering if my parents were aware of these disturbing facts. Did they realize Sean was experimenting with drugs far more harmful than marijuana?

Dead tired, I finally dropped into bed beside Marmalade, who sat patiently waiting for me, kneading on a blanket. "Are you making biscuits for me, sweetie?" She flopped down close to my side and purred up a contented storm. Sleep should have come immediately, but instead I tossed and turned, unable to shut off the troubling thoughts ricocheting around my brain like ping pong balls. After checking the clock for the umpteenth time, I gave up, threw off the covers and padded back to the kitchen. The best way to attack this problem was to arm myself with facts. I sat down at my computer and began to surf the Web for information. Two hours later, dog-tired and bleary-eyed, I had to take a break from the online craziness. What kind of a mixed-up world were we living in? Why did people feel compelled to post their most private acts and thoughts on the Internet for all to see—especially under the influence of drugs and alcohol? And the more I learned about the proliferation of drugs, the drug culture, victims of drug-related crimes, the insidious effects that some of the new synthetic drugs had on the user and the user's family, friends and co-workers, the more pessimistic I felt, the more 'old school' I felt. We now lived in a society that seemed to lack a moral compass or boundaries on any kind of aberrant behavior. And my brother was now a part of it. A player. How had such a wide chasm of philosophies developed between us? We had been raised in the same stable two-parent household where traditional values such as honesty, virtue, integrity, respect, hard work and achievement were taught and held in high regard.

I yawned and stretched, noting with dismay that it was after 3 am. I pressed a hand against my hollow stomach. How was it possible that I was hungry again? "Because you're not asleep, that's why," I murmured aloud. Was there any point in even going back to bed? Apparently Marmalade had heard me because she suddenly appeared and jumped up on my lap, vying for attention. "Okay, what should I do?" I asked my cat, stroking her velvety, orange fur, "Try to sleep for two hours or make a strong pot of coffee and just stay up?" She fixed me with her luminous turquoise eyes and meowed twice. "I'll take that as a yes on the second suggestion," I said rising. Caffeine was going to be my best friend today.

I brewed coffee and continued to research people's mindset for consuming illicit drugs. Wow. The escalation of pot use among older Americans was kind of surprising, but the rampant use of readily available drugs among young people was downright disturbing. It appeared there was an entire generation, mine, whose main aspiration in life was getting high—at parties, work and even during school hours. In my mind I could only equate it to abusing alcohol and indeed, many people made little distinction other than drugs produced an easier and faster high, and when mixed with alcohol, enhanced the sensation of euphoria. Statistics showed that while some individuals could use cannabis occasionally with no visible side effects and scores of others attested to its medicinal properties, some researchers claimed that heavy pot use over time tended to lower IQs, stunt intellectual development and, for some, created the desire to experiment with more dangerous drugs.

I'd often seen the term, 'they walk among us,' but now it took on a whole new meaning. The number of people wrecking their lives and those of others by getting hooked on methamphetamine, crack cocaine, heroin, prescription and designer drugs like MDMA, or 'ecstasy,' was staggering. I viewed several disturbing videos featuring a young man addicted to OxyContin ('oxy' as it is known on the street) extoling the virtues of this powerful narcotic. He claimed it produced the best high ever, but also warned that once you were hooked, it could cost up to $300 a day to maintain a feeling that he described as 'just feeling normal,' He warned viewers that there was no getting off the drug without horrible withdrawal symptoms and recommended not trying to kick the habit alone, but to instead check into a detox clinic.

Closer to home, the Phoenix newspaper reported a recent crackdown on formerly legal synthetic drugs known as 'spice,' K-2 'bath salts' and another concoction called 2C-T-7, spurred on by a flood of frantic teens showing up at emergency rooms. In addition to that, the wave of ghastly crimes committed by people strung-out on these drugs read like scenes from a horror movie. Meanwhile, the manufacturers of these drugs cleverly attempted to stay one step ahead of increasing sanctions by slightly changing the chemical compounds in an attempt to skirt the new laws.

Being a reporter, I'd done my share of stories on society's lowlifes, but the more I read, the more I felt as if I'd been living a sheltered life, just going about my business while an entire sub-culture of zombie people existed just under the radar. It appeared that some individuals would inhale, swallow or inject just about anything to fit in with their peers, produce a buzz, or escape from the realities of life. A large number had no compunction about lying, cheating, stealing, even committing murder to feed their insatiable habits. One blogger equated them to parasites— leeching off the productive members of society, existing on taxpayer-funded government disability checks, grants, housing, food stamps and healthcare, not contributing to the economy, their lives in limbo.

Sipping a second cup of hot coffee, I watched video

after video featuring teens, some as young as thirteen, blatantly bragging about their drug use. The videos of pot parties were actually kind of boring—people either staring blankly at an object or endlessly pontificating about some inane subject, so I moved on to personal experiences of other juveniles experimenting with harder drugs. In none of the posted videos did any of the young people appear to give a flying crap that what they were doing was illegal, stupid and, in some cases, lethal. As far as they were concerned, anything in moderation was cool. They drifted through school learning little, had no aspirations to pursue a career, cast no judgments on the behaviors of others and seemed unconcerned about the possible dire consequences of continued substance abuse. There were, however, a significant number of firsthand accounts from others describing their frightening descent into the hell of addiction and the agonizing road to recovery in rehab. They appeared to be genuinely chastened by their experiences and solemnly advised viewers to avoid using illicit drugs at all cost. And then there were the tragic stories of people who did not seek help in time. With a dull ache in my heart, I sat there watching a series of videos featuring tearful, hollow-eyed people reporting harrowing tales of family members or friends who had died after ingesting an unknown recipe made from ingredients cooked up in some makeshift lab. I rested my forehead in one hand. Good God! Had Sean already joined the ranks of these full-blown drug addicts? Was that the reason he appeared to be a willing participant in the seamy, criminal underground drug trade—to support his habit? My stomach turned sour at that dispiriting thought. I set my cup down and pushed away from the computer, my brain fried with information overload and my body amped up on caffeine. Enough!

I paced around the kitchen, fearing for the survival of civil society, the country, the future. Needing to relieve some stress, I put on my running gear and headed outside into the frosty pre-dawn air. I walked for a few minutes, allowing my eyes to adjust to the starlight and waning moon, before breaking into a jog. I picked up speed and pounded along Lost Canyon Road, allowing the serenity of the desert silence to work its magic on my agitated frame of mind. But it wasn't long before my thoughts returned to the issue at hand and forced me to do a little soul searching.

Grounded firmly in the principles instilled in me by my parents and grandparents, I was having great difficulty understanding why so many people chose to use drugs or alcohol to escape into a counterfeit reality instead of relying on faith or inner strength. After watching the troubling videos of people acting like out of control idiots, deliberately destroying their lives and those of others, I began to have second thoughts about my own alcohol use. Coming from an Irish family where liquor flowed freely, I had never thought twice about enjoying a glass of wine with dinner, having a cocktail or a margarita or two. But did I really need artificial stimulation when I could create my own natural highs with exercise, laughter or inspiring music? What about the euphoric adrenalin rush of chasing down an intriguing story? And how about the best natural stimulant of all—love? Why wasn't that enough? Amid the noisy chatter of birds welcoming a primrose dawn, I arrived back at my front door with a heavy heart, doubting that I'd ever learn the answer.

CHAPTER
12

Revitalized by a bracing shower, I dressed for the car trip in comfortable jeans and a long sleeved T-shirt and finished packing for the four nights I'd be away before waking Sean. "Rise and shine, buddy!" I sang out, using our grandfather's favorite expression. "Time to get your lazy butt up."

He groaned and waved me away. "Go away. I'm tired."

"Oh, no, you don't." I yanked the covers off him. "You're not going to ruin my great Arizona adventure plans. We're leaving in twenty minutes. No excuses. Go splash some cold water on your face and I'll have coffee waiting for you in the kitchen." And a lecture waiting for you in the car, I thought to myself.

I went online to check the day's weather and came across additional information regarding the car accident that had caused the traffic pileup on Thursday morning. Authorities reported that drugs had been found in the car of the driver who had crossed the centerline, killing a mother and her two small children. An autopsy was scheduled to determine if the man, identified as Juan Ochoa, age 19, had been impaired. It was yet another example of the tragic ramifications of excessive drug use.

Chewing on a protein bar, I tried to get my mind off the story by staying busy. I unloaded the dishwasher and loaded the cooler with drinks, fruit and snacks before grabbing the bag of dry cat food. Thankfully, Ginger's brother, Brian, had agreed to come and stay at the house with Marmalade during my absence. She was bumping my ankles and purring as I mounded the food in her bowl. "There you go, baby. That should keep you until I get back tonight and I promise I won't be late again." She meowed her appreciation just as Sean entered the room looking grumpy and disheveled, his clothing wrinkled.

"You talk to your cat?" he asked, yawning.

A tad grouchy from a lack of sleep and still incensed about the fact that he'd so glibly lied to me, I snapped, "She's better company than you were last night."

"Whoa, what's up your kilt this morning?"

"You." I poured steaming coffee into a Styrofoam cup, secured the plastic lid and handed it to him. "Let's go." I shrugged into my coat, grabbed my purse, and pushed him towards the door.

Outside in the invigorating air, he hugged his coat tighter and griped, "Son-of-a-bitch! I thought you said it was gonna be warm here."

"Don't worry. It'll be nice when the sun comes up," I assured him as we climbed into the Jeep. Nevertheless, I turned up the heat and we rode in silence while I contemplated what questions to ask that would best expose his mindset without alienating him. Until last night, I thought I knew my brother pretty well. Not now. At his age and younger, the drive to achieve my dream of becoming the best investigative reporter on the planet consumed me. Along the way, I'd encountered numerous obstacles, but I'd never once been deterred—the same for my older brother Patrick and my dad and mom. My quick glance revealed him calmly sipping coffee. "So, what do you think?" I began, pointing towards the faint moon hanging above the western horizon. "Does it still look like a glowing cashew nut this morning?"

He stared at me slack-jawed. "What are you talking about?"

"The moon. Don't you remember telling me that last night?"

He shifted his weight. "Um...no."

"Well, you did. And you also thought the saguaro cactus were waving hello to you."

His response was to burst out laughing. "No shit! You must have been freaked out!"

"A little. No doubt you burned off several thousand working brain cells during your little psychedelic trip last night."

"Come on, Kenny, you're way too uptight! Lighten up, have some fun!"

I shook my head slowly. "That didn't look like fun to me."

"Well, it was. I can't ever remember feeling that good before. It was totally awesome."

Had he always sounded this immature? "You think being literally drugged out of your mind is awesome?"

"We were just kickin' back and chillin'. You know what? Mom and Dad are getting to be old fuds and you're starting to sound just like them."

I scowled at him. "So, I'm a young fud just because I don't agree with your lifestyle? I don't need drugs to get high. My drug of choice is called endorphins. They're safe, a natural high, cheap, and always available. And they're legal!"

"Boring."

His blasé attitude really worried me. "If you could get a hold of the same drug you did last night, you'd do it again?"

"Sure! Why not?"

The whole concept seemed foreign to me. "Sean, it sounds to me like you arrange your life around getting high and that you use whatever substance you can get your hands on."

"Ever been to a party where you were the only one sober?" he continued as though I hadn't spoken. "It's no frikkin' fun, so don't knock it if you haven't tried it."

"Thanks, but no. I'm not interested in frying my brain, losing control and maybe killing myself in the process."

His laugh held a hard edge. "Hate to break it to you, Sis, but you're in the minority."

Now that was a scary thought. "And the fact that you're breaking the law doesn't bother you at all?"

He swatted away my question. "Government imposed its will on the people banning alcohol during Prohibition, remember? It didn't work then and it won't work now with drugs. I think everybody deserves to have the opportunity to feel that stoked at least once in their life."

He looked so self-satisfied. Arrogant little shit. "I don't think your self-destructive behavior is anything to brag about."

He let out a groan of exasperation. "Oh man! Are

you gonna bust my chops about this all day?"

I glanced over at his sullen, angry expression. No point in beating around the bush. "Be honest with me. How often are you using?"

An indifferent shrug. "Every now and then."

I would have believed him before. Now I didn't. And I couldn't stop thinking about the video of the hapless young guy addicted to OxyContin. "Do you feel compelled to do drugs everyday?"

"No, I don't," he fired back, sounding defensive. "What about you?"

"What about me?"

"I saw you putting away the margaritas last night. Maybe you're the one with the problem."

His haughty tone and the knowledge that he wasn't being truthful didn't sit well. "Don't try to put this off on me! I don't drink to the point of hallucinating, until I see shit that isn't there. And if I do drink, I at least know what I'm ingesting. I don't understand how you can accept some unknown substance given to you by a stranger and snort it up your nose. Now that is crazy."

He waved away my concerns. "So, I was a little baked last night. If I'd gotten shitfaced on booze, I'd be hung over today. And I probably wouldn't have to listen to a lecture from you. I'm fine, except," he tacked on, "that maybe I could've used a little more sleep."

"You could have used a little more sleep?" My voice actually squawked, I was so incensed. "I was awake all night worrying about you."

"Well, quit worrying. It's all good. I'm not hurting anyone."

The more he talked, the more disheartened I became. "You don't think you're hurting yourself?"

"Not really."

Clearly, I was getting nowhere fast, but gave it one final shot. "You don't think getting high all the time is stifling your initiative and preventing you from facing your problems?"

"What problems?"

"You're kidding, right?"

"Okay, maybe I have a few."

Indeed he did. When I turned onto the main highway, the brilliant rays of sunlight beaming over the top of Castle Rock temporarily blinded me. I reached for my sunglasses. Neither of us said a word for another five minutes. As we reached the outskirts of town, I wrestled with how best to approach his duplicity. I desperately wanted to give my brother the benefit of the doubt, but decided to test his honesty. "So, just between you and me, what really happened between you and Robin?"

"Why do you care?"

I darted a look at his shuttered expression. "Last I heard you two were madly in love. Just curious as to why you suddenly broke up with her." I held my breath waiting for his answer.

"She's been giving me grief about my friends and I'm sick of it. So, I'm cutting her loose."

"That's too bad. And your job? How's that going?"

"Everything's cool."

Not a trace of remorse showed as he lied through his teeth. I bit my lip. The fact that his lies came so easily really pissed me off. But I kept my tone level as I continued, "Refresh my memory. What's the name of the place you're working again?"

"I told you. I'm helping out a buddy at his uncle's bar."

Now thoroughly disheartened, I weighed my next words carefully, hoping he wouldn't shut me out entirely. "Sean, I'm going to be up-front with you. I think you've got a serious problem with drugs, and it appears to be trashing your life."

His cynical expression revealed his disdain. "I told you, everything is fine."

I shot him a 'don't mess with me look.' "I know more than you think I do. I saw the text Robin sent you last night."

I pulled into the motel parking lot and braked near his room as he let loose with a rather impressive string of expletives.

"You have no right to read my private messages!"

"It wasn't my intention," I fired back. "I was throwing a blanket over you when it came in. And since you'd drugged yourself into a coma, I checked to make sure it wasn't one of your new best friends. When I realized you'd lied to me, I followed the string of texts back."

He threw the door open. "You know what? If you're going to spy on me this entire trip, I'm outta here."

My simmering agitation mushroomed into a fiery inferno. "Then stop lying to me," I yelled. "It's insulting. And it's shameful that you're so nonchalant about dealing drugs, getting busted and having Dad pay for your legal expenses." I cautioned myself to calm down. Modulating my tone, I continued, "I'm afraid if you keep this up, you're going to end up dead in some rundown crack house. I don't want to lose you, so you need to get a handle on this addiction before it's too late."

He clapped his hands to his head. "Jeezuz! I am not an addict! I can stop anytime I want. Stop hassling me!"

At that point, I decided the best course of action was to diffuse the argument before it escalated further. "Okay. Okay. If you don't end up in jail, what are you going to do when you get back home? Where are you going live, what do you plan to live on?"

He shrugged one shoulder. "I don't know. Probably hang with one of my buddies 'til I can find something. I'll figure it out."

My unease about his well-being deepened. "Do Mom and Dad know about any of this?"

He managed to look contrite. "No."

"Don't you think you should tell them the truth?"

"I don't know." His voice turned petulant so I decided that even though I had a lot more to say, I'd said enough for now. I could only hope that I'd planted the seed that perhaps he should reevaluate his life.

"Go get cleaned up. We're leaving for Prescott in half an hour."

"Yeah. What's the name of the place we're going after that?"

"Jerome."

I put my hand on his arm. "Promise me that at least while you're here you'll cool it on the drug use, okay? As a favor to me?"

Without another word, he hopped out and sauntered to his room. His cocky attitude and the fact that he seemed unaffected by the consequences of his actions or my heartfelt plea to him bugged the hell out of me, spawning the beginnings of a headache. Too much caffeine? Stress?

Both? Fighting off a mounting sense of gloom, I grabbed my phone and sent a text to Tally confirming dinner plans.

Moments later, trudging towards my parent's room, I felt as if there was a bowling ball lodged in my chest. Would I be enabling Sean's behavior if I did not tell them about last night's activities and probably everything else I'd learned about him? If I did, it was sure to generate a heated exchange, initiate a big family squabble and most assuredly spoil the day. One by one, my carefully thought-out plans for a fun-filled visit were slowly evaporating. Perhaps it would be best to wait until tomorrow or even the next day. With Sean present on the car trip today, what were the chances I would get the opportunity to speak to my parents alone anyway? Or was I just avoiding the inevitable?

I was poised to knock on the door when my cell phone rang. I dug it out of my pocket, thinking it was Tally, but saw a number I didn't recognize. Puzzled, I tapped the call button. "Hello?"

"Kendall, it's Lavelle." She sounded kind of breathless. "Sorry to bother you so early in the morning, but I'm afraid I've got some bad news."

"What's going on?"

"Walter's in the hospital."

CHAPTER
13

My mouth was still hanging open when my dad whipped the door open. "Goooood morning, Pumpkin! Your mother needs a few more minutes…" Noting my obvious distress, his cheery smile evaporated. "What's wrong?"

I put up a silencing finger and continued listening to Lavelle recount the events from the night before and their frantic 3 am trip to a Phoenix hospital after Walter passed out in the bathroom. "He was so dehydrated and getting worse by the minute. He said he felt so bad he wished he could die," she exclaimed shrilly, "so I decided we shouldn't even wait to pick up his prescription this morning."

Genuinely worried, my throat felt like I'd swallowed a handful of dry cereal. "What…what do they think is wrong with him?"

"They're not sure yet. He's on fluids. They haven't ruled out food poisoning and have ordered some tests." Her voice quavered. "Kendall, I'm really scared. I've never seen him so sick. Ever."

"I'm so sorry!"

"He wanted me to tell you that he feels really bad leaving you in such a bind with your family here and all. I have no idea how long he'll be here."

"Tell him not to worry about that for a second. We'll manage. Please tell him just to concentrate on getting well."

But even as the words left my mouth, the serious ramifications of her news hit home. Minus both Walter and Ginger, how could I even think about going out of town on Monday, leaving only Tugg and Jim to handle the entire workload? I felt confident they could muddle through for a few days, but it would create a real hardship. It also meant that my promise to follow up on Jenessa's death was out the window, especially since Walter had not even begun the groundwork. What was I going to do now?

"I'll let him know," Lavelle confirmed with a morose sigh. "Gotta go now."

"Keep me posted." Feeling completely deflated, I tapped the END button.

"Everything okay, kiddo?" my dad inquired, his keen gaze probing mine.

"Um…I've had better days." This latest catastrophe, coupled with my emotional turmoil over events of the past two days and lack of sleep hammered the final nail into the coffin of my well-laid plans. I blinked away the tears loitering behind my eyes.

He shrugged into his jacket. "How about we sit over there on that bench in this nice warm sunshine and wait for your mother?"

Once we were seated, he propped his booted foot on a nearby rock and turned to me. "You were never very good about hiding your feelings. Want to talk?"

I hadn't planned to, but ended up pouring my heart out to him. I shared my intense frustrations about Ruth, the tragic situation with Ginger, Walter's untimely illness and finally blurted out my worries concerning Sean.

When I'd concluded, my dad laced his fingers together, bowed his head and sat in silence before looking up to stare off towards the distant mountains, his jaw muscles clenched, his eyes filled with anguished melancholy. "Well, you're not telling me anything we haven't suspected. We've all known about his pot smoking since he was in high school." He turned back to me, a faint glimmer of anger in his eyes. "But, getting himself arrested for dealing it and knowing he's actually experimenting with other drugs and maybe selling them too makes me sick to my stomach." He shook his head in disgust. "Damn him! His behavior last night is inexcusable and I'm ticked off big time about Robin. She's a nice girl and doesn't deserve to be treated like this."

"He doesn't seem to have a problem playing fast and loose with the truth," I remarked grimly. "That seems to go hand in hand with the drug culture and it really worries me that he's twenty-five years old and seems to possess no moral compass."

His face reddened. "Tell me about it. I had to come up with bail money, hire him an expensive lawyer, and now finding out that he's not even working makes me feel like even more of a horse's rear end."

"What do you mean more?"

He exhaled an audible sigh and ruffled his hair. "For the past six months, I've also been sending him money for rent and food, plus paying his phone bill to supposedly help him get on his feet."

"He's just using you, Dad."

We traded a look of intense exasperation before he echoed my earlier thought. "Let's not mention this to your mother just yet or we'll have World War Three on our hands today, which is the last thing you need right now."

"I have a feeling she wouldn't be that surprised," I said, "but we're definitely going to have to figure out what to do about this situation pretty soon. It's serious. How do you feel about having a family intervention when Pat gets here? See if we can convince him to go into rehab."

"That's not going to be pretty," he responded, his expression forlorn.

"I know. And if he refuses," I added softly, "you have to cut him off, Dad. I mean everything, including his legal expenses. I know it sounds cruel, but if we don't all stand as a unit and employ some tough love and force him to take responsibility for his actions, who knows what will become of him."

A glum nod. "Yeah, you're right. It's time."

The motel room door opened and my mom stuck her head out. "Oh, there you are," she said, looking at my dad and then waving at me. "I'm ready to go now."

I had just gotten my dad and his crutches situated in the Jeep when Sean finally emerged from his room looking considerably better-groomed than before, but I could tell by his closed, insolent expression that he was still pissed at me. My dad and I swapped a conspiratorial glance as he wordlessly slid into the back seat next to my mother and inserted his ear buds, indicating that he intended to tune us out. My mother murmured hello, but was so busy fiddling with her camera, she didn't appear to notice or perhaps just chose to ignore his boorish behavior.

I started the engine and within minutes we were on the open road. Still agitated, tired and weighed down by the magnitude of problems facing me, I was determined to push them to the furthest regions of my mind and enjoy myself. As we skimmed along the highway, I enthusiastically pointed out local landmarks. We breezed through the sleepy community of Congress and then had to stop while my mother took photos of a giant frog-shaped rock formation that had been painted green and white and sprinkled with black & white dots. When viewed from the proper angle, the sixty-ton boulder did indeed resemble a frog and was whimsically referred to by the locals as 'Rocky the Frog'.

"I've never seen anything quite like this," my mother remarked, inclining her head to one side. "It's rather original rock art."

"From what I've read, a homesteader's wife first painted it green back in 1928," I informed them. "She and her family continued its upkeep for years and now it's maintained by the townspeople as a tourist attraction."

Wearing a look of feigned incredulity, Sean deadpanned, "Rocky the Frog? Frogs need water, don't they? Look around, people! Does anybody see anything resembling water around here? Rocky the toad is more like it."

That brought a roar of laughter from my parents and I couldn't help but grin and nod my agreement. His droll remark sounded like the Sean I knew and it lightened my heart somewhat. After that, we began the steep ascent up boulder-strewn Yarnell Hill. When we reached the crest, I stopped to show them the spectacular view of the valley below and pointed out the exact spot where Tally and I had first met the previous April after he had 'rescued' me from a herd of javelinas. Smiling, I pulled out my phone, snapped a photo and sent it along to him with a message proclaiming my love and suggesting that we rendezvous at my house after dinner. It was a warm and fuzzy moment. Within sixty seconds he had fired back, 'YOU'RE ON!' With a thrill of delight, I pocketed my phone, thinking that a little alone time with Tally was just what I needed.

Five minutes later, we drove along the quiet streets of Yarnell and then, within minutes, cruised through the picturesque ranching community of Peeples Valley. My mother, busily taking more photos, seemed happier and more relaxed now that we'd left the prickly, unforgiving landscape behind and entered greener wide-open pasturelands graced with tall trees and scattered herds of grazing horses and cattle. Shortly after that, we breezed through the quirky little town of Wilhoit, and as we headed into the mountains, I deftly maneuvered my new Jeep up the two-lane road that soon turned into a series of dizzying switchbacks. Within a few miles, the high desert scrub gave way to stands of stately Ponderosa pines, and when we entered Prescott my mother exclaimed that its quaint, tree-lined streets and midwestern architecture reminded her of home. She was especially taken with the "jewel" of the mile-high city—the stately columned beauty of the 1916 Yavapai County Courthouse residing in the middle of the tree-framed downtown square. I had felt much the same way when I'd first visited this colorful Western town that bordered the foothills of the rugged Bradshaw Mountains. I decided to take a few minutes to drive around some of the residential streets to show off some of the gracious Victorian homes before heading to the restaurant.

Apparently everyone else in Prescott had heard about the mouth-watering breakfasts being served up, so finding a close parking space became a vexing challenge. After circling the block five times, I finally slid into a spot adjacent to three aqua-green Prescott National Forest vehicles. The sight of them reminded me of the puzzle of the closed Forest Service road that became the frozen deathtrap for Jenessa and Nathan, along with my desire to be working on this case.

The tantalizing aroma of frying bacon, coffee and pancakes met us as we stepped inside the warm, crowded restaurant, where we were informed by our cheerful hostess that we'd have to wait a few minutes until a table became available. By that time my belly was rolling with hunger, so it was encouraging when a party of five green-uniformed Forest Service employees all pushed back their chairs, stood up and filed past us towards the door. Focused on the bus boy clearing away the dishes, I wasn't paying too much attention to the hostess bidding them goodbye until I heard her say, "Take it easy, Burton."

Burton? I swung around in time to see a middle-aged guy with thinning brown hair and wire-rimmed glasses waving as he pushed out the door. I searched my memory. Wasn't that the name of the forest ranger Marshall had mentioned in his report? Burton was not a common first name, so I felt pretty confident it must be him. Though the urge to follow him and pepper him with questions was intense, I willed myself to stay in the moment and followed the hostess to our table. Nonetheless, after we were seated, the haunting questions as to why and how the young couple ended up dead on the deserted road lurked in the corners of my mind, overshadowing the cheerful banter with my family.

My dad must have been channeling my thoughts because during the sumptuous breakfast, consisting of waffles, bacon, eggs, hash browns and coffee, he began to grill me for additional details regarding Ginger's cousin. I filled him in on the latest developments. The more I talked, the more his eyes glittered with speculative interest. When I finished, he let out a low whistle. "So, I'm guessing you're thinking the same thing as this old newshound?"

"Something's definitely not adding up," I replied, careful to keep my tone light, hoping they wouldn't fathom just how much I yearned to investigate this intriguing case further.

"Bet you wish you were out working on this story instead of sitting here with us, don't you?" Sean ventured, apparently only half kidding and sounding far more perceptive than I would have given him credit for.

"Shut up! That's not true and you know it," I snapped back, immediately regretting my dismissive tone when I noticed the startled look cross my mother's face.

"Everybody okay here?" Her bemused gaze bounced between the two of us.

"Absolutely." I wrestled the bill from my dad, paid it, and after posing for several photos in the courthouse gazebo, we continued towards our destination, winding our way through golden grasslands dotted with antelope herds and then up the serpentine road leading to the once-bustling copper mining town of Jerome. The mishmash of charming old houses and buildings, now home to art galleries, coffee houses, shops and top-rated restaurants, sat perched atop Cleopatra Hill, which overlooked the broad Verde Valley and coral-colored cliffs surrounding Sedona. The snow-capped

San Francisco Peaks could be seen in the distance.

While my folks chatted amiably, asking non-stop questions about the various locales, Sean appeared withdrawn and spent the time alternately listening to music, fiddling with his phone and napping. I tried not to be annoyed that he showed no interest in the sightseeing trip I had so carefully planned out weeks in advance. When it came time to get out and explore Jerome, he opted to stay in the car and sleep. My mother, raising a skeptical brow, questioned his odd decision. Deliberately avoiding eye contact with me, he lamely explained how late he'd been out the night before and his subsequent fatigue. Without a word, she turned away and cast a suspicious glance at my dad who just shrugged. Me? I was seething inwardly. Because of his actions, I'd had no sleep and yet he was so tired he had to take a nap.

We left him there curled up on the back seat and began our slow walking tour of the old mining town. An hour later, my dad, pale-faced and breathing hard, most likely from the higher altitude plus increased pain in his ankle, proclaimed that he could not walk another step, so the two of us found a nearby bench and sat chatting and munching on nut-infused fudge while my mother continued her exploration of the remaining shops and art galleries along the main street.

As we basked in the toasty sunshine and savored the soft breeze whispering through the nearby Piñon pines, my dad began to nod off and soon my eyelids felt as if they each weighed a thousand pounds. I fought hard to keep them open but lost the battle. The next thing I knew a thunderous roar and the ground vibrating beneath my feet jolted me awake. Blinking in confusion, I sat bolt upright and exchanged a startled look with my dad, who'd apparently been sleeping as well. I checked the time. Holy cow! I'd slept for thirty minutes! Together we surveyed the noisy parade of motorcyclists rolling along the street, revving their engines for maximum effect. Most rode Harleys, some wore helmets, some not, and while about half rode solo, the rest were couples. Because this was my third trip to Jerome, I knew that the bar at the end of the street not far from where Sean lay snoozing in the Jeep, was a favorite destination for bikers. No doubt the noise would wake him as well. I sent him a text telling him where we were and to come join us.

Another smaller group of riders rumbled into town and I couldn't help but notice my dad's wistful expression. "Perfect day for a ride," he remarked as they rode by.

"Is that on your bucket list?" I joked, watching the rough-looking leather-clad group, women included, glide by.

"If I was Sean's age..." his voice trailed off as he turned his bright green eyes on me. "And speaking of Sean, I think your brother is right."

"About what?"

"About you."

I stared at him, mystified. "What are you saying?"

"Come on! You're a news junkie just like me. I can read you like a book. Why aren't you jumping on this story?"

My mouth fell open. "Dad! How can I?"

"How can you not?" he countered. "Look here, Pumpkin, don't pass up this opportunity because of us. Your mother and I are big people and we're perfectly capable of renting a car, reading a map or following GPS directions to find the locations you've arranged for us to see. We'll figure it out and be back together at the end of the week. You've already visited all these places, right?"

"Well, yes, but…but that's not the point…"

"It's exactly the point," he responded, impatiently waving away my objection. "You need to get your priorities straight. Right now, nobody knows more about this story than you do. You made a promise to your friend and it's yours to break."

Before I could formulate a suitable response, my phone's robust Latin tune sounded from my pocket. I fished it out, noting Tugg's home number on the screen. "Excuse me for a second, Dad. Hello?"

"Kendall?"

I paused, recognizing Mary's voice. Why would she be calling me? "Yes?"

"I'm sorry to bother you, but Mort told me about Walter being in the hospital and…well…" she lowered her voice. "He'll be really mad if he knows I'm calling you, but I'm worried about him trying to handle everything at the paper next week with all three of you gone and Louise out of town…"

"I'm not happy about it either, Mary, but it's only for a couple of days and…"

"He shouldn't be under that kind of pressure for even one day."

Gripped with helpless agitation, I replied, "Well, Mary, I don't know what to tell you…"

She cut in brusquely, "Did Mort tell you his doctor put him on blood pressure medication last week?" Her voice sounded a tad shrill.

Feeling completely deflated, I sighed, "No, he didn't."

CHAPTER
14

"Ah-hah!" she crowed in my ear. "I didn't think so. Now listen, Tugg's doctor was adamant that he avoid stress…"

"Gaawd damn it, Mary!" Tugg's angry voice boomed from the background. "Who are you talking to?"

"It's Kendall…"

"Hell's bells, woman! I told you not to tell anybody!"

"You stubborn old donkey! Do you want to die of a stroke?" came her high-pitched retort. A clunking sound and then Tugg came on the line. "Don't pay any attention to her, she's exaggerating. I'm perfectly fine. You go ahead with your trip."

My spirits plummeted lower. I'd thought the news about Walter was bad, but this was the proverbial icing on the cake. How could everything I'd planned to go so right be going so wrong? Again, my intuitive dad observed my crestfallen expression and frowned his concern. "What's wrong?"

"Just a second," I answered him before saying to Tugg, "I have to agree with Mary on this one. We need to talk about our options…'

"No, we don't. I can handle it."

"Tugg…"

"Send me a postcard. I'm hanging up now."

And he did. He was a stubborn old donkey.

"Yoo-hoo! Kendall! Can you come here for a minute?" I turned to see my mother signaling me from the doorway of an art gallery. "I need your opinion on something!"

Out of control. My life was spiraling out of control and it was all I could do to maintain the tumultuous surge of emotions engulfing me. My cheeks burning, I wondered if perhaps I could use some blood pressure meds myself. I stood and inhaled a deep breath to calm my erratic heartbeat. Following a measured exhale, I forced a serene smile and stated to my dad, "I'll be back in a few minutes."

"Hold on. What's going on with Tugg?"

"His doctor put him on blood pressure meds and he's supposed to avoid stress, which I don't see as being even remotely possible with me out of town for ten days." I didn't realize until that second how tightly my jaw was clenched.

My dad's face softened. "I'm sorry, kiddo. Sometimes the winds of fate turn against us. I'm sure you've heard that old saying, 'Men plan, God laughs,' right?"

"No, but it's certainly appropriate for my situation."

"Keeeennnnndaaaaaallllll," shouted my mother, "are you coming or not?"

I glanced over, noting her agitated expression, yelled back "Yes!" and to my dad, "Be right back."

Wrestling with the magnitude of problems confronting me, it took extensive willpower for me to keep it together and focus on what seemed now to be the innocuous determination as to which of the two Arizona landscape paintings my mother should buy—really, really low on my priority list. But I gave her my considered opinion and of course, she chose the other one. It was a real effort to concentrate as she chattered on about the Native American art and jewelry. She finally got around to talking to me about Ruth's unconscionable behavior at the barbeque and I shared with her Tally's vow to banish his mother from our engagement party if she didn't clean up her act. It was uplifting to see the glimmer of approval in my mother's eyes.

Over an hour had elapsed before we returned to the bench where my father sat talking in an animated tone to someone on his cell phone. When he looked up and saw me approaching, he hastily ended his conversation. His self-satisfied expression mystified me. Strange. Who had he been talking with? Before I could ask him, my phone's text alert sounded. It was from Sean and read: @ THE BAR HAVING A COLD ONE. I noted the time. If we were to make it back to Castle Valley for dinner, we needed to get on the road soon.

The late afternoon sun cast long checkered shadows across the street and there was a distinct chill in the air by the time we returned to the Jeep and piled my mom's painting and other purchases into the back. While she munched on a protein bar and my dad admired the row of Harley Davidson motorcycles backed into parking spaces in front of the bar, I went to find Sean. I canvassed the interior of the noisy bar without success and felt my chest tightening with irritation. Please, not again! I stepped out the side door and looked up and down the street. No sign of him. Where was the brat this time? Beyond frustrated, I dug out my phone and was in the process of messaging him when I heard the sound of masculine voices from somewhere at the end of the short, narrow side street. I didn't pay too much attention to it until I heard a familiar laugh. I cocked my head to one side, listening closely. Sounded like Sean. More hoots of laughter. Yep. Definitely him. Now super curious, I pocketed my phone and walked downhill, avoiding deep cracks where the crumbling sidewalk had fallen away. A partially collapsed house stood to my left and through a gaping hole in the wall, I had a clear view of the vast Verde Valley below. I rounded the corner of an abandoned building and stopped short, shock rooting me in place. There was Sean, straddling a black Harley, immersed in conversation with the Hinkle brothers. What the hell? I was too far away to hear what they were saying, but I immediately realized that their rendezvous could not possibly be coincidence. Had these plans been hatched at the desert party last night or since then? What for? And why hook up here?

When I heard the distinctive clatter of another Harley approaching from behind, I ducked into a shadowy doorway just as a big-bellied man with a salt and pepper beard and ponytail glided past. He also wore the signature Harley attire—leather, ultra-dark sunglasses and a bandana. I peeked around the corner and watched with interest as the brothers crossed to meet the rider on the opposite side of the dead-end street from Sean. They greeted the newcomer with one of those macho handclasps and then Danny, the one without the spike through his ear, handed the guy something, which he pocketed in his jacket. It was reminiscent of the scene I'd witnessed in the parking lot of the Rattlesnake Saloon last night. My intuition told me that whatever was going on here could not be good. The fact that Sean had chosen to continue involvement with these two characters, even after I'd warned him, really frosted me. While the Hinkles had their backs turned towards me, I sprinted towards Sean, who seemed unruffled by my sudden appearance. One look at his goofy smile and vacant glassy eyes revealed the reason why. "Are you high on something again?" I demanded just barely above a whisper.

Lips pinched together in a cagey smile, he giggled, "Maybe a little."

"Are you friggin' kidding me?" I seethed through clenched teeth, "You couldn't manage to stay sober for one day?"

"I only had a few hits for...for..." he frowned, staring blankly for a few seconds while he struggled to find the words, "medicinal purposes," he concluded with an expression of sublime accomplishment.

I fisted hands on my hips. "Medicinal purposes?"

Another mellow grin. "Yeah. I was carsick and now I feel a whole lot better."

"Uh-huh. Where'd you get the weed? At the bar?" I asked, thumbing over my shoulder.

"From Daryl."

I nodded. "Of course you did."

"Don't be mad. It's totally legal. He's got a medical marijuana card, so he just shared a little bit with me."

"Is that a fact?" I glanced over at the strapping bull of a guy. "He doesn't appear to have any health issues."

"Yeah, he does. Umm...he says...yeah, ah, he's got chronic pain from getting thrown off his horse."

"Sure he does." I struggled to keep my temper at

bay. "Sean, what are you doing hanging around with those two losers again anyway? Are you too stoned to remember what I told you about them?"

First, he looked perplexed, then taken aback for a second before stating earnestly, "They're my friends, Kenny. Why are you always so...so...touchy and negative about everything?"

A combination of hopeless, helpless anger consumed me. I stood there holding my breath, fighting back the desire to throttle him for his stupidity, when I heard a sarcastic voice behind me. "Well, look who's here. Dude! Is that the wicked bitch of the West stalking you again?" Raucous laughter.

I turned slowly and glared at the Hinkle twins' smirking faces and beady, steely-blue eyes. The air of smarminess surrounding these two lowlifes made my skin crawl and the childish remark only served to compound my escalating dislike. "I don't know who you think you are, calling me a bitch, but that's the second time and I'd strongly advise that it be the last. Got it?"

"Ooooohhhh! I'm so scared," Daryl jeered, stretching his stocking cap down over his ears.

Laughing gruffly, Danny punched his brother in the shoulder, "Guess she told your sorry ass off, didn't she?"

Tiring of their adolescent game, I returned my attention to Sean. "It's getting late. We have to go now."

I could see his mouth moving, but couldn't hear his answer because at that moment, the ponytailed guy revved up his Harley and roared up the street out of sight. In the ensuing silence, and obviously still spoiling for a fight, Daryl piped up again. "Why don't you butt out of your brother's business? We were just having a nice friendly visit and here you go again, barging in and ruining everybody's fun. Why don't you leave him alone? You're not his mommy."

It took herculean effort to suppress a caustic comeback. Squaring my shoulders, I scowled at him. "I don't remember asking for your opinion."

"Yeah," Danny concurred, his tone mocking, "She didn't ask for your opinion, you dumb shit."

I turned back to Sean. "We're leaving right now."

He stared at me inanely, then mumbled, "But...but, I um...can't really go with you."

"Why not?"

"Because Danny promised me a ride on this Harley and I wanna go."

He sounded like a petulant little kid. Thoroughly disheartened, I groused, "Are you crazy? You're not going to operate this thing in your condition on that winding road, or any road for that matter!"

"Chill, lady," Danny interjected sternly. "I'm cool. Just had one beer. I'll give him a ride back to Castle Valley."

To his credit, at least he didn't call me a bitch again. Yet. "I don't know what you guys are up to, but whatever it is, I don't want my brother involved in it."

Danny drew back, appearing offended. "What's wrong with trying to show him a good time while he's here?"

"Come on, Kenny," Sean whined. "He's right. I'm not a kid. You can't tell me what to do. Quit trying to deprive me of my great Arizona adventure."

I paused a few seconds to gauge the situation. It was apparent that he wasn't as addlebrained as last night, so short of dragging him off the Harley, there didn't seem to be much I could do. He was beyond reasoning with. And, unfortunately, he was right. He wasn't a kid. I was not responsible for his behavior and couldn't force him to come with me. I turned to meet Danny's penetrating gaze. His hooded eyes looked clear. Sinister, but clear. And sober. "Six o'clock at the Crab Shack." I turned on heel and hiked up the street, my earlier elation diminished. When I reached the corner, I cast one last glance over my shoulder in time to see Daryl hand something to Sean, which he popped in his mouth. Profoundly troubled by my brother's reckless behavior, I continued up the hill, more aware than ever that I was up against a powerful adversary. Addiction.

CHAPTER
15

What a shitty day it was turning out to be. Torn as to what I should do, what I could do, I approached my parents conversing on a bench adjacent to my Jeep. Should I fess up to my mother about Sean's activities or continue to keep it between my dad and me? Poised to lay it all out, I braced for the inevitable fireworks. But the confession froze on my tongue when she noticed me and smiled brightly. She looked so happy and relaxed I decided the details of his accelerated substance abuse would keep a while longer.

"Where's Sean?" she asked, puzzlement crinkling her sun-tinted face as she searched the distance behind me.

"Oh…ah…he met up with a couple of the guys from the party he attended last night and he a…wants to hang with them for a while." Lame. That sounded so lame

"Really?" Indignation evident in her voice, she added, "And just how is he planning to get back to Castle Valley?"

Should I tell her he would be returning on the back of a Harley with a person I could only pray would be sober while traversing the steep winding road that lacked guard rails in some places? Nope. Best not. Why worry her? I couldn't change anything anyway. "Um…he's getting a ride back with one of his…new buddies."

The corners of her mouth turned down. "So typical of him to prefer the company of strangers over us and I have a pretty good idea of the caliber of friends he's chosen." It was hard to miss the flash of suspicion in her eyes as she rose abruptly and headed towards the Jeep. My mother wasn't stupid. She had to know something was amiss and it only intensified my growing sense of guilt. I glanced over and caught my dad's look of warning. He mouthed, 'not yet,' so I swallowed the words back once again.

All during the drive back to Castle Valley, sandwiched in between conversation with my parents, I contemplated again how to resolve the issues dogging me and came up with no satisfactory solution. As the lavender-blue dusk spread across the landscape, my sleep deprivation finally caught up with me. Fighting to stay awake, my eyes sandpaper-dry, I chewed gum and drank caffeine-laden sodas while maneuvering down the switchbacks. Intense relief flowed through me when we finally rolled into Castle Valley. As we pulled up in front of the brightly-lit restaurant, the overpowering smell of fish and French fries permeated the night air. I was in the process of handing my dad his crutches when my cell phone sounded. It was Fritzy. Finally! "Hey, I need to take this call," I told my parents. "I'll meet you inside in a few minutes, okay?"

They nodded agreement so I slid back into the Jeep and closed the door. "Hey, busy lady, I was wondering when I'd hear from you."

"Sorry. It's been pretty hectic at work, but I wanted to touch base with you before you take off with your family. Tomorrow, right?"

"Bright and early. Got any news for me?"

"Yes, but probably not what you're expecting. My examination confirms the cause of death to be CO_2–carbon monoxide–poisoning."

"So, you believe this was simply an accident?"

"Right now, there's no evidence to suggest otherwise."

So that was that. Case closed. For some strange reason, I could not shake the underlying sense of skepticism. I pressed her again. "So…in your professional opinion, there was nothing at the scene to raise any suspicions of…"

"I know you're always on the lookout for an intriguing story, Stick," she said, intercepting my line of thought, "but again, unless you can produce evidence to the contrary, it appears to be an accident."

"Wow."

"Why wow? These types of things do happen."

After I filled her in on the details Marcelene had shared surrounding the death of Jenessa's childhood friend, she mused, "Okay, I can see why she might be unsure. And you." She was silent a few more seconds before tacking on, "Listen, I was there for two days and there was nothing, and I mean nothing, to indicate foul play. I do have a question for you, however. Do you know if this girl was experimenting with drugs?"

"Why do you ask?"

"Because we discovered some pills in the pocket of her jeans. They're at the lab now being evaluated, but we suspect they're probably MDMA, which is a street drug with a lot of different names, but you might know it as Molly or Ecstasy or a hybrid."

I stared straight ahead, mildly shocked. What an odd coincidence. I had just been reading about this subject last night. It was disturbing enough to know that my own brother was dabbling in drugs, but being involved in the party scene seemed totally out of character for a straitlaced person like Jenessa. I finally found my voice. "Well...how soon will you know whether either of them had used drugs prior to their deaths?" I asked hoarsely, still feeling disbelief. Marcelene and Ginger would be horrified to learn this. Was this the confidential information Marshall had been unable to share with me?

"Could take three to six months to verify."

"Are you kidding me? Why that long?"

"A big backlog of cases ahead this one."

False. Something about this scenario felt false. "I'll do a little investigating and see what I can find out from Ginger."

"No rush. Try to relax and have a good time with your family, okay? I'll see you next Saturday at the party."

"Okay." I tapped the END button and just sat there absorbing this new and provocative information. No matter how I tried, I could not reconcile the idea of Jenessa using these types of drugs. She had been as far from a party girl as one could get. No. Nathan must have been the corrupting influence in her life. But that was just conjecture on my part. To verify my suspicions, I needed to contact his relatives and friends to find out more about his personal life. He had been close to Sean's age, and like many young people had most likely experimented with pot and perhaps other stimulants. But wait, how would that work? Hadn't Ginger told me that he'd participated in all manner of extreme sports? Wouldn't that require him to be in excellent physical shape and have his wits about him? I could buy the fact that he might have used steroids, but hallucinogenic drugs? That didn't make any sense. I pressed a hand to my head, admonishing myself. Stop it! Quit torturing yourself, O'Dell! You can't do a damn thing about it until next week anyway. Would the story be stone cold by then?

I had my hand on the door handle when I felt strong vibrations and a thunderous roar filled the air. Seconds later, three Harleys rumbled past me and stopped near the restaurant's main entrance. When I recognized Sean perched behind Danny Hinkle, irritation-infused relief streamed through me. At least he'd made it back in one piece. I was buoyed by the fact that by this time tomorrow night, he'd be far away from the influence of the Hinkles. Sean dismounted, gave each brother a firm high-five handclasp before crossing to converse with the third individual whose face was hidden behind a helmet. Following a short exchange and another macho handshake, all the bikers hit the gas and disappeared onto the highway. Sean was ambling towards the entrance when I pushed the door open and shouted, "Sean! Wait up!" I slid out and hurried to his side. "Well, was it everything you hoped for?"

"Whoo-hoo! It was only like freakin' awesome!"

"I'm so glad you're having a good time," I commented dryly.

Completely missing the nuance of my remark he crowed, "You shoulda been with me!" Giggling like a kid at a carnival, he grabbed me and twirled me in a circle, gushing, "I am lovin' Arizona and...and...I love you too, Kenny! I mean it! You totally rock!"

If I hadn't known he was high as a kite, I would have been flattered, but I wriggled out of his grasp and focused on his flushed face and dilated pupils. There was no logical reason he would be this effusive or affectionate, and I wondered what concoction of drugs he'd recently ingested. Whatever it was had transformed him from being withdrawn and angry into a happy, sociable guy.

"Man oh man somethin' smells good!" He sniffed the air kind of like a dog would, his nostrils flaring in and out. "I am so starving!" He was chattering away like a girl about the wind, the stars, pine trees and some song he'd heard on his magical motorcycle trip when we stepped inside the crowded Crab Shack. Over the din, I introduced Sean to several of the locals waiting for tables and then looked around for our parents. I finally spotted Tally sitting at a corner table engaged in conversation with my dad and another man seated next to him with his back to us. Advancing closer, I was sure my eyes were deceiving me because the bald-headed guy looked an awful lot like Tugg. It couldn't be. Nothing ever got in the way of his Saturday night poker game. Wait a minute. It was Tugg. "Well, this is a surprise! I didn't know you were coming tonight."

"Hey, Kendall! I wanted to have a little more time to visit with your old dad here," he said, patting him on the shoulder affectionately. "You don't mind me crashing your party, do you?"

"Of course not."

I could hear Sean babbling excitedly about his ride to my mother, who sat eyeing him with a look of wary bemusement as I slid into the chair next to Tally. I momentarily forgot about my frustrations when he folded my hand in his. "Hey, cowboy."

"Hey, yourself."

I leaned close and whispered in his ear, "You're still coming over after dinner, right?"

His tone low and intimate, he answered gruffly, "That is my plan." His grin widened and he just kept on grinning. "You have a good time today?"

"I…it had a few challenges, but yes." By now I was pretty good at reading Tally and the inscrutable expression in his deep brown eyes puzzled me. I searched his face closely. "What's going on?"

He shrugged. "Nothing. Can't I be glad to see you?"

"Sure. Everything okay with you?"

"Couldn't be better."

"Good." I edged him a final glance of uncertainty before turning my attention back to Tugg. "Any more news about Walter?"

"Yeah, Lavelle called me a little while ago from the hospital." He fished a piece of paper from his shirt pocket. "He's suffering from a serious foodborne bacteria called…and I'm not sure I'm pronouncing it right…Campylobacter Jejuni."

"I've never heard of that in my life."

"Me neither. It's a long word for serious food poisoning. The doctor told her it's the second most common type after Salmonella. Apparently you can contract it from eating undercooked poultry or beef or even from unsafe food handling practices."

"Like in a bowling alley kitchen perhaps?" Tally chimed in, arching one dark brow.

"Could be," Tugg commented grimly. "Lavelle

looked it up online and it can sometimes be fatal."

"Shit," I murmured, a little shockwave running through me.

"Don't panic. She thinks maybe he'll be released on Tuesday or Wednesday, but doubts he'll be up to working until the following week."

"Oh my," I groaned. What was I to do? It seemed no matter which decision I reached, it would be the wrong one.

I must have looked pretty glum because Tally inquired, "You okay?" I waved away his concern. "I'm just under a lot of pressure right now."

His gaze strayed from me to Tugg and then my dad. Was I mistaken or did they all exchange a conspiratorial look? "I think I can be of some help to you," Tally stated, his eyes twinkling with mischief.

I stared at him. "How?"

"You want to tell her, Bill?" he asked, addressing my dad.

"Tell me what?" All three men wore the same secretive grin.

"We've talked it over and reached a consensus," Tugg announced with a wink.

"Okay," I demanded, "what are you guys up to?"

"Unpack your bags, honey," my father announced. "We're setting you free to do what you do best."

I stared at him, shaking my head. "I...I'm not following you."

He extended his palm towards Tally. "Meet our new tour guide."

With a playful smile pasted on his lips, Tally inclined his head towards me. "As always, I am at your service, Ma'am."

CHAPTER
16

I fired a stunned looked at my mother. Her benevolent smile conveyed knowing approval, and my dad admitted that he'd hatched the plan after I'd received Mary's troubling call, phoning both Tugg and Tally while Mom and I were shopping.

While I appreciated his efforts and certainly didn't want to appear ungrateful, I wasn't quite sure how I felt about the unexpected proposal. Part of me was anxious to jump on the story, but it didn't seem right to abandon my family. I protested to no avail and should have kicked up more of a fuss, but the arrangement solved a host of vexing problems, so it was hard to be upset with them. Before heading home, I hugged and thanked them all for their generosity and confirmed plans to meet for breakfast.

Hours later, as Tally and I lay cuddled together, tiny flashes of doubt still assailed me. Was I making a mistake accepting his offer? What if I was giving up this precious time with my family for nothing? Even though the initial investigation suggested accidental death, what if there was something to Marcelene's suspicions? Didn't I owe it to her to at least follow up? Tally, bless his heart, had done a superb job of convincing me the situation was a win-win. Not only did it present a unique opportunity for my family to get to know him, he'd explained, it also freed me to pursue the story. And, with gentle good humor, he reminded me that his intimate knowledge of Arizona and its history made him a far superior tour guide. Of that I had no doubt.

I propped myself up on one elbow and studied the outline of his lean, muscular body illuminated in the faint moonlight streaming in the window. I trailed my fingers lightly along his hip and thighs. He was a mighty fine specimen of a man. "So, did you volunteer for this gig or did my dad back you into a corner?"

He turned on his back and stretched his arms above his head. "Mmmm...I'd say a little of both."

"I thought so."

"He's pretty persuasive. After he filled me in on everything going on, we both came to the conclusion that you needed to stay and take care of things here, especially with Tugg's health situation and Walter being out of the picture for now."

"Tell the truth. You don't really want me investigating this story, do you?"

He turned towards me, his facial features unreadable in the low light. "No, not really."

"Then why did you agree to it?"

His resigned sigh filled the room. "Because whether it's now, next week or next month, you're going get involved, especially if there's an element of danger."

"Wow. Am I that transparent?"

"You're kidding, right? You've been dying to look into this ever since you heard about it. And before you get all defensive, I've come to terms with the fact that this is who you are. This is your passion and I can't change you." He chuckled softly. "And it's also a waste of breath for me to try and talk you out of it."

"You continue to amaze me, Bradley James Talverson." I leaned in and kissed his sensuous mouth tenderly. "I hope you know how much I love you for doing this."

"Consider it another engagement gift."

That earned him another kiss, but then he suddenly pulled back. "One favor."

"What's that?"

He reached out and caressed my cheek. "Try not to get yourself killed."

"Deal." I placed my hand over his and a companionable silence fell between us momentarily before he spoke up again. "So, what's the plan? You heading out that way tomorrow?"

"Absolutely. Might as well get started."

"I'm very familiar with that area."

"Really? That's pretty far from the Starfire Ranch, isn't it?"

"Yeah, but we've been doing business with the McCracken Ranch for a long time," he informed me and then cautioned, "Just so you know, Raven Creek has a pretty bad reputation, so be extra careful."

"Yeah, Marshall told me."

"Take your phone and your gun."

"I intend to," I said, turning to pet Marmalade who

had jumped onto the bed between us, vying for attention. "How long since you've been out there?"

"A while." He told me that after Buster McCracken died, he'd continued doing business with Elizabeth McCracken until she married John Hinkle, who then split his time between running his own spread while making improvements on his new wife's ranch prior to his death last year. Once again, my heart went out to her. Not only had she been left alone to deal with two ranch properties, she also had to contend with his two errant sons. "How does she manage to run both places?"

"Not too well. She's got her hands full trying to run the Circle H, but she's still running a couple of hundred head of cattle in the hills out there, mostly on BLM land. I heard she's got a manager there now, but it's still not being kept up like it should be."

"Yeah, Marshall told me it's the same guy who found Jenessa and Nathan."

"Harvel Brickhouse?"

"You know him?"

"Met him a few times. He was in the process of applying for permits to try and re-open the old Thunderbolt mine when John decided to lease that section of land to a sand and gravel operation three or four years back."

"Why would he do that?"

"Money. Elizabeth told me Harvel was pretty ticked off about it, but said they needed the extra revenue to help cover the taxes. Turns out it was a good thing or she would've lost that place by now, I'm sure."

Marmalade bumped her head against me for attention, so I scratched her chin. "I was wondering why Elizabeth would hire an ex-con. Marshall said he'd done time about thirty years ago," I murmured. "Maybe hiring him to work there was her way of smoothing ruffled feathers?"

"Maybe." He yawned widely again, adding, "As you're finding out, ranching isn't as profitable as it used to be. Most of the mom and pop ranches are gone, turned into housing tracts and shopping centers, or the owner's got to have additional sources of income to maintain it."

"So that's why you diversified into horse breeding?"

"Yep." He thumped the pillow and pulled the covers higher. "I gotta get some shut-eye now. I'm fading."

"Me too. Thirty minutes of sleep last night didn't quite cut it." I snuggled next to him. "Oh. Just one more question. What's the best route to Raven Creek?"

"Pick up I-17, head north and get off at the Bumble Bee exit just past Black Canyon City. You'll be on pavement for a little while before you hit the gravel road, which is pretty well-maintained. but some of the other back roads aren't and can be pretty dicey depending on the weather."

"Is that the only route?"

"Nope. You could take the old road just past Yarnell. It's kind of a long way around and pretty rough in places."

"I'll check Google Earth to get my bearings before I leave."

"You'll be in your glory as soon as you're knee-deep in another assignment and jacked up on adrenalin."

"You think so?" I teased, delighting in the feel of his smooth skin against mine.

"I know so," he countered lazily, adding, "So in the words of your dad, I'm setting you free to do what you do best." He gathered me closer, murmuring, "Well, maybe second-best."

Feeling content and full of optimism, I fell asleep in his arms and slept like I was in a coma until the alarm buzzed at seven. I smacked the button and collapsed back onto the pillow watching the grey dawn light filtering through the blinds. I knew I had to get up, but my body felt like it was super-glued to the sheets. I could have easily used another twelve hours of sleep. As always, Marmalade lay curled at my side waiting for my eyes to open. Her morning ritual began by bounding onto my chest, followed by furious kneading, accompanied by her musical purr. "Good morning, you little cutie pie," I mumbled drowsily, stroking her soft orange fur until it crackled with static electricity. Tally, always an early riser, had left at some point, probably before daylight, and was no doubt already at the ranch making last minute preparations for his spur-of-the-moment journey. And thinking of that, I grabbed my phone from the night stand and tapped out a quick text to Brian informing him that he didn't need to cat-sit as I wouldn't be leaving town as planned. "That's right," I told Marmalade, staring into her luminous eyes, "Mom will be home tonight after all."

Feeling wistful and maybe just a tad envious of missing all the fun, I almost regretted my decision. But when I remembered Ginger's mournful face and Marcelene's ardent plea for help, the determination to ferret out all the facts returned with a vengeance. If nothing more, I would confirm law enforcement's assessment that Jenessa's death was indeed accidental, granting them closure and perhaps a little bit of peace. I'd learned over my years of reporting that most people could eventually come to terms with a loved one's death and move on if all parts of the 'who, what, why, where, when and how' equation were present. But if the vital questions of *where* or *why* remained unanswered, it tended to haunt the survivors for a lifetime. In this instance, I only had to concentrate on the why.

With that thought at the forefront of my mind, I threw off the bed covers. It took me a while to unpack the suitcases, setting aside the clothing that I would now need for travel to higher altitudes. I dressed in layers and checked the weather forecast and road conditions. I fed Marmalade and then loaded the Jeep with water, snacks and emergency supplies before heading out to meet everyone at the Iron Skillet. Wow. I couldn't have ordered up a more gorgeous day. Accelerating along Lost Canyon Road, I reveled in the sight of cottony puffball clouds gliding swiftly across the robin's-egg-blue sky while strong gusts of wind, no doubt a precursor to the weather change predicted for later today or tomorrow, buffeted the Jeep.

Seated with my family inside the Iron Skillet moments later, I watched Lucinda, wearing her 'spray on jeans,' flit about being her usual annoying self. Even though I tried mightily to ignore her blatant sexual advances directed at Tally, it irritated the shit out of me. She didn't appear to be abandoning her quest just because we were getting married. Tally, Sean and my dad seemed greatly amused, while my mother and I traded looks of shared exasperation.

I was actually glad when breakfast ended. Outside, after an emotional farewell with promises to send photos and video back and forth, I stood in the mounting wind, hair whipping my face, fighting off a sudden sense of gloom as Tally's big SUV disappeared into the distance. I was getting what I wanted, wasn't I? So why should I feel sorry for myself? "Get over it," I muttered aloud as the melodic peal of church bells galvanized me into action. If I were to get on the road by ten, I'd have to catch Marcelene before she left for church.

Tingling with nervous energy, I drove along mostly deserted streets to the Desert Sky Motel, busily compiling a mental to-do list. Besides having additional questions for her regarding Jenessa's recent activities, I also needed to talk to the girl's friends and acquaintances. It was nothing short of amazing how some seemingly unimportant detail, obscure story or almost-forgotten event could deliver bountiful information that might prove to be significant. I hated to heap any more misery on the grief-stricken woman, but I would have to ask Marcelene about Jenessa's possible drug use, grill her with more questions regarding her daughter's relationship with Nathan Taylor and then ask if she would grant me permission to go through Jenessa's things—a depressing job, but it had to be done. I parked near the cottage and jotted another reminder to myself. Since Walter had not been able to review the files on Friday regarding the two other deaths in that vicinity, I would have to research that as well. Oh, boy. I still hadn't ordered flowers or picked up a card for Walter.

I composed a quick text to Ginger. SURPRISE! TALLY CHAUFFERING FAMILY ON SIGHTSEEING TRIP. MY BUTT'S OFFICIALLY IN GEAR AS U REQUESTED! ☺ NEED A FAVOR. PLS SEND FLOWERS & CARD 2 WALTER. THX! TALK SOON. I tapped the SEND button. That should get her attention.

I hurried to the front door, knocked and then stood listening to the soothing jingle of wind chimes and winter birds tweeting until the door swung open. Marcelene stared at me in surprise, and after I told her about the change of plans, she blinked back tears. "God bless you. Ginger and I are so grateful to you for doing this," she said, her voice tremulous as she pulled on her coat and shouldered her purse. "And we'll say a special prayer for both you and Tally today."

"Thank you. Do you have a few minutes to talk?" I tensed. This wasn't going to be pleasant.

Her dark-circled eyes darted at her watch. "Well...I have to teach a Bible study class this morning. I only have a few minutes. What about later this afternoon?"

"Can't. I'll be somewhere in the Bradshaws by then. Just one quick question," I pressed. "To your knowledge, do you know if Jenessa was using any...illegal substances?"

Her eyes widened as tiny dots of scarlet appeared on her pale, sunken cheeks. "What? What are you asking me? Do you mean was she using drugs?"

"Yes."

Face contorted in shocked rage, she spluttered, "Why...why are you asking me such a...a...horrible question, Kendall?"

"Because the forensics specialist found drugs in the pocket of her jeans." I laid a comforting hand on her arm. "This is not an accusation, Marcelene, but your answer is important."

"Oh good Lord," she whispered, her expression softening from outrage to bewilderment. "I...I...never... she wouldn't..." She paused, her lips twitching, obviously trying to gather her wits before barking out a forceful, "No! I know her...I mean, I knew her too well. She would never use drugs! We talked about things like that. She didn't drink. She didn't smoke. She went to church every Sunday. She...she was a good girl. No, I refuse to believe..."

"What about Nathan?" I cut in, "Where did she meet him?"

"One of her friends introduced them."

"Did he live here in town?"

She shook her head. "No. He lived with his father in Surprise."

"Did he ever display any surreptitious or odd behavior?"

Appearing ill at ease, she glanced away. "I suppose it depends on a person's definition of odd."

Intrigued, my interest level climbed. "What do you mean?"

She needlessly fiddled with her purse strap. "He seemed like a nice-enough young man. Very good-looking. Jenessa was certainly bedazzled by him but I had reservations."

"Because...?"

"His wild streak worried me."

"In what way?"

She drew in a deep breath and expelled the air slowly, apparently considering her answer. "Nathan was a daredevil. Not like the other boys she had dated. I worried about him pushing her into something...dangerous. The higher the risk, the better. He didn't seem to have any life goals other than trying to figure out what crazy stunt to try next."

"And you worried that he might have a corrupting influence on her?" I suggested.

"Yes."

Might as well get to the point. "Marcelene, do you think he was doing drugs?"

Lips pinched together, she hesitated before whispering, "I don't know." She eyed her watch again. "I have to go now."

"Okay, just one final thing. Would you mind if I look around Jenessa's room? I'll lock the front door when I leave."

Deep sadness invaded my heart when she pressed a hand to her mouth. "I...I haven't been able to bring myself to go in there yet." She locked eyes with me and thumbed behind her. "Down the little hallway behind the kitchen. Last door on the left." Swiping away tears, she marched past me to her car and drove away. I had no doubt she was trying desperately to keep it together.

Sighing heavily, I stepped inside and closed the door. Within seconds I felt it, the same haunting sensation I'd experienced walking through the hushed rooms in my grandmother's house four years ago a few days after she died—the aura of emptiness, of grief, of irreplaceable loss. Even though her physical body was gone, it seemed that remnants of her powerful essence, her fiery spirit still remained. I also remembered the phenomenon of the inexplicable silence, an extreme dense hollowness that seemed to inhabit the house after her passing. With those gut-wrenching memories still fresh in my mind, I walked through the living room, hearing only the muted ticking of clocks. Yep. A familiar feeling. And a little eerie.

I forced myself to concentrate, pondering Marcelene's emotional response to my questions. What if Nathan had been using drugs, but had not exhibited any obvious signs like my brother? Had he pressured Jenessa into trying them? In order to please him, had she abandoned her principles? But why were the pills found only in her pocket? If Nathan had provided them, why were none found on his person? I was positive the camper must have been searched from end to end, with no other pills being found. Thought-provoking indeed.

With the curtains drawn at all the windows, I had to stop momentarily when I entered the narrow hallway so my eyes could adjust to the low light before continuing. Several feet from the last door, I paused again, unable to identify the dark lump on the floor in front of Jenessa's room. My heart did a nervous little dance. What the hell was that? I sidestepped to the nearest window and pulled the curtains apart, revealing one of the saddest things I've ever seen. A fuzzy, black cat, head bowed, body curled in a tight ball, lay pressed against the closed door. Cold relief mixed with sympathy streamed through me. Oh my. Was the poor thing waiting for Jenessa's return? How long had it been there? "Hey, there, little one." I knelt, allowed the cat to smell my hand and then reached out to stroke the silky fur. A round nametag dangled from the pink collar so I angled it towards the window. Fiona. Obviously female. "Well, hello there, Fiona." The cat slowly raised her head, fastened glowing emerald eyes on me and stared intently as if she were trying to telepathically convey a message. A sorrowful breath caught in my throat. Over these past few months of being a cat owner, I'd learned how intuitive and complex these remarkable creatures could be. More than likely, she was suffering from depression. The urge to comfort her was overwhelming. Should I pick her up? Nope, might spook her. Besides, I knew what she wanted. Rising to my feet, I simply opened the door. Unexpectedly, an icy breeze, almost tomblike, rushed out, sending goose bumps skimming up my arms. The ghostly flutter of sheer white curtains at the open windows added to the surreal atmosphere. But, it didn't deter Fiona. She streaked into the room and leaped onto the stuffed-toy-littered bed. Only then did I realize that she had only one hind leg. Surprised by her agility, I watched as she searched the bed, dropped to the floor, sniffed all around, then looked up at me expectantly as if to say, 'Okay, where is she?'

"Can't help you, honey," I whispered, crossing to close the window before beginning my own quest for answers. Even though I was on a worthwhile mission, I still felt like an interloper rummaging through the personal possessions of a young woman who'd only been gone from this earth for a week and a half. Just like I'd experienced with my grandmother's death, the strong perception of her life force remained. Fiona apparently sensed it too because she seemed more at ease lying on a round throw rug, lazily flicking her tail. However, she never took her eyes off of me as I moved around the room taking photos, recording notes and learning far more about the attractive, flaxen-haired girl than I'd ever known while she was alive. That thought sent waves of regret coursing through me. I wished I hadn't been so preoccupied with my own life, wished I'd taken the time to get to know her better. I would have known that her favorite color was lavender; favorite flower was daisies and that she preferred perfumes with a light and airy scent. Resentment joined with regret at the unfairness of it all. What was that old adage—only the good die young? Conversely, why did it often seem that rotten people lived forever? With difficulty,

I shook off my growing despair and focused on the task at hand. I had work to do. No time to be fanciful.

Jenessa's bookcase revealed more about her character. It was packed with sheet music for piano, books on religion, including several beautifully bound Bibles, a pile of BLM and Prescott National Forest maps, a stack of *Arizona Highways* magazines and other publications featuring various outdoor activities, as well as informative pamphlets about no-kill animal shelters. The mauve-tinted walls were adorned with colorful photographs depicting various Arizona landscapes, and in one corner stood a glass display cabinet containing an array of quirky ceramic animals and dolls. Her dresser drawers and desk were orderly, as well as the clothes and shoes in her closet. And something else was strikingly evident. Everything in that room reflected goodness, innocence, optimism and compassion. There were no slick posters of Hollywood entertainers or grungy pop stars, no hint of porn, no references to alcohol, cigarettes, illicit drugs, nothing to indicate that she dabbled in anything improper, which made the situation decidedly more bizarre. Nathan must have been the corrupting influence in her life. The urgent desire to find out more about him and his activities was now high on my priority list.

A tree branch rocking in the wind scratched the windowpane rhythmically as I sifted through a box of receipts on her desk, noting some recent purchases—hiking boots, backpack, sleeping bag, freeze-dried food and a flashlight. She'd bought new blue jeans, shampoo, conditioner, hair ties, earrings, and there was paperwork indicating that she'd recently upgraded her cellphone. Yeah. That was one of the things bothering me the most. What had happened to the cellphones? What were the odds that they would both lose them at the same time? And if they had, where were they?

Barely halfway through the pile, I found several letters thanking her for generous donations to various Arizona animal shelters, and a receipt for cat food, cat toys, collar and nametag. I checked the date. They'd been purchased three weeks ago. Did that mean she'd recently adopted Fiona or just bought replacement items? I'd have to ask Marcelene. I returned all the receipts to the box. Then I made the poignant discovery of her calendar where she'd circled the date for our engagement party. There was a little notation marked in the square. *So excited!* There was also a cryptic notation for the previous Tuesday, the day she and Nathan should have come home. *Pick up SG.* What did that mean? My cell phone chimed and I glanced at Ginger's text. TALLY'S A SWEETHEART! IF U EVER DECIDE 2 THROW THAT MAN BACK, HE'S MINE! ☺ WILL TAKE CARE OF WALTER'S DEAL. GOOD LUCK! KEEP ME POSTED!!

A loud crash from behind made me flinch so violently, I almost dropped my phone. I whirled around to see Fiona perched on the edge of the dresser calmly staring at me. A few tense seconds passed before I noticed the picture frame lying facedown on the wood floor below her. Still feeling light-headed from the sudden shock, I knelt down, flipped it over and stared through the cracked glass at a photo of Jenessa and a very good-looking dark-haired young man standing in front of a row of mailboxes on a dirt road. Was this Nathan Taylor? I studied the photo carefully. They were both smiling, attired in outdoor gear, and she was clutching a black cat in her arms. I glanced up at Fiona and back to the photo. I could not tell for sure if it was the same cat. Directly behind them, nestled between thick foliage, stood several small buildings and further in the background a steep, rocky incline. I wondered if Marcelene could tell me where and when the photo had been taken and by whom.

Careful to avoid the shards of glass, I removed it and took a picture of it with my phone before looking around for others. I searched the room, finally discovering a few more in the nightstand drawer. There was one of Nathan jumping an ATV over a dry wash, another of him rollerblading, several showed him hang gliding and the last one pictured the laughing couple kayaking on a lake. I rummaged around in the second nightstand looking for more photos and came across two faded ones at the very bottom along with an assortment of greeting cards she'd saved. The first one pictured a smiling Jenessa posing with Kailey and two adults that I assumed were Kailey's parents. Both appeared slender, the man quite tall. They were backlit so it was difficult to see their faces clearly.

The second photograph appeared to have been taken at a fair or amusement park and showed both young girls riding a merry-go-round. When I turned it over, my throat closed with emotion and my eyes glazed with tears reading the inscription *See you in Heaven.* There was no way to tell when it had been written, and I wondered if the sentiment reflected her state of mind immediately following the tragedy, or had it been penned more recently? I carefully replaced them, hoping her wish had been fulfilled.

When I couldn't find any others, I figured the bulk of them were probably on her laptop, which sat closed on her desk. I opened the lid, disappointed to see it was password protected. Being fully aware that Marcelene knew next to nothing about computers meant I'd have to ask Ginger's brother, Brian, for help. He'd know how to get into the files so I could check out her emails and hopefully find more photos.

The cuckoo bird in the kitchen chirped ten times, reminding me that it was time to hit the road. As I turned to leave, Fiona bounded back on the bed and settled herself comfortably. "Sleep well, little one," I murmured, careful to leave the door open, my heart heavy with the thought that she was waiting for someone who would never return.

Anxious to tackle my new assignment, I left the cottage feeling certain about only two things. I'd seen nothing in Jenessa's room to indicate that she was anything other than a sweet, loving person. No way would this girl be experimenting with street drugs, prescription drugs or any other drugs. The two words she'd scribbled on her calendar indicated that she'd been looking forward to performing at our party. In my mind, that pretty much ruled out suicide. It boiled down to an accident or foul play. Driving out of town towards my destination, I was filled with a new sense of purpose. If there was something sinister going on out there, I intended to find out what it was.

CHAPTER
17

Strong tailwinds and scarce northbound traffic on I-17 allowed me to peg the speedometer at 80, so in no time at all I skimmed past the small, mountain-rimmed communities of New River, Rock Springs and Black Canyon City, where I began the steep ascent towards Sunset Point. I arrived at the Bumble Bee exit in just over an hour and twenty minutes, and headed downhill into the remote valley, dazzled by the breathtaking scenery. It was an optical illusion of course, but somehow the intermittent patches of snow decorating the craggy tops of the Bradshaw Mountains made them appear higher, more imposing and majestic. Fast-moving clouds patterned the vast juniper-mesquite-and cactus-dotted slopes with irregular shadows, adding rich texture to the deep canyons and jagged rock outcroppings. The ribbons of narrow dirt roads and ATV tracks snaking away into the wilderness beckoned to me, firing up my imagination. Would the brooding peaks hold fast to their secrets, or would I eventually be able to pry loose some answers to my

209

questions? Even though my instincts told me there must be more to this story, I still had to fight off the fleeting notion that I might also be on the mother of all wild goose chases.

Rounding a sharp bend, my approach startled a small herd of javelinas munching on prickly pear cactus and scattered them into the dense brush. The recent winter rains and snowfall had rejuvenated the arid Sonoran desert and transformed it into a succulent, green garden. I cracked the window a little more, relishing the invigorating wind blowing in my face. And only then did it hit me—the full ramifications of what Tally's benevolent gift had granted me. Freedom. Adventure. Pursuit of the truth. I could not resist smiling. It was a supremely reassuring feeling to realize that after all these months of verbalizing his displeasure, Tally finally got me. Instead of expected resistance, this time he'd actually encouraged me to follow my passion, pursue my 'adrenalin fix' as he laughingly called it. Our relationship was definitely maturing.

The pavement ended abruptly after a mile or so and, other than two pickups and a handful of RVs sitting in a wide parking area, there was no sign of civilization. Driving on, I crossed over a little stone bridge and spotted a rectangular yellow sign that read: **WELCOME TO BUMBLE BEE, AZ. Est. 1864, Ranch 1/4 MI Town 1/2 MI Population 19 People, 45 Horses, 161 Cattle, Drive With Care.**

I zoomed past the entrance to the Bumble Bee Ranch and drove into the tiny village of Bumble Bee itself. There wasn't much to the place and if I'd looked away for even a minute, I would have missed it completely. I pulled onto the shoulder and slid out to take a few photos, which I forwarded to my dad, Sean and Tally. I looked around, taking it all in. There didn't appear to be more than a dozen structures still standing and they looked deserted. Except for the crunch of my boots in the gravel and the soft whistle of the wind scattering a few pieces of paper along the road, there were no other sounds. To the west stood a row of small wooden houses, along with an old stone building that looked like it might have once been a bar or store. It was boarded up tight, but there was no missing the prominent hand-painted signs nailed to the door. **Tell ADOT No to the highway in the canyon! HELL NO TO ADOT!!!** What was this? The Department of Transportation was going to build a freeway through this picturesque place? There were several other homes, including a rough-hewn stone house in good condition on the east side of the road. And there were other telltale signs of the residents' strong opinions nailed to a nearby fence. **NO FREEWAY HERE! LEAVE BUMBLE BEE IN PEACE! IF YOU TRY TO BUILD IT, EXPECT A LOAD OF BUCKSHOT IN YOUR ASS!** I totally agreed and could not blame people for voicing their written displeasure. It would be a shame to ruin the peace and quiet of this tiny ranching community by carving a freeway through here. I shook my head, wondering what bureaucrat would make such a boneheaded decision. The expense of such a project would be astronomical.

Looking further down the road, I noticed an old yellow school bus with the windows blacked out and a TV antenna sticking out of the roof. Yep. Definitely a unique place.

All at once, the serene silence was broken by loud, ferocious barks. Startled, I glanced around and my heart rate surged when I saw two dogs, teeth bared, rushing at me. Uh-oh. I backed towards the Jeep. To be on the safe side, I jumped inside, noting that the curtains in one of the small cabins moved slightly. Okay. Apparently one of the 19 residents was watching me and whoever it was had knowingly let the dogs out, no doubt in an attempt to scare me away. I found that annoying and just a little disturbing. Did they think I was with the Department of Transportation? I waited another minute, and when no one appeared and the dogs continued their frenzied yowling, I decided it was time to go. I sprayed a little gravel as I pulled away and within seconds the tiny town vanished in my rearview mirror.

Accelerating along the well-graded road, with the Sunset Point rest stop towering above me to the right and flanked by rolling foothills to the west, I passed by a rusting stock tank on an abandoned ranch and followed the sign towards the little hamlet of Cleator, still having not seen a single soul since leaving the freeway. Just when I was starting to feel like I was the only person on earth, I turned a corner and stared in wonderment at the unexpected scene ahead. The road was completely blocked by a dump truck. A mud-caked red and white pickup, probably at least 40 model years old, sat sideways in front of it, debris all over the ground. A short, rotund woman wearing a floppy brown hat and overalls stood toe-to-toe with a tall, wiry man. She appeared to be shouting and was shaking her finger in his face. And there were chickens—lots of chickens running around in panicked circles. Brimming with curiosity, I eased to a stop and lowered the window. The woman's angry voice, plus the rumble of the truck's idling engine, apparently masked my arrival. What in the world was going on?

Upon closer inspection, I determined that the rubble strewn on the ground consisted of damaged wooden cages and scores of egg cartons, the contents now undoubtedly smashed. I pulled out my phone and took a series of photos as I eavesdropped on the fierce verbal altercation.

"What do you mean it was my fault?" the woman shrieked, gesturing at the chaotic scene around her. "You're the one who hit me, you idiot!"

"How the hell did I know you were gonna slam on the brakes for no good reason? I can't stop this thing on a dime, you know."

"I had a reason," she fired back. "If you people would quit tearing up the road with your damn trucks, I wouldn't have to slow down every two minutes to avoid all the gigantic potholes!" She threw her hands up, gesturing wildly. "Look at this mess. You, Mister, owe me big bucks for scattering my chickens to hell and gone and breaking all my eggs. And look at the damage to my truck!"

The driver, who I judged to be in his late 40s or early 50s, rubbed the dark stubble on his chin and appeared to be baiting her when he glanced towards her pickup and responded with an insolent, "This shit wagon? How can you tell?"

"It's *vintage,*" she squealed, her face now beet-red and contorted with rage, "and happens to be worth a lot of money."

The man pulled himself up to his full height, towering over the diminutive woman. "I ain't payin' you squat. This was your doin', you dumb bitch."

"Who are you calling a bitch?" She poked him hard in the chest. "I've got a good mind to shoot your boney ass!"

At that his expression turned cautious and he took a step back, palming his hands forward as if in surrender. "Look, Lady, I don't want no trouble, but I'm warning you.

Keep your hands off me!" He fished a cell phone from his shirt pocket and tapped the screen.

I could tell by their rigid body language that the dispute was escalating to a dangerous level. So, what could I do about it? I hesitated. Should I involve myself in yet another dicey situation? Impatiently, I checked the time. While the confrontation was certainly entertaining, and at times bordered on amusing, nevertheless my frustration level climbed. With less than five hours of daylight left, I didn't have any more time to waste listening to them squabble. Unfortunately, there was no way to get around the truck because of the steep inclines on either side of the narrow road. But, the urgent need to do something to break the impasse persisted and I was all set to get out and try to convince the man to move his rig when the sound of another vehicle approaching from behind caught my attention. It was only then that the two of them looked over and saw me. Their jaws dropped in surprise before they switched their attention to the aqua-blue pickup braking to a stop on the far side of the road.

With interest, I noted the Prescott National Forest emblem on the door. Maybe this guy could get things moving. The ranger or whoever he was had a cell phone pressed to his ear, but within thirty seconds terminated the call and exited the pickup, his lips pressed together in obvious agitation. I judged him to be in his middle-to late-30s, of medium height and build. He had a round, nondescript face and wore wire-rimmed glasses. Shrugging into a jacket, he secured a ball cap over thinning brown hair and, after shooting me an inquiring glance, trudged towards the feuding couple. I sat up straighter when I suddenly recognized him as the same man I'd seen at breakfast in Prescott yesterday. "What's going on here, Darcy?" His arrival momentarily diffused the volatile confrontation as both of them began talking at once, each of them stating their own version of the story. "Slow down," he finally ordered. "One at a time, please."

Two of the chickens were clucking and scratching in the dirt around my Jeep, so I pocketed my phone and stepped outside just as a second pickup rolled to a stop. This one was white and belonged to the Bureau of Land Management. A tall, muscular woman with a tight, blonde ponytail emerged, wearing a tan uniform, badge, radio and a sidearm. After pausing to assess the situation, she turned to me. "Any idea what's going on here?"

I told her what I'd overheard concerning the accident and she inquired, "You a witness?"

"No. This was already in progress when I arrived." The rising wind was making a complete mess of my long curly hair, which maddeningly kept blowing across my face as I rummaged in my purse and handed her a business card. "Kendall O'Dell. I'm here to do a follow-up story on the recent deaths of a young couple somewhere up the mountain there," I said, gesturing towards the jagged ridgeline. "You're probably familiar with it."

"Very much so." She studied the card briefly and then fished one from her shirt pocket. "Linda Tressick. I'm the Law Enforcement Ranger for this district." We shook hands. "You know where you're going?"

"Ah...not exactly."

"Well, you're in luck. That gentleman over there in the green uniform is Burton Carr. He's with the Forest Service and he'll be able to provide you with more information since the place where those kids died lies within his jurisdiction. Mine officially ends there at the cattle guard," she stated with a wry smile, pointing to where the truck's front tires rested. "Although there's always cooperation and cross-delegation between the two agencies when need be and it looks like this is one of those times."

I glanced over at Burton Carr. Was this fortuitous or what? He was another of the people high on my list to interview. At least something right was happening today. "May I ask you a few questions?"

She raised a hand. "Another time. I need to deal with this situation right now," she said, moving towards the trio. "My number is on the card." She walked right into the middle of the ongoing fracas, which had fired up again with the irate woman stubbornly standing her ground.

"He's a lying bastard! He was too close and going way too fast! You need to arrest him for reckless driving!" The tip of her bulbous nose was so red it almost glowed. This was one pissed-off lady.

"That's horseshit! How about you arrest this wing nut?" the driver challenged, his expression turning surly. "More than likely she's high on some the of that weed she's growing up there in her little backyard pot garden." And in an apparent move to add fuel to the fire, he tacked on, "Or have you moved on to cooking meth?"

Bristling, she pulled herself up to her full height, which was probably about five feet tall at best. "For your information, *numbnuts*, I've got a certificate from the state granting me permission to grow it!" Then she switched gears, modulating her tone, assuming a beleaguered demeanor designed to elicit sympathy, no doubt. "As a caregiver, I need it for my suffering patients." She turned to Burton Carr, her brow furrowed with disappointment. "What's wrong with you? Why are you just standing there like a bump on a log?" Really? This abrasive little woman was a caregiver? She must have a hidden compassion bone not readily evident to me.

The forest ranger managed a conciliatory smile. "It's not necessary to use such inflammatory language. What do you say we try a little harder to work this out, okay?"

"Oh, Burton, I'm glad your dear mother isn't here to see this, God rest her soul. She'd hate to see you acting like such a wimp." Fisting hands on broad hips, she lamented, "You didn't like being bullied by that brother of yours, did you?" Without waiting for his response, she resumed, "And I'm not gonna stand here and be bullied by this idiot!"

Eyes bulging, the driver screeched, "Who the hell are you calling an idiot?"

I noted the brief flash of resentment in Burton Carr's eyes before he shot Linda Tressick one of those 'what are you gonna do' looks. "Okay, Darcy," the woman stated firmly. "Enough. You need to calm yourself down so we can find a solution to this problem. And if you two can't come to an agreement, I'll have to settle it for you. We can't have this road blocked all day while you two continue your pissing match." She pointed at the driver. "You, sir, need to move that truck out of the way right now." And in a no-nonsense tone, she addressed Darcy again. "Does your pickup still run or do I need to give you a tow?"

The petite woman folded her arms and planted booted feet. "It runs, but I'm not going anyplace until I get paid for the damages he caused. You can't just let him off the hook! Someone's got to pay for fixing my truck. I lost a week's worth of eggs and somebody's got to help me find my chickens!"

As I stood there wondering how the scene was going to play out, yet another pickup arrived, this time from the opposite direction. It pulled up behind the gravel truck and a chunky, square-jawed guy clad in jeans, checkered shirt and dark glasses emerged. He raised a hand in greeting and strode purposefully into the fray. "Jack, how you doin'?" Linda inquired while he shook hands with her and Burton Carr.

"I'm good." Exuding an air of all business, he said crisply, "Rod, let's you and me have a little confab." Their heads bowed in conversation, the two men walked to the truck and then Rod climbed into the cab. Jack trudged back and without pretense said to Darcy, "Ms. Dorsett, I apologize for any inconvenience or damage to your vehicle. Besides Linda here, do you want to get additional law enforcement or the insurance companies involved, or do you want to settle this now ourselves?"

She reached up and straightened her hat. "Settle it how?"

"It's our goal to be good neighbors, and we don't want any trouble. So, what's it going to take to make this go away?"

His thin smile struck me as disingenuous and just a touch intimidating, so I shifted my attention to Darcy's reaction. At first she appeared taken aback and then her eyes narrowed with suspicion as her gaze bounced back and forth between Linda and Burton Carr. "Okay, Mr. Loomis, what are you offering?"

"Five hundred and we all walk away happy."

A cunning gleam entered the woman's eyes. "My neck really hurts," she complained, rubbing it gingerly. "Most likely, I have whiplash."

Jack Loomis looked like he was chewing a hole on the inside of one cheek. "One thousand."

"Two," she countered. "Cash."

He countered, "Fifteen hundred and that's my final offer."

Wow. Fifteen hundred dollars for a little dent and some broken eggs? Quite a generous offer.

While she hesitated, Burton and Linda traded an amused glance before the BLM agent volunteered, "I'll help you round up the chickens if that will help conclude this matter."

Darcy gave Jack a curt nod. "Deal."

He unsnapped his shirt pocket and pulled out a sizeable wad of bills. He peeled off fifteen, but instead of handing them to her, he held the money away from her grasp. "These two government officials are witnesses that you are being paid in full for any and all damages and that this matter is closed forever. Agreed?"

She snatched the money. "Agreed."

He issued Linda and Burton a two-fingered salute, strode back to the truck, signaled to the driver and then jockeyed his polished bronze pickup until he got turned around and headed back in the direction he'd come. Interesting. I could only gather that he was the owner or supervisor for the sand and gravel company. And no doubt the truck driver had called to alert him of the situation. On the one hand, I had to admire his slick handling of the circumstances, but it struck me as mighty odd that he would be carrying around that much cash.

CHAPTER
18

Things happened swiftly after that. Darcy moved her weather-beaten pickup out of the way, her whiplash having apparently vanished, and Burton walked back to his vehicle while Rod shoved the big gravel truck in gear. He roared by wearing an unpleasant smirk, leaving a thin trail of dust in his wake. As if on cue, a grey van, a battered, orange pickup and two ATV riders, having luckily missed the roadblock, rounded the corner and proceeded along the road. While Darcy and Linda went chicken hunting in the sagebrush, I hurried to catch Burton Carr before he could get away. Phone to his ear once again, he was already executing a U-turn as I sprinted towards his vehicle, shouting, "Mr. Carr, wait!"

Appearing distracted, he flicked me a startled look as I rushed up to his window. He lowered the phone and thumbed the OFF button when I handed my business card to him. "Kendall O'Dell. I'm a reporter with the *Castle Valley Sun*. Linda Tressick said you'd be able to help me."

He stared briefly at my card before looking up. "Help you with what?"

"Find the spot where the two bodies were discovered last week."

Fixing me with an expression of genuine puzzlement, he absently smoothed his uneven mustache. "What for? There's really nothing to see now."

"I'm working on a possible story angle and I thought I'd get a few photos and talk to some of the people involved, such as yourself."

Apparently considering my request, he continued to stare at me questioningly for additional seconds. "Personally, I think you'll be wasting your time. The officials have concluded their investigation, the vehicle has been towed and just this morning I relocked the gate." He glanced upward. "In addition to that, I'd be wary of venturing up the mountain today considering the weather conditions."

I shaded my eyes against the bright sunshine, following his gaze to the ragged clouds swirling around the top of the peaks. "Looks pretty nice to me. I checked the forecast online earlier. The storm front isn't supposed to move in until tomorrow or maybe the next day."

His look of disdain cancelled out his indulgent smile. Apparently, he didn't appreciate me challenging his prognostication. "I'm more than familiar with this area," he responded coolly. "Believe me when I tell you that the mountain tends to generate its own weather patterns. They can sometimes be unpredictable and take people by surprise... like those two young folks unfortunately discovered."

Duly chastised, my face warmed with chagrin. "I came prepared for bad weather."

He heaved a sigh and consulted his watch. "I'd normally be happy to escort you there, but I've got a mandatory meeting in Prescott within the hour."

I squared my shoulders. I hadn't come all this way to turn back now. "If you'll point me in the right direction, I'm sure I can find it myself."

His brows dropped lower as he tapped his fingertips on the steering wheel. "I'd really feel more comfortable showing you the spot myself. Is there any chance you could come back tomorrow?"

"Not really. My plan is to go there today."

"Can't you wait one day? I'll be in this general area and could meet up with you at your convenience."

I pondered his suggestion for long seconds. My agenda for Monday was packed. "Thanks, but it really fits my schedule better today."

A quick flash of exasperation crossed his face. "I hope you're prepared to take a hike...literally. That road is closed for a reason and has been for quite a while. It's in terrible condition and unless you know where you're going, I'm not sure you'll be able to find the exact location anyway. There's nothing much left there to see except a bunch of muddy tire tracks from all the emergency vehicles and everything."

Was I mistaken or did it seem like he was trying to discourage me? "Well, yes, I am prepared to walk. Approximately how far is it from the junction?"

He reached into the door's side pocket and pulled out a map.

"I won't need that," I stated breezily, holding up my phone. "I've got GPS..."

He waved away the end of my sentence. "Lots of dead zones up there, so you can't always count on it unless you've already downloaded the area maps. Have you done that?"

I'd meant to, but had run out of time. "No, not yet."

A tight, humorless smile. "Well then, it's always smart to have an old-fashioned paper map as a backup. Trust me."

"I have one. Thanks."

"Really? You have a Forest Service motor vehicle use map and an interactive travel map?"

I hesitated. "Well, no. Is that really necessary?"

"You may not think so, but I happen to know what I'm talking about."

I felt a bit taken aback by his curt, defensive demeanor. Either he was super-sensitive and had misconstrued my responses as criticism, or he was still ticked off about Darcy's wimp remark and taking it out on me. Whatever, I really didn't have the time or patience to be lectured. "I'll take your advice and download the maps."

"Good." He snagged a pen from his shirt pocket and began marking the map anyway. "The online maps are good, but my directions may differ just a bit."

I decided that alienating this guy would not be smart, so I graciously thanked him, tacking on "Oh, one more thing before you go. I understand you're acquainted with Harvel Brickhouse?"

"I know him."

"He's on my list of people to interview, but I understand he moves around a lot."

A cagey smile hovered around the corners of his mouth. "He's not an easy guy to find. You might try reaching him at the McCracken Ranch first, but if he's not there, he could be at his cabin or out working one of his mining claims."

In my haste to follow the story, it didn't dawn on me until that particular moment that I didn't have the slightest idea what Harvel Brickhouse looked like. Just how did I intend to find him as I tromped through the brush hunting for him? "Could you give me a brief description of him, so I know who I'm looking for?"

"You can't miss him. Just look for a big, brawny guy about six foot six with mutton chops wearing a shaggy old hat. That's Harvel. But, even if you do locate him, he may not talk to you. He's a pretty unsociable guy." He paused, apparently weighing my reaction. When I showed no signs of abandoning my goal, he concluded, "Okay, I'll indicate how to get to his cabin and the mining claims accessible by four-wheel-drive vehicles." He made several more notations on the map, handed it to me and then cautioned, "Ah...there are some...peculiar and disreputable individuals living around that area, so I'd be real careful if you insist on going alone."

As if to defy his words another dump truck driven by a young Hispanic guy roared by, followed by a pickup and four young guys on quads. I smiled. "Looks like I'll have plenty of company." My attempt at humor fell flat, so I inquired, "I gather you're referring to some of the inhabitants of Raven Creek?"

"I am."

"I've already been warned, but thank you for your concern. By the way, do you have a card? I'd like to ask you a few questions at some point."

He pushed his glasses higher on the bridge of his nose. "About what?"

"Your involvement in the discovery of the bodies." He removed a card from his shirt pocket and handed it to me. "My cell number's there if you change your mind about going today. Good luck." He waved a quick goodbye and drove away. Noting the time on my cell phone, I turned and hotfooted it to my Jeep. Crap! The delay had cost me over an hour. I started the engine and as I rumbled over the cattle guard, it was amusing to see Linda Tressick in full pursuit of a clucking brown chicken while Darcy clutched another one tightly to her breast as she held a cell phone pressed to her ear.

Raring to continue my quest, I bounced along the washboard road and in less than ten minutes passed through Cleator, another of the numerous out-of-the-way communities that had flourished in the hinterlands of Arizona, fed by the discovery of gold, silver and copper, only to become ghost towns when the mines finally played out. I often wondered why some people chose to stay on when there appeared to be no reason for the town's continued existence. Hardly more than a wide spot in the road, the main focal point of the tiny cluster of ramshackle tin-roofed houses and rusted trailers was the James P. Cleator General Store and Bar. There were two pickups, a dirt-encrusted Jeep and several quads parked outside. Other than a few people drinking on the open patio and a couple of mangy-looking dogs running around, there were few signs of life. There was, however, a plethora of crudely drawn and worded signs protesting the possibility of a freeway and a few more condemning the sand and gravel company that left little doubt as to how the residents felt. **POLLUTERS GO TO HELL! SAVE OUR DESERTS and FREEWAYS SUCK!**

The last building in the town that looked like it might have once been a garage was covered with graffiti, witchcraft symbols and swastikas. I'd visited an abundance of these small out-of-the-way communities in Arizona these past nine months while on assignment and found that all manner of eccentricities were free to flourish. That was one of the wonderful things about living in a free country. As long as people operated within the boundaries of the law, they were free to be as weird or stupid as they pleased. But, I'd also discovered that a fair amount of illegal activities operating out of sight thrived as well.

Approximately four miles beyond Cleator I passed the entrance to the Circle M Ranch. A small sign read: **McCracken. Private Property. No Trespassing.** I toyed with the idea of stopping at the ranch first, but decided to press on. Finding the spot where Jenessa died was my priority. The range fence seemed to go on forever and I studied with interest the rough, boulder-strewn terrain where Elizabeth had lived before marrying John Hinkle. What must life have been like growing up out here in such isolation? High on the mesquite-and juniper-covered hillsides to the north, I spied a few grazing cattle. Now that I understood how tough ranching was, I had nothing but admiration for the hardy souls who chose this rigorous way of life, for those who sacrificed to keep these secluded private ranches operating and worked long, hard hours to maintain the vanishing rural western lifestyle. I drove on, cognizant of the deteriorating road conditions. Rocking back and forth, I bounced over the tops of exposed boulders, dipping in and out of deep ruts. Even so, I was making good progress, but then less than a mile later, I ended up behind a truck hauling four modular toilets. I couldn't help but laugh out loud at the original name—GRAB YOUR SEAT PORT-A-POTS—but lamented that the slow-moving vehicle presented yet another impediment to my tight schedule on a road too curved and narrow to safely pass. Fortunately, I didn't have to follow it for long when the driver turned right beneath a sign reading **RAVEN CREEK SAND & GRAVEL CO., Authorized Personnel Only**. The clever slogan below read: **WE'LL ROCK YOUR WORLD!**

My Jeep rattled over a series of extremely deep indentations that literally had my teeth clattering together. Oh man. Darcy was right about the deplorable road conditions. But then, almost immediately after passing the entrance, the graded surface smoothed out, proving that it was most likely the heavily-loaded gravel trucks causing the damage. Within several more miles, I noted a subtle change in the foliage as the elevation increased. The mesquite and chaparral gave way to scrub oak, larger junipers and, ahead on the higher slopes, a sprinkling of skinny ponderosa pines appeared along with a few patches of snow. I pulled to the side of the road, intending to download the maps, only to realize there was no cell service. Grudgingly, I had to admit that Burton Carr had been right and felt a twinge of gratitude as I studied the paper map he'd insisted that I take.

The high-pitched drone of an approaching vehicle split the air, disturbing the peace and solitude broken only by the occasional whisper of the wind through the nearby junipers. An athletically-built young guy, cap on backwards, his face hidden behind a bandana and sunglasses, buzzed by, slowing only briefly to glance in my direction before accelerating up the hill towards Crown King. The idea

227

of tooling around on a quad sounded like fun, but the ear-grating noise was definitely annoying.

Less than a mile later, I turned right and passed a yellow sign warning **UNMAINTAINED ROAD**. I headed northwest, winding my way higher up the switchbacks as sunlight and clouds fought for supremacy. I knew from the quick research I'd done that all of the peaks in this magnificent mountain range were over 7000 feet high. Good Lord! Unmaintained was definitely an understatement. The recent rains and snowmelt had washed enormous rocks down the embankments and created deep grooves and teeth-jarring potholes, some of which were still muddy pools. The rugged terrain made for a challenging drive and it was stomach-swooping scary to maneuver along the narrow ribbon of road with not a guardrail in sight. In some places, significant portions of the road had washed away into the deep ravine. One wrong move could send the vehicle plunging down the steep, rocky slope into the creek below.

Shoulders taut, my eyes straining with concentration, I pushed on and on, climbing continuously as the pines thickened. Shouldn't I be there by now? I couldn't possibly be lost, could I? What if I needed to turn around? What would happen if I met another car on one of the blind corners? Hands clenched tightly on the steering wheel, I executed a series of sharp hairpin turns and then unexpectedly, the road leveled off. I was relieved when the mountainous topography softened onto a flat, narrow shelf where the first signs of civilization since I'd left Cleator began to appear in the form of oxidized fuel drums and vehicle carcasses, piles of trash, old appliances plus a scattering of crumbling, abandoned dwellings.

To my left, set back from the road behind a chain link fence, stood a ramshackle white house along with several pickups and off-road vehicles. A crudely-carved sign above the garage door caught my attention, so I slowed to read it. *If you are found here at night, you will be found here in the morning.* Whoa! Ominous, yet tinged with black humor. A second one read: *If you think there is life after death, trespass and find out.* Okay. No doubt this person meant business. All at once the back of my neck prickled. It wasn't hard to envision someone inside with a shotgun trained on me. Not a happy thought. I moved on quickly. The small patches of snow gradually turned into deep drifts piled up against the boulders. I estimated the elevation probably exceeded 6000 feet by now. The road eased around several gentle turns and then flowed smoothly into a peaceful valley dotted with alligator juniper, scrub oaks and a smattering of spruce and ponderosa pines. There were also groves of leafless deciduous trees. Was this the location of the old apple orchard Marshall had mentioned? There was obviously an abundant water table because the trees were much larger and the vegetation greener and far more abundant compared to the sparse desert landscape below.

As if to confirm Burton Carr's theory that the mountain created its own climate, I stared in awe as billowy clouds cascaded down the rocky cliffs, finally blotting out the sunlight. Well, well. He'd been right about that too and had merely been thinking of my welfare. I cringed inwardly remembering my flippant behavior. I wasn't doing a very good job of living up to my promise to Tally just weeks ago that I would make a sincere effort to be more tactful with people.

The road climbed gently again for a while before I

finally arrived at the junction where I stopped, powered the windows down and just sat relishing the moist, chilly mountain air, totally captivated by the surreal sight of misty tendrils of fog enveloping the secluded valley. Here and there I could see the shadowy tops of pine trees. Who would believe it? Fog twice within a few days and reminiscent of the long, dark, frigid winters I'd left behind in Pennsylvania. On the other hand, the winter season in Arizona was always a welcome event, savored by natives, newcomers and tourists alike. And that thought made me wonder what Tally and my family were up to—probably all clustered around the rim of the Grand Canyon by now marveling at the mother of all chasms. I tapped his number on my phone to no avail, but did capture a few photos to send along later as soon as I had cell service again. Might as well share images of this hidden jewel.

I studied the map, double-checking Burton Carr's clearly marked directions again. The left fork led to the closed Forest Service road, which angled up to the very top of the peak and then down the northeast side culminating near Mayer. The right fork would take me to Raven Creek. I'd no sooner completed that thought when a strange sound caught my attention. Wheep. Wheep. Wheep! I look up in time to see two giant, black birds appear out of the mist. Their expansive wings whipping the air, they landed on a lopsided wooden fence nearby where they proceeded to hop up and down clucking like chickens before settling down to observe me with baleful, ebony eyes. Was this the Raven Creek welcoming committee? The place was most certainly aptly named. And then, as quickly as they'd arrived, they flew away. Odd.

Poised to turn left, I paused when I heard the

unmistakable whine of a vehicle approaching and started violently when a quad rider suddenly roared up beside me. I couldn't be certain, but I was pretty sure it was the same guy I'd seen earlier on the main road. He no longer wore sunglasses, but still had the red and white-checked bandana pulled over the lower half of his face. He looked at me intently for several seconds, his dark eyes unreadable before he revved the engine and turned left. He sped up the hill, turning to cast one last furtive glance at me before disappearing into the mist. Weird.

Slightly uneasy, I sat there mired in indecision. No one had ever accused me of being faint-hearted, and in fact, Tally laughingly teased that when on assignment, I was unstoppable, fearless and sometimes wrong-headed. But given that he, Marshall and now Burton Carr had warned me about the possibility of questionable people skulking about, was it really a good idea to venture alone through the darkening landscape to the abandoned road? As much as I wanted to, common sense prevailed. It could wait until tomorrow. In fact, that might actually be better. Burton Carr could accompany me to the precise location and I would have plenty of time to conduct my interview with him. I swung the Jeep to the right instead. Might as well check out Raven Creek.

I drove slowly along an incredibly furrowed, muddy road thinking that this was quite an initiation for my pristine Jeep, now all mud-splattered. As I bumped and splashed along, I was able to make out only indistinct shapes of various structures and vehicles materializing every so often through the fog bank. One place I passed must have had ten or twelve classic cars parked in the yard. Raven Creek looked nothing like I had envisioned. There seemed to be an unnatural silence, no twitter of birds, no sounds of civilization; definitely eerie. There was also no shortage of **KEEP OUT, PRIVATE ROAD, STAY OUT** and **NO TRESPASSING** signs posted, reinforcing the message that strangers were not welcome. And there were additional warnings analogous to the first set of cautionary signs I'd seen driving in. **IF I DON'T KNOW YOU, DON'T COME HERE. IF YOU MESS WITH ME YOU MESS WITH THE WHOLE TOWN. ARMED AND DANGEROUS! BEWARE OF NASTY-FACED DOG**. I couldn't help smiling at the last one.

I passed a long row of mailboxes, marveling at the fact that mail would even be delivered in this out-of-the-way hamlet, and traveled another fifty yards or so before an odd sensation crept over me. I reduced speed and finally stopped. Something hovered at the edge of my memory. There was something familiar about the place, yet I was positive I'd never been there before. What was I trying to remember? Perplexed, I sat there in the fog, taxing my brain before it suddenly hit me. Holy cow! I shoved the Jeep into reverse. When I pulled even with the mailboxes, I picked up my phone and tabbed to the photo of Jenessa and Nathan posing with the black cat. Bingo! This was the identical spot.

CHAPTER
19

Now that I knew for certain they had been here prior to their deaths, what did this knowledge really tell me? For sure, I needed to know when, why and who had taken the photo. Considering that the road I'd just conquered was made-to-order for adventurous off-road enthusiasts like Nathan probably answered the why. Marcelene should be able to tell me approximately when. But who had taken the photo and how a cat figured into the scenario of two people out exploring mountainous back roads baffled me. I stepped out and tromped through the mud, gingerly sidestepping pools of water as I approached the mailboxes. I counted sixteen of them—some so rusted, faded, flaking and caked with dirt there were few numbers or names visible. But considering that people supposedly came here to get lost, I had a feeling that was just the way the residents wanted it.

I moved along the row, able to make out a few of the names, some looking as if they'd been written with a Magic Marker. All at once, one of those unexplainable sensations like I was being watched shimmied down my spine. Spooksville, Marshall had called it, and I decided my fanciful state was due to the ghostly fog surrounding me.

Just to be cautious however, I glanced behind me. Nothing. I looked carefully in each direction and it was only when I turned back that I drew in a surprised breath. Three Pygmy goats stood behind the chain link fence, staring at me curiously with their strange slotted eyes. And then, in silent procession, two horses, a donkey, a cow, two sheep and a potbellied pig appeared out of the mist. All ambled to the fence and viewed me with interest. Finally one of the goats bleated a soft greeting. "Well, hello, gang," I said, petting each of them through the barrier. I had quite a fan club going, but pulled back as a stunning, rainbow-colored rooster strutted by, eyeing me with arrogant suspicion as if to assert his proprietary authority.

At that moment, a light breeze touched my cheeks and the fleecy clouds, still pouring down the mountainside like waterfalls of frothing milk, began to disperse. Within minutes I could make out the shadowy framework of a barn and two sheds. No, wait. The sloped roof of one identified it as a chicken coop. Then a faded blue mobile home slowly materialized. I looked along the fence line, noting that this property bore no warning signs. I checked out the name on the mailbox nearest to the driveway. **D D Dorcett**. Unreal. It couldn't be anyone other than the same feisty woman I'd seen earlier today near Cleator.

As the cloud layer thinned, sounds that had been muted became more distinct. I could hear chickens clucking, ducks quacking and as I walked along the fence line towards the driveway, the friendly little herd followed along beside me. A sudden cacophony of loud barking stopped me in my tracks. On the opposite side of the wide driveway I counted six dogs of different breeds, all yapping away simultaneously, tails wagging, a pleasant contrast to the vicious-looking ones that had rushed me in Bumble Bee. What a menagerie. It appeared that Darcy was not only a caregiver of people, but animals as well. My initial impression of her mellowed considerably. The barking apparently alerted every other dog in the area, and the sound of their answering yelps echoed from the towering walls of granite in much the same manner as an amphitheater. No doubt everyone in town now knew there was a stranger in their midst. I stopped to allow each dog to sniff my hand and when their curiosity was satisfied they lost interest and wandered off inside the enclosure.

I could now see the chicken coop and feathered residents clearly as fragments of blue sky appeared above the wreaths of swiftly thinning cloud cover. It wasn't until I had reached the dilapidated porch that I noticed the faded sign. *Safe Haven Animal Sanctuary*. Interesting. And out here in the middle of nowhere? I searched my memory, unable to recall if I'd seen the name of this particular rescue group among the piles of brochures in Jenessa's room, or if there had been a donation receipt. I made a note in my phone to check it out.

As I drew closer to the mobile home, a little shock of amazement ran through me. Cats! A whole slew of them. There must have been at least two dozen felines—some hiding beneath the sagging porch, some crouching in the grass, several others lounging and bathing on an old blanket-covered couch or lying in the tall grass, all sizes, all colors. Three sleek black ones studied me with bright green eyes and the two gorgeous orange and white tabbies reminded me of Marmalade.

I about jumped out of my skin when a scratchy, high-pitched voice behind me bellowed, "Who are you? Who are you?" Whirling around, I stared down at a petite woman almost as round as she was tall. Really. Everything about her was round, from her body, to her face to her eyes—the palest, blankest blue eyes I'd ever seen. For a second, I almost mistook her for Darcy. Probably in her fifties or sixties, this woman had similar facial features— same prominent globular nose, mottled skin—but instead of having thick, dark eyebrows, hers were almost nonexistent. Dressed in a red warm-up suit and boots, she wore a black stocking cap pulled down over lank, ear-length white hair. For some reason, she had a wad of tissue or toilet paper stuffed in one nostril. "Who are you? Who are you?" she demanded again in a singsong tone before running her tongue along protruding, yellowed teeth. I couldn't help but notice the bulging cloth laundry bag tied around her waist and was slightly taken aback to see her clutching a ragged stuffed bunny.

"Ahhh, Kendall O'Dell. Is Darcy around?"

Her change of demeanor was lightning swift. Beaming with pleasure, she stuffed the bunny in the bag and grabbed one of my hands in hers, pumping it up and down several times. "You know Darcy! You know Darcy! Did she tell you about me? I'm Daisy. My momma named me after a flower—a yellow flower. Daisy. Daisy is my name. Daisies are very pretty, aren't they?"

Why was she repeating everything? "Well, yes they are. Nice to meet you, Daisy."

"Me and her are twins, you know," she confided, her tone friendly and confidential. "Me and Darcy. She came out first. She's older than me. Twelve minutes older. Twelve minutes."

"I see."

"You're really tall. A tall, tall lady." Wide-eyed, she reached up and stroked my hair, crooning "Such pretty red curls. So, so pretty." Then she dug in one pocket and pulled out a camera. "You look like a movie star. Can I take your picture?"

I smiled down at her. "Um...well, sure, I guess so."

She backed up a little and snapped several before cocking her head to one side. "What about animals? Do you love animals?"

Slightly taken aback at the rapid-fire change of subject matter, I replied, "I do."

"Me too! Me too! I *love* animals. These are all my animal friends," she exclaimed, opening her arms wide, a magnanimous smile softening her weathered features momentarily before her expression altered to a forlorn pout. "Bad people throw them away you know. But, I take care of them. Even the sick ones. Even the hurt ones. That's what I do, yes, that's what I do." Then she fell silent and just stared at me, slack-jawed for extended seconds with slightly crossed eyes.

I filled the sudden void with, "That's very commendable."

"What?"

"Commendable."

"What is commendable?" she asked, her gaze vacant.

"It means...you're doing a wonderful thing,"

"Oh, yes, a wonderful thing. Wonderful. Yes. Yes." She reached down and picked up a grey and white cat that had only one eye. "Would you take this sweet kitty home? There's whole bunches of them here. This is Penelope. She is a snuggle bunny." She hugged and tenderly kissed the cat on the head. "Don't you just love, love, love a snuggle bunny?"

It was now clear to me that the woman was mentally impaired. "I do. But…I already have a cat…" I paused and we both looked around as Darcy's battered red and white pickup rattled along the driveway and stopped. Frowning at me from behind the wheel, she slid out of the truck and five chickens flew out with her, plopping onto the ground. "Aren't you the redhead I just saw down at the bottom of the hill awhile ago?"

"Yes."

"Thought so." She shooed three more squawking hens from the cab of the truck and slammed the door. "Daisy, get these girls back in the coop."

"Why did you bring 'em back?" she asked, furrowing her light brows at Darcy. "Why didn't Emma take 'em to Globe with her?"

She let out an audible groan. "It's a long story. Just put 'em away, okay?"

"But, I'm busy. I'm busy. See? I'm showing this lady Penelope. See? I don't want to do it right now. Don't want to." She sounded obstinate, petulant, childlike.

"Don't argue with me." Darcy peered at her, pointing to her nose. "Your nose bleeding again?"

"A little bit."

"Humph. We'll deal with it later. Hop to it and get these hens rounded up."

Apparently her supposedly compassionate nature didn't extend to her sister. Lips quivering, a defiant light glimmering in her eyes, Daisy hesitated before she set the cat down and stomped by me, muttering in an accusatory tone, "She sucked up all the air, you know. She sucked up all the air." Baffled by her comment, I looked after her while Darcy confronted me with a blunt, "Who are you and why are you here?"

I dragged my gaze away from Daisy and handed her my card. "I'm an investigative reporter with the *Castle Valley Sun.*"

"You're kinda off the beaten track, aren't ya? What d' ya want?"

"To ask a few questions."

"About what?"

I pulled out my phone and located the photo. "Do you recognize either of these two people?"

She looked at the image. "Mmmm. Yeah. I think the girl's name is Jennifer, Janice or something. I can't remember his name."

"Jenessa. And that's her boyfriend, Nathan."

"Uh-huh. And?"

"Did you take this photo?"

"Nope. Daisy must have. That's her thing. She loves to take pictures of everyone and everything," she remarked, sounding mildly derisive. "Drives me nuts. Thank God for digital cameras or I'd have to rent a second storage unit to hold another ten million prints plus all the other crap she drags home. In case you didn't notice she's got a few problems. She's got ADD, she's OCD and a bit of a kleptomaniac, so don't set anything down if you want to see it again." Her

239

gaze strayed to Daisy struggling to round up the chickens and then back to me. "So, what is it that you want?"

"Do you know why Jenessa and Nathan were here in Raven Creek the day this photo was taken?"

"I'm not a mind reader. All I know is I got home from taking care of one of my patients and they were standing here listening to Daisy's nonsensical chatter." Her twisted smile held just a trace of sardonic humor. "Kind of like you."

I ignored her mild ridicule. "Did they stop here for directions? Do you know if they were lost or just out exploring the area?"

"I don't keep a diary."

Oh my. Forthcoming she was not. While pondering my next question something dawned on me. I showed her the photo again. "Did she adopt this cat from you?"

"Maybe."

"And did it have only three legs?"

"I can't tell from that picture, but yeah. We had one here and Daisy pushed 'em pretty hard to take it."

Talking more to myself than her, I mused, "How in the world did Jenessa find you? I mean, how does *anyone* find you up here?"

Her eyes reflected ironic affirmation. "You noticed that we're not exactly a destination. I'll tell you what, it was a hell of a lot easier to get here before the damned Forest Service screwed us over by closing the only good road we had."

That captured my attention. "When was that?"

"I dunno. About four years ago, I think."

"And why exactly was it closed?"

"Because according to the powers that be, it wasn't worth maintaining just for us. They claimed it wasn't needed anymore after the old lookout tower got shut down. And get this," she went on, her ruddy face reddening, "they didn't just close the damn thing, they dug out the culverts and bulldozed it to make *sure* we couldn't use it anymore. And now every time it rains water comes pouring down the hill and washes out part of the canyon road. And adding insult to injury," she went on, brandishing a hand eastward, "Old Buster McCracken always allowed us to use the shortcut across his ranch to the main road. He kept it up real nice, but after he died, the damn gravel company gated it off, supposedly for safety reasons." At that point in her soliloquy, she had to pause for a breath before finishing with a vociferous, "Bunch of heartless bastards!"

I'd obviously hit on a sore point and decided it might be best to gently direct her back to the matter at hand. "It does seem unfair." A fluffy cream-colored cat with no tail rubbed against my leg, sparking the memory of Marcelene's poignant observation regarding her daughter's predisposition to rescue animals and people with disabilities. Had she already known about this place or just stumbled upon it accidentally? I bent down to pet the cat's soft fur. "So, do you advertise your animal sanctuary? I mean, how did Fiona end up here?"

Her shaggy brows edged higher. "Who?"

"The black cat."

"Oh. Well, in case you didn't know, there's a shitload of heartless assholes out there who think nothing of dumping unwanted or injured animals in the desert. The locals find 'em wandering half dead down around Cleator, Cordes and Bumble Bee. They know they can bring 'em to us and we'll care for them."

241

"Sounds like a time-consuming and costly proposition."

"It is. A couple of times a year we make room for more by taking the adoptable ones to a couple of the no-kill shelters in Prescott and Phoenix." She paused, frowning. "So, where are we goin' with this?"

I pointed to the photo once again. "You do know what happened to them, right?" I studied her reaction closely.

She palmed her hands upward with an impatient, "No. What?"

When I explained, her splotchy, sun-wrinkled face crinkled with genuine shock. "I'd heard that some young folks died out there in the snowstorm last week, but didn't have a clue it was them." She shook her head glumly. "That's awful sad. She's…she seemed like a real nice girl. Gave us a generous contribution to boot. And they're tax deductible, you know," she tacked on with a look of hopeful expectation.

Taking the hint, I dug out my wallet, hoping my gesture would buy me some good will and access to more information. "You're doing a wonderful thing here and I'd be happy to make a donation," I said, pressing two twenty dollar bills into her hand accompanied by what I hoped was a charismatic smile.

Her expression mellowed somewhat as she pocketed the cash. "Much obliged. I'll make sure you get a receipt."

"That would be great. Do you happen to remember the approximate date Jenessa adopted the cat?"

She stared over my shoulder, a faraway look glazing her heavy-lidded blue eyes. "Can't say as I do. Last month sometime, I think. I'll have to check the records."

I knew it had to be at least three weeks prior because

of the receipt I'd seen in Jenessa's room for cat food and accessories. "Would Daisy remember?"

Her expression sardonic, she said, "Her? Trust me, the porch light is on, but there's nobody home. Can't you tell?" Her voice had a brusque, critical edge to it.

There didn't appear to be a diplomatic way to respond to her question. "Well, I had my suspicions…"

"Anything else you want? I got animals to feed and broken crates to repair before dark."

I wanted to say that with the amount of money she'd just astutely extracted from the sand and gravel company, she could buy a hundred new ones. But I let it slide. "Do you have a suggestion as to which other residents I should talk to?"

"About what?"

"To find out if anyone saw or heard anything suspicious…"

"Well, good luck with that," she interjected with a meaningful glance.

"Yes, I noticed all the signs. Not exactly welcoming. Some came across as deliberately intimidating."

Her gaze turned shrewd. "I saw you talking to Burton Carr and I'm guessing he filled your head with bloodcurdling stories about some of the people who live here, right?"

"He mentioned that there might be former inmates from various penal and mental institutions living here."

She let out a snort of laughter. "Well, that's a real tactful way of putting it." She scratched her armpit. "I'll admit we've had our share of scoundrels here from time to time and a few folks who probably should be locked up for their own good, but it's damned annoying when law enforcement tries to pin every little thing on us. If someone gets so much as a hangnail within fifty miles of here, they're automatically banging on our doors first."

Oh, good opening for one of my questions. "Are you aware of the other two deaths that occurred in this area within the past year or so?"

She scrunched her substantial, badly blotched nose at me. "Yeah. One of 'em was that pesky filmmaker who was always hanging around."

"Hanging around where?"

"Here. There. Everywhere. The guy was all over the place. Told anyone who'd listen that he was making a documentary on how the locals feel about the environmental impact of the state's plan to build a freeway through Bumble Bee and having a sand and gravel company in their backyards. I think he got an earful."

"Yes, I saw the protest signs. Why do you say he was pesky?"

"Because he was! He was pushy and annoying. Constantly bugging people with questions. Personally, I think he fancied himself to be some kind of big shot Hollywood type, all huff and blow, running around here acting like he was real important. I guess we were supposed to be impressed because he had a friggin' video camera. Big whoop. Some folks around here, well, they don't want to be bothered, let alone wind up on the Internet or some reality TV show."

"Do you know anything about the death of the second man?"

"The road surveyor? Not much. I saw him doing his thing a couple of times down around Cordes and Mayer.

Nice-looking young fellow. Always waved at me real friendly-like. Then I heard through the grapevine he'd had one too many drinks at the Crown King Saloon and offed himself driving over a cliff."

"The sheriff told me it was ruled as accidental death. Have you got any thoughts about that?" I watched her expression change from befuddled to insightful.

"Oh, you mean because he worked for the transportation department? You think one of the pissed-off residents maybe helped him over the side of the road?" An eye roll accompanied her slight shrug. "I wouldn't be surprised, but I also don't think we'll ever know."

At the sound of an approaching car engine, we both looked around. I stared in amazement at the unexpected and rather unnerving sight of the vehicle emerging from the mist—a hearse—a big, long, black hearse.

CHAPTER
20

Undaunted, Darcy raised a hand in greeting and shouted, "Hey, Goose, how ya doing today?"

The driver, a fiftyish-looking man with a short salt and pepper beard, yelled back, "Fair to middling!" before proceeding to slide mail into the boxes.

"Well, that's different," I remarked in wonderment. "Unique choice of vehicles for mail delivery."

"Ain't that a hoot?" Darcy cackled, slapping her thigh. "He gets the biggest kick out of parking that thing in front of the bar down there in Cleator and watching people's expressions as they drive by." Humor sparkled in her cornflower-blue eyes. "Sort of like the look on your face just now."

I grinned. "Well, it's not everyday you see a guy delivering mail in a hearse. Is Goose his real name?"

Now it was her turn to grin. "Naw. It's Percy Cross. I don't remember who pinned that nickname on him."

"Is he an official postal carrier?"

"In a roundabout way. Contract worker. Regular guys won't come up that bad road, so we only get mail once or twice a week unless we want to run over to Black Canyon City."

"I'm surprised he can negotiate the curves in something that substantial."

"He's got a quad if the weather's too bad, but he's got that thing all tricked out and road worthy." Noting my skeptical expression she added, "He restores vintage cars. You passed his place on the way here. Didn't you notice 'em all lined up in his yard?"

"Sort of. It was hard to see anything very clearly in the fog."

"I bought my truck from him," she announced proudly, thumbing behind her. "When she ain't all mud-caked, she's pretty spiffy-looking."

"Yeah, same for me," I murmured, observing my now-filthy Jeep. It was encouraging to see her crusty demeanor softening towards me, and I got the distinct impression that even though she appeared reticent to talk, she was actually in her element sharing the local gossip with me. How lucky was I to have stumbled upon a treasure trove like Darcy Dorcett? Tapping the horn lightly, Goose waved farewell to Darcy and nodded in my direction before driving away. When I turned back to her, Darcy was staring at her cell phone. I drew back, surprised. "Oh. You have cell service here?" I pulled my phone out again to check. Nope. No signal.

"Not really. I was just checking the time." She drew in a huge breath. "Here's the deal. To get a signal, you gotta stand in just the right spot with the phone pointed directly southeast and even then most of the calls fail within a minute or so. But, if you're determined...see that big tree over there?" she asked, pointing across the road.

"Yes."

"If you can shimmy up it and park your butt on the first limb and then hold the phone out at arm's length with your tongue set in just the right place, you might get a decent signal for a few minutes." Her lips curled up at one corner as she enjoyed her own joke. "Up here we rely on good old-fashioned land lines, and even they sometimes fail us if we get a hellacious storm like the last one. The phones can be out for days at a time."

"That must be frustrating. With my job, I'd be lost without my phone."

"We're used to it."

Aware that we were fast running out of daylight, I asked, "When those two guys died, did the authorities question any of the local residents?"

A nod and snort of distain. "You guessed 'er, Chester."

"Anyone in particular?"

Her expression grew furtive. "Ah....that I don't remember." Really? Was her memory actually faulty or was she sticking to the Raven Creek code to not rat out her neighbors? But then, she quickly added the caveat, "I won't lie to you. There are some damaged souls living here. We got a few squirrelly dudes who did some rotten things, but they've paid their debt to society and just want to be left alone. There's also a couple of ex-military guys with pretty severe symptoms of Post Traumatic Stress Disorder and a few like Daisy, a little light in the brain cell department, mostly harmless, but like I said, folks mainly keep to themselves, mind their own business, keep their mouths shut and leave people to live their lives as they see fit. That seems to suit everybody just fine."

I stared at her. "Mostly harmless? So, you never feel concerned for your safety?"

A perfunctory head shake. "We get a bad apple every now and then, but most know better than to shit in their own nest, if you get my drift."

"I see. The honor among thieves principle."

"Pretty much. And if someone gets out of line... word gets back to the mayor, and things...well, they get handled. Of course, we can't do anything about the crazies who camp out in the forest."

I peered across the narrow valley dotted with a conglomeration of cottages, shacks and mobile homes tucked in among the boulders and trees. There couldn't be more than twenty or thirty residents. I turned back to her. "Raven Creek has a mayor?"

"Well, not officially, but everybody kind of refers to him as that since he owns most of the land. All except this property and one other piece," she clarified, gesturing towards Daisy who was calling, "Here chicky, chicky, chickies," as she shooed the flapping hens into the coop. The sharp-eyed rooster, perched atop a rusted-out washer, closely monitored her activities. "Our pappy left us these two acres, so we don't have to pay rent like everybody else."

"Oh, really? I thought this was all part of the Prescott National Forest."

"Nope. Besides the McCracken Ranch, our little paradise is one of those few remaining parcels of private land left around here, but don't you know they'd love to get their grubby hands on it if they could."

"So, who owns the third piece of property?"

"Shitfire, you ask a lot of questions."

Hoping to thaw her crusty demeanor and keep the information flowing, I smiled appreciatively. "Just doing my job, and you've been very helpful."

Apparently unimpressed by my attempt at flattery, she flicked a glance towards the western sky. "I got five more minutes and that's it."

"I really appreciate it." I paused expectantly, waiting for her answer. "The other landowner?"

"Oh, yeah. I can't remember his last name. It's something long and weird-sounding. Everybody here just calls him Stilts. Guy's a real loner. Hardly ever see him unless he goes out for supplies or to sell his honey."

"He's a beekeeper?"

"Uh-huh. But, he's not the only one who raises the critters now. A couple of other people got hives goin', including our mayor. He even recommends honey to his patients. Yep, if you got any questions about bees, Stilts is our resident go-to guy." She pointed across the valley towards the base of the rocky cliff where a sizeable flock of ravens sailed lazily on thermals. "See that goofy-looking house over there?"

I narrowed my gaze, focusing past her finger. "You mean that big, stone structure without a roof and all the chimneys?"

"Yeah. He's been working on that place for the last fifteen years. Never seems to get finished for some reason or another."

"Why do you call him Stilts?"

An extended shrug. " I dunno. I'm guessin' because

he's a real beanpole."

Goose. Stilts. The people living here seemed partial to nicknames. Was that to disguise their real names? "I see. The major landowner sounds like someone I might want to speak with. What's his name?"

"Gabriel Gartiner. Dr. Gartiner."

"Really? What kind of medical doctor is he?"

"Naturopath. He used to teach chemistry before he started his practice about five years ago."

I looked around. "How do patients find him?"

"He runs a real nice clinic in Prescott."

"Does he have a nickname too?" I ventured, unable to suppress an impish smile.

She grinned back. "Nah. We just call him plain old Doc."

I chuckled. "Of course."

I definitely hit the jackpot when I ran into Darcy. She appeared to know everything about everyone. As much as I would have loved to keep her talking, I wanted to locate Harvel Brickhouse before I ran out of daylight, which, as the sun slipped behind the peak, plunging the valley into shadow, I realized would happen soon. "I'd really like to ask you a few more questions, but I need to leave if I want to get out of here before dark. Perhaps when I come back tomorrow…"

Her eyes narrowed with interest. "You're coming back?"

"I'm planning to meet up with Burton Carr." Of course, he didn't know that yet. I would contact him on the drive back to Castle Valley.

A speculative gleam entered her shrewd gaze. "What for?"

"He offered to show me the location where the bodies were found."

She nodded approval. "Well, Burton can be a real pill sometimes, but you couldn't ask for a better guide. He knows every square inch of these mountains."

"Sounds like you're pretty well-acquainted with him."

"Oh yeah. Known him a long time. Knew his whole family actually. His mom, Billie, came here from Casa Grande after her first husband died in the service. Burton was just a toddler and never knew his real daddy. She met Calvin, husband number two, when she lived in Mayer and then they all moved to Crown King after they both went to work for the Forest Service."

"So, Burton followed in their footsteps?"

"Sort of. They manned the old fire tower I mentioned earlier for a long time," she informed me, gesturing westward towards the craggy mountaintop. "That is until Calvin keeled over from a heart attack. After that, Billie stayed on for another four years by herself, but quit the tower when she remarried again."

"This must have been a fascinating place for a kid to grow up," I remarked wistfully, eyeing the fleecy clouds hovering around the peak.

"Maybe. But I think he was a pretty lonely little boy."

"Really? I thought you said he had a brother." One who bullied him, I recalled.

"Step-brother, actually. Darren Pomeroy came into the picture with husband number three, who just happened to be Doc Gartiner's half brother, Chris. He owned a nice motel up there in Crown King. That's how they met. Anyway, Burton was maybe eight or nine at the time and Darren a couple of years older. I never did care for the Pomeroy boy," she remarked, wrinkling her nose in distaste. "He bedeviled the hell out of poor Burton."

"Why?"

"I dunno. Burton was a quiet, sensitive little kid and Darren was aggressive and argumentative. They never got along from day one, but then Burton acted kind of strange sometimes."

"How so?" I was itching to get back to my original topic, but before I could steer her in that direction Darcy continued in a confidential tone, "Billie told me he got real sick and almost died when he was four. She said he must've had one of those near-death experiences because he kept jabbering about seeing God and angels and stuff. He had an odd fixation with death after that. Anyway, when Chris kicked the bucket five years later, Darren took off for Phoenix saying he had bigger fish to fry. Now he's a big shot lawyer down there. Poor Billie," she added with a forlorn smile, "she started calling herself the black widow because she put three husbands in the ground. She was just starting to get her life back together when she got diagnosed with ovarian cancer."

"Is that so?" Good grief. She may have been reluctant to talk initially, but she was on a roll now.

"I was her caregiver those last six months," she tacked on. "Burton was a real devoted son. He moved her down the road into the stone house so she'd be close by me. And Doc Gartiner too. He checked on her almost every day, but that cold-hearted nephew of his only came by to visit her twice that I know of that whole time. Poor Burton, well, he was a complete basket case after Billie passed away. I've never seen anybody so bummed out. And then he had to rely on his stepbrother to untangle the legal mess left behind from all three deceased husbands. Personally, I think Darren Pomeroy monkeyed with the paperwork so he'd inherit the bulk of the inheritance."

"That's too bad," I murmured, struggling to keep from peeking at the time on my phone. "How long ago did that all happen?"

She fiddled with a couple of disturbingly long white hairs on her chin while she contemplated my question. "Three years ago. Poor lady suffered something awful towards the end. Too bad we didn't have the medical pot to offer her back then. She'd have been a whole lot more comfortable that last year."

That got my attention. "I overheard you saying that you're able to cultivate a certain amount for your patients?"

"Yeah, but not for much longer."

"Why's that?"

"Because a guy opened a dispensary in Black Canyon City, which means the state will pull my permit soon."

"Because…?"

"If the patient lives within twenty-five miles of a dispensary as the crow flies, that's where the medical pot has to be purchased." A sniff of distain accompanied her derisive, "Kind of a stupid law if you ask me, and the rules keep changing. It's legal in one state, but not in the next, while other states say recreational marijuana is fine. But then, it's still illegal to possess it at all under federal law. I can't keep up. Typical government mess if you ask me."

"Darceeeeeeeee."

We both looked around as Daisy came trotting up,

out of breath. "There's one missing! One is missing!"

Darcy frowned at her. "One what missing?"

"Chicken."

"No, I got them all."

Daisy stomped her foot. "You didn't! I counted. One is gone."

Darcy leveled me a beleaguered look. "I don't pay much attention to her antics," she muttered under her breath before turning back to Daisy with a dismissive wave of her hand. "You just miscounted. Now run along. It's time to feed your sugar gliders."

Her chubby face growing pink with frustration, Daisy planted her feet firmly. "No. One is missing. Look in the truck," she insisted, her mouth set in an obstinate line. "Go look in the truck."

Darcy threw up her hands, shouting. "All right! But just to prove you're mistaken…" She marched to the pickup, yanked the door open and then sprang back in disbelief as a squawking white hen burst from the cab and flapped towards the coop. I had to stifle the surge of laughter. Perhaps Daisy was not as slow-witted as she appeared.

"What are sugar gliders?" I inquired with a curious smile.

"Oh! You don't know? Wait until you see them!" Daisy crowed, clapping her hands. "Just wait. I'll show you a picture." She grappled in her pocket and retrieved her camera. "They are so cute! Cute, cute, cutie pies!"

"Not now," Darcy interjected gruffly. "I need your help getting those crates out of the truck. We have to get 'em fixed so I can get those hens to Emma tomorrow. Chop, Chop."

Daisy's face drooped with disappointment. "Maybe when I come back tomorrow you could show them to me." I grinned at her and was rewarded with a toothsome smile before she hurried to the pickup and began pulling the broken crates out of the bed. "So you sell your chickens as well as the eggs?" I asked, returning my attention to Darcy.

She glared at me. "Don't you ever stop asking questions?"

"No."

"If you must know, Emma is our cousin from Globe," Darcy explained. "She's taking the hens to a friend of hers in Thatcher who wants to start her own flock. Emma's a part-time cook for a really nice boutique hotel there called Dream Manor Inn and she arranged to have them buy our fresh eggs. Happy now?"

Globe, Miami and Superior, all historical old mining towns I'd read about located east of Phoenix, were on my list of Arizona places I'd yet to visit. "Darcy, thank you so much for your time." I pocketed my phone. "Just one more thing. What's the fastest way to Harvel Brickhouse's cabin from here?"

"Keep heading that-a-way." She pointed past my shoulder towards the east. "It'll take you about thirty minutes. Watch out though, the road further on got washed out even worse than ours in the last storm, so you'll need four-wheel drive. But, if I was you," she advised sternly, "I'd head home now. Nightfall comes pretty quick here in the wintertime and unless you fancy driving those hairpin curves in the dark, I'd skedaddle."

"Got it." I turned to leave, but then hesitated.

She planted her hands on her ample hips. "Yes?"

"Daisy said something earlier that puzzled me?"

"Really? Just one?"

She didn't do a very good job of masking what seemed a deep-seated animosity towards her sister. It had to be a heavy responsibility to care for her sister's welfare. "What did she mean when she said you sucked up all the air?"

"Oh, good Lord," she said with an exasperated head shake. "According to our mother when we were born…"

"You were delivered twelve minutes before her," I interjected with a mischievous grin.

"Right. Daisy got herself tangled up in her own umbilical cord and was oxygen deprived, which accounts for her…slowness, which she blames on me because I came out okay and she didn't. Are we done now?"

"For today, yes."

"Well, thank God for small favors." She stepped inside and shut the door behind her, leaving me a bit nonplussed. Okay. Obviously our conversation was over. I wondered how much of Darcy's crotchety behavior was for show.

With the sunlight gone and the temperature dipping fast, how smart was it to be tromping around alone in the forest hunting for Harvel and then trying to navigate those grueling switchbacks at night? The time spent questioning Darcy had netted me far more material than I'd originally expected, so I decided my interview with him could wait until tomorrow. Plus that my stomach was growling with hunger pangs and I had to admit that I was tired. A good night's sleep was definitely on my agenda.

After calling goodbye to Daisy and petting all my animal admirers, I turned the Jeep around and headed out. Munching on a protein bar, I made it almost to the junction when I came upon a strange sight. Directly ahead, right in the middle of the narrow, rutted road, a raw-boned guy sporting dirty-looking blonde dreadlocks and wearing camouflage, struggled to peddle a bike with a makeshift, junk-filled trailer attached. It looked like he had everything he owned in it. How he was managing to move at all along the muddy track was nothing short of miraculous. The scruffy-looking brown dog trotting beside him kept looking back at me apprehensively. With no way to get around the duo, I slowed to a crawl.

Come on! The guy glanced furtively over his shoulder at me several times, but made no attempt to let me pass. Irritated, I followed him another half mile or so before my patience ran out. I leaned out the open window and shouted, "Excuse me! Would you mind moving over so I can get by?"

His response was to flip me off. What? My temper now fully ignited, I nudged the Jeep a little closer and tapped the horn. He ignored me. What was it with people blocking the roads today? Fuming, I honked again. That caused the dog to let out a couple of sharp yelps as I continued to follow him at an agonizingly slow two miles an hour. Finally, the road widened slightly. I calculated that there was just enough room for me to squeeze by on the right hand side, so I quickly pulled even with him. When I glanced over, I instinctively recoiled at the crazed light reflected in his deep-set eyes. His gaunt face contorted with rage, he shook his fist at me, screaming, "Why are you tailing me? You're here to kill me, aren't you? Are you gonna kill my dog too? I won't let you kill my dog!" I stared back at him in open-mouthed shock as he jumped off the bike and began rummaging around in the trailer, shrieking, "I've got a gun! I'll kill *you* first, I swear I will!"

Holy crap! What the hell was wrong with him? Was he psychotic? Strung out on drugs? Or both? For a fleeting second, I considered pulling my own weapon in self-defense, but wasn't really prepared to get into a gun battle with my limited firearms training. Exit time! Hopped up on adrenalin, my heart thundering madly, I hit the accelerator and rocketed down the winding road as fast as safely possible, certain that I had just encountered one of the damaged souls Darcy had described. After a harrowing, seemingly never-ending drive down the mountainside, foolishly checking the rearview mirror for any sign of a deranged man pursuing me on a bicycle, I turned onto the graded road with a huge sigh of relief, still shaken, but now able to think more clearly. My concealed carry training class had taught me that I had the right to pull my weapon if I feared for my life and I had definitely felt threatened. Perhaps he'd only been bluffing and could be placed in Darcy's 'mostly harmless' category, or perhaps not. Under the circumstances, I felt confident I'd made the right decision to get out of there rather than engage him. That kind of bizarre behavior might not concern Darcy Dorcett, but it certainly bothered me. When I returned to Raven Creek, I vowed to heed all prior warnings I'd been given and remain vigilant.

CHAPTER
21

Even though I'd stayed up much later than planned discussing the days' events on the phone with Tally, I rose at the crack of dawn the following morning, energized, filled with hopeful anticipation and was at my desk by six o'clock. In between my daily duties, I made sure to download the maps to my phone per Burton Carr's suggestion. I'd been heartened by the news that my parents seemed to be having a terrific time. They'd enjoyed the peaceful charm of Flagstaff and were predictably blown away by the ever-captivating beauty of the Grand Canyon. Tally reported that having the time alone with my family was probably the only way he would have ever gotten the opportunity to know them better and vice versa. I wasn't surprised to hear that my mother and Sean were still feuding, but was elated to hear that Tally and my dad had hit it off big time and that he felt he was making inroads with my mom. But when I questioned him further about Sean, he wasn't as upbeat. "Hard to tell. He's been pretty distant with everybody," he'd told me. "Keeping to himself, not talking much, but doing a fair amount of texting." That bugged the ever-loving crap out of me. So far, he'd found time to send me only a short video featuring my parents expressing their awe of the Grand Canyon and two selfies, one picturing him in the process of devouring a substantial hamburger. So, who was he texting? Friends in Pennsylvania? Was he trying to mend his relationship with Robin? Or could it possibly be someone he'd met since arriving here, like the repellant Hinkle brothers? And if that were so, what could be so important that he needed to be in constant contact with them? To obtain more of the hallucinogenic drug he enjoyed tripping out on so much? That sobering thought served to dampen my mood. I had to forcibly banish that line of thinking so I could concentrate on my assignment.

While I sipped a cup of freshly brewed coffee and munched on a sinfully delicious cinnamon roll, I compiled a list of people to interview. The rest of the crew filed in around eight just as vibrant sunbeams slanted through the blinds, blanching the walls a festive, lemony yellow shade. Jim, Harry, Al and Rick all called out greetings before heading to their respective desks. Five minutes later, Tugg strolled in and tossed his coat over the back of his chair. "Well, look who's up with the chickens, bright-eyed, bushy-tailed and raring to go!"

I grinned. "Speaking of chickens, let me tell you about one of the interesting experiences I had yesterday." He turned his computer on and sat twirling a pen in his fingers while I apprised him of my adventures en route to Raven Creek and the disturbing incident on my way home.

"You do meet the strangest people," was his

thoughtful reply, "but then you love that kind of stuff."

I smiled ruefully. "Oh yeah. Nothing like the possibility of getting into a gunfight with some mental case to get the blood running hot." I leaned back in my chair. "So, what do you think?"

In a now familiar gesture, he ran a hand over his balding head and then fluffed the remaining tufts of grey hair above one ear. "Doesn't sound like you've got much to go on."

"Except four dead people within a few square miles of Raven Creek within the past eighteen months. Now don't tell me that doesn't sound just a bit peculiar to you?"

Deep furrows gathered on his forehead. "Definitely peculiar. But, since the authorities have ruled them accidental, where's your story?"

I shrugged. "I could be just chasing shadows for all I know."

"Or not. The day is still young. If there's an angle here, I have no doubt you'll find it."

"Thanks for the vote of confidence." I heaved a dejected sigh. "Sure would've been easier if Walter hadn't poisoned himself on chili. I could really use an extra hand." I pointed at my notepad. "Look at this list of people I still have to interview, Burton Carr, Harvel Brickhouse, Nathan Taylor's father, Linda Tressick, not to mention that I've got to touch bases with Marshall to get more information on those first two guys…"

"I'll do what I can to help," he cut in. "What time are you meeting the forest ranger today?"

"Around noon near Raven Creek, which means I need to get on the road no later than ten. And speaking of

Walter, I literally have not had a minute to call him."

The phone jangled and Tugg grabbed the line. When the second line rang less than thirty seconds later, I answered it, lamenting the fact that Ginger's absence from the reception desk all week was likely to pose a real hardship for everyone. Adept at handling a multitude of problems, she shielded us from annoying sales calls and soothed disgruntled patrons with her quick smile and effervescent personality. I dispensed with the call, headed to the lobby to assist two people, then consulted with Rick and Al before reviewing the day's assignments with Jim and finally returned to my desk to dial Walter's hospital room. After several beeps I heard a muffled voice croak, "Hello?"

"Walter?"

"The one and only," came his weak reply.

"It's Kendall. How are you feeling?"

"Like crap. Honest to God, I can't remember ever feeling this bad."

"I'm really sorry. Tugg gave me the rundown on your condition."

"Yep, Doc says I got a bad bacteria called camping lobaten jujube or something like that. I still don't know how I could have gotten such a thing. I haven't been camping since I was a Boy Scout."

Camping Lobaten? I was pretty certain that wasn't how it was pronounced but, unsure as to whether he was joking or not, I didn't correct him. "Well, take it easy and get well. We miss you."

"I feel like shit, pardon the pun, deserting you like this. If I could stay off the porcelain pot for more than five minutes you know I'd be there."

"Don't sweat it. Just get back on your feet."

"Oh, and thanks for the flowers. They're real pretty."

"Just hoping to cheer you up. Take it easy."

"No choice."

Tugg was juggling two lines when the third one rang and then almost immediately the bell on the front door jingled again. Out of the corner of my eye, I saw Al shuffle towards the lobby just as the wail of a siren filled the room. I had the phone in my hand to call Marshall, when more sirens screamed by. Cradling the receiver, I rushed to the window in time to see two fire engines and an ambulance roar past. Uh oh. For Castle Valley, that meant something big was up. Behind me, Jim shouted, "Fire at the high school! I'm on it!" I swung around and had to sprint along the hall to catch him before he got through the front entrance.

"Jim, wait a second! When will you be back?"

His face flushed with excitement, he struggled into his jacket. "Don't know!"

"I have to leave soon. We can't all be gone at the same time."

He paused, scowling at me as if I'd lost my mind. "You want me to cover it or not?"

"Yes, of course," I replied hastily, feeling foolish. "Just…get back as quickly as you can."

Without another word, he streaked out the door. For a moment, I just stood there half-listening to Joe Shipman from the hardware store haranguing Al while my frustration level mounted. Now what? Should I continue on with my plans or cancel them? Could I reach Burton Carr in time to reschedule our appointment? Should I rethink the whole idea of pursuing the story at all this week?

"Kendall!" Al's agitated voice intruded on my thoughts, "you want to handle this matter? I'm done."

Cognizant of the irate expression plastered on his broad-cheeked face as he stomped from the room, I steeled myself and confronted Joe with a conciliatory tone and cordial smile. "What seems to be the problem?"

Normally a pretty easy-going guy, the owner of Joe's Hardware proceeded to bend my ear about us running the wrong ad copy for the second time in two weeks. He was unmoved by my attempts to mollify him. "Well, sorry isn't going to cut it," he griped, waving the paper in my face. "Your mistakes are costing me a lot of money! Don't you have people to proofread this stuff?"

"Of course we do."

Red-faced, he shouted, "Well, then someone here has his head up his ass!"

I bit back a cutting retort and cautioned myself to be patient. This part of the job was definitely not fun. As he continued piling on his list of complaints, I felt the beginnings of a tension headache. Suddenly I wanted nothing more than to be someplace else. Anyplace else. My mind wandered away as I envisioned myself escaping from the everyday, mundane details and problems of running a newspaper—a position I'd jumped at, but now wished I hadn't. Oh, to be free, out on the open road in my Jeep, top down, wind whistling through my hair…

"Miss O'Dell? Are you even listening to me?"

"What? Oh, yes. Yes, I am. I promise you this will be fixed today and we'll run it an extra three days for no additional charge in both the print and online edition. And I will personally proofread it. Will that make you happy?"

Facing his flinty glare, I hoped my ultra-charming smile would pacify him. The angry light in his eyes gradually dimmed and with a curt nod he turned and wordlessly marched out the door. That crisis averted, I returned to my desk where Tugg informed me that Jim had called to say that no one had been injured in the fire, but the gymnasium had been badly damaged, classes suspended and he'd return as soon as he had a few more shots to accompany his copy. Relieved, I dialed the sheriff's office. "Hi Julie. This is Kendall. I don't suppose Marshall and Duane are there with the fire still in progress?"

"Right. But Marshall said you'd probably be calling. The two files you want are here on my desk."

I checked the time. If I left now, I'd have barely half an hour to go through them. "Great. I'll be right over." I hung up. "Okay, Tugg, I'm out of here." I scooped up my notes, laptop and coat, then paused. "Are you sure you're going to be okay here without me?"

"I'll be fine."

"You'd better be or your dear wife is going to strangle me."

He narrowed his eyes. "Listen, I've been doing this for thirty-five years, young lady. Long before you were even born."

I grinned and saluted. "Yes, sir!"

Chuckling, he added, "Hey, listen. I hate to spring this on you at the last minute, but Mary reminded me I've got a doctor's appointment in Phoenix tomorrow. Think you can stick around here?"

Shit. I'd barely begun my investigation. "No problem," I answered cheerily. "Let's hope I find the people

I need to interview today. If not, I'll push it to Wednesday."

"Good. Now get out of here."

"You're sure?"

Eyes sparkling with good humor he pointed at the door. "Git!"

"Gone." I hurried outside into the crisp morning air, once again experiencing a sweeping sense of freedom and exhilaration. It was time I admitted it to myself. As much as I'd tried to convince myself that this was the life I wanted, I really wasn't cut out to be a newspaper executive anchored to a desk all day, even part time. Tally and my dad were right. I thrived on the excitement of chasing down an interesting story.

It took me all of five minutes to get to the sheriff's office. After chatting with Julie briefly, I settled down to go through the reports. I set the alert on my phone to remind me when I needed to leave and opened the first file on the documentary filmmaker. Reviewing the cause of death was disturbing enough, but the subsequent series of photos made me queasy. Luke "Skip" Campbell, age 36, divorced father of two, had died from anaphylactic shock after being stung multiple times by a swarm of Africanized honeybees. He'd been found early on the morning of July 10th of the previous year by Manuel Dominguez, a two-year employee of the Raven Creek Sand and Gravel Company inside one of the modular toilets, slumped on the seat, pants down, his face swollen beyond recognition. According to the medical examiner's report, he'd been dead for at least 48 hours. Oh man. What a ghastly way to die.

The report stated that he'd last been spotted at the bar in Cleator Friday evening and had told several patrons he was going to take pictures of a strange rock formation he'd stumbled upon the day before. He was not seen again until the discovery of his body. According to Dominguez, the bees flew out when he'd opened the door to enter the toilet. What had the filmmaker been doing at the sand and gravel operation in the first place? What could be worth filming? I continued reading. His car was found parked along the main road near the entrance and inside the glove box authorities found the life saving epinephrine pen. Why would he be tromping around the desert without it? On his person they'd found his driver's license, car keys, credit cards and cell phone. Investigators found nothing significant in the way of photos or videos on his phone. His Nikon camera was discovered on the floor of the toilet, but there were no photos or videos on the memory card. How peculiar. And how on earth had bees gotten inside the modular toilet? From what I recalled, the doors automatically slammed shut after use. Could they have gotten in through the vents? There were additional pages in the file, but since I was short on time, I set it aside and opened the second one.

Benjamin Thomas Halstead Jr., single, age 27, had worked as a surveyor for the Arizona Department of Transportation for two years. The medical examiner's report confirmed that he had died of blunt force trauma to the skull when his car crashed to the bottom of a rocky ravine on March 18th of this year. Witnesses stated he'd been at the Crown King Saloon for hours playing pool with other patrons prior to the accident and had exhibited signs of having had too much to drink when he left. Authorities suspect that he may have made a driving miscalculation or fallen asleep at the wheel. My phone alert sounded so I closed the file. "Thanks, Julie," I said, setting both of them on her desk while slipping into my jacket. "I'll come back and finish reading these tomorrow or Wednesday."

She flipped her dark hair behind one shoulder and dragged her gaze from the computer screen. "Not a problem. They'll be here."

Outside in the Jeep, I sent a quick text to Ginger before heading out, asking how she and Marcelene were doing. I told her how much we all missed her at work, that I was on my way to check out the location of Jenessa's death and would give them a full report later. Knowing there would be no place to eat out in the boonies, I stopped to pick up a sandwich on the way out of town and could not resist pulling into the two-minute car wash. It seemed almost criminal to drive my beautiful new Jeep around caked with mud from top to bottom. While waiting in line, I left a voice message for the sheriff. I told him about Walter and that I would now be following up on the story. I asked him if he'd contacted Nathan Taylor's mother yet and requested that he text me a phone number where I could reach Nathan's father.

The wind had picked up significantly by the time I reached the freeway, and as I traveled northward, the flotilla of charcoal-bellied clouds pushing over the mountains signaled the arrival of the impending weather change—a prelude to supposedly an even bigger storm forecast for the middle of the week. I remained hopeful that my family's sightseeing trip would not be spoiled as I'd learned that these dramatic predictions could also fizzle to almost nothing with a change of wind direction.

By the time I reached Black Canyon City, thunderheads stretched along the crest of the entire Bradshaw range, billowing like smoke from a volcano. There was little doubt I was heading into some bad weather and most likely it had been a complete waste of time and money to wash my Jeep. "Flapdoodle," I muttered, borrowing Ginger's favorite phrase. Moments later, I swerved onto the Bumble Bee exit and headed down the curving road into the still sun-drenched valley.

As I approached the wide gravel pullout at the bottom of the hill, I recognized Linda Tressick's vehicle parked among the handful of motor homes and pickups with empty trailers attached. A glance at my clock confirmed that I had about fifteen minutes to spare, so I decided to take the bird in hand and pulled in behind her white pickup truck. I stepped out into the driving wind and strode to where she stood jotting information from a pickup on a notepad. "Hello again," I said, walking up beside her. "I was driving by and wondered if you had time for a few questions now?"

She glanced up from her paperwork and acknowledged me with a tight-lipped smile. "Sure. What do you need?"

I explained briefly my assignment, my relationship to Jenessa, showed her the photo of them on my phone and asked if she'd seen or interacted with them prior to their deaths.

She cast me an appraising look. "With the Taylor kid, yes. I'd seen him hiking and tearing around the hills on his quad a couple of times in the past few months. Burton Carr told me he'd stopped him from rappelling down the side of several Indian forts too. Idiotic stuff."

"Was he acting irrationally? Like, maybe he was hopped up on something?"

She made a face. "Who knows? Pretty recently, I caught him riding off the designated trails out there," she stated, pointing towards a series of dirt tracks snaking up the mountain into the wilderness. "I informed him he was on BLM land, gave him a warning and less than two weeks ago I issued him a ticket for having an expired OHV Decal." Her brow furrowed in remembered annoyance. "He went ballistic and started ranting about not having the money to pay the fine or renew the decal."

"Does it cost that much? It's like renewing tags on your car, right?"

She waved her hand dismissively. "Exactly. Twenty-five dollars. You can buy them online and they're good for a year, but he made a huge deal about not having the use of his quad for his planned excursion."

I absorbed the information thinking that now it made sense that they'd rented quads in Crown King. "Did you see them together after that day?"

She thought for a few seconds. "As I recall, the young woman didn't enter the picture until several days later. She asked if it would be okay if she left her car here in the staging area because they were going to travel together in his camper."

"Was that the last time you saw her?"

"First and last. After that whopping storm ended and the snow started to melt, I noticed her car was still here and that's when I realized something might be wrong."

"Do you remember what day that was?"

"Last Wednesday. I'd just finished pulling a truck out of a snowdrift and jumping another car when Burton drove up and gave me the bad news. I called the sheriff right away." We exchanged a somber glance and she tacked on, "Pretty sad situation."

"Very. And speaking of tragic situations, I just

finished reading the police report on two men who also died recently in this general vicinity." I filled her in on what I'd learned and asked if she'd had contact with either of them.

She smoothed a few tendrils of wind-ruffled hair behind one ear. "I encountered the filmmaker several times because he hung around here for weeks trying to interview people. His name was Luke something or other. He got really huffy when I declined to be on camera, but I answered all of his questions about what impact I thought a freeway would have on this whole region. He also wanted to know how I felt about the environmental impact of the gravel company."

I tilted my head at her. "And how do you feel about it?"

She chewed her bottom lip. "I don't like it very much, but it's on private land so we can't do anything about it."

I nodded. "What about Benjamin Halstead, the surveyor?" I asked, checking the time on my phone. "Did you have any discussions with him?"

Her features brightened considerably at the mention of his name. "Many. Benjamin was here working on and off for a couple of months." But then her smile faded. "I felt sorry for the poor kid."

"Why?"

"Because, his job with the Department of Transportation put him on everyone's shit list. But he really had two strikes against him."

"How so?"

"Not only do most of the people around here oppose the idea of the freeway, the environmentalists hated him too. A bunch of activists got involved, claiming that John Hinkle and the state were colluding to put the freeway through here because he'd profit from the sand and gravel company selling the product to help build it. They're out here picketing the gravel company every couple of weeks. Anyway, John Hinkle ended up in a protracted legal battle, saying he could do what he damn well pleased with his own property and finally won in court. Folks are still against the freeway, but they've softened their stance against the gravel company because it provides jobs." She grinned wryly. "That's what people call a Catch-22, right?"

"I guess so. So, the locals resented Benjamin because he was the road surveyor? That seems silly."

"In their minds, he was working for the enemy," she responded, her lips pinched together for emphasis. "Hardly any of the residents would talk to him and he seemed genuinely grateful that I would stop and chat with him once in a while."

"Did he commute from Phoenix everyday?"

"No, he was renting a room from some lady in Black Canyon City from what I recall. He said he really loved being in this area since he'd grown up in Cave Creek. I'd see him here sometimes on weekends hiking or camping."

"Anything else you can tell me about him?"

She pondered my question for several seconds. "Nothing much more except that he seemed to be a nice, upstanding young man," she remarked with a veneer of wistfulness entering her voice. "And nice-looking too. It was quite a surprise to hear about his accident. In fact, I was pretty shocked."

"Why's that?"

The cleft between her blonde brows deepened. "Because witnesses reported that he acted drunk or spaced-out before he left the Crown King Saloon and subsequently ran off the road that night."

I eyed her reaction with interest. "You seem skeptical."

"I am."

"Why?"

"Because he told me he was a Mormon. Mormons don't usually drink, do they?"

"Not devout ones, maybe Jack Mormons. Do you know who any of the witnesses are?"

"I don't, but it's probably in the report. Or you could talk to Cal Moreland. He's the bartender up there. He might remember who else was there that night."

The last part of her sentence was almost drowned out when two huge trucks hauling rock roared by in a cloud of dust. They had no sooner disappeared around the corner than another truck appeared and sped by in the opposite direction. She glared after it, lamenting, "Those damn trucks are a nuisance. It was sure a lot quieter around here before the gravel company opened."

For a couple of seconds, I watched the truck until it was out of sight and then turned back to Linda. "Where are they taking the loads, do you know?"

"To a plant in Mesa. Jack Loomis told me that one is open to the public where the Raven Creek operation isn't."

"Does he own the company?"

"No, he's the foreman. Harvel Brickhouse told me it's owned by some big wheeler-dealer in Phoenix. I overheard some of the locals at the Cleator bar saying that he makes an appearance every once in a while, but I've never met him."

I was running short on time, so I thanked her and

returned to my Jeep, mulling over everything she had told me. On the surface, it appeared unlikely that Benjamin Halstead's accident had anything at all to do with what had happened to Jenessa and Nathan, but when I added in the bizarre death of the filmmaker, Luke Campbell, the startling common denominator became apparent. Was it a coincidence that each one of them had been hiking or camping in this general area and that all four deaths had been classified as accidental? As I looked searchingly towards the rugged hills, I could not shake the instinctive feeling that there was something else at play. Now, I was anxious to find out what other pertinent information might be contained in the rest of the report. I also made a note to contact the bartender at the Crown King Saloon.

Tooling along through Bumble Bee, it appeared just as deserted as it had yesterday except for two young men standing near a quad parked in front of the boarded up store. One of them, talking on his cell phone, looked up and stared at me as I drove by. I looked back and he was still watching me. Puzzled, I turned back and continued along the dusty road towards Cleator.

Powerful wind gusts intermittently buffeted the Jeep and sent tumbleweeds skimming across the road. Good thing I was concentrating because all at once two guys racing dune buggies side by side tore around the blind corner headed right at me. Reaction time? Zero. Wrenching the wheel sharply to the right, I careened off the road, skidded through a section of broken range fence and bounced out into the desert, barely avoiding several giant boulders. I crashed through a mesquite thicket before sliding to a stop at the edge of a stock pond. Shaking all over, my heart pounding,

I sat there struggling to catch my breath. Oddly enough, as if something like this happened daily, the half dozen black cows grazing nearby didn't even move and stood observing me with solemn brown eyes. No question about it. That had been a close call. If I'd hit the rocks head-on I could have been toast. What a bunch of irresponsible shitheads! I darted a look out the passenger side window, shouting, "Freakin' morons!" Nothing except a curtain of dust remained in sight, but then another vehicle appeared heading in the same direction. This time though it wasn't an ATV, pickup or dune buggy, but a dark-colored Hummer with heavily tinted windows. The driver appeared to pause for a few seconds before accelerating past. Whoever it was had surely seen what happened and apparently didn't give a crap whether I'd been hurt or not.

"Thanks a pantload!" I yelled, jumping out to inspect the Jeep. My wild charge through the brush had left several ugly scratches in the paint. "Son-of-a-bitch! Are you kidding me?" I screamed aloud, mournfully running my finger along the grooves, thinking that, for outdoor enthusiasts, desert pin striping was like a badge of honor, but for me, not so much. Overcome by intense anger, I just lost it. I kicked the tires, the dirt, the rocks and let loose with a tirade loud enough to finally startle the cows. They galloped away into the brush so I forced myself to calm down. Breathing deeply, I felt the flames of a legendary O'Dell temper tantrum diminishing. What the hell was wrong with people anyway? What possessed them to drive like absolute maniacs on these back roads with total disregard for others? I reached for the door handle and groaned aloud when another thought occurred to me. Oh man! Tally was going to have a field day with this latest scrape and I'd never hear the end of it. I was fast developing a reputation for trashing cars while on assignment. The list now included a Mercedes, a classic Packard, my precious Volvo and, just mere weeks ago, a pickup I'd borrowed from Tally. Not a good track record.

Still fretting, I re-started the engine and resumed travel along the winding road, my pulse rate slowly returning to normal. When I approached the dilapidated bar in Cleator, I had to weave my way around an assortment of pickups, Jeeps, crappy old cars and several ATVs parked at odd angles. Poised to accelerate up the hill, I paused when something caught my eye. The unexpected sight sent my heart rate rocketing right back up again. Braking to a stop, I stared in utter disbelief at the BAD BOY sticker prominently displayed on the back window of a shiny, black pickup truck. It couldn't be! And yet I knew it had to belong to the Hinkle brothers. I felt like I'd swallowed ground glass. "Un-friggin' real," I murmured. Inundated with a strong sense of foreboding, my mind grappled with the question of what these two characters were doing in Cleator of all places. It seemed everywhere I went, there they were—Tally's barbeque, Jerome and now here. No sooner had that thought crossed my mind than the two, of them along with another young guy, emerged from the bar deep in conversation with Jack Loomis from the gravel company. Really? Intrigued, I slid a little lower and cautiously shielded my face behind my hand. I was pretty sure the Hinkles didn't know what kind of a vehicle I owned, but wasn't so sure about Jack Loomis. Bright, iridescent lime-green Jeeps tended to draw attention. I powered the window down, wishing I could hear what they were saying but the wind obscured their voices until I heard a clear, "Better not screw this up or he's gonna have your hide this time!" Jack gave them a taut one-fingered salute and retreated inside the bar while the Hinkle brothers glowered after him before jumping in their truck. Danny or Daryl, I couldn't tell which from this distance, revved it loudly and to my surprise, turned in the same direction I was headed. Relief flowed through me. Good. They hadn't seen me.

Curious as to what the twins were doing with Mr. Moneybags, I followed them for several miles and it wasn't until I crossed over a cattle guard near the entrance to the McCracken Ranch did it dawn on me why they would be in this area. Of course! The realization helped dispel a small measure of discomfort. Most likely they'd been going to the ranch ever since Elizabeth had married John Hinkle. And because the sand and gravel company was located on McCracken property, that probably explained how they knew Jack Loomis. Perhaps it was not unusual for them to be in Cleator after all. Still, I could not shake a lingering apprehension. Maybe if the Hinkle boys weren't so damn smarmy and hadn't established such a problematic connection with Sean, I wouldn't have given it a second thought.

CHAPTER
22

Deep in thought, I continued to follow their pickup from a distance along the dusty, curving road. When four young guys in a Jeep with the top down roared up behind me, music blaring full blast, I eased to the side of the road allowing them to pass. Good. Less chance of the Hinkles spotting me now with another vehicle between us. They disappeared around the bend and when I caught up with them, I had to practically stand on the brakes to keep from slamming into the back of their Jeep. What the...? Pulse throbbing in my throat, I sat there behind the rowdy boys, the Hinkles, an old gray van and two couples astride ATVs, all at a dead stop waiting for two dump trucks from the gravel company to cross the one lane bridge.

"Oh, cut me a break!" I muttered aloud, my belly clenched with aggravation from the constant delays. Already late for my appointment, I grabbed up the phone and dialed Burton Carr's number, only to have it go straight to voicemail. No cell service, of course. Just my luck.

As I sat there studying the weatherworn stone bridge that looked like it had been there forever, I wondered what would happen if it was ever out of commission. No doubt, it would present a vexing problem for people trying to get into or out of Crown King and Raven Creek. As the noisy trucks rumbled by, the young Hispanic man I'd glimpsed yesterday exchanged a greeting with the Hinkle boys and then flashed me a friendly smile and waved. I lifted my hand in response and then noticed that Rod, the same surly guy from yesterday's altercation with Darcy, sat hunched behind the wheel of the second truck. He did not smile or wave, just glared and drove by. Not exactly the friendliest person on earth, to say the least.

A mile later, the twins turned sharply into the gravel company entrance and vanished into the distance. I was not surprised, but wondered what business they would have there. What was their connection with Jack Loomis? Other than the fact that the company was operating on ranch property, why would he have anything to do with those two lowlifes?

My cell phone chimed and I glanced at the screen. Seeing that it was a text from Ginger, I pulled off the road and stopped to read it. DRIVING AUNT MARCELENE 2 PHOENIX 2MORROW 2 GET JENESSA'S IMPOUNDED CAR. FUNERAL ARRANGEMENTS IN PROGRESS. MY SISTER BONNIE IS COMING 2MORROW NIGHT. DON'T WORRY. STILL WORKING ON PARTY PLANS IN BETWEEN. DO YOUR THING, GIRL! YAK AT YA LATER. ☺ HUGS!

Hmmm. Well there went my opportunity to question Marcelene. Now it would have to wait until Wednesday. I texted her back. ALMOST THERE. WILL TAKE PHOTOS

FOR YOU AND MARCELENE. HUGS BACK AT YA!

I shifted into a lower gear and continued up the hill to the turnoff. Half an hour later, I arrived at the junction and spied Burton Carr's aqua-blue vehicle parked on the north side of the left hand fork. As I pulled along side he looked up from whatever he was reading and greeted me with a polite nod. I slid from the Jeep, calling out, "Hi there! Sorry I'm late."

"No problem."

The escalating wind tore at my hair, whipping it across my eyes and making me wish I'd taken the time to corral it into a ponytail. "Thanks for meeting me. So, what's the game plan?"

"Follow me to the gate. It's only a mile or so. You can leave your vehicle at the road entrance and ride with me." He patted his shirt pocket. "I have a permission slip for you to sign."

I balked. "Why can't I drive my own car?"

He shook his head while simultaneously extracting a pen and picking up a clipboard from the passenger seat. "Against the rules, I'm afraid. And too dangerous. The road is decommissioned, so if you're caught driving on it by one of our law enforcement officers, you could be ticketed and I doubt you'd want that, am I correct?"

"You are."

A thin smile. "I thought so."

Still not crazy about the idea of leaving my brand new Jeep sitting alone in the forest, I hesitated a few more seconds. "So, you think it's safe to leave it unattended?"

He didn't look overly concerned and his demeanor seemed cool. "We shouldn't be gone long. Just make sure it's locked." He handed me the form to sign.

Okay. He was either a really mild-mannered guy or still annoyed about my snippy behavior yesterday. If he were that easily offended, I'd best try and get in his good graces if I planned to earn his cooperation.

"All right." The temperature appeared to be dropping by the second and I shivered slightly as I scanned through the flapping papers, signed, and handed him the clipboard, thinking that I'd definitely be trading my light coat for the down jacket. I started towards my Jeep and then wheeled around. "By the way, you were right about the mountain producing its own weather patterns. The fog was pretty dense here yesterday. And your assessment concerning some of the people was correct as well," I acknowledged with a sheepish smile.

Apparently mollified, his sullen expression softened to one of gratitude. "Thank you. It's nice to hear an appreciative word now and then and actually get credit for knowing a thing or two once in a while."

I gathered there was a story behind his cryptic remark but doubted I'd ever find out what it was. I returned to my Jeep, still feeling doubtful about leaving it unattended, and followed behind him, jostling from side to side on the primitive road flanked by intermittent patches of dirty snow. Constantly dipping in and out of bright sunlight and deep shadow made it hard to navigate. I drove past several secluded cabins and rusted mobile homes tucked back in the groves of trees and continued climbing the rough, zigzagging road. As the pines and ground cover grew thicker, I tried to imagine the area buried in three feet of snow and wondered again what Jenessa and Nathan had been doing here. Had they taken a wrong turn in low visibility, or were they hunting for a place to camp for the night and wait out the storm? All at once, Burton Carr's brake lights lit up and he motioned for me to pull into a narrow clearing adjacent to a sizeable mound of tree limbs, dirt and brush.

He leaned out the window and yelled, "I'll unlock the gate. You can meet me there when you're ready." He pointed to his right and then drove around the pile. I craned my neck, just barely able to see the gate almost hidden from view.

I parked and, when I slid out, the frigid wind sent goose bumps racing up my forearms. Shedding the lighter coat, I pulled on my down jacket, secured a stocking cap over my hair, tied up my hiking boots, grabbed my notepad and, after locking the door, made my way around the brushy barrier in time to see Burton Carr unlocking a gate that warned: AREA CLOSED DUE TO RESOURCE PROTECTION. NO ENTRY.

"Why is all that brush piled up there?" I asked, thumbing behind me.

"To discourage people from driving their vehicles here."

It was interesting to note that except for perhaps twenty feet of wire fencing beyond the gate, plus a row of good-sized boulders that extended five or six yards on both sides, there really was nothing to stop someone from driving onto the road. I walked up beside him. "So, I hear that, much to the consternation of the good citizens of Raven Creek, the Forest Service has no plans to reopen this road."

He flicked me an inquisitive look and unloaded what sounded like pent-up frustration. "Consternation? That's putting it mildly. They're mad as hell, along with hikers, campers, rock climbers and these crazy, destructive off-road riders who call me every name in the book and then go out and carve their own trails through the forest regardless of the damage they cause."

Crazy and destructive was right, I thought, remembering the two wild dune buggy drivers. "So you're saying it wasn't a good decision to close it?"

A shrug and head roll. "The order came down from on high. I'm not in charge, I'm not a supervisor and it's not for me to say. I know everyone around here is upset, but then why should public funds be used to maintain a road solely for private landowners? And as a geologist, I have to say it has had some positive effects."

"Such as?'

"Keeping people away from some of the dangerous old mining areas, discouraging vandalism at many of the archaeological sites like the Indian forts and petroglyphs, in addition to the old fire lookout. Eventually nature will reclaim it and someday you'll never know there was ever a road here." He gazed nostalgically into the forest. Was he reliving events from his past?

"Darcy said you spent a lot of time in the tower as a young boy."

He turned questioning eyes on me. "When did she tell you that?"

I explained how I'd happened upon their place and as he listened, he pushed his glasses higher on his nose. "Sounds like she told you my whole life story," he observed with a hint of impatience as he opened the passenger door for me. As I climbed in he asked pointedly, "You're still sure you want to do this?"

"Yes."

"It's going to be a rough ride." After he shut the door, started the engine and turned up the heat, I said quietly, "This is more than just another assignment for me. It's personal. I knew Jenessa and I promised her mother that I'd check out the place where her daughter died."

His eyes rounded in surprise. "Oh. I didn't realize that." He looked away quickly, his nondescript face compressed into a troubled frown that accentuated his weak chin. He drove through the gate, stopped, got out and locked it before sliding behind the wheel once more. We drove in silence for a few minutes. He was right. Again. The road was in terrible shape—overgrown with foliage, deeply furrowed, rocky and very muddy. We jostled, bucked, pitched back and forth and in one particular spot, splashed through a water-filled channel so deep, I didn't think we'd make it, but he forged ahead. "This is where we removed the culvert which restored the natural runoff patterns," he explained, his jaw tight with concentration as he maneuvered across the gully.

So, this was most likely the source of Darcy's complaint about water cascading down the hill, washing out sections of the road below. When the terrain leveled out a bit, I was able to talk without fear of biting my tongue. "I spoke with Linda Tressick earlier today and she told me about her confrontations with Nathan Taylor, the young man that died here. She said you'd also had dealings with him?"

Keeping his eyes pinned ahead, he answered, "Yeah, I had the same issues Linda experienced. I had to cite him for tearing up the forest driving his ATV off the designated trails several months back. Some of these kids have no regard for rules," he added, a touch of exasperation coloring his tone, "or for much of anything else for that matter."

"Tell me about it. On the way here, a couple of young guys racing dune buggies ran me off the road. If I'd hit one of the boulders in my path, I might have been killed."

"Really?" He tossed me a look of displeasure. "Where did that happen?"

"A half a mile past Bumble Bee."

"Irresponsible kids," he groused. "Did you get a look at them?"

"Not really. They had dust masks and sunglasses on."

A deep sigh. "Well, that proves my point. Reckless disregard for anyone and anything but themselves."

"And on that note," I remarked, holding onto the handle as we lurched from side to side. "With the exception of those two encounters, how many confrontations did you have with Nathan?"

He didn't answer immediately. "He was preparing to rappel from the top of one of the old Indian forts the first time I saw him. Now that's just crazy stuff. Besides damaging a historical site, he could have killed himself right then and there. I warned him that he was trespassing on BLM land without a permit."

"And his response was?"

A disdainful sniff. "Let's just say he used some pretty disrespectful language and ignored me. But when I threatened to call one of the law enforcement rangers, he finally backed down." He shook his head briefly, adding, "Reckless, wild kid. Abrasive too."

While a part of me could not help but admire Nathan's adventurous spirit, it appeared more and more likely that he'd been a corrupting influence on Jenessa. "Tell me something.

In your opinion, did he act as if he might be on some kind of stimulant?"

"You mean drugs? Who knows nowadays? It seems like all the kids are high on something. Or, and I hate to say this now, but maybe he had a death wish. I also caught him trying to rappel down a vertical mine shaft not too far from here."

"When was that?"

"Couple of weeks ago."

I digested that sobering thought, calculating that the incident must have occurred near the beginning of his fatal trip. "Was Jenessa with him?"

He hesitated. "I...don't remember seeing her that day."

"Did you see them together at any other time these past two weeks?"

Swallowing hard, he stated somberly, "Not alive. Not until last Wednesday when I followed Harvel back to their camper and...well, you know."

"Tell me more about that day," I interjected. "Where were you and what time of day did he flag you down?"

"Around noon. I was just coming to the turnoff when Harvel came tearing down the hill on his snowmobile."

"I read in the sheriff's report that you were unable to get a cell signal. That's weird, because I just got a text from my friend at about the same spot a short while ago."

"I'm not surprised," he said, lifting one shoulder. "We call them dead zones. You can be in the same place one day and have it work fine and then depending on weather conditions and other factors, not the next. It's a crap shoot."

"I see. So, you drove down the hill and that's when

you met up with Linda?"

"No. That was later. I felt it was my duty to check things out for myself first. It took me awhile to get the chains on the truck and even then the road was difficult to navigate because of the ice sheet beneath the snow. It was a challenge to keep from sliding over the edge, believe me. I kept hoping that maybe Harvel was mistaken and they were still alive, but when I got here…well, it was not a pretty sight."

I could only imagine. He glanced over at me fleetingly, his downward sloping eyes giving him a perpetually melancholy expression. "I guess the only good thing you can say is that they didn't suffer at the end like a lot of people do."

The grave undertone in his voice convinced me that he was probably referring to his mother's battle with cancer. "I certainly hope that was the case."

"This is as far as we can go," he announced, slowing to a stop. "You ready to hike?"

I looked up at the swiftly darkening sky and saw that it was beginning to spit rain. "Looks like we're going to get wet."

"And muddy." He opened the door and the sudden blast of icy air chilled me. I buttoned the collar of my coat, tucked my hair beneath the stocking cap and pulled the hood over my head. No turning back now. Rain spattering on us, we trudged through the mud, uphill, downhill and sloshed through puddles. The rain eventually turned to sleet and the wind whistled eerily through the pines. We descended into a particularly dark ravine and he put up a hand. "This is it."

With thunder rumbling overhead and sleet now coming down so hard that photos were impossible, I just stood there with my shoulders hunched, absorbing the forlorn scene. It was easy to surmise how the young couple had gotten stranded in this deep gulch and again, Burton Carr had been correct. At this point in time, there was no evidence that anyone or anything had ever been here. If there were tire tracks, I couldn't discern them. Nothing remained except the sorrowful aura of death. Saddened, I thought how unfair it was that their young lives had been snuffed out so soon and in such a tragic fashion. But now that I knew more about Nathan's foolhardy exploits, it seemed plausible that he'd made a hasty and reckless decision to tackle this road in bad weather, fully aware that entry was prohibited, but willing to risk the consequences. And he had paid dearly for it. Poor Jenessa. Her attraction to his adventurous lifestyle, extraordinary good looks and capricious personality had sealed her fate.

Standing there in the freezing rain, I knew the misery I felt couldn't begin to compare with the heart-crushing anguish that had befallen Marcelene and Ginger. Tears stung my eyes, and when the vision of Jenessa's poor little cat waiting in vain for her return popped into my mind, a sob caught in my throat. Blinking fast, I looked away and stared at the thrashing treetops, still haunted by a host of unanswered questions. Some facts that appeared to be a given to law enforcement just didn't compute. Since it seemed most likely that it was Nathan experimenting with drugs, why had the pills only been found in Jenessa's pocket? Had drugs contributed to their demise? But, now that I knew about Nathan's fearless personality, I wondered why this thrill-seeking young risk-taker would passively lie around and freeze to death. Why wouldn't he take the bull by the horns and strike out on his own to find help? He was within two miles of Raven Creek. It just didn't make any sense.

I looked back, staring at the muddy pools, wondering how to describe this lonesome, totally depressing scene to Marcelene and Ginger. Maybe I wouldn't. Viewing the photos taken by law enforcement would be the only way any of us would ever know how the bodies appeared after six days of decomposition. Did I even want to see them now? Why implant that disturbing memory in my mind?

"Satisfied?"

I glanced over at Burton. He looked as miserable as I felt, his shoulders hunched against the howling wind, his coat and slacks drenched.

"Yes." Hiking dejectedly towards the truck, I asked him, "Did you go inside the camper when you came back here with Harvel?"

A momentary hesitation. "No. I couldn't. Opening the door was enough to convince me. The smell was… overpowering. It was the most terrible odor. Nauseating. I've never experienced anything like that before."

"Tell me something. The times that you came into contact with Nathan, did you notice whether he had a cell phone?"

Eyes narrowed in thought, he pushed his fogged glasses higher on the bridge of his nose. "I honestly don't remember. Why?"

"Because the authorities never found his or Jenessa's phone. Don't you think that's awfully strange?"

"Considering that kids don't go anywhere without them, it does seem peculiar."

Perhaps to fill the void as we tromped back through

the mud, Burton asked me about my job, and after I'd told him about some of the bizarre stories I'd investigated over the past few months, he darted me an inquisitive look. "So, is that what this was all about?"

"What do you mean?"

"Maybe you're reading more into this situation than is really there, hoping for another big story."

"I'm after the truth, whatever that is."

Breathing heavily from exertion, he huffed, "So…I'm gathering that you're not convinced it was an accident?"

"I don't know yet. There are a few things still bothering me," I said through chattering teeth. Chilled to the bone and pooped from the hike, pure relief surged through me at the sight of his truck. I could hardly get inside fast enough. He swiped the water off his coat, jumped in and started the engine. Within a few minutes warm air blew from the vents. "Sorry about messing up your truck," I said apologetically, looking down at my mud-caked boots.

He shifted into gear. "Don't worry about it. I gave up years ago trying to keep a vehicle clean on these roads."

"What an interesting experience it must have been growing up in these mountains and your mother having such a unique job."

His gaze turned wistful. "I don't know if it was all that interesting, unless there was a fire, but it was the happiest time of my life."

"Darcy told me she'd taken care of your mother during her illness."

His jaw muscles twitched slightly. "Yeah. I don't like to dwell on that part. I'd rather remember how great it was spending long summer days with her in the lookout when it was just the two of us."

"You must know everyone around here," I remarked, holding my cold fingertips to the vents.

"Pretty much."

"Do you know the Hinkle twins?"

A rapid sidelong glance. "Yeah. Known 'em since they were kids. Troublemakers. Both of them. Why do you ask?"

Did I detect a tinge of irritation in his voice? "I spotted them earlier at the bar in Cleator and, then on the way here to meet you, I noticed they turned off at the Raven Creek Sand and Gravel Company."

His brows dipped noticeably lower. "That place is a nuisance."

"People around here seem to either love it or hate it, depending on whether they're employed there."

"That's true. I tend to sympathize with the environmental point of view. I'm not crazy about companies or people destructive to nature." He gave me a brief smile. "Part of my job, I guess."

"What business would they have there?"

"Maybe Elizabeth asked them to check things out since those people are operating on her land."

"I don't know about that. I've been told that she doesn't have much to do with them since her husband died."

Burton returned his attention to the road. "I wished she had listened to me. I warned her not to marry John Hinkle. Big mistake. Huge mistake. I tried to tell her he was just using her to raise those obnoxious boys. He never really cared about her like...what the hell?" Staring intently through the fogged-up windshield, he braked unexpectedly.

I followed his stricken gaze to the side of the road and drew in a startled breath at the sight of a blood-splattered deer lying on the ground, weakly thrashing her legs in an attempt to get to her feet. Two skinny golden-eyed coyotes paced nervously nearby while at least a dozen ravens sat perched on the pine branches above, patiently waiting. We'd obviously interrupted a scene from nature's food chain.

Burton shoved the truck into park, jumped out and I was right behind him. The coyotes glared at us and stood their ground for a few seconds then, after casting baleful glances in our direction, slinked off into the forest. Once we got close enough, we could see the deep wound on the deer's left hind leg. This didn't look good at all. And the expression of abject terror reflected in the doomed animal's soft brown eyes, filled me with sorrow. Burton surveyed the situation glumly. "Looks like she got entangled in some barbed wire fencing," he said, pointing to the coil of jagged wire still attached to a piece of what had probably been a fence post. "You might want to go back to the truck now."

"Why?"

He drew his service revolver. "I'm not going to leave her here to suffer. You think you can stomach this?"

Horror welled up in my chest when I realized what he was about to do. "Wait a minute! Isn't there something we can do to save her?"

"No," he stated with a note of finality. "She can't walk, so she can't survive. What's it going to be?"

I hesitated, torn as to whether I wanted to witness such a traumatic, yet inevitable event, and decided that I'd come off looking like a coward if I didn't stay. "Do what you have to do."

His hand shaking slightly, he placed the barrel close to the deer's skull.

Throat tight, belly quaking with expectation, I swear the doe gave me a resigned look as if she knew what was about to transpire. Even though I'd steeled myself, I flinched violently when the shot rang out. The reverberation echoed through the rain-soaked trees, sending the flock of ravens flapping away, cawing loudly, their long wings whipping the air around us. As I watched the life seep from the deer's eyes, I had to admit that the scene had disturbed me far more than I dared let on. It was one thing to fire at paper and metal at the target range but quite another to shoot a living thing. I darted a look at Burton Carr and it was enlightening to note the look of distress etched on his face as he wordlessly turned away, holstering his weapon. Out of the corner of my eye, I noticed the two coyotes skulking in the nearby brush, salivating. They would soon be feasting on the doe's carcass. On a logical level I accepted the fact that this was nature's way, but emotionally I had no stomach to witness it. I hurried to the truck.

We rode in silence back to the gate and it was a great relief to see my Jeep still sitting there where I'd left it. When I slid out of the truck, weak sunlight peeked through the fast-moving clouds. Considering that I had a lot more to do this afternoon, I felt grateful for a break in the weather. I pulled off the stocking cap and shook my hair loose. "Thanks for driving me out there," I said, shaking his hand. "I appreciate your efforts."

"Got a little more than you bargained for, didn't you?"

"Yeah, a little."

"You do realize I had no choice, right?" His

beseeching gaze held such a look of utter torment I got the odd impression that he was seeking my approval.

"Yes, of course."

"I had to put her out of her misery. I couldn't let her suffer."

Was I mistaken or did it seem there was a trace of moisture glistening in his hazel eyes? I disagreed with Darcy. Burton Carr did not strike me as a wimp. He struck me as a caring, but perhaps slightly hyper-sensitive guy, and it wasn't hard to visualize him being bullied by someone with a stronger personality. "You did the right thing," I assured him.

"Thank you. I try. Some people just don't understand that."

He was still busy fiddling with the gate lock when I pulled away and began the arduous drive back down the slushy road. With the memory of the dismal, secluded spot where Jenessa and Nathan had drawn their last breaths still fresh in my mind, along with that of the unexpected deer execution, I felt emotionally drained and heavy-hearted. I was no closer to knowing what happened than before I came. How would Marcelene and Ginger react when I confessed that I'd come away unable to provide anything at all to allay their suspicions? When I reached the fork in the road and turned towards Raven Creek, it was still bugging me why a savvy, skilled outdoorsman like Nathan Taylor had been here in the first place in the middle of a snowstorm. And what was the attraction to this particular region of the Bradshaws anyway, when the entire mountain range was out there to explore? Why had they kept returning to Raven Creek? At this point in time, it appeared likely that no one would ever know for sure.

CHAPTER

23

As I bumped and rocked along the deserted mud track leading into Raven Creek, I passed by an incredibly junk-littered yard where two small boys stood throwing rocks into a pool of water in front of a rundown, rambling stone house with all of the windows shuttered. Could this be the same house where Burton Carr's mother had stayed before she died? There were two rusty pickups and several older model cars parked in the long, gated driveway with the inevitable **NO TRESSPASSING** sign prominently posted. The two boys were giggling and obviously having a great time when all at once, the front door flew open. A gaunt-looking young blonde woman holding a baby on her hip rushed out shouting tersely for the kids to come. I was taken aback when she glared at me, eyes bright with fearful suspicion before swiftly herding the children inside and slamming the door behind her.

I frowned and drove on. What the hell was that all about? What was she afraid of? Did she perceive me as some kind of threat? I remembered Marshall's assertion that authorities suspected that many of the residents were cooking meth or guarding other personal secrets. Was there something going on behind those covered windows that I dare not see? Raven Creek definitely had its share of strange people. And speaking of strange, directly ahead of me, I recognized Daisy Dorcett plodding through the muck in knee-high boots and wearing a yellow rain slicker. She held out her camera, snapped a photo of something, then stooped low to retrieve an item from the tall grass alongside the road, which she then stuffed into the drawstring bag tied around her waist. All the while, she wore a serene smile as if she were out strolling on a beautiful, sunny day. Pulling even with her, I powered the window down and waved a friendly greeting. "Hey, Daisy! Where are you headed this cold, rainy afternoon?"

She stared at me with an ultra-blank expression for a few seconds before her blue eyes brightened with pleasure. "Oh! You came back! You came back to visit my sugar gliders, didn't you?"

I checked the clock on the dashboard. I had about three hours of daylight left. "I'd love to see them if it doesn't take too long."

"Okay! Okay!" She wheeled around as if she were about to bolt in the opposite direction, then hesitated, her pale brows knitting together in a puzzled frown. "But, first I have to get honey. Darcy told me to get more honey today. I'm going to see the bee man. Sometimes he lets me help him with the hives. I like the smoker and he lets me wear the...the...long funny face thing."

"The veil," I interjected with a smile.

"Yes! The veil! Yes! One day he showed me the queen bee!" She paused, her expression growing concerned as she groped in one pocket. "Darcy gave me money." Finding nothing, she searched the other pocket and pulled out some bills, crowing, "There it is! Money for honey. Money for honey!"

She exuded an air of such delightful, childlike innocence I could not help grinning. "Would you like me to give you a ride to his house?"

"But, I'm all muddy," she said, observing her boots. "Your car will get very, very dirty."

"It's already dirty." I gestured for her to come. "Get in."

She hurried around to the passenger side and heaved her bulk up onto the seat, announcing happily, "I walk a lot. I walk all around everywhere. I hear everything. I see everything."

"Well, that's great. It's a beautiful place to live."

"Turn around and go up that road," she exclaimed, pointing over my shoulder. "The bee man lives beside the funny-looking house. He works and works every day, but he never gets done. Never. Never gets done."

"I wonder why?" I mused aloud, executing the turn.

She fiddled with the drawstring bag on her lap. "I think he's too sad. He's a very sad man."

Interesting. What she lacked in intellect, she made up for in keen observation. In fact, she seemed far more perceptive than Darcy gave her credit for. "Why is he so sad?"

"I don't know. He doesn't talk much. He has a silly name."

The idea of visiting the beekeeper sounded intriguing,

but also resurrected the memory of the ghastly file photos of Luke Campbell's bloated body in the modular toilet. Why not take advantage of the opportunity to pick the brain of an expert on honey bee behavior? I smiled at her. "You're right. Stilts is a silly name."

She gave me one of those vacant looks as if she didn't quite understand me. "He has a different name."

"Yes, it's very different."

And then in a lightning-quick change of subject, she thrust her camera in my face. "Want to see my pictures?"

"Sure." I stopped alongside the road and she held the camera up so I could view the screen as she scrolled swiftly from one to another. Many of them were nothing noteworthy, just endless landscape shots, the surrounding homes, her animals and then the ones she'd taken of me just yesterday. "Very nice," I murmured and then a thought struck me so I dug out my phone. "Want to see one of my pictures?"

"Oh, yes," she said, her cheeks flushing a rosy pink. "Please! Please!"

I swiped the screen until I found the photo of Jenessa and Nathan. "Do you remember meeting these two people?"

She stared hard at the photo then looked up at me. "The pretty girl! She took Blacky home with her!" She touched the photo with her forefinger. "Poor kitty only had three legs. Three little legs."

"Darcy told me that you took this photo, right?"

A wide-toothed grin accompanied her eager nod. "With *her* phone. Then she took a picture of me." But then her smile faded swiftly. "She promised to come back. I marked it down. She never came back. No, never came back." She blinked at me several times, appearing slightly befuddled and I didn't have the heart to tell her I knew why. While she continued tabbing through my photos, I turned onto an even narrower, rougher dirt road and soon arrived at the unfinished house. The six rain-darkened chimneys jutting skyward into the gray storm clouds presented a rather forbidding sight. To me, the stone pillars looked like grave monuments. Piles of river rock surrounded the base of the empty shell along with mounds of wooden planks, sodden bags of cement and an array of tools. Why had it remained incomplete after so many years? Lack of funds? Lack of motivation? What a weird-looking place. I pulled out my phone and took a few photos.

"She came for honey," Daisy murmured with a faraway expression glazing her eyes.

I looked at her sharply. "Who did?"

"The girl in the picture."

I drew back in surprise. "Really? How do you know that?"

"I showed her where he lives. She talked to Stilts and then ran away, laughing." She blinked fast. "No wait. Maybe she was crying," she whispered, appearing troubled and uncertain. "Did I make her cry? I didn't mean to. Didn't mean to."

My mind whirled in confusion. Her statement made no sense at all. "Well, I'm sure it wasn't anything you did," I soothed her, patting her shoulder.

Without responding, she turned away, pushed the door open and headed towards the gate. Grateful that the wind had died down, I got out and followed her, but flinched when a muscular-looking boxer rushed up to us, barking ferociously.

"Hi, Oscar! Hi there, boy!" Daisy called out, calmly approaching the yapping dog without fear. He settled down immediately and licked her hand before warily approaching me.

"Hi, fellah," I said, tentatively extending my palm. He sniffed it and then apparently lost interest. Stubby tail wagging, he wandered away into the brush as we continued across the overgrown, unkempt yard. Daisy rapped on the metal door of a mobile home that displayed more rust than paint while I took note of the rows of white wooden beehives lined up at the far corner of the property. It was so quiet I could hear the steady musical drone of their wings.

"Mr. Stilts!" When she got no response, she knocked several more times, rattling a faded plaque beside the door that read: **IF YOU DON'T HAVE BUSINESS WITH ME, MIND YOUR OWN.** Out of the corner of my eye, I noticed the curtain move slightly in the adjacent window before hearing a gruff, masculine voice inquire, "What do you want? Who's that with you, Daisy?"

"She's my friend. My new friend. I need honey." Daisy pulled out the bills again. "Three jars." She held up three fingers. "Exactly three."

The curtain dropped back into place and after another minute or so the door slowly opened to reveal a tall, gangly man that Ginger would have dubbed 'a long, tall drink of water.' A tangled mass of shoulder-length graying-blonde hair surrounded his gaunt, unsmiling face. His dark green eyes, flinty and intimidating, probed mine with a look of suspicion. "And you?"

"Um...sure, I'll take a jar, Mr. ah..."

I waited for him to fill in the blank but all he said was,

"Wait here." He closed the door again. Daisy was right. He didn't talk much. He also struck me as introverted and very unsociable. When he returned, we paid for the honey and I decided what the hell, nothing ventured, nothing gained. A question unasked is a question unanswered. I handed him my card.

"Kendall O'Dell. I'm in the area following up on two recent fatalities and also wanted to find out if you could shed any light on the death of a man by the name of Luke Campbell. He was stung by a swarm of bees inside a modular toilet down at the gravel company. Are you familiar with that story?" I issued him a hopeful smile.

He studied the card and then looked up at me. Apparently hugely unimpressed by my credentials, his dark brows inverted into a deep V over his oddly misshapen nose. In fact it was so crooked, it seemed misplaced on his face like a broken Mr. Potato Head doll. "You talking about that arrogant, officious asshole who called himself a documentary filmmaker?"

"Yes."

His lip curled in disgust. "He kept pestering me with foolish questions until I had to threaten to shoot him if he came on my property again. And yes, the sheriff's people already questioned me about him. Several times."

I opened my mouth to ask the next question, but he cut me off with, "Yes, bees sometimes leave the hive. No, they weren't my bees. They could have come from someone else's hive or been wild. I don't know how they got inside that glorified outhouse unless someone left the door open. Yes, sometimes people do stupid things to provoke an attack. It's possible he was being pursued and a few of them got inside. Anything else?"

His callous reaction to what must have been an agonizing death disturbed me greatly. Man oh man. Talk about cold-hearted. Watching his expression closely, I thrust Jenessa's photo in his face. "Do you recognize this girl?"

He stared at the photo, jaw muscles clenching and unclenching. When he looked up at me, the depth of hatred reflected in his hollow gaze sent a painful shock zinging through my gut. "What about her?"

"Daisy said she came here to buy honey from you. Is that right?"

"Maybe."

What reason would he have to be evasive? "Well, was she here or not?"

"Twice. Did she send you here to grovel on her behalf?" Eyes deadly cold, he shook his head and stabbed his finger against his chest. "There's no forgiveness in here, never will be, so you might as well be on your way."

My head reeled. Grovel? Forgiveness? For what? What was he talking about? "So, you're saying that she came here a second time after she bought the honey from you. Why?"

"You're kinda pushy, ain't ya?"

I gave him a thin smile. "I can be. Daisy told me she was crying after her last visit. Why was that?"

His gaze turned arctic. "I don't want to talk about it and it's none of your goddamn business anyway." He turned to Daisy and modulated his tone. "You don't need to be carrying tales like your sister does. Now, why don't you run along?" But to me he commanded, "*You*, get the hell off my property."

Goggle-eyed with confusion, Daisy clutched the honey jars to her breast while her head swiveled back and forth between us.

His abrasive, insensitive, downright weird behavior both confounded and intrigued me. I didn't budge. "Are you aware that she and her boyfriend were found dead less than two miles from here last week?"

His sneer switched to that of a 'deer in the headlights' expression and he appeared to stop breathing. "How did she die?" he whispered hoarsely.

"Carbon monoxide poisoning."

He stood unmoving, staring at me in utter disbelief before his eyes ignited with a gleam of what I can only describe as triumphant vindication. A tiny smile blossomed at the corners of his mouth and he began to tremble all over.

Daisy and I exchanged a startled look. Was he having a seizure or something? I was poised to ask him if he was all right when suddenly he jammed his fist skyward and burst forth with a shout of guttural laughter that seemed to emanate from the depths of his bowels. "Yeeeeeeesss!" he bellowed. "At long last!"

What? His monstrous declaration left me stunned and speechless for long seconds. And then, consumed with breathless outrage, my reporter's objectivity flying out the window, I blurted out, "How can you say something...so... horrible, so inhumane? What's wrong with you?"

The fiery glint in his eyes was that of a madman. "What goes around comes around. There will be no tears of sorrow shed here," he intoned, his words laced with venomous sarcasm, "Why should I be the only one to suffer? Time to spread it around. Good riddance." His bitter laughter echoed through the trees and off the steep cliff walls, creating an eerie feedback that chilled my bone marrow. What kind of a person would be celebrating the tragic death of an innocent young woman?

"Who are you?" I demanded. "Do you have information about Jenessa's death? Maybe the sheriff would be interested in talking to you again."

Teeth gritted, he growled, "Don't threaten me! And don't try to involve me in any of this." He took a step backwards and right before he slammed the door, he muttered, "An eye for an eye, a tooth for a tooth."

CHAPTER
24

Unable to shake the sickening sensation lodged in my gut, I trudged through the mud listening to Daisy chanting a nonsensical little tune in an off-key singsong voice, "I have eyes and I have teeth, you have eyes and you have teeth..." while I struggled to understand what had just transpired. Was this guy a total psycho? His professed hatred for a person as sweet and kind as Jenessa seemed misguided, vindictive, incomprehensible and left me feeling incensed, mystified and just plain dumbfounded. While he appeared to be genuinely surprised to hear about her, I couldn't help but wonder if he was acting. Had he played some role in Jenessa's death? But how was that even possible? The whole uncomfortable scene made no sense at all. What would have caused her to make a return trip to apologize to him? Obviously Stilts was not his real name. So who was he? I was anxious now to talk with Marshall and find out what was known about this peculiar man and his background. But why wait? I made a beeline for his mailbox. Just like the ones I'd looked at yesterday, this one was rusted, dented and I could only make out two faint remaining letters. I used my fingernail to pick off some of the grime, hoping to reveal more of the name, but all I could make out was a G and T. Well, that wasn't going to help much. If Darcy didn't know his real identity, then surely the mail carrier Percy 'Goose' Cross would. Did I have time to detour to his place? And if I did that, would I still have time to find and interview Harvel Brickhouse before darkness settled in?

The answer to my question came in the form of huge drops splattering on my head. Great. Round two of the storm system. By the time I made it back to the Jeep, we were in the middle of another cloudburst. I turned the ignition key and switched on the wipers full speed while a hard knot of frustration gathered in my chest. Well, crap on a cracker. I glanced up at the gray curtain of rain and decided once again that venturing into the forest to try and hunt down the elusive miner would be sheer folly. I had no desire to be stranded out in the boonies overnight in the rain with no cell service, especially considering the caliber of people skulking about. "Okay, let's go to your place," I said to Daisy, exhaling a sigh of pure exasperation.

"Goody, goody, goody!" She clapped her hands with glee, and as I negotiated the slushy road it occurred to me that if the rain continued at this rate, I might not be able to get out of here at all, even with four-wheel drive. Common sense told me I should leave pronto, but now that I'd made Daisy a promise it seemed cruel to disappoint her. "I can only stay a few minutes," I informed her. "If it keeps raining like this, I won't be able to get back down the road."

She turned those amazing, fathomless eyes on me.

"I can show you a shortcut! A shortcut through the woods." She put one finger to her lips. "Shhhhhh! It's a secret. We're not supposed to go there. No, not supposed to. No. Not ever."

Was she referring to the road Darcy had mentioned? "You mean the one that leads to the McCracken Ranch? The one that was closed several years ago?"

She nodded and lowered her voice to a whisper. "Some people still use it. They don't know it, but I see them. I see them go through the gate."

"Really?"

"I have pictures," she announced, patting her camera. "But I won't go there. Never, never, never."

"Why not?"

A troubled frown creased her sun-freckled forehead. "Because of the skeleton head. I'm scared of the head. Big scary head," she added, spreading her arms wide.

Uncomprehending, I just stared at her and then thought, okay, O'Dell, you're an idiot. Why are you wasting one second of your time trying to make sense of this woman's gibberish? Look who you're dealing with here. She was probably on the intellectual level of a three-year-old. A very slow-witted three-year-old. I grinned at her. "Why don't you show me the sugar gliders now."

Rocking along the slushy road once again, I glanced at the satisfied smile pasted on Daisy's lips. She appeared to be immensely enjoying the ride when she suddenly pointed to the right. "That's old Suzie's house."

I looked over at an unpainted, ramshackle house almost hidden among the trees. "Is there something special about her?"

"She's a witch."

Why not humor her? I grinned. "Does she mix up potions, cast spells and keep a black cat?"

Daisy turned to me wide-eyed, her jaw sagging open. "You know about her?"

"Lucky guess," I murmured, pulling into her driveway. My theory about eccentric people hiding away in these isolated communities held true. I realized that I'd never eaten my sandwich and I badly needed to make a pit stop before hitting the road again. We jumped out into the driving rain and bolted for the front door of her mobile home. Unlike yesterday, there wasn't an animal in sight. At least they had the good sense to take cover from the rain, I thought ruefully, splashing through deep puddles before rushing up the stairs to the porch. Daisy threw open the unlocked door and a chorus of barking met us when we stepped inside, shed our wet coats and removed our muddy boots. After I'd greeted three small dogs and four friendly cats, I looked around the modestly furnished rooms with interest. The place was bigger than it looked. I hadn't realized it was a doublewide and wondered how on earth had they gotten the thing up that narrow, twisting road.

"Come to my room! Come on!" Daisy shouted with gusto, gesturing for me to follow her down the narrow hallway.

"I'm going to stop here for a minute," I said, pointing to the bathroom. Once inside the small, but tidy room, I couldn't help but chuckle at the sign hanging behind the toilet. **JIGGLE HANDLE AFTER FLUSHING OR DON'T COME BACK!** After I'd tended to business and washed the dirt off my hands, I used a towel to pat some of the rain off my sodden hair. The steady drum of the raindrops on the metal roof diminished and it appeared the deluge was tapering off for now. A quick glance out the small, smudged window revealed a still-overcast sky. Best get out of here soon. When I stepped into the hallway, Daisy, holding the ragged stuffed bunny, stood waiting and led me to her bedroom. Holy cow! I'd never seen such an assortment of items outside of a yard sale. Every nook and cranny was filled with stacks of plastic bins, bric-a-brac, clothing, dolls, shoes, games, puzzles and just plain junk, leaving barely enough room for the bed, desk, chest of drawers and a tall wire cage wedged in one corner. Had she innocently collected this enormous pile of stuff on her scavenger hunts or was Darcy right about her sister being a kleptomaniac? "Daisy, where did you get all these things?"

A shadow of remorse crossed her face and she ducked her chin, glancing up at me furtively. "Are you mad? Are you mad at me like Darcy?"

She looked so pitiful, my heart melted with compassion. "I'm not mad at you."

"I don't mean to take things. Sometimes, I just… borrow them." She chewed nervously on a fingernail then her eyes lit up. "I can take it all back! I will! You can help me!" Excitedly, she ran over to a wall shelf, grabbed a handful of books and shoved them at me. "Here! Here! We can take them back!"

"No! No, Daisy. That's all right." The pile of books tipped forward and landed on the floor with a thud. "Let's put them all away, shall we?" I knelt to gather the books, absently reading the titles as I handed them back to her one by one. Quite a variety—*Alice in Wonderland*, a biography of George Washington, *The Beginner's Guide to Trout Fishing, Easy Meal Planner* and *Final Departure, Assisted Suicide for the Dying.* The last one caught my eye and I pulled it back. A curious subject matter for Daisy to have in her collection. I opened the front cover and drew back when I saw the inscription. Billie Carr. How interesting. "Where did you get this?" I asked gently, not wanting to spook her. "Did you know Billie Carr?"

"She's gone to Heaven," she said simply.

"Did she give this to you?"

"No."

"Did you take this from her house?"

Her furtive gaze shifted away. "Maybe." She stared blankly into the distance for a few seconds and then disconnected from the conversation. Humming happily to herself, she crossed the room and began to replace the books on the shelf. At that second, it occurred to me that Daisy had probably accompanied Darcy when she had gone to care for the dying woman and helped herself to the book or books while there. I leafed through several chapter headings that outlined the numerous ways patients could take their own lives—starvation, various combinations of drugs, poisons, and the proper use of plastic bags to smother the patient. Pretty grim stuff. It was doubtful Daisy had read any of it. She'd most likely just taken it...just because she felt compelled to take something.

"Come see them now!" Daisy pleaded, beckoning me as she opened the cage door and reached inside to pull out a small, multi-colored, possum-like creature with bulbous black eyes. "This is Henry," she announced, beaming. "And that one is Lolita," she said pointing to a second, smaller one hanging by its tail from the top of the cage. Daisy set the sugar glider on my shoulder and I stroked its soft fur as we sized each other up eyeball-to-eyeball. "Well, aren't you the cutest little thing," I whispered. I'd never seen anything quite like them before. "Where did you come from, little one?"

"Australia!" Daisy exclaimed. "They have big, big eyes to hunt at night." She studied my face. "Do you like him?"

"He's adorable." I glanced inside the cage and pointed at little bags hanging from the top of the cage. "What are those for?"

"For sleeping," she announced with pride in her voice. "They sleep in the little bags and run on those little wheels."

"How fun." I pulled my phone out and handed it to Daisy. "Take a picture. Just tap the button at the bottom."

She tapped away and then picked up her camera and took several shots. "You can take him home. You can take both of them," she announced with wide-eyed eagerness. "I can't keep them. No, I can't keep them."

"Why not?"

"Darcy says they cost too much. They eat too much!"

"What kinds of things do they eat?" I asked, marveling at the unique creature.

"Look! Look at these," she said grabbing two small containers from the floor and screwing the lid off one of them. "Meal worms! And wax worms! They eat lots of these and fruit and vegetables. Avocados! They eat avocados and eggs too."

"That's a lot of food."

Her lips gathered in a forlorn pout. "It costs too much. And Darcy says it costs too much to keep them warm.

They take too much work. That's what she says," Daisy complained despondently. "Too much work. That's what Darcy says. Yeah. Too much work."

"Well, I'll sure ask around when I get back home," I promised her as the energetic creature leaped, or should I say flew like a flying squirrel from my shoulder to the top of her bureau. It actually looked like it had wings, and at that moment it dawned on me why they were called gliders. "Well, this has been quite educational," I said, noting the time, "but I have to go now."

Disappointment clouded her face as she picked up the unique creature and gently placed him on a perch in the cage. "You don't want to take them?"

"I'm sorry...I just can't." I turned and headed for the door when I heard her say softly, "The pretty girl said she would take them."

I whirled around to stare at her. "What?"

"The pretty girl. In the picture."

My heart stilled. "You mean Jenessa?"

"She never came back. She never came back and now she's in Heaven. Yes, in Heaven," she murmured to herself then fixed me with a questioning look. "Is she there with Billie Carr?"

"I'm sure she is," I answered, her surprising revelation kicking up my pulse rate. Very interesting. I now knew at least one of the reasons that she and Nathan had returned to Raven Creek. "Daisy, do you remember what day Jenessa was supposed to come back to get the sugar gliders?"

Another blank look and then her eyes brightened. "I do! I do! I wrote it down," she said breathlessly, rushing to the cluttered desk to scoop up a notebook depicting several kittens cavorting on the cover. Tongue clenched firmly between her irregular teeth, she leafed through it and then shoved the page so close to my eyes everything blurred. "Right here! Right here! See? I wrote it down on my calendar."

I pushed the notebook away, focused on the date and my heart faltered. If this entry was correct, Jenessa had intended to pick them up last Tuesday—the same day she'd been expected to return home. And then the memory of the strange notation on the calendar I'd seen in her room jumped to mind. Of course! Pick up SG had to mean sugar gliders. "Daisy, can you show me exactly which day she came to see you?"

Daisy tilted her head sideways and pointed to a small x she had marked on Tuesday of the previous week. "See here? See this x? She said, "I will come back in one week." She held up one stubby finger. "One week. That's what she said. Exactly."

If Daisy was right, that meant only three days elapsed between the day they were here and the day they died. If I recalled correctly, the big snowstorm had indeed blown in on that Friday. "Did Jenessa say anything to you about where she and Nathan were going or what they planned to do before they returned?"

She chewed on her thumbnail, her face a mask of intense concentration. After an extended silence she finally said, "In the morning. She said they would go in the morning to Crown King to rent the…the little car things."

"You mean an ATV?"

She nodded affirmatively. "ATVs. Yes, ATVs!"

"Did she say anything else? Did she say where they were going on the ATVs?"

She pursed her lips. "Mmmmmmmm. Riding on the mountain. I think…to Horse Thief Basin and look for old mines and camp and hike! Hike in the moonlight. Moonlight hiking, she said!"

Hiking around on this rugged mountain terrain in daylight looked to be daunting enough, but attempting it solely by the light of the moon seemed dicey to me. Remembering Nathan's penchant for extreme sports, no doubt meant he would relish the challenge and the risk involved. But why drag Jenessa along on such a perilous journey? I made a note in my phone to find out what date they'd returned the ATVs. But as I tapped the reminder out something occurred to me. If they had planned to be gone for another week, why had they returned the ATVs after only two days? I'd have to double check with Marshall, but I didn't remember him saying they'd found ATVs on the closed road. Just the camper. And if they'd been coming back to Raven Creek, it made no logical sense for them to drive in the opposite direction. The list of questions without answers grew larger by the day. Yeah, I definitely had my work cut out for me. "Daisy, I really have to go now."

"No! Don't go yet!" she implored. "Stay longer. Just a little longer. I can show you more pictures!" She rushed to the stack of plastic tubs and began to excitedly pile them on the bed. "I have a hundred thousand million pictures to show you! A hundred million!" Her face aglow, she pulled photo after photo out, spreading them out on the bed. Her childlike enthusiasm was contagious, but I had to say gently, "I'd love to look at them another time, but right now I have a lot of things I need to do, okay?"

Her face crumpled in disappointment. "Oh. Darcy

says I have too many. Too many pictures. A hundred million zillion is too many, she says."

She seemed lonely and I felt bad, but time was getting away from me. "Thank you, Daisy." When I reached the front door to pull on my boots and coat, I added, "You've been a really big help today."

Expectant blue eyes sparkling with pride, her whole persona seemed to light up. "I can be a good helper! A good, good helper!"

"You certainly can be." I had the impression that Darcy probably never praised her for anything and that was sad. And then something occurred to me. "Daisy, do you have any more pictures of Jenessa? I know her mother would like to see them."

She stared at me with a searching look for long seconds and then clapped her hands together. "I do! I do have some! Do you want to see them?"

"You bet! Are they on your camera?"

She wrinkled her nose. "I have real pictures too! Darcy makes me pictures on her…on her…" She paused and her eyes went blank.

"Her printer?" I filled in hopefully.

Her face lit up. "Yes! The printer! The printer! I have lots and lots to show you!" Again like a child, she skipped back to her bedroom and I watched while she rummaged through the plastic tubs, humming a little tune. How she managed to find them so quickly from among the thousands of photos, I'll never know, but within five minutes she exclaimed happily, "Here! Here she is!"

I sifted through at least a dozen photos of a smiling Jenessa holding the sugar gliders and several others of her posing with some of the dogs and cats. I dug out my phone again and recorded them. With a twinge of sadness, it occurred to me that these were probably the last pictures ever taken of her while she was alive. "These are really special," I remarked, smiling at Daisy. "Thank you."

"I have more! Bunches and bunches more!" She pulled out handfuls of photos and spread them out on the bed. "Do you want to see pictures of the nice boy too?" she announced in an eager-to-please tone as she continued to rummage through the tub.

"You mean Nathan?"

"Yes. Yes. Nathan. The boy Nathan."

"I would like to see them," I answered, thinking it was strange that I was actually becoming accustomed to her odd repetitive sentence structure.

While she hunted, I sat on the edge of the bed absently fingering through the pile, looking at pictures of plants, flowers, animals, bugs, structures and a lot of people I didn't recognize, but deduced that most of them were probably residents of Raven Creek. There were also images of things that I had no idea what they were or where they were taken. She had a sizeable number of photos of Percy Cross's vintage cars, photographed from every conceivable angle, including several of him delivering mail in his hearse. But my breath caught in surprise when I noticed one in particular. I held it closer. There was Percy in his hearse parked beside a familiar black pickup truck. Really? What reason would the Hinkle brothers have to be in Raven Creek? "Daisy, do you know the men who own this truck?" I held up the picture and her round face crinkled with concern. "Oh! Darcy says those are bad, bad boys. I don't like them. No. Don't like them. They are mean. Mean, mean boys."

Of that, I had no doubt. "I'm not too crazy about them myself. Do they come here often? Who do they visit?"

Preoccupied still searching for photos, she answered vaguely, "Mmmmm. Mostly to see the doctor."

"Doctor Gartiner?"

"I think they are sick a lot. Darcy says he's a good doctor. Good doctor. Good." She picked up another photo, stared at it and then let out a sheepish giggle. "He didn't know I took this. He would be mad. Real, real mad."

"Who? Nathan?"

"No. Mr. Stilts. He told me to never take his picture. Never, never."

"Let's see." She handed it to me and just for the hell of it, I took a photo of the print, thanked her again and headed for the door. She trotted along behind me. "Will you come back again to see me?"

"Absolutely," I replied, shouldering my purse. "And, thank you, Daisy. You really were more help than you can imagine. See you later." I patted her spongy shoulder and stepped outside. The air smelled amazing, saturated with the musky scents of wet earth, leaves and pines. That part was nice, but I could not help but bemoan the fact that my plans to find Harvel Brickhouse, the person I most wanted to interview, continued to be thwarted by inclement weather. Trudging towards the Jeep, a twinge of surprise zinged through me at the sight of Burton Carr's pickup cruising by the mouth of the driveway. He waved and shouted, "Just checking to see if you were okay. We're going to get slammed by this next storm front. Want me to follow you down the hill?"

I looked up at the mass of gray clouds hovering over the treetops and yelled back, "I'll be fine, but thanks."

"I'd get a move on real soon if I were you," he advised sternly, then acknowledged Daisy with a smile and friendly wave. "How are you doin' today, Miss Daisy?"

When she didn't answer, I turned around in time to witness her staring at him in goggle-eyed, open-mouthed alarm. No, actually it was more than that. She looked petrified. Was she worried that I might tell him about the book she'd stolen from his mother's house? She didn't respond to his inquiry and seconds before she darted back inside the trailer, her startled gaze met mine and I heard her mutter, "He sucked up all the air. He sucked up all the air." Well, that was just plain weird. I glanced back at Burton, but he had already pulled away. Before I could even begin to analyze her peculiar statement, a powerful gust of wind roared down the mountainside, almost knocking me off my feet. Oh brother! I could only hope my family wasn't experiencing the same fate in Monument Valley. I grabbed up my cell phone and then my heart fell when I remembered there was no cell service.

"Crap." Please don't let their tour be cancelled, I prayed. The excursion had cost me almost a week's salary.

I hopped inside the Jeep and sat there trying to shake off my escalating blue funk. Was it the cloudy weather? Over these past nine months, I had become totally addicted to sunshine and sharp blue skies. My complaining stomach reminded me that I'd never eaten lunch, so, with the insistent wind as my companion, I ate my sandwich and mulled over the day's events.

Merely summoning up the unhappy recollection

of Jenessa and Nathan's watery grave depressed me even further and made it difficult to swallow. The now-dried-out bread hit my belly like a brick and formed a hard lump. And the unnerving encounter with the very strange 'bee man' known only as Stilts was as distressing as it was puzzling. For the life of me I could not fathom what could have transpired to cause a display of such intense hatred toward a kind and gentle human being like Jenessa. And his cruel exultation following the announcement of her death totally mystified me. What could possibly be the basis for such shocking behavior? Had Jenessa's confrontation with Stilts taken place the same day she'd visited Daisy? Cognizant of the woman's limited mental capabilities, could I really rely on anything she had told me so far? Was I wasting my time?

I laid my head back and let out a long breath. Either there really was no story here or I just couldn't find it. Besides scratching the paint on my new Jeep, what had I really accomplished driving around the Bradshaws these past two days? I started the engine. Marcelene and Ginger were counting on me to find some answers to the puzzle and so far all I had to report back to them was…nothing—a big, fat stupid zero. Boy, had I made a wrong decision. If I hadn't suffered a weak moment and instead stuck with my original plans, I'd be having fun vacationing with my family right now instead of sitting on this stormy, lonesome mountaintop.

Matching my dismal mood, random drops splattered on the windshield. Of course it was going to rain again. I turned on the windshield wipers and made my way slowly along the sloshy, deeply furrowed road. I was rocking past Percy Cross's place when I glanced over towards the dark spires of the unfinished house. Overcome by a powerful impulse, I turned into his driveway and parked behind the creepy-looking old hearse. I could almost hear my dad's admonishment ringing in my ears. 'Pumpkin, it's too soon to throw in the towel.' It would be far easier to accept the fact that Jenessa's death was truly an accident, but try as I might, I could not extinguish the lingering sense of doubt.

So, why was I here? Who better than the mail carrier to know something about everyone residing in or around Raven Creek? Why not take just a few minutes to pick his brain? Perhaps he could provide additional information about the mysterious beekeeper. He might even know the man's real name. Couldn't hurt to ask.

I reached beneath my seat, pulled out my seldom-used umbrella and stepped into the driving rain. Sprinting by the jumble of vintage cars in his front yard, I could smell the tantalizing odor of mesquite smoke pouring from the chimney of the small wooden house. Two quick steps up to the porch and I was out of the downpour. I raised my hand to knock when I heard a peculiar sound emanating from within. Honk! Honk! Honk! It sounded like a goose. I rapped on the door and when it swung open, I stood face to face with a watery-eyed Percy Cross, wiping his nose with a dishtowel. Oh. I now understood the source of his nickname.

After I'd introduced myself and told him why I was there, he croaked, "Yeah, I remember seeing you at Darcy's place." He paused. "Look here, I got me a real bad cold, so I jest thought I'd warn ya, ifn ya don't want to come in."

I hesitated. I couldn't very well question him with the rain pounding on the roof, but I wasn't thrilled about catching a cold either. Decision time. I told him I wouldn't stay long and he invited me inside, where I stood in front of the crackling woodstove fire warming my cold hands.

"Join me in a cup o' hot cider?" he inquired, his friendly gap-toothed smile lighting up his watery brown eyes while he tightened the belt on his flannel checked bathrobe.

"Sounds good to me," I answered, gazing around the crowded, unkempt wood-paneled room. It looked like a bachelor pad—frayed armchairs, dusty, dated furniture piled with newspapers and magazines, the remains of frozen meal containers scattered about along with empty beer and soda cans.

A few minutes later, he joined me in front of the stove, handing me the steaming cup of spicy-smelling liquid. "You might want to wait a minute. It's pretty hot."

"Thank you."

Blowing his nose with a resounding honk again, he shuffled back to the kitchen, returning with a cup in one hand and a bottle of whisky in the other. "I got me a touch of Jack Daniels in mine. You want a little nip too?"

I smiled wryly. "If I didn't have to conquer that winding road, I would definitely join you."

"Ya get used to it after awhile." He moved across the room and settled himself into a chair. "I'm gonna sit over here so I don't give you this creeping crud, okay?"

"I appreciate that." I sat down near the fire.

"So, what is it you'd be wanting to know about old Stilts?" he asked, taking a drink of his cider.

I filled him in on my strange encounter and he nodded sagely. "Yeah, he's an odd bird, I'll give ya that. I don't know a whole hell of a lot about him 'cept I understand he's been living here close on to fifteen years. Keeps to himself, never talks about where he come from, don't seem to have no friends and for some dang reason, never finishes building that house." He sipped more cider continuing with, "Wish I could help ya out with his real name, but ya see, I don't deliver his mail. He uses a PO Box in Black Canyon City."

Now I was even more curious. Using a Post Office box is the best way for a person to go underground. "But he must have had mail delivered at one time. There used to be a name on the mailbox, but all that I could make out was a G and a T."

"A G and a T," he repeated, stroking his beard. "Well, I jest took this gig over about six years ago after Millard Boggs passed on. The name on that old box might've belonged to someone who lived there before him." He paused and his eyes lit up. "You know what? I think I remember hearing that Doc Gartiner's brother once owned that property. So, there ya go! There's your G and T," he announced with a look of supreme satisfaction. "Anything else ya want to know?"

I pulled out my phone, tabbed to the photo of Jenessa and Nathan and after a brief explanation, crossed to where he sat and held it out to him. "I was wondering if you recalled seeing them anytime during the past few weeks and if so, where?"

He grabbed a pair of reading glasses from the cluttered side table and perched them on his beet-red nose. He studied the photo for a long time before looking up to meet my inquiring gaze. "I wish I could help ya, but, ya know, I see so many of these kids tearin' around up and down the roads on their cycles and quads, I'm just not certain. Sorry."

Well, great. Every path of questioning I started down seemed to lead to the same dead end. I returned to my seat and took a swallow of the cider. Tasty!

"Anything else?" he inquired, pouring more of the amber liquid into his cup.

"What can you tell me about Harvel Brickhouse? You know him, right?"

He made a face. "Yeah, I know him. What do you want to know about the old skunk?"

Skunk? I smiled. "Whatever you want to tell me."

"I know he works a bunch of mining claims back here in the hills," he said, thumbing over his shoulder.

"The sheriff told me he was convicted of involuntary manslaughter quite a few years ago. Do you know anything about that?"

"I heard he beat a guy to death with his bare fists down at the Cleator bar a long time back."

"Do you know who and why?"

He scratched his disheveled hair. "Well, I don't know if it's true or not, but I heard he was once sweet on Elizabeth McCracken. Her name's Hinkle now, and that this feller he coldcocked had made some derogatory remark about her and that's when the fightin' started. When Harvel got out of prison, I think it might've been five years later, Buster McCracken hired him on as a ranch hand and now he's kind of the part-time caretaker when he ain't out workin' his claims."

"I'd like to talk with him. Do you have any idea where I could find him?"

He let out a humongous sneeze and goose-honked into the dishtowel again before proceeding to have a coughing fit. My stomach churned when he finally hawked something up. He noisily cleared this throat. "Sorry about that. What'd you ask me?"

"Do you know where I could locate him?"

"Harvel's a hard guy to find. He don't stay in one spot very long."

It was only then that I realized the rain had stopped and even though it was only three-thirty, early twilight was fast descending. I rose hastily. "Well, thanks for your help." I headed for the door.

"Well now, hold your horses a minute," came his voice from behind. "I can't tell you where he is at this very second, but I can for certain tell you where he'll be on Wednesday."

I swung around. "Where?"

He edged me a crafty smile. "No matter how far he roams, he manages to truck it on back to the McCracken Ranch by two o'clock in the afternoon the second Wednesday of the month."

"Why?"

"I deliver his monthly check that day."

At last something I could actually bank on. I thanked him for the cider and drove out of Raven Creek with a little prayer that the canyon road wouldn't be a perilous river of mud. Even though I hadn't made much progress on the side of finding any concrete proof to reinforce Marcelene's theory, I was convinced that there had to be something more going on here than met the eye. There just had to be. There were too many unanswered questions, too many suspicious events. All I needed was one small piece of tangible evidence to prove it.

CHAPTER
25

What a difference four thousand feet makes. By the time I reached the turnoff at the bottom of the hill, the wind had died down considerably and streams of sunlight intermittently punched through the ragged, fast-moving clouds. Amazing. Behind me, the summit was still shrouded in a misty cloud cap of charcoal grey. The mountain did indeed create its own weather patterns.

Back in the land of cell service, my phone started dinging like a pinball machine as message after message came through. I pulled to the side of the road to scroll through them. The first one was from my dad and included several photos of the family standing at the entrance of Monument Valley. REALLY WINDY BUT HAVING A BALL! WISH U WERE HERE WITH US. He wore a cheerful grin, but Sean and my mother were not smiling. In fact, they both looked peeved. Oh boy. No doubt they were still at each other's throats and I wondered again what we were going to do about his destructive behavior and drug use. Should

I plan a family intervention after our engagement party? It would be more effective if our brother, Patrick, were present. He was a level-headed, no-nonsense type of guy and would most likely concur with my assessment of the situation. But the mere thought of what could prove to be a volcanic family upheaval with possibly no resolution sent my spirits spiraling downward again. There seemed to be no good solution to the dilemma.

I tapped the next message from Marshall Turnbull. NOT SURPRISED! I NU YOU'D END UP WORKING THIS CASE! ☺ HAVE NOT BEEN ABLE 2 CONTACT THE TAYLOR BOY'S MOTHER YET. WORKING ON IT. He also included the phone number for Nathan's father. Good. At least I could call him tonight or tomorrow.

I scrolled to the next message. CAN'T WAIT TO HEAR WHAT U FIND OUT, GIRLFRIEND! CALL ME LATER. COME OVER 2 MARCELENE'S 2MORROW NITE AROUND 6. POTLUCK. BRING CHIPS & DIP. BONNIE, TOM, NONA AND BRIAN WILL BE THERE 2. WE CAN TALK ABOUT THE PARTY PLANS 2. ☺

Perfect. I always enjoyed visiting with Ginger's sister and especially their colorful grandmother, Nona. Plus that, it would be a good time to find out if Brian would be able to access the information on Jenessa's laptop and there might even be time to go through the rest of her receipts to determine if they contained any significant information.

There was also a text from Tugg reminding me that he would not be in the office until Wednesday morning. Time wise, that would work out well for me. I would make sure I was at the McCracken Ranch that afternoon well before two o'clock. Tally had left me a message commenting on the photos I'd sent, reminded me again to be careful and that he missed and loved me. That alone made my day. Feeling more optimistic, I set the phone down and shoved the Jeep into drive.

Traffic was pretty light on the way towards Cleator, but when I heard the distinctive whine of ATVs behind me, I pulled to the side. Two young guys raced by and bolt of surprise shot through me. Wait a minute. Was the second guy with his hat turned backwards the same one I'd seen twice in the past two days? I was pretty sure it was. A fluke or did he live somewhere around here? A tight, uncomfortable knot formed in my stomach when he briefly glanced over his shoulder at me. I don't know why the notion that he might be tailing me flashed through my mind, but it did. I waited until they were out of sight and then continued on my way.

When I neared the entrance to the gravel company, the unexpected sight of more than a half a dozen cars parked along both sides of the road caught my attention. What was this? I eased to a stop behind a white van plastered with an array of bumper stickers and decals all warning of mankind's destruction of Mother Earth. I counted eight women and two men, arms locked together, blocking the driveway and waving signs protesting the company's alleged desecration of the desert landscape. **SAVE OUR PRISTINE DESERTS, FRIENDS OF THE LAND** and **GREEDY CORPORATIONS DESTROY THE EARTH! THIS COMPANY COLLUDES WITH ADOT!! DELIVER US FROM THIS EVIL!**

I looked up and down the empty road. Since there were so few passersby, whom were these people attempting to influence with their inflammatory signs? Obviously, this demonstration was meant solely for employees and management of the sand and gravel company. I shook my head. They were wasting their time, but I shouldn't waste mine. Adversity always presents a good story opportunity. I smiled to myself. Tugg's sage prediction that I'd find some angle to write about echoed loudly in my ears. Okay. Since I wasn't making much headway on the exposé I was hoping for, why not take advantage of the human-interest story right in front of me? What did my dad always say? When life hands you lemons, make lemonade or, better yet, a lemon meringue pie.

I grabbed my notepad and approached the group. After my introduction, they eagerly seized on the publicity aspect for their cause, posed for pictures and passionately voiced their opinions regarding the grave environmental impact of the gravel company. There were vociferous accusations that the company was systematically destroying the landscape, flora and fauna, birds, bats, lizards and toads, plus a flagrant disregard for EPA safety rules. In regards to the impending freeway construction and the supposed collusion between Raven Creek Sand and Gravel Company and the Department of Transportation, they uttered a barrage of words I could not print. I was happily jotting down their concerns on my notepad when I felt first the vibrations and then heard the roar of one of the big gravel trucks fast approaching.

The group quickly hoisted their signs and locked arms again. Well, this ought to be interesting. I swiped to my camera icon fully expecting the truck to reduce speed and stop for the chanting chain of humanity. Not only did the driver not slow down, to my horror, he accelerated and bore down on us. I barely had time to leap to the side of the driveway. "Run!" I shouted, scrambling up the side of the knoll. "He's not kidding!"

Screaming like banshees, the protesters scattered like frightened sheep in all directions. From my awkward position on the embankment, I managed to raise my phone and tap the screen multiple times as the giant vehicle rumbled through the gate in a choking cloud of dust. Good God! What was he thinking? He could have killed all of us. Short of breath, heart thundering in my ears, I sat down on the sloped ground to collect my thoughts. Was it possible he'd been blinded by the late afternoon sunlight and hadn't seen us? Surely, he wouldn't have intentionally mowed us down? I scanned my photos but they were backlit and out of focus except for the blurry outline of the man's profile. Could that possibly be Rod, the surly driver who'd been in the dust-up with Darcy, or was it the young Hispanic guy? I enlarged the photo, but could not nail down the driver's identity.

I glanced back toward the group of protesters. Faces ashen with shock, some exchanged looks of wide-eyed disbelief while several of the women wept. The group swiftly dispersed and within minutes all the cars had vanished, leaving discarded protest signs scattered in the road. As my own shock dissipated, white-hot fury took its place. Someone needed to report such reckless, irresponsible behavior to the management. And that someone was going to be me. I marched to my Jeep and without a clearly defined plan of action, accelerated through the gate.

I'd traveled a mile or so when I encountered a second chain link fence bearing the name of the company and product list. **RIPRAP. LEACH ROCK. FLAGSTONE.**

ABC. ADOT CERTIFIED PIT. Another sign announced: **HARD HAT AREA – KEEP OUT**. And beneath it a smaller sign read: *Authorized personnel only beyond this point*. Inside the double gate, an idle water truck sat beside a green storage tank. Nearby loomed a large concrete building with wide double doors. Adjacent to it were several smaller structures, a trailer and several pickups, and beyond that rows of heavy equipment, two dump trucks and cone-shaped piles of various-sized rocks and gravel. In the distance, I could hear the roar of some type of heavy machinery and saw a plume of dust rising into the air. Eyeing my phone, I surmised it must be near closing time. But, the gate was still open, so I parked, walked inside the enclosure and approached the trailer, which bore the sign: OFFICE. I tried the door, which was locked and then knocked repeatedly. No answer. I tried to peek in the window, but the blinds were closed. Consumed with pent-up frustration, I looked around, wondering what to do. Should I drive towards the column of dust in hopes of finding someone I could report the driver's dangerous behavior to?

And then I spotted a row of blue modular toilets nestled in the shadow of a hill perhaps a hundred yards away. Was this where the documentary filmmaker had died? My interest in his bizarre death rekindled, I gravitated toward them. Just to satisfy my curiosity, I opened the door of the first one, let go, and it slammed shut. Yep. As anticipated, the door operated as designed. I opened the second one, let go and *bang!* So how had a swarm of bees flown inside that fast? Why hadn't the guy simply run out when he realized he was in trouble? Was it possible that the lock had somehow become jammed? I opened a third door and released it to slam shut.

"You got some kind of a problem, lady?"

My heart jolted painfully against my chest. Robbed of breath, I spun around to meet the accusatory stare of Jack Loomis. Where had he come from so suddenly? Close up, his six-foot-plus height and beefy frame made him appear even more intimidating than he had during the altercation with Darcy. Before I could speak he seethed, "I don't know how many times I have to tell you damn tree huggers to quit trespassing on private land." He nodded curtly towards the toilet. "Do your business and get the hell off this property."

Incensed by his churlish conduct, I drew myself up to my full five foot eight height and returned his glare. "You are mistaken," I informed him coolly. "I'm not part of the protest group."

He looked momentarily taken aback before his eyes narrowed with suspicion. "Whoever you are, you're trespassing on private property. Can't you read?" He pointed to the **KEEP OUT** sign.

Boy, talk about testy. "I apologize. I was trying to find someone to talk to. Do you always treat potential customers in this fashion?"

Unfazed by my bravado, he studied me for a few seconds and then pointed his forefinger at me. "Didn't I see you yesterday with that bunch near Cleator?"

"Yes."

"Thought so. We don't serve the public here. This is a commercial enterprise. If you're interested in buying a finished product, you'll have to visit one of our retail outlets in either Tempe or Mesa."

I dug out a card and handed it to him. "Kendall

O'Dell from the *Castle Valley Sun*." Of course I knew who he was, but he didn't know that. "And you are?"

"Jack Loomis. I'm the foreman here. So what do you want?"

"I was in the process of interviewing some of the protesters when one of your truck drivers came within inches of plowing into all of us a few minutes ago."

He glanced down at my card before saying in a slightly more conciliatory tone, "Sorry about that. He probably didn't see you."

I raised a skeptical brow. "Really? You think he didn't see eleven people standing there?"

"I'm sure it was unintentional," he insisted brusquely, pocketing my card. His cell phone beeped and he muttered, "Excuse me." He stared at the screen and typed something before looking up to meet my eyes.

Aware that I'd get nowhere if I remained obstinate with him, I modulated my voice. "Unintentional or not, I'm sure that you don't need any more bad publicity."

"More?" His sun-tanned features crinkled into a puzzled frown. "What do you mean?"

"I'm sure you're aware of the body discovered here awhile back," I said, pointing behind me. "I'm following up on that as well as a couple of other deaths that have occurred in this area. Perhaps you could answer a few questions?"

"We didn't have anything to do with that...unfortunate event." He widened his stance and crossed his arms. "Look, the guy had been hanging around here for weeks stirring up trouble between us and these...uninformed idiots who don't like the way we run our business. He was trying to promote hatred and manufacture a situation when there isn't one.

Then or now."

I fired off the list of infractions inferred by the environmental activists and he bristled. "They're full of shit. We follow all the rules we're required to. As far as the EPA, they've got no jurisdiction over us because we're operating on private property. If they come sniffing around, I just tell them to go kick rocks." He exhaled a long breath and moderated his tone. "Look, we try to be good neighbors, keep the noise down, keep the dust down. Besides providing a product people want, we employ as many of the locals as are qualified. I don't think that's a bad thing."

"Very commendable, but it's also important for the public to hear both sides of the issue. I thought you handled the situation with Darcy Dorcett yesterday very ah... diplomatically." I was dying to ask him if he always carried that much cash around, but refrained. My observation appeared to please him and his tense shoulders relaxed somewhat. "But," I continued, "according to the medical examiner's report Mr. Campbell had been dead more than forty-eight hours when he was discovered. How do you suppose he got through the gate after hours? Is this property completely fenced off?"

"Every foot of it. And there are signs posted all over the place." A giant shrug. "I can only figure he sneaked in here before we closed that Friday and was hiding out someplace. Or, maybe he somehow got through or over the fence, I don't know."

"Why? What would be the point? What would he have been looking for?"

"Beats the hell out of me." He rubbed a forefinger along his upper lip. "All I know is he was dead when we found him. There isn't much else I can tell you."

"That reminds me," I remarked, assessing my notes. "Would it be possible for me to speak to Manuel Dominguez? I understand he's the person who found the body."

"Can't help you. He's no longer with us."

Rats! I hid my disappointment and yanked open one of the modular toilet doors before releasing it to shut with a bang. "I know the case has been classified as accidental, but I'm still trying to figure out how so many bees could have gotten inside when, as you can see, the doors don't stay open but a few seconds. And I don't understand how he could have gotten trapped inside."

He cast me an appraising 'so that's what you were doing' look and his jaw muscles twitched repeatedly. When he spoke, I detected a hint of irritation in his tone. "Like I told the sheriff, once a week, the shit wagon…er, the pumper truck comes to empty them. While Lloyd's got the vacuum hose going in there the door is open for a certain amount of time depending on how much cleanup is required. As to why Mr. Campbell didn't come out, well, maybe the latch stuck or something. I don't know. Maybe that's where he was hiding when he entered the property."

His distracted look told me that I'd milked that subject dry, so before he could brush me off, I inquired, "Tell me something, is this the same road the residents of Raven Creek used as a shortcut before you closed it off to traffic?"

"Yeah." The hard light in his dark eyes returned.

I smiled. "I guess you know you're not very popular with them either."

"There's nuthin' I can do about that. It's a safety and liability issue." He thumbed over his shoulder. "We've got a lot of equipment running, and besides that we had to keep people, especially those crazy kids, from snooping around inside the old mine. We had a study done by several mining safety engineers and they declared it structurally unsafe. Plus while old man McCracken was alive, tweakers used it to dump their garbage. It's a mess and a health hazard. It's closed off for everyone's safety."

I tilted my head in question. "Tweakers?"

"Meth heads."

"Oh. Well, that's different from the story I heard."

His mouth twisted into a smirk, he fisted both hands on his hips. "Oh yeah? And what did you hear?"

"That a local miner was in the process of obtaining permits to reopen the Thunderbolt Mine before you leased the property out from under him."

Annoyance colored his heavy features and his nostrils flared so wide I could see the nest of hairs in each. "You mean Harvel Brickhouse? That drunken old fool! He doesn't know his ass from a hole in the ground." He dismissed my statement with a flick of his hand. "That's a pipe dream if there ever was one. That place is a deathtrap. It would take mega millions to shore up that old mine. Hell, the supporting timbers are sagging and half the tunnels are flooded. He could have never done anything with it."

My goodness. I seemed to have hit a sore spot. "You'd think being a miner that he would have known that, wouldn't you?"

"Are you going to believe him or the experienced engineers we paid to do the study?" he challenged, his eyes glinting with anger.

"Speaking of that, who is the owner of this company?"

The barest hesitation. "The Sweetland Corporation."

I glanced up at him. Why the hesitancy? "Is that based in Phoenix?" I asked, jotting more notes.

"I believe so." He shifted his weight from one foot to another and his eyes darted again to his phone, signaling that he was growing restless.

"In order to give my readers a fair view of both sides, I'd like to learn a little more about your operation here," I ventured, "and take some photos to accompany my story."

"That's not happening today. I've got too many things to finish up before I go."

"Oh. Well, another day then? Perhaps Wednesday?" I issued him a hopeful smile.

Frowning, he tapped his phone. "No. It'll have to be later in the week." His open-handed gesture towards my Jeep confirmed that the interview was concluded. I flipped my notepad shut as he accompanied me to the gate. I stepped through and he closed it behind me with a resounding clang. "Oh, just one more question, Mr. Loomis."

"Yes?"

"What's your connection with the Hinkle brothers?"

For a split second, his eyes widened before his thick brows dipped lower. "I'm not sure what you mean by connection."

"I saw them turn in the gate earlier, so I'm assuming you know them."

"I do," he growled, securing a padlock on the gate. "Their step-mother sends them here once a month to collect the lease payment from us."

"So, you're saying that you're not well-acquainted with them?"

"That's what I'm saying. And that's fine by me. I'm not interested in associating with those punks any more than I have to."

When his cell phone rang, he whipped it to his ear and listened intently. He nodded curtly in my direction, swiveled around and strode to his truck. As I watched him head towards the distant dust cloud, I could not shake my escalating unease. If I hadn't overheard the exchange between him and the Hinkle brothers at the Cleator bar, I wouldn't have known that Jack Loomis was lying through his teeth. But why? What reason would he have to lie about his relationship with the Hinkle twins?

Intrigued, I slid into my Jeep and continued to mull over the day's vexing events. Even if I took into consideration everything I'd learned to date, it still netted me nothing more than a series of unconnected tidbits of information that brought me no closer to my goal. I wondered if it was even worth my time and effort to make yet another trip to interview Harvel Brickhouse. He sounded like an interesting character, but could he shed any new light on this perplexing case? At this point, it seemed doubtful.

All during the drive along the dusty Bumble Bee Road, I chastised myself for failing to come up with anything substantial to report to Marcelene and Ginger. Acutely aware of their high expectations, they were bound to be disappointed. Yes, I had my share of shortcomings, but being a quitter wasn't among them. Lord knows, I'd followed up on every possibility, interviewed a bunch of quirky people and yet, even considering all the baffling circumstances, Marshall appeared to be right. There was nothing to indicate anything at play other than accidental death. As strange as it sounded, I could understand how it might be easier for them to believe that foul play was a factor rather than having to accept the fact that the young couple had simply made a stupid, fatal mistake.

As I sped westward towards Castle Valley filled with mixed emotions, I was treated to a spectacular sunset. Awestruck, I watched fiery shafts of scarlet and tangerine shoot skyward from the horizon, illuminating the mound of creampuff clouds, slowly transforming them into a kaleidoscope of iridescent pink, blue and gold. Even though my investigation appeared to be at a dead end, the fact that my family and Tally would be back tomorrow night buoyed my flagging spirits. And best of all, our engagement party was now only four days away.

CHAPTER
26

Anxious to get a jump on the day, I pulled into the office parking lot as the first golden rays of sunlight spilled over the rugged peaks. Instilled with restless energy, I walked inside only to discover there was no electricity. "Are you kidding me?" I shouted, slamming my purse on the desk. "I don't have time for this!" After the usual, exasperating journey through the automated voice prompts, my call to the power company netted me ten minutes on hold listening to the worst music I'd ever heard in my life. When a live person finally came on the line, I was informed that the power would probably be out for several more hours. I hung up and yelled to no one. "Well, that's just great!" The office phones didn't work, we had no heat and I couldn't even brew a pot of coffee. After a few minutes of useless fuming, I decided that it was actually a good thing that I was here instead of Tugg. He didn't need this kind of aggravation.

Needless to say, news of the power outage threw my co-workers into a tizzy as we struggled to figure out how to do business and make our deadlines. Being shy three employees placed a painful strain on our skeleton staff, creating friction and frayed tempers.

With no working computers, Jim typed laboriously on his cell phone trying to put the gymnasium fire story to bed while Al and I dealt with a host of other issues including impatient advertisers crowding into the lobby. Boy, did I ever miss Ginger and Walter. Four hours later, collective shouts of relief echoed through the offices when the lights and computers blinked on. The outage turned out to be a story in itself, having been caused by a hot air balloon getting snagged in a power line west of town. So, we were down to a staff of two after I sent Jim to cover the story. By four o'clock, Al and I finally got a handle on everything and my tension headache began to subside. I pulled out my notebook and checked the remaining items on my list. What I'd really wanted to do all day was tie up the loose ends of my investigation before having to face what I suspected would be a long list of questions by Marcelene at the potluck tonight. I asked Al to cover the phones and dialed the number for Nathan Taylor's father. As I waited for him to answer, I circled the reminder to contact Cal Moreland at the bar in Crown King.

"Hullo?"

"Am I speaking to Stuart Taylor?"

"Yeah. Who's this?"

I told him who I was and the reason for my call. A few seconds of silence followed before his wary, "I don't know what I can tell ya that will change anything. My boy is gone and that's that."

"I'm looking to get a little basic information on you

and your late son for my article." Of course, I wanted a lot more than that, but sensed I needed to proceed slowly.

"I don't want my personal business spread all over the Internet."

"If there's anything you'd like me to keep off the record, I'm happy to do that." He seemed reluctant to talk at first, but I managed to drag out of him that he'd lived in Cottonwood most of his life before moving to Surprise five years earlier and that he owned a small plumbing company. "I understand Nathan had a passion for sports," I said, hoping to segue into the topic I really wanted to discuss.

"Oh yeah. From the time he was a little guy. He loved basketball, soccer, hiking, everything. Got a baseball scholarship to college, but he dropped out after only a year when he got interested in this extreme sports craze. I thought it was just plain nuts. I warned him to stop it before he got himself killed. But, he wouldn't listen. The more dangerous it was the better he liked it. I don't understand what got into him…" he paused, then sounding grim, he tacked on, "well maybe I do. Maybe he needed the adrenalin lift to get through the day."

I could certainly identify with that. He'd provided the opening I was hoping for so I pressed ahead. "I understand from speaking with Jenessa Wooten's mother that he seemed depressed over your recent separation?"

"He was depressed before Brice and I split up," he grumbled. "She made both of our lives a living hell, what with her drug use and whoring around. You'd think she'd at least've had the decency to try and clean up her act for Nate's sake but no! It got worse and worse. We finally had to arrange an intervention and got her into rehab."

"And how did that work out?"

"Things were okay for awhile, but she didn't have no will power. Turns out she couldn't stay away from the drugs and went right back to her old habits after a couple of months." His words hit disturbingly close to home and made me uncomfortable. "She'd disappear for days at a time," he continued, his tone turning bitter, "and come home looking like shit! After a while, she was nuthin' but a stranger to me. But Nate, he'd always forgive her. He was real protective. The counselor called it something but I can't think of the word."

"Enabling?"

"Yeah. That's it. He enabled her bad behavior and she was real conniving to get what she wanted."

He paused and I could hear his uneven breathing. "Next thing I know she'd run off to Seattle with some dude, some meth head probably ten years younger'n her."

"The sheriff told me they've been unable to locate her whereabouts. Do you have any idea where she could be?"

"Last I heard she was someplace up in Alaska. She...she don't even know Nate's dead! Can you believe that? Probably passed out in some crack house right now. What kind of a woman would do that? She ain't even close to the person I married." His voice faltered with emotion. "That person is gone. Gone forever." He tried to disguise the quaver in his voice with a manly throat clearing.

Judging by his distressed tone, it was pretty obvious that the poor guy had a lot to get off his chest. "I'm very sorry about your son's death."

A hesitation followed by a gruff, "Thanks."

"Mr. Taylor, when you loaned your son the camper,

did he tell you where he was going?"

"He was kinda vague. Just that he was headin' up into the Bradshaws with his new girl for a couple of weeks of camping and hiking."

"Did you ever meet Jenessa Wooten?"

"Naw. Sorry to say I didn't. I seen her picture. He was real sweet on her and said he was gonna bring her to meet me but… that ain't never gonna happen…" his voice trailed off.

"Mr. Taylor, do you know if Nathan ever experimented with any sort of…mood enhancers?"

A heavy silence. "Are you asking me if he was doing drugs?"

"Yes."

A protracted sigh in my ear. "Brice was an awful influence on the kid. Got him started smokin' pot with her when he was fourteen. Who knows if she got him to try anything else? After she bailed on us, him and me had some knock-down, drag-out fights about it. I told him he oughta stop or he'd end up just like her."

"What was his state of mind when she left?"

"Pretty bummed out. He quit school. Quit his job. Moped around for awhile doin' nuthin'. Then one of his buddies got him into ridin' his mountain bike along the edge of a cliff and other risky stunts like cave jumping down in Mexico and the Bahamas."

I wondered if Nathan had posted videos of himself online. I'd have to check that out. "Sounds like an expensive hobby. If he wasn't working, where did he get the money for something like that?"

His sharp laugh had a caustic edge to it. "He didn't

get it from me, that's for sure. His grandma left him a little money and he started spending it like water." Then he quickly added the caveat, "Don't get me wrong. I loved my son a whole lot. He was a good kid, but we wasn't too close after he started acting real squirrelly."

Real squirrelly? Did that mean he *was* on drugs? My instincts were probably correct. Most likely he was doing steroids and possibly other mood-enhancing drugs like Mollys to help boost his spirits after his mother walked out. That most likely explained the pills found in Jenessa's pocket. I heard another phone ringing in the background and he said hastily, "Hold on." He was gone for a few minutes and then came back on the line. "Sorry about that. I gotta go unplug a toilet. Anything else?"

"Do you know if Nathan had his cell phone with him?"

"He never went no place without it."

"Did you have any communication from him after he left?" I asked.

"Well, let's see. He did call me once about the BLM giving him grief about a sticker on my ATV bein' expired. I told him I'd take care of it when he got back, but he said they was just gonna rent one up in Crown King."

"Did the sheriff tell you they were unable to find his cell phone, or hers for that matter?"

Total silence while he absorbed my news. "No. Something 'bout that don't sound right to me."

"Jenessa's mother didn't think so either. That's why I'm following up. There are quite a few unanswered questions."

Another very, very long silence. "What are you

sayin'? You think them two kids dying out there in the snow wasn't no accident?" His voice rang with incredulity.

"I have no proof that it wasn't, but I'm not discounting anything until I've completed my investigation."

"Are you some kind of a detective?"

"In a manner of speaking. I always tell people that investigative reporters are simply underpaid detectives. Are you aware that two other people died in that general vicinity within the past year?"

"Mmmmm...I don't think so."

"I talked to the BLM ranger for that region yesterday and also a Forest Service ranger. Both of them had encountered Nathan several times in the past few months. Do you know why he was attracted to that particular area?"

"Because it's dang purty country, that's why. And we had us some really fun times out there over the years deer hunting, fishing, camping and the like."

"Did he ever talk about meeting anyone specific on any of his recent trips?"

"Um...I don't think so."

"Do the names Luke Campbell or Benjamin Halstead mean anything to you?"

"Nope, but since you're lookin' into it, I'm here to tell you that this whole thing don't make a lick o' sense to me. It wasn't like Nate was some green city kid. He was pretty savvy when it come to the outdoors."

"Mr. Taylor, are we speaking on your cell phone?" I inquired, eyeing the time on the wall clock.

"Yep."

"You have my number on your phone now. If you remember anything else that might be relevant, will you please call me?"

"I'll do that."

I thanked him and tapped the END button, feeling both perplexed and vaguely dissatisfied. How interesting that he was having the same misgivings as Marcelene. And Ginger. And me. I fanned through my notebook. It seemed as though I was amassing a mountain of unconnected minutiae that took me nowhere. I tabbed to the Internet and looked up the number for the saloon in Crown King. Following six rings, a woman answered crisply, "Crown King Saloon."

"Is Cal Moreland available?"

"Hang on." I heard her drop the receiver and amid background noise consisting of loud country music intermingled with animated conversation, she screeched, "Cal, you got a phone call!"

A minute later, a pleasant male voice came on the line. "This is Cal."

I went through the same drill, introducing myself and explaining the nature of my inquiry regarding the last evening of Benjamin Halstead's life.

"*Castle Valley Sun?* Well, there's not a whole lot more to say that I didn't already tell the sheriff's deputies. Ben came in here occasionally for lunch or after work and would have a drink and maybe play a couple games of pool. Sometimes he'd just sit and talk with other customers and watch TV. If we had live music, once in a while he'd get out and hoof it with some of the girls."

"I'm interested in the last time you saw him. Did anything out of the ordinary happen? What time of day did he come in? How long did he stay? Did he talk to you or anyone else? What was the weather like...?"

347

"Whoa, whoa, whoa! Slow down! Too many questions in a row. One at a time, please."

"Sorry. Okay, let's start with the last day you saw him."

"Mmmmm, That's been a while ago now, but I'm thinking he came in around four, four-thirty."

"And the weather?"

"I remember it was pretty cold. We'd had some rain and a little snow, but nothing serious."

"Do you live in Crown King?"

"Yep."

"So you don't know the condition of the road that day?"

"Not really. But the place was pretty busy, so I'm guessing people weren't having any particular problem negotiating it. Depending on the weather, it can be treacherous, and believe me, there are times you wouldn't want to be driving on it."

"So I've heard. What did Benjamin do when he came in that evening?"

"The usual. He ordered a drink, talked a little about this and that, had a conversation with a couple of guys at the bar and then he spent the rest of the time playing pool."

"What did he normally order?"

"Sodas mostly. Once in a while he'd have a beer. Nothing stronger."

"Did he say anything that stands out in your mind?"

"Let me think..." Following a few seconds of silence he said, "I remember he was starting to tell me about something he'd seen on one of his hikes, but I got interrupted and...of course I never did find out what it was."

As if to validate his statement, I heard someone shout, "Hey! Any chance I can get a beer down here! I'm dyin' of thirst!"

"Hang on, Roscoe. I'll be right with you," came Cal's rejoinder.

Well, this conversation wasn't netting me anything helpful. "Was he sober when he left? According to the sheriff's report, several witnesses stated that he appeared to be weaving a little like he was drunk."

A hesitation. "That doesn't sound right. I only served him one beer. Listen, I know drunk when I see it and he wasn't. Plus that, I'd be liable if I sent him out of here if he was too intoxicated to drive."

"So…what could account for the witness statements?"

"I don't know. I think I remember him saying his stomach wasn't feeling too good and he felt light-headed, like he might be coming down with the flu or something, but that's all. He was *not* drunk when he left here."

"I see." Might as well wind this up.

"Are we done? I gotta get back to work."

"Anything out of the ordinary happen that night? Anyone in particular stand out? Do you remember who was there?"

"I can't remember everybody who comes in here. We have regulars who live here and others from the surrounding area, but we also get a lot of visitors passing through on their quads and ATVs. We get our share of Snowbirds and lowlanders from the valley too."

"Who would you consider a regular?"

"I dunno. All the townspeople. Local miners, ranchers and the residents of Raven Creek. Our area BLM ranger comes in after work sometimes."

"Yes, I've met Linda Tressick and also Burton Carr."

"Yeah. Burt usually stops in for lunch 'bout once a week. I think he may have been here that night, but I'm not positive."

"So, nothing about that night stands out in your mind? Benjamin Halstead came in, ordered a drink, talked, played pool and then left."

"That's about it. Oh...wait. I do remember one thing different. I had to break up a fistfight between a couple of roughnecks and two of our local boys."

"From Crown King?"

"No, from the McCracken Ranch."

My breath caught in my throat. "Are you talking about the Hinkle brothers?"

"You know 'em?"

"Yeah, we've met a few times." *Another* coincidence? How was that even possible? I thanked him and hurriedly dialed the sheriff's office. "Julie! I need a favor. I don't have time to get over there today to finish reading those two files, so could you scan the tox report on Benjamin Halstead and send it over to me?"

"Sure, give me a few minutes."

It was a quarter after five by the time I got her email. Knowing I still had to stop at the store to buy chips and dip for the potluck, I skimmed through the toxicology report as quickly as I could. Holy flippin' cow! The report showed documented evidence of the powerful painkiller OxyContin in Benjamin Halstead's system.

CHAPTER
27

Deeply troubled and more intrigued than ever, there were so many thoughts knocking around in my head it was difficult to stay focused on the task at hand. Lost in a fog, I locked up, rushed to the store, grabbed a cart and headed down the aisle. I paused in front of the potato and tortilla chips section thinking that I needed to contact some of Benjamin Halstead's friends and relatives to find out more information about him. Had the young man been abusing OxyContin and perhaps other stimulants prior to that night? Or had he, as my Internet research illustrated, been out partying and ingested a dangerous cocktail of drugs and alcohol before driving off the cliff? Where had he obtained the drugs?

After witnessing the alarming conduct of the drug-addled teens in the desert, my own brother's bizarre behavior and what I suspect had been a drug deal going down in Jerome, it seemed a certainty that the Hinkles were involved. Had Benjamin Halstead met them there to make a purchase? Had he taken too much and fallen asleep at the wheel? Or was I reading too much into the fact that the two men just happened to be at the saloon that particular night? Was I using twisted logic to cast blame because I found them repugnant and harbored resentment towards them for providing my brother with illicit drugs?

But was it a coincidence that they appeared to be connected with every single person I had met in and around Raven Creek? And what about their access to the gravel company property? If Jack Loomis was associated with them, was it possible that Luke Campbell had also come in contact with them during his weeks of gathering interviews for his documentary film? And if so, was it conceivable the brothers had been entangled in the strange circumstances surrounding his death? But, how would that have been possible? And the most important question had to be, why? Was there a connection between him and Benjamin Halstead? And if there was, what possible motive could the Hinkle brothers have to silence these two men?

The next thought that popped into my head took my breath away. Oh my God! Could they somehow be linked to the deaths of Nathan and Jenessa? Was it mere coincidence all four people had been found dead within a few miles of Raven Creek? Could that be the key? Or was I way, way out in left field? My supposition sounded logical. The problem was, I possessed not one single shred of evidence to prove it. All I had to go on was the grinding apprehension lodged deep inside me.

"Excuse me. Would you please move your cart?"

Startled, I looked up to realize I was blocking the aisle and had to issue a sheepish smile to the exasperated elderly woman. "Sorry, I was thinking about something…"

As she rushed by with a curt nod, I glanced at my phone. Oh crap! I was really late now. Haphazardly, I chose several bags of chips, threw four containers of dip into the cart and checked out. Still preoccupied, I drove across town towards Marcelene's cottage, wondering why I was so hungry. Then it dawned on me. I'd been too busy to eat lunch.

No sooner had I pulled into the motel parking lot, gathered up the grocery bags and started towards the cottage than my cell phone sounded. Awkwardly, I slid the bags up my arms and fished out my phone. When I saw Tally's name on the screen, my heart did a happy, little dance. "Hey, Cowboy! I was wondering why you hadn't called."

"Sorry, we were out on the Jeep tour. No cell towers in the middle of Monument Valley."

"I'm so jealous I missed it."

He chuckled. "You would have loved every minute."

"I know. How's my dad holding up?"

"He's a real trouper, but I can tell his ankle is bothering him."

I sighed. "I'll bet he's not taking his pain pills again. Poor guy." A sudden gust of wind rattled the plastic bags. "Well, how are Sean and my mom doing?"

Dead air. "They're tolerating each other."

"That means they've been at each other's throats the whole trip, doesn't it?"

"Sort of. Listen, some problems have come up and we're going to have to skip the last leg of the trip to Canyon de Chelly and head back tomorrow morning."

His somber tone sent a pang of concern sweeping through me. "Why? What's wrong? Is it because of the bad weather coming?"

"That could be a factor, but secondary. Got a couple of other problems."

Was I going to have to drag it out of him? "Such as?"

"Ronda left me a message earlier. She's been pushing Ma hard to take her meds. She finally did and overdosed."

Taken aback, I gasped, "You're kidding!"

"Nope. Ronda rushed her to the emergency room and they had to pump her stomach."

"Is she going to be okay?"

"As far as I know. Ronda's there with her now, but she said Ma is raising a ruckus asking for me."

Immediately suspicious, I wondered if this was a deliberate ploy by Ruth to get Tally away from my family and back in her clutches? She was a master manipulator and I would put nothing past the conniving old witch. "Why am I not surprised?"

"Before you get your panties in a twist, you might want to know the second reason."

"What?"

"Your brother's sick."

"Really? What's wrong with him?"

"I dunno. He's blaming the Indian fry bread and says traveling in the car is bothering his stomach."

All the years we'd been together growing up I'd never known him to have motion sickness. Did that mean he would try to opt out of our driving excursion to southern Arizona next week? "I see. Well, what are your plans? Are you coming back tonight?"

"I don't think that's necessary. Ronda's going to stay overnight and everybody's too tired to travel now. I'll let everyone sleep in a little bit and we'll head back right after breakfast tomorrow."

"What time do you think you'll get in?"

"I'm shooting for noon or so. I'll drop your family at the motel and go on to Phoenix."

"We'll probably pass each other going opposite directions on the freeway. I have one more guy to interview in the Bumble Bee area around two. I'm going to invest a few more hours and then I'm done with this story."

"That so?"

"Yeah." Chagrined, I swiftly changed the subject. "Hey, any chance you'll get back in time to meet us for dinner tomorrow at the Barbeque Pit around six?"

"Can't say for sure yet. But that's a good pick. Your family will like the Old West ambiance and the ribs for sure."

"I wonder if Sean will feel up to going."

"I wouldn't count on it. Even if he wasn't feeling sick, I think he and your mom need a break from each other. They had a pretty big blow-up this morning."

"What about?"

"Not sure. I came in on the tail end of it."

"Oh man. Sorry about that."

"Even with the squabbling, I've enjoyed getting to know your family, especially your dad."

"I knew you two would hit it off."

Apparently not willing to let go of my earlier pronouncement he inquired softly, "You glossed over it pretty fast, but I gather your investigation didn't pan out?"

"No, it hasn't. At least not the way Marcelene and Ginger hoped. Granted, I met some colorful characters, but so far I haven't been able to come up with a workable theory or even one miniscule crumb of evidence to prove that what happened to Jenessa and Nathan was not accidental." I blew out a dejected sigh. "Now I have to go in and tell them that I failed."

"I wouldn't say you failed, Kendall. It is what it is. They'll just have to accept the truth."

"It's not like there isn't still a boatload of unanswered questions. Wish I could get the toxicology report from Fritzy now," I lamented, staring up at the brilliant starlit sky, "instead of having to wait months."

"Why so long?"

"She's backlogged with too many cases. Oh well, maybe I'll learn something new tomorrow."

"You're by far the toughest taskmaster of yourself," he consoled me with a chuckle. "You did your best. That's all you can do."

"I'll get over it."

"I know one thing for sure," he added, his tone turning husky, "I could sure use some alone time with you, pretty lady."

His intimate suggestion sent a surge of warmth coursing through me. "Cowboy, you can count on it."

After we exchanged goodbyes, I stood there in the cold night air for another minute, savoring the image of his invitation, then headed for the cottage. I rang the doorbell and was still formulating what I should say when the door swung open. "Well, it's about time you showed up, girl!" Ginger reached out and crushed both the chips and me in an enthusiastic embrace. "Come on into the kitchen. Everybody's been waitin' on ya."

"Sorry, it was a hellish day at work, I got away late..."

"Don't fret none," she said, reaching for the plastic

grocery bags. "Now that Bonnie and Tom are here to help out, guess what?"

I eyed her with puzzlement. "What?"

She treated me to her dimpled, pixie-faced grin. "I'm gonna be back at my desk first thing in the mornin'!"

"Oh, that's great news! You have no idea how much we've missed you."

"I figured that might make your day."

"It sure does." When we reached the doorway, I asked in a low voice, "How's everyone holding up?"

"Well as can be expected. Lot of waterworks around here. I know I've bawled so much I ain't got a tear left to shed right now. It was pretty rough pickin' up Jenessa's car today and just now Aunt Marcelene got a phone call sayin' they're releasing her body to the funeral home tomorrow." Looking morose, she tacked on, "It still don't seem real."

"I know."

She searched my face expectantly. "Did ya find out anything new?"

I was in no hurry to admit I hadn't. "How about we eat first. I'm starving."

"Come on into kitchen. Nona rustled up her famous chicken casserole, I brung that corn bake you like so much and Bonnie's whipped up a snazzy-lookin' salad. Oh! And Brian brought ice cream. I think we can get ya filled up."

"Let's get started."

Bonnie and Tom greeted me with animated smiles and hugs, while Brian called out, "Hey, how's it going?" from across the room. As always, it was a pleasure to visit with their grandmother, Nona, who delighted in concocting a different pronunciation of my name almost every time we met. With her hearing almost gone, she'd pronounced my name as 'candle' at our first encounter and, continuing her tongue-in-cheek tradition, she asked with a merry twinkle in her eyes, "How you doin' tonight, Scandal?"

"That's a new one!" I grinned and bent down to kiss her withered cheek. "I'm doing okay." True to staying in character as a former Broadway leading lady, she wore an over-abundance of blush and sported an outlandish feather hat—both endearing aspects of her playful personality.

While everyone ate and conversed, keeping to light topics like the weather, amusing stories about Bonnie and Tom's baby and the upcoming engagement party, the underlying sadness was palpable as everyone verbally tiptoed around the somber subject matter. For me, conjuring up the image of Jenessa's cold body lying in the funeral home proved to be an exceedingly effective appetite suppressant. After dinner, while everyone pitched in to clean up, with the exception of Nona, who had nodded off in her wheelchair, Marcelene caught my eye. She and Ginger traded expectant glances before she motioned for me to follow them into the living room. Hating to admit that I'd come up empty-handed, I filled them in on what I'd learned, omitting some of the more depressing details. The entire time, Marcelene sat there shaking her head no and when I concluded with a sheepish shrug, she snapped, "I can't be wrong. I am certain that something terrible happened to her. I refuse to accept the premise that it was an accident. I...I feel it right here." She pressed her hands to her middle and her stricken expression turned my heart inside out.

"I do too," Ginger concurred in a tremulous voice, pinning me with a look of mild reproof. "Don't you?"

I threw up my hands in frustration. "Yes! I do! Look, I believe there *is* something weird going on out there, but for the life of me, I can't logically connect whatever it is with Jenessa. And if there isn't any evidence, there's nothing I or anyone else can do. I can't magically create it."

My passionate declaration was met with stone-cold silence from both women. I shrank beneath their disapproving stares, unable to remember being this disappointed in myself, and my abilities as an investigative reporter. Marcelene's crestfallen gaze slid away from mine, but Ginger reached out to pat my knee. "We ain't mad at ya, sugar. And well, we both feel bad about even askin' you with your family here and all, but it's just that we both feel real strong about this and it don't seem like Marshall is taking it seriously."

"He's in the same boat I am. Listen, I haven't given up yet. I'm going out there again tomorrow. I've got one more person left to interview. He's the man who found...the... them. I'm hoping maybe he'll have some new information." I directed my attention back to Marcelene. "If it's okay with you I'd like to go through her room one more time in case I may have missed something. But, I could use your help as well." I repeated my conversation with Stuart Taylor. "He told me that Nathan called him at some point during their trip. Did you have any communication from Jenessa after she left here?"

Marcelene nodded. She called me two...maybe three times."

"From her cell phone."

"Yes."

"Did she say where she was calling from?"

"Not specifically. Out in the forest someplace."

"Did she say what they were doing?"

She massaged the deep frown lines on her forehead. "Um…it was hard to understand her because she kept cutting out, but I know she said they'd been hiking. She said they'd found some Indian ruins with petroglyphs, seen some baby javelinas, deer and some other strange little creatures. I can't remember what she called them…"

"Sugar gliders?" I cut in hopefully.

Appearing surprised, she said, "Why, yes. I never heard of them before. How did you know that?"

So, Daisy had been right. I hurriedly grappled for my phone. "I have some pictures I thought you'd like to see." I told them about Daisy's propensity for photographing everything. "I think these were taken just a few days before Jenessa died and perhaps on one of the days she called you."

Marcelene stared at them with an inscrutable expression, then solemnly handed the phone to Ginger, who blinked back tears before she passed it back to me. Absently, I swiped to the very last picture. Ah yes. The mysterious Stilts. Hoping to spare her sensibilities, I'd deliberately left out his hurtful diatribe. Why torture her further? But, maybe that was wrong. Every possibility should be explored. She would expect that of me. I leaned forward. "There is one more thing. Did Jenessa ever mention meeting a man who calls himself Stilts?"

She drew back, frowning. "Stilts? Not that I can remember."

As I recapped the inflammatory conversation, Marclene's expression of bewilderment switched to horror. Her face turning scarlet, she gasped, "What? What possible reason would that…that *monster* have to say such despicable things about my sweet girl?" Tears flooded her eyes. "He must be insane!" Marcelene grabbed several tissues from a box.

"Well, that's one possibility," I answered dryly. "But, somehow I got the impression that it was more than that. His remarks seemed...calculated and personal."

I turned the screen to face her. "Have you ever seen this guy before?"

Marcelene squinted at the photo and shook her head. "I don't think so. Can you make the face larger?"

"Sure." I expanded his face to fill the screen and handed her the phone again. This time she stared in open-mouthed astonishment and murmured, "Oh my God!"

"What?" Ginger interjected, her startled gaze darting back and forth between her aunt's stricken face and the phone.

Marcelene's breathing was so erratic, I was afraid she might be hyperventilating. She looked up to meet my eyes. "Do you remember the story I told you about Jenessa's friend Kailey?"

"Of course," I replied. "The little girl who drowned at Lake Powell."

She pointed a shaky finger at my phone. "This man looks much older, but I'm 99 percent sure this is her father. John Higglebottom."

CHAPTER
28

Statues. We must have looked like three stone statues, sitting there in frozen wonder. I'm sure I looked especially dumbfounded. Her revelation blew my theory about the Hinkles to smithereens. "Are you positive about this?"

Marcelene let out an anguished wail that made my hair stand on end. "I'm sure! Call the sheriff. This man murdered my daughter!" She sprang from the chair, grabbed my shoulder and I winced when she dug her nails in like cat claws. Her flushed face only inches from mine, she held the phone up and shrieked, "Don't you see? An eye for an eye! He...he...he's punishing me for killing Kailey! He did it! He got even with me by killing *my* little girl!" She shoved the phone into my hands. "Do it! Call Marshall right now! Hurry!"

Her accusation certainly cast a whole new light on Jenessa's mysterious death and sent my imagination skyrocketing. The callous proclamation made perfect sense to me now. And that also explained the G and T on the mailbox. My mind flashed back to Daisy. She'd told me he had a different name but I had put no stock in her odd statement. Why had he chosen to hide out in Raven Creek all these years? And if he had somehow orchestrated that Jenessa die in the same manner as his daughter, how had he carried it out and left no evidence behind?

Marcelene's hysterical screams brought Bonnie, Tom and Brian rushing into the room, and for what seemed like an hour, sheer pandemonium reigned. Everyone talked at once, demanding to know what was happening, while Ginger and I tried to calm the situation. "Aunt Marcelene!" she finally commanded in a kind but stern tone, attempting to slide one arm around the flailing woman, "You gotta calm yourself down! You're scarin' the bejeezus out of everybody!"

Undeterred, Marcelene shook her off. "He killed her! He killed my baby!" Eyes brimming with anguish, she glowered at me. "Tell Marshall to arrest this man for murder!"

Even though I knew calling him would be a wasted effort, I soothed her with, "Okay, Marcelene. Calm down. I promise I will call him."

Her whole body shook with uncontrollable sobs as we all stood there wondering what to do. As her cries grew louder and more frantic, Bonnie burst into tears, Squirt began to howl and the men shrank into the furthest corner watching in helpless horror. Apparently Marcelene's shouts were shrill enough to awaken Nona, who rolled into the doorway and sat in bleary-eyed puzzlement, surveying the chaotic scene. "What the hell is all the commotion about?" she demanded, banging her hand on the arm of her wheelchair.

"Aunt Marcelene is havin' a nervous breakdown." Ginger turned startled eyes on me. "I got some sedatives Dr.

Garcia prescribed for her nerves. I'd best go get one!"

"Better get two," I urged as she hurried from the room.

Ginger finally got her settled down enough to get the pills down her throat, and to everyone's relief, her sobbing began to gradually subside to shuddery moans as we helped her onto the sofa. Poor little Squirt nervously whirled in circles, his little face scrunched in concern while Bonnie clasped Marcelene's hand and Ginger tucked a blanket around her. When I looked around for Brian, I caught him charging towards the front door. I sprinted across the room to intercept him. "Hey, don't go yet! I need your help."

"I don't do family drama real well," he said, his lips twisting with chagrin as he struggled into his jacket. "I'm outta here."

"Wait!" I pulled him aside and explained what I needed.

"If you just need photos and files I can take the hard drive out and connect it to my computer and pull the files off as long as the drive is not encrypted."

"So, I'll be able to log in?"

"Sure. I can run a utility on it that will change the password."

"What about her emails?" I inquired, glancing over my shoulder, relieved to see that Marcelene seemed under control.

"Depends on if it's password protected. Most times it isn't. I can go get it and take it home with me to work on if you like."

"That would be great." Hurrying towards her room, I could hardly wait to pull out the old photo in the nightstand to verify Marcelene's allegation.

When we arrived at the bedroom door, my heart ached at the sight of the lonesome cat still crouched in a tight ball on the floor. "Hello, Fiona," I said softly. She looked up at me and we made immediate eye contact. Approaching with stealth, I knelt down and experienced a mild twinge of surprise when she allowed me to pick her up and stroke her luxurious black fur. Within seconds, her rumbling purr filled the hallway. "What's going to become of this poor kitty?" I murmured as Brian ambled across the room towards the desk.

"I dunno," came his disinterested answer. "Aunt Marcelene's allergic to her long hair and wants to get rid of her."

"Really? That's a shame."

He unplugged the laptop. "Yeah, I overheard her telling Ginger that she's going to have to go back where she came from."

My heart contracted with pity. The cat had obviously bonded big-time with Jenessa and even though I felt certain she would be in good hands with Daisy, somehow returning her seemed cruel.

He grabbed up the power cord and laptop and swept past me. "I'll let you know when I get into the files."

"Thank you, Brian," I said, setting the cat on the bed. "I'm mainly interested in any photos, messages or emails within the past month."

"Gotcha." He disappeared around the corner, and as the same gloomy silence I'd experienced before settled over the room, I made a beeline for the nightstand and pulled out the faded photo. I pointed my phone flashlight directly on it and gasped in disbelief. There was no mistaking that crooked nose, that gangly frame. Marcelene was right. Marshall should know immediately about this embittered, vindictive man who possessed the motive, means and opportunity to have committed this vengeful crime. It was clear to me that he was a man consumed with unending hatred for those responsible for his daughter's death. I could only conclude that the unfinished house served as a reflection of his unfinished life, or perhaps unfinished business?

Deeply disturbed, I took a picture of the print and laid it on the desk before I methodically began to sort through the receipts a second time. I was disappointed when I got to the bottom of the box. I'd found nothing of significant interest. As I was scooping up the papers, I felt Fiona rub against my leg. I stooped to pet her again, and when I did, one of the receipts fluttered to the floor. I picked it up, noting it was the one for Jenessa's new cell phone purchase. I gave it a cursory once-over, thinking that she'd badly overpaid, and was poised to return it to the box when one of the items caught my attention. I stared hard as the significance gradually sunk in. *Jenessa had purchased two phones.* Pausing, I looked up, staring unseeing at the wall. *Where was the second one?* Wait a minute! What if...?

I turned around so fast I tripped over the cat, then executed a series of short hops, careened off the dresser and finally grabbed the bedpost to keep from falling. My awkward ballet sent the poor animal into a panic. Fur puffed, her back arched like a Halloween cat, Fiona streaked under the bed. "Sorry, girl," I called out before dashing towards the living room, my mind whirling. Why hadn't Marcelene mentioned this very important fact? My breath coming in short gasps, I barreled into the room where Bonnie and Ginger hovered over Marcelene. Obviously taken aback by my dramatic entrance, both women gawked at me before Ginger placed her forefinger to her lips.

"I need to talk to her!" I said in an urgent whisper. "Right now!"

Bonnie pinned with me an incredulous look. "You can't. We just now got her settled down."

I waved the receipt in front of Ginger. "Jenessa bought two new cell phones before she left. Do you know where the other one is?" Her blank expression answered my question. I pointed to the sofa. "She's got to have it. I need to find out where it is. Jenessa may have left a voice message, a text or a photo that could pinpoint her location before her phone disappeared!"

The two women exchanged a look of uncertainty before Ginger replied in a doubtful voice, "That can't be right. Marcelene never mentioned nuthin' about havin' a cell phone. And even if she had one, she wouldn't know what to do with it. You know how she is with computer stuff."

Consumed with helpless frustration, I said, "Look. You both wanted answers and this could be it." Ignoring Bonnie's request, I pushed between them and knelt down beside the sofa. Marcelene was totally zonked out. I shook the woman's bony shoulder. "Marcelene, wake up! I have to talk to you!"

"Sugar pie," Ginger whispered in my ear. "Are you sure this can't wait until mornin'?"

"No!" I shook her again. Stirring, her eyes fluttered open and I could tell she was having trouble focusing.

"What? Whaaaat's happening?" she slurred.

"Did Jenessa give you a cell phone?"

Blinking fast, her eyes kept rolling back in her head.

I glanced questioningly at Ginger, thinking the tranquilizers must have been pretty potent. Ginger looked perplexed. "What? Why are you givin' me the stink eye? You told me to give her two."

Sighing, I turned back to Marcelene. "Did she buy you a cell phone? That's all I need to know."

Struggling to keep her eyes open, she licked her dry lips. "I...I...yes, she did. But...I...don't how to use it. She said she'd...show me. But...she's never..." Her eyelids fluttered closed again and I decided it was useless to continue browbeating the poor woman. My blood burning with curiosity, I jumped up to face Ginger.

"We have to find the other phone. Where would she have put it?"

"I ain't a mind reader," my friend complained, her gaze sweeping around the room. "Bon Bon," she said, addressing her sister, "stay here with her, would ya?" And to me she added, "Let's start lookin' in every drawer and cupboard. You take the kitchen and I'll check out her bedroom. It's gotta be around here someplace."

It took fifteen minutes of rifling around the small house but I finally heard Ginger's triumphant shout. "I got it! I got it!" We almost collided in the kitchen as she bolted in and thrust a cell phone into my waiting hands. "I like to have never found it! She had it setting up on top of the TV with the remote."

Eagerly, I pressed the ON button. Nothing. It was only after repeatedly pressing the power button that I realized that the battery had most likely never been charged. "Rats," I murmured just as the cuckcoo clock chirped ten times. Suppressing my agitation, I looked up at Ginger. "Do you know where the charger is for this phone?"

"Oh, good gravy," she muttered, tossing her head impatiently. "Come on, let's both look for it."

Ten minutes later, we found it underneath a stack of magazines. "Listen," I said, wrapping the cord up next to the phone. "I don't have time to hang around here all night waiting for this to charge. I'm going to take it home with me."

"Fine by me," said Ginger, trotting after me as I grabbed my coat and strode to the front door. "You are gonna call Marshall, right?"

"Yes." I hated to tell her that without evidence it would be a futile effort, but I did plan to text him the photo along with Marcelene's suspicion. Armed with the new information, he could decide whether John Higglebottom would now become a person of interest.

Ginger added, "Let us know what you find out."

"Of course."

"Hey, Kendie, we didn't get a chance to talk about the party plans, but," she lowered her voice and flicked a worried look at Marcelene sprawled on the sofa, "I'm workin' on it and maybe we can have a little chat tomorrow?"

Distracted and anxious to get home and charge the phone, I murmured, "Sure, that sounds fine." I hurried out the door, but Ginger ran after me.

"Wait a minute. I forgot to mention something." Even in the deep shadows, I could see her biting her lower lip. "Marcelene wanted to know if you could do her a big favor and…"

Resentful, I turned back to her, snapping, "I know. I heard. She wants me to take Fiona back to the shelter. Personally, I think that's heartless. Why can't you take her home with you?"

She scrunched up her nose. "I'd love to but I can't. Churchill's real territorial. He don't mind the dog, but he sure don't much care for other cats. He'd probably skin the poor thing alive. Why don't you take her?"

"Ginger, I've kind of got my hands full right now. Can't you find someone else to take her in?"

"I've tried. Believe me, I've tried, but nobody wants a three-legged cat."

I stood there mired in indecision for long seconds. "Okay. I'll stop by and pick her up on my way out of town tomorrow. Do you have a carrier?"

"I'll get it out for you." Stepping forward, she hugged my stiff shoulders. "You're a real peach. I'm sorry to lay this on you, Sugar!" Then she drew back, looking chagrined. "I'm just trying to help simplify Aunt Marcelene's life. That cat is a constant reminder of Jenessa. She cries every time she lays eyes on it."

After promising to do it, I revved up the Jeep and headed home bursting with expectation. Would I find anything significant on Marcelene's cell phone? Anxious to find out, I floored it. Fortunately, I didn't meet any other oncoming traffic as I sped through the cold, starry night along Lost Canyon Road. When I reached the house and hurried inside, Marmelade met me at the door, mewing loudly. Flooded with the usual self-reproach for leaving her alone so much of the time, I crooned, "I'm sorry, baby," and lifted her into my arms. "I didn't mean to be so late." Hurriedly, I plugged in the phone and opened a can of cat food. While waiting, I sent a quick email to Tugg explaining what had happened and that I'd need to leave a little earlier than planned tomorrow. Then I sent the photo of Stilts and a text to Marshall. I checked the phone. Still not charged up enough. Impatiently, I stared at the green light in vain before one of my grandmother's old sayings crept into my head. *A watched pot never boils.* Okay. I headed for the shower. By the time I returned to the kitchen, the phone was charged up enough for me to turn it on. Nerves as tight as a stretched rubber band, I tapped the icons. The e-mailbox was empty, of course, but there were three text messages from Jenessa. I checked my calendar. If I was calculating correctly, the first one had been sent near the beginning of their trip. CELL SERVICE TERRIBLE OUT HERE! ONLY HAVE 1 BAR BUT HOPE YOU GET THIS. HAVING LOADS OF FUN! GREAT HIKING. GORGEOUS MOUNTAIN TRAILS! CAMPED BY A LITTLE WATERFALL LAST NIGHT. She'd attached several photos in separate texts. One showed her smiling, wearing a backpack, standing on the edge of a precipice back-dropped by a pine-filled valley spread out below. No telling where the photo was taken, so that didn't really help me. The second one looked to be a selfie, and pictured her and Nathan each making a goofy face. I studied the rocky background, but again had no clue where it had been taken. The third one, also a selfie, featured a smiling Jenessa standing beside Daisy, holding one of the sugar gliders. The photos were disconcerting enough, but when I noticed there was a voicemail message, I instinctively tensed. Oh boy. This would be difficult.

I tapped the screen and listened to Jenessa's message. *"Hi Mom! Did you see... pictures I...you?"* The dropped words confirmed poor cell service. After a few more seconds of silence and several unintelligible words, I made out, *"It's easy!"* The sound of her tinkling laughter cocooned my heart in melancholy. *"You can...it. Tap on...icon and scroll down. Hiked.... moonlight. ....old mine b... we got chased off... some.....trespassing...guys....nd of creepy ....really cold so...leave... early. I love you! Be home soon!"*

I listened to the voice message several more times and my pulse rate ramped up as I interpreted her broken sentences. So, they'd been hiking at night and were chased away from an old mine somewhere. Which old mine? Good grief. The Bradshaw Mountains were pockmarked with hundreds of them. Had they stumbled upon a mining claim on BLM or Forest Service land? But wait. If they'd been chased away for trespassing that meant they'd been on private land. Was it possible that she'd been referring to Harvel Brickhouse, whom everyone described as unfriendly and reclusive? Would he have evicted them from one of his mining claims? If so, I'd be able to pinpoint exactly where they had been the day prior to their deaths. I sent the photos to my cell phone for future reference.

It was getting late, so I finally climbed into bed and lay there analyzing all the events of the past several days that had so far added up to zero. Wouldn't it be great if my luck changed and Harvel Brickhouse was able to provide some significant, breakthrough information? With questions circling endlessly in my head like a flock of ravens, I tossed and turned for a long time. I remember thinking just before falling into a deep sleep that tomorrow couldn't come nearly soon enough.

CHAPTER
29

BIZZ! BIZZ! BIZZ! The irritating buzz of my alarm jolted me awake. I slapped the button to silence it. Marmelade stretched, yawned and planted herself on my chest, purring. "Good morning, you little orange love bucket," I murmured, stroking her soft fur. What a luxury to sleep in until seven o'clock! I turned towards the window and was treated to a spectacular sight. Dawn appeared as a thin, luminescent ribbon of scarlet on the horizon and swiftly spread across the sky, lighting the mountains on fire and painting the desert floor a luscious rose color. The phrase *Red in the morning, sailor take warning*—the time-tested precursor to an impending weather change — flashed through my mind. Instilled with eager anticipation, I threw off the covers and hurried through the morning routine, checking the weather forecast online several times. The report confirmed that a winter storm warning had been issued for the high country with predictions that it would blow in later tonight or tomorrow morning, with expectations of a foot or more of snow at higher elevations and up to two inches of rain in the lower deserts. That would be a bummer for my family, who'd been enjoying the warm sunshine. Hopefully, it wouldn't hang around as long as the previous storm.

If my day went as planned, I'd get back to town in time to meet up with them and Tally for a scrumptious barbeque dinner, providing he could escape the clutches of his wily mother. Dressed in black jeans, hiking shoes and a flannel, emerald-green shirt, I cinched the leather belt with the turquoise buckle around my waist and surveyed my reflection with satisfaction. Good. This way, I'd already be dressed for the evening when I returned from the McCracken Ranch. After a quick breakfast of toast and oatmeal, I hurried out into the frosty morning air and drove towards town, as always, delighting in the stark beauty of the sun-splashed Sonoran desert. And who could find fault with the glorious weather? But as I drew closer to the Desert Sky Motel, my stomach soured at what promised to be another emotional encounter with Marcelene. Considering her fragile emotional state, I feared her distress level would go off the charts when I shared the messages on her cell phone. Did I really want to be present when she listened to the final voicemail from her daughter? What choice did I have? And when I added to that the heartbreaking chore of transporting Fiona back to Raven Creek, I winced. It was all I could do to keep from turning around. But I didn't. Reluctantly, I got out and rang the front doorbell. Might as well get it over with.

Marcelene answered, clutching Squirt in one hand. She looked like hell-clad in a rumpled purple bathrobe, her pinched face colorless, the dark circles beneath her red-rimmed eyes more pronounced than ever. When I stepped inside, the pall hanging over the cottage weighed down on me heavily.

"I want to apologize for my behavior last night, Kendall," she croaked, inviting me into the living room. "I...I guess I got a little hysterical when you showed me that picture."

A little hysterical? "It's understandable. I did text Marshall all the information. I haven't had a chance to touch base with him yet this morning."

Looking glum, she sat down hard on the couch, still holding tightly to Squirt for comfort. I reached into my purse for the phone, but hesitated when she said, "Ginger told me you'd be by this morning to pick up the cat."

"I was hoping maybe you'd changed your mind," I said, struggling to subdue my agitation.

A look of genuine remorse crossed her careworn face. "I know you think I'm heartless, but I'm terribly allergic to her long fur and to be frank, I'm not much of a cat person. She'll be better off someplace else."

Resentment burned my chest. I silently agreed that she was being heartless and waved away her explanation. "I don't agree with your decision, but I promised Ginger I'd do this."

"Thank you."

No point in trying to put it off any longer. Dreading her reaction, I pulled the phone out. "I don't know how much you remember from last night, but...we found the cell phone that Jenessa bought you." I set it on the coffee table. "There are a couple of text messages, a few pictures and...a voicemail from her."

Face blanched ghost-white, Marcelene stared straight

ahead, unmoving, not seeming to breathe for long seconds. She pressed one hand against her mouth and I braced for another round of hysteria. But after a minute or so, she seemed to regain her composure. "She was going to teach me how to use it when she got back," she whispered, barely loud enough for me to hear.

"If you want, I can show you how to access everything."

"Maybe later," came her morose response. "Or Bonnie can do it when she gets back. I don't think I can bear it right now."

I really wanted to go over all the particulars in this strange story, but wondered at this point what good it would do. Marshall would more than likely question Stilts again, but to what end if there was no solid evidence of foul play? And if he had somehow played a part in their deaths, how had he carried it out and left not a scintilla of evidence behind?

"Are you going to be alright?" I inquired, studying her haggard expression. I had never seen anyone look quite as grief-stricken as she did at that moment.

"I don't know if I'll ever be all right again," she answered faintly, bowing her head. "Just so you know, I was planning to have her funeral on Saturday, but because of your engagement party, I'm waiting until Sunday to bury my...sweet angel." her voice cracked and as dismayed as I was with her lack of compassion regarding Fiona, my heart shriveled with remorse, and my earlier exasperation vanished. "That's really very kind of you. And...I'm so sorry about Jenessa and I'm doubly sorry I wasn't able to bring some closure for you. It hasn't been for lack of trying."

She locked anguished eyes with mine. "I know that.

I appreciate you trying and sacrificing this time you should have been with your family." She cleared her throat and swallowed hard. "Children aren't supposed to die before their parents. This will haunt me the rest of my days on Earth."

I couldn't think of a single thing to say to comfort her. "I'll go get the cat now."

She nodded and her empty gaze turned inward. I left her there drowning in her grief, gripping the now-squirming Squirt, who appeared as anxious as I was to escape the somber atmosphere.

Dragging my feet, I made my way half-heartedly towards Jenessa's bedroom. The door was open this time and my throat closed up when I spotted Fiona sleeping peacefully on the bed. The carrier sat nearby on the floor. Oh man! Why had I ever agreed to this? As I approached, the cat's head popped up and when she fixed her luminous eyes on me, I got the distinct impression that she already knew why I was there. I was quickly learning that cats really do seem to possess a sixth sense and noted with wonderment that she didn't object when I picked her up and lowered her into the carrier.

As I drove out of town beneath a cobalt blue sky dotted with wispy white clouds, I kept glancing over at her little face. Was I imagining it, or was it possible for a cat to look heartbroken? I tried to ignore the burgeoning guilt gnawing at my conscience as Ginger's words echoed over and over in my head. *Nobody wants a three-legged cat. Why don't you take her?* I made it all the way to the freeway before I finally caved. Wrenching the steering wheel into a sharp U turn, I doubled back towards Castle Valley. There really wasn't any good reason I couldn't take her. And the fact that she only had three legs made not a bit of difference to me. She seemed like a sweet and gentle cat. Of course, I had no idea how Marmalade would react, but suspected she might actually appreciate having some company. It cost me an extra two hours by the time I detoured to the pet store. I had to purchase another cat box, more litter and food and some new cat toys, but the warm, fuzzy sensation glowing in my abdomen convinced me that I'd made the right decision. When I finally pulled into the driveway, my heart felt significantly lighter.

To be on the safe side, I closed Fiona in the spare room until I could be present for the formal introduction. "Make yourself at home," I said brightly, watching her explore her new surroundings. Being the inquisitive, perceptive creature she is, Marmalade eyed me with intense curiosity when I stepped into the hallway and shut the door behind me. After pinning me with a long, questioning stare, she settled onto the floor and stuck her nose under the door. She knew. I had a strong feeling that they'd be playing "paw" pat-a-cake long before my return. Supremely satisfied, I hopped in the Jeep and resumed my trip alone, guilt-free and relieved that I circumvented the dismal task of having to return Fiona to Daisy's shelter. One less homeless cat for her to feed and care for, and a new friend for Marmalade.

Tooling along the freeway, I used the travel time to complete several phone calls. I filled Tugg in on yesterday's events at the office and then informed him that this was my final trip to the Bumble Bee area for the foreseeable future. When I told him I'd be back at my desk in the morning, his enthusiastic response conveyed that he was pleased by my decision. I hung up and dialed Walter. The welcome news that he was making rapid progress and would probably leave the hospital by day's end sent my spirits sky-high. Hooray! With Ginger back at the reception desk and Walter hopefully back to work by Friday, things were finally turning around in my direction again. For that I sent up a little prayer of thanks.

As I drew closer to the Bradshaw range, it was interesting to note that while the desert landscape was still awash in brilliant sunlight, billowy cathedrals of thunderheads pushed towards the majestic peaks. Would it soon be raining in Raven Creek? At least I wouldn't have to tackle that harrowing road again today. I sighed with relief. One of the best things about living in Arizona was the diverse topography. When winter hit at home in Pennsylvania, it stayed cold and grey and miserable until late spring. Not in Arizona. In a matter of a few hours a person could drive north to ski or play in the snow, then jump back in the car and return to the warm sunshine all in the same day. Heaven!

I zoomed through Black Canyon City and was primed to call Marshall Turnbull when the car phone rang. I glanced at the Caller ID on the screen and tapped the CALL button. "Hey, Marshall, I was just getting ready to call you."

"That so? How're you doing today?"

"Okay. What did you think of the new information in my text?"

"I just hung up from talking to Marcelene about it."

"Are you going to bring him in for more questioning?" I asked, accelerating up the hill past a slow-moving truck.

"We can certainly do that," he intoned thoughtfully, "but like I told her, we have to be able to produce some kind of evidence, even circumstantial, in order to hold him and right now I don't have it. I can't arrest the guy for shooting off his mouth."

"True, but now that you are aware of his background, it does throw a suspicious light on him, don't you think?"

"It could. But, first thing I have to do is verify if he really is John Higglebottom and then we'll go from there."

Beep. Beep. I glanced over at the screen and saw that Brian was trying to reach me. That sparked my curiosity. "Marshall, I've got to take another call. Talk to you soon."

"Sure thing."

I touched the button again. "Brian, what's up?" I asked, easing off the accelerator to turn onto the Bumble Bee exit.

"I got into the emails on her laptop."

"Fantastic! Anything jump out at you?"

"Mmmm, no, but I'm not sure what you're looking for. You want me to bring it by your office?"

"I'm not there right now. Did you check out her Photo folder?"

"Oh, yeah. Lots of 'em. Mostly animals, family, and just...I don't know. Stuff. She took a ton of the black cat. There's a shitload of photos of Nathan and a bunch of selfies of the two of them hiking, biking, riding ATVs...looks like they're at a lake in a couple...uh..."

The pavement ended abruptly and the Jeep bounced along the washboard dirt road once again. "Well, thanks for doing that," I murmured, disappointed. "I was hoping you might find something significant."

"Nothing much interesting that I can see...whoa! This last one's kinda weird."

Senses on alert, I asked, "What do you mean?"

"There's a picture of Nathan leaning against a

humongous rock that someone painted white to look like a human skull."

I frowned. A skull? It took a few seconds for it to come to me but when it did, Daisy's words came rushing back to me. *'I'm scared of the head. Big scary head.'*

For no discernable reason, icy pinpricks of apprehension invaded my gut. "You're sure that's the last photo?"

"Positive. It was the last one uploaded from the Cloud."

"Brian, would you do me a favor and text it to me? Cell service out here is sporadic at best, so, please do it right now. Include the date too."

"Sure. On its way."

I thanked him and searched for a place to pull over. The photo might or might not have any bearing on my investigation. Either way, I was eager to see it. There was no safe spot along the winding road, so I drove on, finally stopping in front of the old stone structure in Bumble Bee I'd passed by several times before.

I grabbed up my phone and swiftly checked my text messages. Nothing new yet. "Come on," I whispered, unable to explain the anxious knot in my stomach. In reality it was only a minute but it seemed like thirty before I heard the familiar chime. I scrolled to the photo and a cold shiver brushed the nape of my neck. No wonder Daisy was scared. The ominous skeleton face painted on the skull-shaped rock was definitely unnerving, but more important was the date the photo was taken. If my calculations were correct, it had been taken the week before the young couple's bodies had been discovered. And if Daisy was correct, the rock was located somewhere between Raven Creek and the McCracken Ranch on property adjacent to the closed road. I studied the photo again. Judging by the soft lighting and long shadows it appeared to have been taken in the late afternoon.

I drummed my fingers on the steering wheel as I absorbed the information. If this was in fact the last photo Jenessa had taken, it confirmed they had been somewhere in that area the last day or two of their lives. I thought about Jenessa's voice message. The closest mine that I knew of located on private property was the old Thunderbolt Mine, now owned by the Raven Creek Gravel Company. My mind created a likely scenario. Nathan, who seemed to have little regard for rules, had ventured onto the property with plans to snoop around the old mine. He and Jenessa had been caught trespassing and chased off by…someone—someone creepy, she'd said. And then…what? How did knowing this make any difference in the scheme of things?

Totally frustrated, I returned the phone to my purse and sped towards the McCracken Ranch. Now that I felt fairly certain of their last whereabouts, what good did it do me? What did I really know? I could wish, I could hope, but there was still nothing solid to connect Jenessa's photo, her voice message and all the other leads I'd gathered over the past few days to any of the four supposedly accidental deaths. And at this juncture, it was highly unlikely that Harvel Brickhouse could add anything to the disjointed mix, so I was probably wasting my time. Why not just turn around and go back to Castle Valley right now and be with my family? Torn, I struggled to make the right decision, but hard as I tried, I could not ignore the shadowy weight pressing down on me. I glanced up towards the charcoal clouds shrouding the mountaintops. The secret had to be up there somewhere. All I needed was one significant clue to break this story wide open.

CHAPTER
30

Powerful, intermittent wind gusts rocked my Jeep and stirred up massive dust devils alongside the dirt road as I resumed my trip towards the McCracken Ranch. Even with the inclement weather now imminent, the joyriders were still out in force. I pulled to the side to allow two couples on quads and a dirty, white Jeep that had been riding my tail zoom by, followed by a dune buggy and a shiny, black pickup that looked like it was traveling a hundred miles an hour. Left in a cloud of choking dust, I flinched with surprised recognition. What? The Hinkles were here again? I no longer believed it was coincidental that they seemed to show up everywhere I went. But I also had no logical explanation for their blatant and continuing attempts at intimidation.

Nerves on edge, I pushed ahead, but had to swerve suddenly when two dump trucks rounded a sharp curve and roared by only inches from me. Good God! Why did everyone feel compelled to drive like it was the Daytona 500 on this road? What was the hurry? I finally reached the cattle guard that marked the delineation between BLM and Forest Service land. Two vehicles facing opposite directions blocking the road caught my attention. Drawing closer, I realized it was Linda Tressick and Burton Carr seated in their respective trucks visiting through the driver's side windows.

At the sound of my approach, Linda looked over her shoulder, while Burton lifted a hand in greeting. She backed her truck up and then, with a cordial wave in my direction, drove past me heading towards Bumble Bee. I returned her wave and then bumped over the cattle guard. As I passed by Burton Carr's truck, he motioned for me to stop. I did so and powered my window down. "How are you today?"

"I'm good." He inclined his head towards the thunderheads towering over the mountain. "I'm surprised you came back today with this big storm brewing. I'm going home now and if I were you…"

Grinning, I cut him off with, "I know. I know. I'm not going anywhere near Raven Creek today. Believe me, I trust your judgment."

His round face flushed pink and he practically preened. "I appreciate that. More than you know."

"You bet."

"What brings you back here today? Still hunting for a headline?"

"This is probably my last trip for a while."

"Did you ever find Harvel?" he inquired, tilting his head to one side.

"On my way to the McCracken Ranch now. I'm hoping to find him."

"Well, good luck." He started his engine. "You take care now." He glanced up at the sky again. "It's going to start snowing here soon. I'd make it a short visit."

"That's my plan." He gave me a friendly salute and drove away. I continued on and, within two miles, first a row of mailboxes and then the first few houses in Cleator popped into sight. Cruising by the dilapidated bar, a cursory glance revealed an old white van, two pickups, a couple of quads and a dark, green Hummer parked in front. I frowned and did a double take, thinking that such an expensive vehicle seemed oddly out of place in this setting. Could it possibly be the same vehicle I'd seen cruising by after I'd been run off the road by the two dune buggies? The one which the driver didn't have the courtesy to stop and see if I was all right?

I drove past the few remaining structures and within seconds the tiny community disappeared from sight. I gunned it along the uneven road towards the heart of the Bradshaw Mountains, anxious to reach the ranch, question Harvel and then get home before the storm front arrived with full force. The repeated chiming from my phone signaled incoming texts, so I finally pulled onto the shoulder. I grabbed an apple from the cooler and chewed as I read the messages. The first one from my dad made me smile. FANTASTIC TRIP! CAN'T THANK U ENOUGH! MONUMENT VALLEY IS AWE INSPIRING. BACK @ THE MOTEL. SEAN'S NAPPING. THINK WE'LL GRAB A FEW WINKS 2. DARN FOOT HURTS! SEE U THIS EVENING. LOVE, DAD

The joyous tingle running through me was tempered somewhat by a pang of disappointment. I felt badly that our phone communication had been nonexistent due to the sporadic cell service. I should have been with them on the trip to share in all the fun. Oh well, no use dwelling on it. I swiped to the second message, from Tally. ON THE ROAD

2 PHOENIX. HOSPITAL PLANS 2 RELEASE MA IN THE MORNING. WILL DO MY BEST 2 MEET U FOR DINNER LTR. LUV U.

All right! My postponed vacation was about to begin. Feeling slightly more optimistic, I slid the phone back in my purse and shifted into drive. No sooner had I pulled onto the road than I heard the familiar roaring whine of an ATV behind me. I flicked a look in the rearview mirror and the shock of recognition made the half-eaten apple stick in my throat. It was the same young guy I'd already encountered three times before. Same hat on backwards, same kerchief covering his face. My stomach went hollow when he accelerated around the Jeep and came abreast of me. I fired him a startled look and sped up. He sped up. I slowed down. He slowed down. Then he swerved sharply towards the Jeep, forcing me to wrench the wheel to the right to avoid a collision. My adrenalin kicked into overdrive, catapulting my pulse rate skyward. What kind of an insane game was this idiot playing? Refusing to be intimidated, I powered the window down and shouted, "What the hell are you doing?" I jammed the brakes so hard I almost skidded off the road. He edged a glance over his shoulder at me, floored it and then flipped me off before he disappeared around the bend.

Breathing heavily, my heart thudding in my throat, I had to forcibly calm myself down before continuing the journey. Was this creep just another nut job, or was there something more sinister going on? Was there any question that the guy was keeping me under surveillance? Why? What was going on? Both perplexed and agitated, I reached over and felt around in my purse until my fingers curled around the holster of my .38. The likelihood of ever having to use it for self-defense had always seemed remote, but now it made me feel just a little safer knowing that I had it as a deterrent, if necessary. All the rules I'd learned in my concealed-carry course paraded through my head as I warily rounded a blind curve. The road ahead was clear, but the faint remains of a dust plume rising from a narrow trail snaking its way into the foothills signaled his whereabouts and afforded me only a temporary sense of relief. My stalker might be gone for the moment, but I had a strange feeling that I'd be seeing him again.

Lost in thought, I almost overshot the entrance to the McCracken Ranch. Slowing, I turned right onto a wide, well-maintained dirt road, and within a half a mile passed a corroded stock tank surrounded by at least a dozen head of skinny brown and white cattle. A quarter of a mile later, a low-slung ranch house came into view. I eased to a stop beside an incredibly mud-splattered red pickup and spotted a man seated on the front porch apparently asleep with a shotgun cradled in his lap. I knew I'd found the right person. Harvel Brickhouse fit Burton Carr's description to a T—salt and pepper mutton chops and a ragged brown hat. A yellow Lab rose to its feet and barked. The man's head jerked up and he surveyed me with a look of curiosity laced with suspicion. I slid out into the chill wind and approached the porch, taking note of three empty beer bottles on the chipped wooden table beside his chair. "Are you Harvel Brickhouse?"

"Who wants to know?" he countered slyly, brushing his hand along the barrel of the shotgun in a mildly threatening gesture.

"Kendall O'Dell. I'm a reporter with the *Castle Valley Sun*. How are you today?"

"Still on this side of the dirt," came his laconic reply while he eyed me with skepticism.

I grinned. "That's always a good thing."

"Whatcha want?"

"To ask you a few questions about the young couple you found near Raven Creek last week," I stated, gesturing westward towards the imposing heights.

"I only got a few minutes," he grumbled, darting a look at his watch.

"That's all I need."

Apparently pondering my request, he sat in silent reflection for a few seconds before asking, "What do ya wanna know?"

The capricious wind whipped my hair into a frenzy as I walked up the four steps onto the creaky wooden porch, but I froze in my tracks when the dog issued a low warning growl. He rested a hand on the dog's back. "It's okay. Go lay down, Willie."

Willie did as he was told, but never took his deep brown eyes off me as I pulled out my phone, scrolled to a photo of Jenessa and Nathan and held it out to Harvel. "Ever seen either of these two people around here?"

He fished reading glasses from the pocket of his sheepskin coat and studied the photo for a long time before meeting my gaze. "I ain't never seen that girl, but I sure seen this young fellah before," he replied, pulling the reading glasses lower on the bridge of his blotchy nose. "I had to run him off after I caught him gettin' ready to do a swan dive down a vertical mine on one of my claims."

"When was that?"

He puckered his lips up until they met the end of his

nose. "Mmmmm…about a month back, six weeks maybe?"

"Any other time?"

A shrug. "Seen him tearing around the hills on his quad a number of times."

I tapped the screen. "Are you aware that these are the people you found in the camper last week?"

His jaw dropped. "No. They…uh…didn't look like…that when I found 'em," he muttered, obviously shaken by my statement.

I relayed all the information I'd learned from Marshall and Burton Carr. "So, you just happened to be riding by on your snowmobile when you discovered the camper, is that correct?"

"Yep. I was checking on some of my equipment after that big snowstorm. I thought it was kinda strange that camper'd been there in the same spot so long."

My heart skipped a beat. "You noticed it prior to last Wednesday morning?"

His thoughtful gaze took on a faraway sheen. "Mmmm. Saturday? Maybe Sunday."

"Really? Weren't you curious as to why it was parked on the closed road? Why didn't you check it out sooner? Why didn't you report it to Burton Carr or contact the sheriff?"

"People camp all over creation 'round these parts," he griped, irritability smoldering in his light brown eyes. "I mind my own business and don't much like folks pryin' into mine." He heaved his bulk out of the chair and stood up with the shotgun clasped in one hand. Burton was right. He was at least six and a half feet tall. Quite an imposing figure.

"What made you decide to stop and check out the

camper that particular day?"

He inclined his head toward the dog. "Willie. He kept sniffin' around it and actin' real strange, whimperin' sort of. I thought maybe someone might be stranded, so I banged on the door and when no one answered I pulled it open and...well...I ain't never smelled nuthin' like that before. Putrid, it was." He paused and swallowed. "The tires was stuck in the mud and snow. There wasn't no way they could've got out. I'm thinkin' they froze to death."

"Not exactly."

His bloodshot eyes reflected surprise when I explained the manner of death. "Carbon monoxide poisoning, huh? Damn shame." He paused and took a swig of beer. "Seems odd one or both of 'em didn't just hightail it down the road. They wasn't all that far from Raven Creek," he ruminated, almost to himself.

"That's the question I'd like answered."

He looked at his watch again and I suspected he was waiting for Percy Cross to deliver his monthly check. When a loud screeching, grinding sound split the air, I looked around searching for the source.

"If you're wondering what that gawd-awful noise is ridin' the wind, it's coming from the rock crushers over at the gravel company," he intoned gravely. "Them greedy bastards never stop. Sometimes they even work at night just to hack everybody off."

His surly tone signified that he was still smarting from losing his bid to re-open the Thunderbolt Mine. I turned back to him, perplexed. Hadn't Jack Loomis told me they closed at five? "You're saying they run the equipment all night?"

He downed the remainder of the beer and placed the bottle beside the other three empty ones before picking up a pack of cigarettes. After several tries with his hands cupped tightly, he lit one and I was glad the wind grabbed the acrid smoke and blew it away from me. "Well, no. I don't hear nuthin' but sometimes I see lights at all hours of the night up there on the hill," he said, pointing to a prominent limestone outcropping. "Sorta strange, if you ask me."

That jacked up my interest level considerably. "You sure it's the gravel company? Moonlight hikes are pretty popular now. We know from a text that Nathan and Jenessa were doing just that not long before the...accident."

A puzzled frown crinkled his sun-leathered face. "Imagine that. You'd never catch me trompin' around the mountain after dark. Too dangerous. Might fall and break my neck."

I thought about Jenessa's injury. Had she fallen during their night hike? My gaze returned to the jagged rocks crowning the hill. I could just barely see the outline of some kind of structure. "What's that up there?" I asked, pointing. "The tall brown thing."

He peered into the distance. "You must be lookin' at what's left of the old head frame. There's an old vertical shaft up there that connects to one of the main tunnels in the mine." His eyes hardened. "Damn John Hinkle's dead hide. If he hadn't leased it to them people I could've pulled a couple million dollars worth of gold out of there."

I stared at him. *An old vertical shaft.* What if...? My pulse quickened. Sounded like just the type of thing that would attract a daredevil like Nathan. I quickly found the photo of the painted skull rock. "This was the last photo that we know of taken by Jenessa before she died. Do you know where this is?"

He pushed the reading glasses higher, focused on the screen and nodded. "Of course I do. Everybody 'round here calls it the skeleton rock. It's just down the hill from the mine," he informed me, pointing to the northwest. "John Hinkle's two boys painted it up like that when they was about fourteen. Bad news, them two."

Unable to keep a note of derision from sneaking into my voice, I remarked dryly, "And still are if you ask me."

His feathery brows edged higher. "You know them Hinkle boys?"

"We've met. Do they still work here at the ranch?"

"Nah. They got a couple quads stored over there in the bunkhouse they ride every so often. Otherwise, they don't have no interest in being here."

"I heard that's why Elizabeth Hinkle hired you to watch out for the place."

At the mention of her name, his rough features softened, and for a fleeting second, his eyes reflected a fierce yearning. Perhaps the rumor that he was still in love with her might actually be true. My insatiable curiosity had me wondering again what had really happened at the Cleator saloon that would have caused him to beat another man to death. That was a story I'd like to hear someday.

"Yeah," he confirmed gruffly, "she can't depend on them to do shit."

It was obvious he had no use for them either. "The foreman at the gravel company told me they come around once a month or so to collect the lease payment."

"Loomis?" He frowned his disagreement. "Well,

that ain't hardly true."

My scalp prickled with irritation. Why would Jack Loomis lie about that? "So, how often *do* you see them around here?"

"Don't know exactly, but I see 'em comin' an' goin' in and out of there more than once a month." He hesitated, then quickly added the caveat, "But then, it's none of my business."

Harvel reminded me a lot of Darcy Dorcett. He didn't want to be known as a gossip, didn't want people prying into his own affairs or carrying tales about him, but like so many people in small communities, seemed keenly aware of just about everything his neighbors were doing. "So, you don't think it's unusual for them to be in this area that often even though Castle Valley is quite a drive from here."

He shrugged indifference. "They been coming here since they was kids."

"So, that would mean they're pretty well-acquainted with most of the people around here, right?"

"Oh yeah. Just yesterday, I seen 'em with their heads together drinkin' a beer with that quack doctor from Raven Creek."

"The holistic doctor?"

"Yeah. Gartiner's his name."

"You mean the mayor?" I quipped.

A derisive sniff. "That's what he calls himself anyway."

"Why do you think he's a quack?"

"I went up there to his clinic in Prescott one time…" he said, pausing to cover a combination belch and hiccup with his fist before continuing with, "I was sicker 'n a dog and all he did was mix me up a batch of herbs and stuff that didn't do squat for me."

Again, I found it curious that the doctor would be so chummy with the likes of the Hinkles. It sounded farfetched, but I detected an aura of evil surrounding the duo. And the fact that they'd befriended my brother really bothered me. I glanced up at the brooding peaks again. Something unholy was going on out here and it bugged the crap out of me that I didn't have time to delve into it. All I could do was try to conclude my present assignment. "Getting back to this photo," I urged Harvel, redirecting his attention to my phone, "Can you tell me how to find this place?"

He inhaled deeply on the cigarette, his eyes straying to the road at the sound of an approaching vehicle. "I can, but you can't git to it no more."

"Why not?"

"Gravel company people put up a fence and gated the shortcut two years ago. It's sure made my life a whole hell of a lot harder."

"Because...?"

"Now, I gotta drive all the way around the mountain and up the long way just to get to my cabin," he groused, gesturing westward toward the snow-dusted peaks.

I shook my head in amazement. "You're kidding. You work here and you're forbidden to use the ranch road?"

Scowling, he said, "They control that end of the property now. I used to go around the first little gate they put up, but they caught me and built a bigger gate 'bout a year ago. One of their guys said he'd shoot me if'n I did it again, so I ain't been over there since." His features scrunched with annoyance. "But, get this, them squirrelly Hinkle boys got permission to use it."

"Why would they need to?"

"To race them quads, I guess." A mischievous gleam entered in his eyes. "But, I can tell you how to get to that rock if you ain't afraid to do a little trespassin'."

"I'll take my chances," I responded, a small flare of anticipation warming my insides.

The roar of the car engine grew louder until Percy "Goose" Cross's hearse eased to a stop beside my Jeep. He got out and walked up to us just as Harvel finished giving me directions. "Well, hello there, purty lady," Goose said, flicking me a conspiratorial wink. "Fancy seeing you here." I returned his secretive grin as he handed Harvel several envelopes. "I'd recommend you head home soon," he advised me, inclining his head towards the roiling grey clouds. "Betcha a dollar to a donut it's already starting to snow up top, so I'm done for the day. See ya!" He turned and trotted to his hearse.

"Yep," concurred Harvel, tucking the envelopes in his coat pocket. "I gotta git down to Black Canyon City." He stubbed out his cigarette, threw all the bottles into a nearby barrel and whistled for the dog to follow him. As I watched Goose back up the hearse, I wondered if Jack Loomis might be right about Harvel being an alcoholic. But was he also a liar?

"Just one more question before you leave," I called after him.

Harvel halted and turned back to me. "Yeah?"

"I'm curious as to how you planned to reopen the Thunderbolt Mine. Jack Loomis told me it's too dangerous to enter and had been boarded up."

He blinked disbelief. "I don't know what that guy is smokin'," he retorted, his face reddening. "You think I'd 've had financial backers if it wasn't safe? I didn't just fall off a cattle truck yesterday. Sure, it was gonna cost some time and money to bring everything up to code, but that mine's been sitting there for a hundred years and now I'm supposed to believe the tunnels caved in within the past three?" He jerked the door open. "That's bullshit."

Obviously one of the men was lying. Surprised by his forceful response, I concluded with, "I appreciate your time."

"No problem." He touched the brim of his tattered hat, let Willie jump into the cab of his truck first and then followed.

I stood there and watched both vehicles disappear into the distance while contemplating what to do next. Logic would dictate that I leave immediately, but a strong premonition glued my feet to the porch. The close proximity of the painted skull rock to the hilltop mine pretty much guaranteed it was the location Nathan and Jenessa had been summarily banished from—by someone creepy, according to her final voicemail. No question that I'd met a number of people these past couple of days who would qualify, especially the two men who had access to the closed road—the Hinkle brothers.

The thundering din from the rock crushers wafted through the air again as I mulled over the new and conflicting information. If the Thunderbolt Mine had been sealed up due to dangerous conditions, what reason would anyone have to be hanging around on the hill in the dark? What would be the motivation for either Jack Loomis or Harvel Brickhouse to lie about it? Conversely, if the mine was indeed still operable, why would gravel company employees be working up there at night? Shouldn't I check it out for myself? At least I would be able to tell Marcelene that, before admitting defeat, I'd done my best to follow up on every possible lead.

CHAPTER
31

I drove north on the ranch road for two miles, turned west and traveled for another mile or so along an unmaintained road peppered with potholes. Harvel had informed me that I would be able to see the skull rock perched on the east side of the hill and that it was within easy walking distance if I chose to trespass. What was that old axiom my grandmother used to say? *It's better to ask for forgiveness than permission.*

Even though I'd already seen the painted rock in the photo, a little shudder forked through me when the hideous face jumped into view. What kind of mind would create something so repulsive? The black empty sockets set against the white face seemed to stare right through me and the twisted, demonic smile raised a host of goose bumps on my arms. And the really disquieting fact was that it looked freshly painted. Sick. The Hinkles were definitely sick.

Less than a quarter of a mile later, I coasted to a stop in front of the infamous gate where a prominently posted sign screamed out: **NO ENTRY! PRIVATE PROPERTY, NO TRESPASSING! VIOLATORS WILL BE PROSECUTED!**

According to Harvel, the distance to the old mine entrance at the top of the rocky mound was less than a mile from the gate. I'd best not waste a minute.

Serenaded by the song of the relentless wind whipping through the mesquite, scrub oak and nearby palo verde trees, I prepared for my hike, gathering my down jacket, gloves and stocking cap. Primed to get out, my gaze strayed to the creepy-looking skull face and I stopped. How sane was it to wander off alone with a winter storm bearing down? It had always been my nature to be impulsive. I had never shied away from entangling myself in perilous situations in order to scoop an intriguing story. I thrived on the challenge, endorphins and adrenalin rush. I loved it. It was a high like no other. But, should I permit my zeal to overrule common sense?

I pulled my hand away from the door handle, unable to understand my sudden hesitancy. Did this inexplicable restraint have anything to do with the fact that I was engaged to be married now and should begin thinking twice before charging into possibly dicey circumstances? Was Tally's calm logic and quiet urging to examine my priorities beginning to rub off on me? Should I follow my heart and check out the old mine or use my head and go home? With a deep sigh of disappointment, I made the decision to pack it in.

I turned the Jeep around and headed towards the Bumble Bee road. Whatever was going on out here would have to keep until another time. I'd no sooner passed through Cleator than I heard the familiar drone of quads. I flicked a startled glance in the rearview mirror and sure enough there he was again—my stalker. But this time he had an accomplice who wore an evil clown mask. "Are you kidding me?" I murmured as a feeling of dark certainty consumed me. They had obviously been waiting for me. My apprehension increased when I stepped on the gas. My stalker stayed right on my tail while the second rider sped past me and stayed right in front of me. If I'd had any doubt that someone wanted me out of town, I no longer did.

Part of me wanted to stop and confront them. But how wise would that be? I couldn't really even report it because I had no idea of their identities. It wasn't against the law to wear a mask. Could I prove they were harassing me and not just having a little fun? "I'm leaving now!" I shouted. "You can stop following me!"

But they didn't. I was escorted all the way to the freeway on-ramp. Their mission accomplished, they swung around and vanished around the curve. Grimly, I promised myself that at some point I'd return and delve into this baffling story again. I'd driven no more than a mile when my phone rang. I glanced at the caller ID, surprised to see my mother's name displayed. She hardly ever called me on her cell phone. "Hi, Mom. How are you?"

"Not good." Her clipped tone put me on alert.

"Is Dad all right?"

"Yes, yes. He's finally sleeping."

"You sound upset. What's going on?" I pressed.

"It's your brother."

"Oh my. What's he done now?"

"He's gone."

A little tremor of concern raced through me. "What do you mean he's gone?"

"I mean he's *gone!*" came her harsh reply. "Disappeared. After Tally dropped us off we had a huge fight." She paused, then added, "I can't handle these wild mood swings any more. He acts like someone I don't even know."

"Mom, you do realize he's got a drug problem, right?"

"Don't you think I know that?" she informed me, her voice raising an octave. "Sean said he's got a job offer here and he's not coming home."

"A job offer? That's crazy! Doesn't he have to go back and face charges?"

"Of course he does!" She fell silent for a few seconds, and when she spoke again her voice quavered with emotion. "If he skips out on bail it will disastrous! He'll be in even worse trouble and the authorities will send a bounty hunter after him. He's going to ruin your father's reputation!" she shrieked, her voice breaking. "And...this could ruin us financially."

"What do you mean?"

"We borrowed money and mortgaged the house to post his bail."

Furious with my brother's rash behavior, I listened to her heart-wrenching sobs. "Hang in there, Mom. I'll be back in an hour and a half. He can't have gone far on foot."

"He...he wasn't on foot. I saw him come out of his room with two men. He was stumbling around and talking gibberish. They all left together in a pickup."

A sickening stomach plunge. Breathlessly, I asked, "What color was it?"

"What?"

"The truck! What color was it?"

"Black."

"What time did they leave?"

"I don't know. Maybe one-thirty." Plaintively, she added, "Where could he be? We're worried sick about him."

And with good reason. Who knows what kind of a drug he'd taken this time? My heart ached remembering the horrific stories I'd read online describing the fate of teens and young adults who had experimented with unknown combinations of illegal drugs. Some had ended up in a coma while others suffered a horrible death. The memory of the Hinkles' pickup streaking past me on the Bumble Bee road flashed through my mind. "Don't worry, Mom. I have a pretty good idea where he might be."

Amped up on adrenalin and not really sure what I was going to do, I took the Black Canyon City exit, crossed under the freeway and reversed course back towards the McCracken Ranch, my thoughts churning madly. Was there any doubt that the only job the Hinkles could possibly offer Sean would be dealing drugs? Everything seemed to point in that direction. And there was no question someone didn't want me there snooping around. It was a well-known fact to law enforcement agencies that there was an abundance of people cooking meth in isolated communities all over Arizona. I had no doubt that I'd witnessed a drug deal going down in Jerome on Saturday. If the Hinkles were running a lab someplace, how did that involve the gravel company? Is that what Nathan and Jenessa had stumbled across? Without proof it was pure speculation, but seemed a likely scenario.

My brain was on overload, sifting through all the clues I'd garnered since first hearing about Jenessa. I tore along the Bumble Bee road for the second time that day and stared up at the misty peaks. "What is it?" I whispered. "What am I missing?"

And then all at once the answer to the puzzle hit me like a sharp blow to the stomach. "Holeee crap!" It had been in front of me all along—the common denominator linking the four supposedly accidental deaths. They had all been in the vicinity of the Raven Creek Sand and Gravel Company and *they had all stumbled upon something they weren't supposed to see.* My heart began to thump erratically and I broke into a cold sweat. If Jack Loomis was lying about the status of the Thunderbolt, then the nocturnal activity at the vertical mine became a key element. There had to be something more than rock crushing going on out there. And with the Hinkle twins involved, I had a strong suspicion it must be drug-related. Did that explain the lights on the hill at night? Were they hosting desert rave parties to serve copious quantities of illegal substances? Then another thought occurred to me. What if the victims had taken photos of something incriminating? Would that explain the missing cell phones and the blank memory card taken from Luke Campbell's camera? My mind swam with possibilities. The more I thought about it, the more my insides burned with excitement. But, this time I would be smart. No running willy-nilly into danger as I'd done on my last four assignments. This time I would keep the solemn promise Tally had extracted from me and alert the sheriff *before* striking out on my own.

I pressed my phone button. "Call Marshall Turnbull." It rang four times and went to voicemail. Damn! I left a voice message explaining where I was going and then called his office. Julie answered tersely, "Sheriff's Office."

"It's Kendall. Is Marshall in?"

"No."

"How about Duane?"

"They're both out investigating a fatal accident on 89. A wrong-way driver plowed into a family in a minivan. Two of the kids were killed. They're going to be a while."

"That's terrible." I chewed my lower lip for a few seconds. "Well, when Marshall is available tell him I think he should check out the Raven Creek Sand and Gravel Company. There's something weird going on there."

"What?"

"I don't know. But it's possible there may be some connection to Jenessa Wooten's death. He should get a search warrant."

"Can you be more specific?"

"Uh…no."

Silence. "Well, he's got to show probable cause to get it. What is he looking for?"

"I'm not sure yet." I must have sounded lame. I checked the time on the dashboard. Less than two hours of daylight remained.

"So, what do you want me to tell him?" Julie persisted with an undertone of impatience entering her voice.

"It's just a guess, but the Hinkle brothers may be running a meth lab or something there."

"Okay, I'll tell him."

"Thanks, Julie."

One thing I knew for certain. I couldn't drive through the front gate of the gravel company, so I'd do the next best thing and sneak in the back way. I retraced my route to the ranch and when the gate appeared, I pulled off the road and maneuvered the Jeep into a secluded grove of scrub oaks. Armed with my .38 in one pocket of my jacket and my phone and car keys in the other, I slipped through the barbed wire. I was now officially trespassing. I zigzagged my way up the steep rock-and-cactus covered hill, keeping an eye on the advancing clouds that had finally snuffed out the sunlight, casting dark shadows over the mountain. The swift plunge in temperature had me zipping the jacket up to my chin as the first snowflakes pelted my cheeks. But I hardly felt them. Seething with fury, heat radiated throughout my entire body. I could gladly strangle Sean for his irresponsible behavior. He couldn't possibly be in his right mind to think he could skip out on bail and ignore the fact that he had serious charges pending against him back in Pennsylvania. But then, if he was wasted on whatever drug he was experimenting with now, he probably wasn't thinking rationally.

Within minutes I arrived at the painted skeleton rock. It was gigantic and downright spooky up close. What I hadn't seen in the photo or from my vantage point below was the multitude of expletives, lewd pictures and satanic symbols carved into it. Repulsive. Nauseating. Hideous. No question. The Hinkle brothers bordered on psychopathic. Little wonder Elizabeth didn't want them anywhere near her and why everyone else referred to them as bad news. And now they had lured my drug-addled brother into their seamy clutches. At that moment I loved and hated Sean equally. What a friggin' mess he'd caused!

My heart pounded with exertion as the hill grew steeper, but I could now clearly see the splintered wood on the old head frame looming above the limestone rock outcropping. I sprinted the last few hundred yards and arrived at the mouth of the old mine, which was liberally sprinkled with warning signs to stay away. A makeshift chain-link fence surrounded the dark hole. I moved forward for a better look and that's when I heard a whining roar from behind that turned my blood to ice water. Oh my God! For precious seconds indecision held me immobile before I got my mushy legs to cooperate. I broke into a run, frantically searching for a hiding place, finally flattening myself to the ground behind a thicket of mesquite bushes nanoseconds before an off-road vehicle rumbled to a stop. Laughter and masculine shouts reached my ears. With a stab of alarm, I recognized the familiar voices of the Hinkle brothers. Would they hear my tortured breathing? Did I dare even look up? I had to. Ever so slightly, I raised my head and had to stifle a horrified gasp at the sight of my brother seated in the quad with the two men. Sean looked completely out of it, his face ghostly white, his eyes glazed and unfocused. Danny and Daryl hopped out, but when Sean tried, he stumbled and fell to the ground like a rag doll and flailed about, speaking gibberish. The Hinkles turned to glare down at him. "The dude's not supposed to be sampling the shit, he's supposed to sell it!" Danny stated in a disgusted tone, eyeing his brother coldly.

Daryl gave him a sideways grin. "He's really trippin' out on it."

"How much did you give him?"

"Hey, don't blame me. I told him it was something new and to go easy."

Danny's upper lip curled into a sneer. "You dumbass! The big man is coming today. We can't have this guy checkin' out on us or we're gonna be up shit creek!"

"It was your idea to bring his ass here, not mine,"

Daryl shot back, punching his brother in the shoulder.

Danny swiped his hand away. "You better keep an eye on him. Come on, we gotta get this stuff unloaded." He pulled a box from the floor of the quad, shoved it under one arm and handed another one to Daryl before moving a section of the fencing aside. "Bring him over here," he demanded curtly.

"Come on, bro, get it together." Daryl reached down, dragged Sean to his feet and pushed him towards the mine opening, where Sean teetered dangerously on the edge. It took every ounce of willpower I possessed not to jump up and race to his side. Danny leaned over and yelled into the opening, "Catch!" then dropped the boxes. Then he climbed down into the hole and reached up to grab Sean's arm, shouting, "Put your foot on the ladder, dude!" Working together, the Hinkles managed to pull him down and then all three of them disappeared from sight. I had never felt so utterly helpless.

The snow was coming down heavier now and for another few minutes, I laid on the ground, shivering from dread as much as the cold. What kind of drug had they given Sean? Had they been seriously discussing the possibility that he might die? I waited another few minutes to see if they'd return, then cautiously rose to my feet. The knowledge that Sean was in grave danger made my heart shrivel in horror. Stiff from the cold, I ran to the edge of the mine opening and peeked down. I couldn't see anything, but could hear the hum of what might be a generator operating below. A peculiar odor wafted up the shaft along with the echo of masculine laughter. What was the right decision? Storm down the ladder and try to rescue my baby brother or run for help? Torn, I crouched in the fierce wind for another minute before deciding it would be sheer insanity for me to play the hero. No. Not this time. I had no idea what I'd be getting myself into if I followed him down the mineshaft. I took a few deep breaths of the icy air. I must not panic and do something stupid. Call! Call for help. I sprinted further up the hill, pulled off one glove, dug out my phone and dialed 911. Nothing. I wiped the snow off the screen and my heart sank. CALL FAILED. I dialed again. Nothing. I must be in one of the dead zones. Now what? I turned and charged downhill in the blinding snow, slipping and sliding, gasping for breath, trying to suppress the sobs rising in my throat. I had to get to the Jeep. I had to get help.

I figured I was about half way down when I saw the skull rock, barely visible in the blowing snow. And then my toe struck something. I pitched forward, my phone flying from my icy fingers. I landed hard and crashed into a rock or tree stump. I could actually hear the sickening crack of my arm breaking. For I don't know how long, I lay there in a daze and then pushed to my knees. I'd never had a broken bone before. I expected to feel pain, and perhaps it was the adrenalin or the freezing cold or both, but strangely all I felt was numbness. It was more disturbing to me that I'd lost my phone. Groping on the ground, I searched around for it, but with more than an inch of snow already accumulated I knew I was wasting valuable time. Forget the phone! Get to the Jeep!

I tucked my left hand into my pocket for support and continued downward, moving a little slower now, finally feeling the dull throbbing in my arm. What a boneheaded move that was, O'Dell! The bare outline of the open gate brought a measure of relief, but it was short-lived. Fear coiled around my heart when the dreaded sound of more quads met my ears. *Get to the Jeep!* With nowhere to hide, I made a mad dash towards the trees, fumbling for my keys. Behind me, the whining drone grew to a deafening roar and then deadly silence before the thud of footsteps. "We got ourselves a trespasser!" came a triumphant shout. I pushed myself as hard as I could, but the footsteps were now directly behind me. All the air rushed from my lungs when powerful arms wrapped around me.

"Take your hands off me!" I screamed, struggling mightily, jabbing my attacker in the ribs with my right elbow, struggling and kicking until we both went down. I face-planted on the snowy ground. Pinned down, his added weight on top of me generated a searing pain in my broken arm so intense it brought tears to my eyes. *Don't pass out!*

Grunting and panting with exertion, the man wrestled me onto my back and straddled me. Gasping, I looked up into the face of a young guy probably around my age. The futility of my dire situation came home to me when a second man appeared and stared down at me with a malevolent grin. "Well, lookee who we got here." He reached down and whipped my stocking cap off. "You should've stayed gone!" I squinted up through the blowing snow, almost certain I was seeing my stalker's face for the first time without the kerchief. He was actually not bad-looking. A pity he had such menacing dark eyes.

The first guy rolled off, grabbed my injured arm and yanked me to my feet. "Come on. We're goin' for a little ride," he announced, tightening his grip. Nauseated from the blinding pain, I swayed dizzily trying to gather my wits. And then I remembered the gun in my jacket pocket. Everything seemed surreal, like a scene from a movie, like it was happening to someone else. I needed to keep a cool head. Perhaps a show of bravado would put them off balance.

"A lot of people, including the sheriff, know I'm here, so I'm not going anywhere with you two freaks," I replied firmly, sliding my right hand into my pocket. But just as my finger curled around the trigger, he jerked my arm and slammed me against the quad.

"You're lying! Get in!" he shouted through gritted teeth.

My stalker jumped behind the wheel and revved the engine. It was now or never. There was no time to pull out my weapon and take steady aim like I was accustomed to doing at the shooting range. There wasn't even time to pull it out of my pocket, so I just turned and fired a round through my jacket. His face a frozen mask of dumbfounded rage, my attacker released me and lurched backwards.

"She shot me!" he shrieked, clutching his thigh. "The bitch shot me!" He slumped into the snow, moaning. Inanely, I marveled at how red his blood looked against the pristine white snow. I turned towards my stalker, but before I could fire off another round, he leaped from behind the wheel and knocked me to the ground again. I lost my grip on the trigger. In a frantic fight for my life, I bit, clawed and kicked. Teeth bared, his face contorted in rage, he punched me in the jaw, then followed up with a vicious bare-knuckled blow to my temple and a second to my left eye. A kaleidoscope of stars exploded in my head. And then he had his cold hands around my throat, squeezing hard. Desperate for air, I fought valiantly to remain conscious, only vaguely aware that another vehicle had arrived. My vision already blurred, the landscape began to spiral in a circle. I knew I was going to die, but I was too weakened to fight him off. Black. Everything was going black.

But then I heard a masculine voice shout, "Stop it, you fool!" and my stalker released his hold. "Get him out of here!"

I gulped in deep breaths of the blessed cold air and tried to move, but the combination of searing pain in my arm, jaw and head was so severe, I felt myself losing consciousness.

"Drink this," said the kindly voice, cradling my head. I swallowed the hot liquid gratefully. He stroked my hair. "Don't worry. I won't let you suffer."

What? What did that mean? My ears were ringing so loud I couldn't quite recognize the voice. It sounded familiar. Who was it? I strained to open my eyes, but my lids felt massive. It didn't matter. I was saved. I welcomed the blissful peace washing over me, the ebbing of pain. On some level I was aware of being carried by someone and lying on something soft and being warm again. I had the sense of being in a different place, a strange place, a hazy awareness of movement, of a lightness of being. Euphoric beyond anything I had ever experienced. I was flying now, soaring high above brilliantly colored hills that shone like jewels, deep valleys and shining streams among a flock of black ravens. I had wings! How cool was this? I wouldn't have minded staying there forever, but then, the dream was interrupted by the sound of new voices, this time muffled and far away as if spoken from another room. I tried to understand, but the words made no sense. Was I hallucinating? I simply could not put a cogent thought together, so I gave up and faded into a comforting, velvety soft abyss.

Time. I was aware of the passage of time. Again, I struggled to open my eyes and when I finally managed to crack them open a slit, I fought to understand where I was. I wasn't outside in the snow anymore. I was lying in a small, dimly lit room made of rock. Rock walls. Rock ceiling. Where was I? How had I gotten here? I couldn't seem to differentiate between the mishmash of distorted memories, dreams and reality. Why did I feel so woozy and disoriented? I slept again for an indeterminate amount of time and when I awoke again my mind felt clearer.

My insides trembled as the memories of my attack came rushing back full force and the dim recollection of someone coming to my rescue. Sean? What had happened to Sean? I heard the rustle of clothing and, instinctively sensing danger, closed my eyes again. I turned my head slightly at the sound of footsteps passing by my head and peered through half open lids. Golden light poured through an arched doorway illuminating a man's silhouette. I remained perfectly still, feigning unconsciousness, but almost gasped aloud when he stepped into the next room and the light struck his face. My rescuer was none other than Burton Carr.

CHAPTER
32

Shockwaves coursed throughout my body when it dawned on me where I was. For confirmation, I reached out and felt the cool rock wall. So, this was the interior of the old Thunderbolt Mine. I was lying on a blanket. Rolling onto my side, I pushed myself to a sitting position, noting with alarm that I no longer had my coat, which meant no gun and no car keys. Had they found my cell phone? I stayed motionless for a while trying to clear the fogginess from my head.

My arm throbbed dully along with my head. I waited for another wave of dizziness to diminish, gently massaging my sore jaw and temple before slowly rising to my feet. I held onto the rock wall for support, then tiptoed to the doorway and paused, listening. I could hear voices, movement and faint music. I wrinkled my nose at the sharp, distasteful odor. What was that? Warily, I peeked around the corner into a massive chamber and as my gaze swept from right to left and back again, it took a few seconds to absorb what I was seeing. Spellbound, I gaped at the stacks of storage containers, cardboard boxes, plastic buckets, gallon containers of chemicals, detergents, plastic bags and gloves, cans, tubes, packing materials, bottles, pans, cooking materials. Holy cow! My hunch had been right. I'd hit the mother lode all right, but it wasn't gold. Spread out before me were all the ingredients needed to produce large quantities of black market synthetic drugs. In fact, it looked like a veritable supermarket for the mass production of street drugs. This was it. The mountain's hidden secret and the motivation for the deaths of four innocent people who'd ventured too close to the truth—a homegrown drug cartel. I eased back around the corner, breathing heavily, trying to stave off my growing panic. I was now a witness as well. In the murky light, I frantically searched the room looking for an exit. Nothing. Nothing but solid rock. How was I going to get out of here alive? It was difficult for me to imagine that Burton Carr was the unscrupulous brainchild of such a vast operation. He seemed so passive, so compassionate. He could have easily stood by while my stalker strangled me…and then suddenly the words whispered in my ear right before I'd blacked out reverberated in my ears. *Don't worry. I won't let you suffer.* The hot drink! Grimly, I realized he'd drugged me. So that's what it meant to 'trip out.' I'd definitely been given some sort of psychedelic drug along with a painkiller. What had he given me and why had he spared me? Why bring me here? I dug deep inside, mining for inner strength, battling the overwhelming fear crushing my heart. Please God! I needed the courage to find Sean and somehow execute our escape. I stifled the sobs building in my throat when I thought about my beloved Tally, my parents, cherished friends and my precious cats waiting for my return. I had so much to live for. *Don't give up!*

Footsteps coming my way. Pulse galloping erratically, I hastened back to my original spot, lay down and closed my eyes. Heavy steps crunched near my head. Someone was standing over me. It took a herculean effort to keep my breathing shallow and my eyes closed. A kick to my left shoulder sending spasms of pain sizzling through me, but I remained limp. "Stupid bitch is still out."

I recognized Danny Hinkle's grating voice. I dared not move a muscle or blink.

"What are we gonna do with her?" It took extraordinary willpower not to react when I recognized the voice of my would-be killer.

"I dunno. I'm sure Darren has a plan. He'll figure out what to do. He always does."

I tensed. Darren? Where had I heard that name before?

"What about her shit-for-brains brother?"

"The dude's of no use to us now. He's a goner anyway. Come on."

My heart thundered like a thousand drums pounding in my head. Where was Sean? What had they done with him? Again, I waited, my stomach constricted into a hard, cold ball for their footsteps to fade away and then with no workable plan in mind, I stealthily made my way across the immense chamber only to realize that there were tributary tunnels leading off in all directions. I had no clue as to which one would lead to freedom. I flinched violently when a harsh voice from somewhere to my right boomed, "I've had it with you screw-ups!" I ducked behind a stack of boxes and ever so carefully peered around the corner. Inside an alcove, the Hinkles and my stalker stood watching a tall, slender, nice-looking man wearing a white shirt and dark tie, pace back and forth behind a paper-strewn desk. He raked a hand through thick, light-brown hair and turned to face them, his eyes flaming with anger. "You assured me that she was gone!"

"Sorry, Mr. Pomeroy. We chased her clear to the freeway this time, but she keeps coming back," my stalker complained, glowering.

"I'm out of patience with all of you. I can't afford any more mistakes."

"It wouldn't be a problem if Burton hadn't interfered," the younger guy retorted, folding his arms defensively.

"I am surrounded by inferiors!" he railed, throwing his hands up. "So you don't think her being found strangled would have raised any red flags?"

Following a brief silence, Danny Hinkle helpfully suggested, "Why not have Burton devise another accident? His ideas worked out great for all the other ones." His pleasant conversational tone chilled me.

"It's not that simple," the man fumed, resuming his lion-like pacing behind the desk. "Too many people know she's been out here asking questions. No one is going to believe another accidental death so soon after those two kids."

"All anyone will know is she came out here looking for her brother, took a header down one of the shafts and broke her neck," Danny chimed in, appearing mightily pleased. "Problem solved!"

Hearing them ruthlessly discussing my death in such blasé terms had me close to hyperventilating. More aware than ever of my predicament, I felt like a cat teetering on the edge of its ninth life. *Keep it together*, I warned myself, trying to control the waves of panic slapping at my sensibilities.

The man stopped pacing and pinned the three men with a glacial stare. "There are a host of reasons why I'm in charge and you're not," he said succinctly. "Now get out of my sight, all of you! I need to think."

I stood stone-still as the three men trooped by and then heard him shout after them, "And tell that spineless brother of mine to get in here!"

As I waited in the shadows with bated breath, the magnitude of his statement slowly sunk in. OMG! Darren Pomeroy was Burton Carr's stepbrother, the prominent Phoenix attorney and, by his own admission, apparently the head honcho of the illegal drug trafficking operation.

Moments later, Burton Carr strode across the room with a look of steadfast resignation on his face. Involuntarily, I shrank back as far as I could into the shadows, but my slight shift of weight moved one of the boxes. He paused and glanced in my direction. Intense fear clawed at my senses when our eyes locked. I know my heart didn't really stop, but it sure felt like it. This was it. I was dead.

He ran one forefinger across his mustache and then vertically along his lips in an almost imperceptible movement, then continued towards the makeshift office. It took my panicked brain several seconds to realize he was signaling me to be quiet. A couple of long, deep breaths helped restore a modicum of calm. Positive I'd been granted at least a temporary reprieve, I checked to make sure the other three men weren't around, and then edged a look around the corner again.

"Sit down! We need to talk," Darren commanded in

a brusque tone, pointing to a white, plastic chair.

"Don't patronize me. I'm not one of your underlings," Burton shot back, setting his stance. "And stop undermining me in front of the others."

"It's your own fault. That woman is dangerous. Your stupid decision to bring her here has created an unnecessary crisis. So," he said, rubbing his palms together, "your job tonight will be to arrange an unfortunate accident for Miss O'Dell. A very tragic accident." He steepled his fingers together and rolled his eyes upward in a cynical display of thoughtful consideration. "What about this option? She slipped and fell into one of the rock crushers." His self-congratulatory smile was positively diabolical. "Or perhaps she fell down one of the vertical shafts? You're the expert on death. I'm sure you'll come up with something creative."

Overwhelmed with a staggering sense of danger, I knew I should be running for my life, but could not pull myself away from the drama unfolding before me. Eyes ablaze with hatred, Burton set his jaw and stated quietly, "It's over, Darren. No more killing."

Darren placed both palms on the desk and leaned forward, his expression deadly. "It's a little late in the game for you to suddenly grow a pair."

"She was nice to me," he said, ignoring the insult. "She showed me a little respect, which is something you've never done."

His stepbrother's eyes narrowed to slits. "You simpering weasel. Don't ever think that you can defy me, or I'll make sure everyone knows what you did."

"You don't scare me anymore. I'm at peace with myself now."

"Tell that to the judge and see how far it gets you," came his mocking rejoinder. "I can hear you pleading now. Your honor, I didn't physically kill those innocent people, someone else actually carried out the deed. All I did was devise the methods to make it look like an accident. You think any jury is going to believe that? Especially when they find out you murdered your poor, dear mother."

Burton glared at him. "She begged me to help end her misery and I found a way to do it humanely." He shook his head sadly, continuing in a placid tone, "You are cruel and coldhearted. You don't possess an ounce of decency. Gabriel shared that information in confidence and you betrayed it. You've tortured me with it for three years, but not anymore."

"You've been well-paid, little brother."

As I stood listening to Burton's calm narration, the strangest feeling flowed over me. My mind raced back to last Friday night. I was almost a hundred percent sure these were the two men I'd overhead arguing in the parking lot of the Rattlesnake Saloon. The leaden apprehension in my gut convinced me that I was hearing more than an exchange of words. *He wanted me to overhear this conversation.* I was witnessing his confession.

"We're not brothers and I'm finished doing your dirty work."

"You're finished all right," Darren jeered. "You won't last a week in prison."

Burton shoved both hands in his coat pockets. "I will never go to prison." His words had a ring of serene finality about them. "But you will." I inhaled a startled breath when he pulled his service revolver from his pocket and aimed it squarely at Darren, who at first appeared taken aback before his lips curled in sardonic amusement.

"You pasty-faced momma's boy. You don't have the guts to look me in the eye and…" The remainder of his sentence was aborted when Burton fired three times, aiming his shots strategically. One shot to the right shoulder, one shot to each thigh. Screaming with astonished rage, Darren collapsed to the floor writhing in pain. When the Hinkles and my stalker raced into the big room, Burton turned and fired in their direction. They scattered like frightened cats. Then he calmly emptied the remaining bullets into his hand and laid the gun on the desk. Ignoring the stream of expletives pouring from Darren's lips, he announced softly, "The sheriff is on his way. Rot in hell." With a smile of supreme satisfaction, he turned, made brief eye contact with me, and then vanished into the tunnel.

CHAPTER
33

The powerful snowstorm blew itself out by Friday morning, but the firestorm of controversy in regards to the astonishing discovery of the clandestine drug lab was just heating up. Because the investigation was in its infancy and the justice system tends to move at a snail's pace, I knew it would be months and perhaps years before all the salacious details of the extraordinary story would come to light.

Burton's Carr's body wasn't discovered until late Thursday afternoon and only then because of Daisy Dorcett's annoying persistence. True to her compulsive nature, she'd been out walking in the storm the previous evening photographing snowflakes when she'd seen his truck heading up the mountain towards the closed Forest Service road. She'd hurried home to tell Darcy, who had at first blown her off, but after hearing the news the next morning, began to take her sister seriously and reported it to the sheriff. She'd also told him that three years earlier, Daisy had tried to tell her that Burton Carr had killed his mother but she'd dismissed it as nonsense.

After fleeing the Thunderbolt Mine, Burton Carr had returned to the abandoned fire tower where he'd spent his happiest days as a child and taken his own life. Apparently carefully planned in advance, he'd mixed up a cocktail of lethal drugs and gone to sleep. He'd left behind a detailed suicide note confessing his limited, but deadly involvement and implicated his stepbrother as the ringleader of the sophisticated, synthetic drug manufacturing and distribution operation. He'd also provided the names of the other minions and saved incriminating documents and photos. The vexing question of the missing cell phones was also answered when authorities found them hidden in a metal box that acted as a Faraday cage, blocking the electromagnetic waves and thereby making it impossible for the phones to be tracked.

The Hinkles, my stalker, his accomplice, Jack Loomis, four of the truck drivers and a number of employees at the processing plants in Mesa and Tempe were apprehended. Within hours, the revelation was the top story on every Phoenix radio and television station, major Internet news site and social media. Darren Pomeroy remained hospitalized in stable condition but refused to speak with detectives after retaining counsel. His uncle, Dr. Gabriel Gartiner, surrendered without incident and was cooperating with the authorities, most likely in hopes of wrangling a reduced sentence. But, as happens all too often in cases where the perpetrators take themselves out, it's difficult to fully reconstruct the whole picture or to ever know their true motivation for committing the crime. Instead, everyone is left to speculate unless confessions or additional physical evidence is obtained. I thought about all of these things as I struggled to cobble together the most disturbing and convoluted story of my career based on facts emerging over the past forty-eight hours.

Only minutes before Marshall, Duane and reinforcements from the Yavapai County Sheriff's office stormed in, I'd finally located Sean lying in a narrow, dank passageway, cold and unresponsive. Anguished tears blurred my vision as I frantically checked for a pulse. I massaged his arms and legs to increase circulation and sent up a prayer of eternal thanks when he jerked and moaned weakly. After wrapping him in the blanket that Burton Carr had kindly provided for me, I stayed with him until help arrived. He and Darren Pomeroy were transported to the Maricopa County Hospital in Phoenix by ambulance because high winds and low visibility prevented a helicopter landing. By the time I'd finished giving my statement to Marshall, officials from the DEA Task Force rolled in. Tally came rushing in amid the myriad of flashing lights, his dark brown eyes reflecting deep concern. When I hadn't shown up for dinner, he'd phoned Marshall, only to find out he'd already been called to the area. "What the hell happened here?" Tally demanded, surveying my disheveled appearance. Following a brief rundown of the disturbing situation, he lectured me on my penchant for getting myself in trouble and then spirited me away for medical attention.

The six inches of accumulated snow in the mountains, coupled with driving rain and fog in the lower desert regions, created hazardous driving conditions on all the roads, making the trip to Castle Valley much longer than expected. The painkillers Burton had forced down my throat were wearing off and I felt like I'd been run over by one of the gravel trucks. Since my cell phone was still lying somewhere on the snowy hillside, I used Tally's to let my parents know that I was all right. After hearing some of the harrowing details, both of them were understandably upset. My mother admonished me for my over-the-top heroics, babbling something about the 'Wild West' but when I told her about Sean, she fell silent.

"He was in real danger," I stated firmly. "I didn't have much choice." I made a second phone call to Ginger, explained the circumstances and asked if she could drive my parents to Phoenix to be with Sean.

"I knew it! I knew you'd get to the bottom of it. Now, don't you fret, girlfriend!" she exclaimed excitedly. "I am on this."

With the exception of bruises on my throat, a knot on my head and confirmation of my broken arm, Dr. Garcia pronounced me in excellent physical shape. But he also gravely added the caveat that I was damn lucky to be alive. I couldn't have agreed more.

Later that night, after a meal and hot shower, Tally enfolded me in his arms and held me for the longest time. "Good God, Kendall, that was a close call. I'm glad you had the presence of mind to use your weapons training." He pulled back and cupped my face in his hands, his eyes probing deep into my psyche. "No question in my mind that you are one amazingly gutsy lady, but I don't think I'm going to let you out of my sight for awhile."

I had to acknowledge to myself that the ordeal had shaken me more than I cared to admit, even though I thought I'd made every attempt to do things right this time. I'd told everyone where I was going, fulfilled my promise to Tally by informing law enforcement, had my .38 for protection and still, I'd gotten myself into a precarious predicament. Was it worth the sky-high adrenalin rush? Perhaps it really was time to reevaluate my priorities. A Pulitzer Prize awarded posthumously wasn't exactly what I'd had in mind.

My dad phoned the following morning to tell me that Sean was expected to make a full recovery. They'd had a serious heart-to-heart talk with him, and he had agreed to consider rehab. After having experienced what would be my one and only psychedelic trip, I had a new insight on why he'd been drawn into that lifestyle. Why not feel that good all the time? "All we can do is pray he actually does it," I told my dad. "There is no guarantee rehab will be successful unless he truly wants to get sober and stay sober."

"I agree. But he was pretty upset when I told him the high price you paid to rescue him. I think that may have been a factor in him agreeing to do it."

Ruefully, I looked down at my left arm encased in the pink cast. "Yeah, that was a little bigger enterprise than the run-of-the-mill meth lab I was expecting to find. But I went with my instincts just like you always told me."

My dad was quiet for extended seconds before saying gruffly, "I'm really proud of you, Pumpkin. If it hadn't been for this damned foot, I'd have been there with you."

"Mom's not too happy about my decision to tackle it alone and neither is Tally."

"Let's not dwell on that. You were doing your job, you got through it, got your story and kiddo, you've got more courage than most men I've met during my lifetime." It was heartening that the two most important men in my life had the same thought. "Thanks, Dad," I replied, my throat closing with emotion. It was a somber moment so I lightened it with, "We'll be quite a pair with our matching casts at the party tomorrow night."

Ever the optimist, he said brightly, "And we're going to dance the night away celebrating if it kills us, right, Pumpkin?"

"Ginger has promised it will be a one-of-a-kind evening, so yes, I can hardly wait to see everyone."

"That reminds me, we got a note from Tally's mother apologizing for her bad behavior at the barbeque. We accepted it, so I'm guessing she's going to be there."

As usual, the mere mention of Ruth sent a shiver of irritation waltzing down my spine. "Crap! I was hoping she'd stay home. She's hot one minute and cold the next. There's never a dull moment with that woman around. Let's hope she's properly medicated, and we have to keep her away from the champagne."

My dad chuckled. "The Starfire is a pretty big place. Maybe you could talk Tally into building your new house an additional ten miles further away."

"Not a bad idea. Well, I've got to get this story filed before I leave. See you later, Dad!"

By the time the staff assembled for our editorial meeting later that afternoon, my conversations with Marshall had netted additional evidence that helped tie up a few loose ends. A search of Burton Carr's home in Mayer had shed some light on his mental and emotional state and yielded more information regarding the deaths of Luke Campbell, Benjamin Halstead, Jenessa and Nathan.

"Gaawd damn it!" Walter exclaimed, shaking his head in amazement. "I eat one bowl of rotten chili and miss out on all the excitement."

I eyed my cast. "And a broken arm."

"Yeah, but the upside is you got the byline on one hell of a story," Tugg crowed, clapping his hands together. "I swear the headlines you provide are keeping this paper afloat."

I grinned my appreciation and looked around the room at the expectant faces of my treasured co-workers and friends, once again thankful to be alive. The only missing faces were Tally and Ginger. Tally had agreed to pick up my brother Patrick, his family and my cousins at the airport in Phoenix and transport them to the Desert Sky Motel while Ginger had left early to finalize arrangements for the engagement party.

"So, let's hear all the juicy details," Walter demanded eagerly, appearing pale and noticeably thinner since his illness. "You said this guy Pomeroy was a kick-ass rich lawyer. Why get involved in such a risky venture?"

"Money. More money than he could ever make practicing law or from all his legitimate real estate investments. He very cleverly drafted paperwork to make sure that this endeavor would never lead back to him by setting up several interlocking LLCs listing front men as the owners of the gravel company, the processing plants and the two trendy nightclubs in Scottsdale, which by the way, is where he met the Hinkle brothers. They were already dealing on the side and it didn't take Darren long to figure out how lucrative it could be on a much larger scale. Danny Hinkle hooked Pomeroy up with one of his contacts who worked closely with one of the cartels in Mexico."

"If Pomeroy isn't talking," Tugg remarked, "how do they know this?"

"Sheriff's detectives obtained a signed confession from Daryl Hinkle, who is the weaker of the twins."

"So, if the lawyer was getting the goods from Mexico, whose idea was it to set up shop in that old mine?" Jim asked, twirling a pencil between his fingers.

"Pomeroy's. And I have to admit it was a brilliant scheme." I went on to explain how ramped up security at the Arizona/Mexico border was making it more and more difficult for the cartels to get their loads into the States. Increased arrests and confiscation of large amounts of contraband by Border Patrol units and other federal agencies were affecting Darren Pomeroy's supply, and he began to worry that the escalating network of contacts could eventually lead back to him. "That's when he came up with the ingenious idea of producing the stuff himself," I said. "But he needed to find a location way off the grid. The Thunderbolt Mine proved to be the perfect solution. He was already leasing the property for the sand and gravel operation and had been able to safely transport the drugs hidden beneath the rocks in the trucks. When they arrived at the processing plants in Mesa and Tempe, which he also owned, the drugs were unloaded, distributed to the dealers and sold to customers at his nightclubs and smoke shops. It was a foolproof plan. Because he was operating a legitimate business *within* the United States, who would ever have reason to inspect the truck loads for drugs? Now all he needed was someone with a background in chemistry to formulate and tweak the various compounds. He knew his uncle was a free spirit, a big proponent of medical marijuana, a user himself, and had no quarrel with other people using controlled substances to enhance their quality of life. Apparently, the doctor was also enriching himself by dispensing the illicit drugs through his clinic in Prescott along with his own herbal blends."

"Pomeroy is one smart cookie," Tugg commented astutely. "But, I thought you said he and Burton Carr were at odds. Why were they working together?"

I shared the details of the heated exchange I'd overheard in the mine, adding, "Dr. Gartiner is also a big proponent of assisted suicide. He loaned Burton the book *Final Departure*, which outlines various methods people can use to…check out, so to speak. Burton chose to suffocate his mother with a plastic bag."

The three of them stared at me in open-mouthed shock. "Ouch," Walter finally managed to murmur. "That guy was one sick puppy."

I shrugged. "Complex, that's for sure. Strange as it sounds, if he hadn't been a super-sensitive guy, I wouldn't be sitting here right now."

"Yeah, a real sweetheart," Jim observed with a hint of sarcasm. "Crying over a deer and yet able to kill his own mother and those innocent people. Kinda twisted logic. Sounds like Dr. Jekyll and Mr. Hyde to me."

"Good analogy."

Appearing confused, Walter asked, "So, why do you suppose he let you live?"

I gave him a solemn look. "He saw me hiding in the corner, but he didn't give me away. I think he wanted me to hear his final confession. Maybe it was his shot at redemption or his way of making sure his stepbrother got taken down. Who knows? Burton was terrified he'd be sent to prison, so to save his own butt and justify his actions, he devised ways to humanely do away with the witnesses knowing that if Pomeroy and his toadies got hold of them it wouldn't be pretty." I looked up at my captive audience and tacked on, "Speaking from my recent experience, I believe he was right. These people are every bit as ruthless as any of the Mexican drug cartels."

Tugg leaned forward, one brow arched in question. "Correct me if I'm wrong, but how does a guy getting stung to death by bees qualify as humane?"

"That puzzled me from the start. According to Daryl Hinkle's confession, he claims the first death actually *was* an accident. Apparently they caught Mr. Campbell trespassing on the property taking pictures of the Hinkles' rock artwork, but they didn't know what else he'd seen and decided to lock him in the modular toilet until they could figure out what to do with him. Daryl swears he didn't know there were bees inside and when they found him dead the next morning, they erased the memory card in his camera and just left him there until he was discovered two days later. When his death was ruled accidental, that set the paradigm. Should any other incidents occur in the future, the deaths would appear to be accidental. Nothing happened for nine months until Benjamin Halstead began asking questions about unusual activity he'd witnessed near the vertical mine entrance while he'd been hiking."

"Why did they use the entrance on the hill to transport supplies?" Tugg asked, drumming his fingers on the desk. "Why didn't they just bring 'em in the main gate?"

I consulted my notes again. "Apparently not all of the employees at the sand and gravel company were aware of what was going on inside the mine. It was a legitimate business by day, and at night the drugs were concealed in the trucks for transport the next morning."

"Clever," muttered Tugg. "So who slipped the OxyContin into the Halstead boy's drink?"

"Daryl Hinkle claims it was Burton Carr, but then he's no longer here to defend himself. It could have been any one of them, but there's no way to prove it now. It was pretty simple to make his death appear accidental, but pulling off the deaths of Jenessa and Nathan was a lot more complicated."

All three of them leaned forward in anticipation. "So tell us how he did it," Jim urged.

"I don't have all the answers yet," I replied. "But, I've got an inside source who tells me that sheriff's detectives found more incriminating evidence at Burton Carr's house today and he's promised to share some of it with me tomorrow."

Jim's blue eyes twinkled with mirth. "And that inside source wouldn't happen to be the charismatic, got-the-hots-for-you Duane Potts, would it?"

I gave him a sly grin. "Possibly."

CHAPTER
34

True to his word, Duane Potts did provide me with most of the answers to the mystery of how Burton Carr had cleverly orchestrated the deaths of Jenessa and Nathan when he contacted me with the disturbing facts on Saturday, just hours before Tally was scheduled to pick me up for the engagement party. "Thanks, Duane. Would you scan that last document you mentioned to me?"

"I sure will," he agreed amiably before adding in an insinuating tone, "I'll be expecting at least one dance with you this evening. A nice, slow song."

Good grief. The payoff. Oh well, I could survive a few minutes of his unwanted attentions to get what I needed.

"As long as your wife doesn't mind." Without waiting for his response, I hung up and glanced down at my injured arm with a rueful smile. The cast would prevent him from having much bodily contact and for that I was thankful. I was thankful for so many things—the emotional reunion I'd enjoyed with my family the previous evening, the warm sunshine pouring down from an electric blue sky and the fact that my furry feline companions had bonded much faster than I'd expected and now lay close to each other on the couch. My heart swelled with happiness knowing that Marmalade would never be lonesome again and Fiona's sad vigil outside Jenessa's bedroom door was over forever.

The chime on my phone alerted me to Duane's email and as I read over the document, I shook my head in disbelief, realizing that without it no one would have ever figured out how the young couple had actually died. I checked the time and sent Tally a text asking him to come by a half hour earlier than planned. Marcelene deserved to know as soon as possible that her instincts concerning Jenessa were correct.

The evening sky was ablaze with fluffy lavender and gold tinged clouds when Tally arrived looking more handsome than ever in his well-cut, black western suit, polished boots and black felt hat. The original dress I'd bought especially for the occasion still hung in my closet because the sleeves were too narrow to wear with my cast. Ginger had jokingly suggested that I cut the left sleeve off, but instead, I opted for wide black velvet slacks and a sleeveless peach-colored top. "Not exactly the outfit I had planned," I sighed, as he draped my coat over my shoulders.

He turned me to face him and eyed me appreciatively from head to toe. "You look mighty fine to me, Miss O'Dell. In fact, that pink cast is pretty damn sexy," he murmured, leaning in to plant a warm, sensuous kiss on my lips. As always, his touch sent a fiery tingle coursing through my veins and I thanked my lucky stars that I had found this exceptional man. In a gallant gesture, he hooked his arm through mine, led me outside into the cool, desert air and helped me into his truck. On the way into town my emotions fluctuated wildly between exhilaration, anger and sorrow as we discussed the tumultuous events of the past week. The ordeal had left me both physically and emotionally drained, and now I had one more uncomfortable stop to make before I could relax and celebrate.

"Are you okay with my mother being there tonight?" Tally asked with a note of hesitancy.

"As long as she behaves herself," I answered before adding coyly, "Sean is going to be there too. Are you okay with that?"

His sidelong glance held a spark of mischievous humor. "As long as he behaves himself."

I couldn't resist smiling. "Touché."

We rode in companionable silence until the Castle Valley city limits sign popped into view. "I thought your folks already had a ride to the community center?" Tally asked, turning off the highway.

"Ginger and my mom have been there for hours." I checked the time on my phone, adding, "And Brian should have already picked up my dad and Sean."

"So why are we stopping at the motel?"

Sighing, I answered, "I've got news for Marcelene and I want her to hear it from me before I file my story on Monday."

He raised one dark brow. "Is it so important that you have to tell her right now?"

"Yes." I shared the information I'd gotten from Duane and his expression grew somber. "All things considered, I'm a fortunate man to still have you sitting here next to me."

I beamed him a loving smile. "I was just thinking the

same thing about you."

We pulled into the motel parking lot just as the sun vanished behind the jagged purple mountains, leaving in its wake a brilliant sky of molten cinnamon sprinkled with chocolate gold-rimmed clouds. For a long moment, we both sat staring in reverence, savoring the magnificent tapestry of colorful splendor, before I finally turned to him. "Do you want to come in with me, or have I injected enough drama into your life for a while?"

After hesitating a few seconds, he said, "I think I'll wait here." He reached over to push my door open. "Don't be too long. Half the town is waiting for us."

"Gotcha. Fifteen minutes." I hurried up the steps, rang the bell, and when the door swung open, Marcelene gaped at me in surprise.

"Kendall! What are you doing here? I thought you'd be at the party by now." She dropped her gaze. "I apologize for not attending. It's just that..."

I knew she was remembering that Jenessa would have been playing the piano for our celebration. "No need to apologize," I said softly. "I have something to tell you. May I come in?"

"Of course." Squirt rushed up to greet me, making little grunting noises and twirling excitedly in a circle as Marcelene led me into the darkened living room, turned on a table lamp and gestured for me to sit. "I feel terrible about your arm," she fretted, pulling the Pug into her lap. "Please believe me when I say that if I had known for one minute you were going to be in harm's way, I would have never..."

I interrupted her with, "I'll be all right. Listen, I want you to know that your suspicions regarding Jenessa were correct."

She inhaled sharply and pressed a hand to her breast. "I knew it. My baby was murdered. It was John Higglebottom, wasn't it?" Her breathing was so ragged, her complexion so pale, I was afraid she was going to faint.

I reached out and touched her knee. "No, it wasn't. He had nothing to do with what happened. He's just a bitter old man who chose to hide away in Raven Creek, and if Daisy hadn't brought Jenessa to his place to buy honey, we wouldn't have ever known he was there. I'm afraid it's much more diabolical than simple revenge. The forensics team and sheriff's detectives still don't know all the details, and more facts will come to light as the investigation progresses, but if you're up to hearing it, I can tell you what I've been able to piece together so far."

She took several shuddery breaths and listened intently as I gave her a brief synopsis of the clandestine drug lab, Daryl Hinkle's confession and the information contained in Burton Carr's suicide, before adding in the new findings provided by Duane. "Daryl Hinkle stated that Jenessa and Nathan were caught trespassing near the vertical mine entrance and witnessed them delivering supplies. The Hinkles chased them off and that's probably when Jenessa fell and broke her ankle. Danny reported the incident to Darren Pomeroy, who decided he couldn't chance them telling anyone what they'd seen."

"Dear Lord," she whispered, her eyes reflecting horrified anguish.

"We don't know where they went or where they camped during the night," I continued, "but we do know they returned their rented quad to Crown King the next day and picked up their camper. Burton Carr wrote in his suicide note that he'd intercepted them with news that the road was shut down due to an accident and offered to show them a shortcut. That's when he led them to the closed forest service road, where he knew they'd get stranded in the muddy ravine. He closed and locked the gate behind them, so that's why they weren't found until last week."

One hand pressed to her mouth, Marcelene's eyes swam with tears as I continued. "It's pure speculation as to what happened from this point because there are no eyewitnesses, but sheriff's detectives believe this was his blueprint." I pulled the article Duane had scanned for me from my purse and as she read it her eyes bugged out. It told the story of a couple who had cooked dinner on their charcoal grill and when they'd finished, had placed the lid on the grill to extinguish the coals, then set it underneath their camper and gone to bed. Sometime during the night, the coals had rekindled and the couple died from carbon monoxide fumes penetrating the floor of the camper. "It's believed that Burton returned sometime during the night on foot and carried out the exact scenario described in this story. Afterwards, he placed the grill inside their camper, making it appear to have been a tragic accident. We can't know for sure, but it's my guess that he probably planted the drugs on Jenessa to make it appear that they were impaired when the decision was made to use the charcoal grill for heat."

"Oh my God," Marcelene whispered. "What kind of a monster would do something like that?"

"They are all monsters," I said grimly, then leaned forward and took her cold hand in mine. "I didn't want to upset you, but you needed to know how she really died."

Weeping profusely, her voice overflowing with emotion, she hugged me and thanked me profusely for risking my life to restore her daughter's reputation and bring her some peace of mind. I left the cottage with mixed emotions. On the one hand I felt gratified that I'd helped put her mind at ease, but my heart ached for her. She'd looked forlorn and lost sitting there in that dark room clutching the dog for comfort. The timing wasn't the best and I had a hard time pumping myself up for the party as we traveled through town towards the community center where we found the parking lot jammed with cars and pickups.

In my high emotional state, I got a little misty-eyed when I noticed that Ginger had outdone herself decorating the outside of the building with colored lights strung along the eaves and wound around the branches of the trees and bushes.

"Pretty snazzy," Tally commented as we walked towards the red brick building. Lively music from the band, excited voices and laughter wafted out as we reached the double doors where Ginger had taped two red hearts with our names written on them. A warm blanket of affection wrapped around my heart. I really was blessed with life, with love, with cherished friends.

Tally took my hand. "Well, my beautiful bride-to-be, are you ready to celebrate?"

"Yes, I am." I looked up into his dark eyes brimming with affection and happiness radiated through every fiber of my being. "And my handsome husband-to be, I know I'm not the easiest person on earth to live with, but I hope you know that I love you with all my heart, and how important it is to me that you be happy."

"I am happy."

I squeezed his warm, calloused hand. "Are you sure you're going to be okay taking on my dysfunctional family?"

He tilted his head to one side and squinted at me quizzically. "You sure you're going to be okay taking on mine?"

Grinning, I held up two fingers. "I promise I'll do my very best."

He stepped close, enfolded me in his strong arms and kissed me until I was breathless. When we drew apart, he pushed the door open and fixed me with that endearing, crooked smile. "All right then. Let's do this."

We hope you enjoyed
FORBIDDEN ENTRY!

If you did, would you take a few minutes to
share your thoughts with us?

_____

_____

_____

_____

_____

_____

We also appreciate reader comments posted on your
favorite online bookseller's website.

I purchased the book at _____

_____

Also, if you would like to receive information regarding
future publications by this author, please return this card or
e-mail us at: **Niteowlbooks@cox.net**

Name_____

Address_____

City_____State_____Zip_____

E-mail:_____

Mail to: Nite Owl Books, 2850 E. Camelback Road #185,
Phoenix, Arizona 85016-4311

Phone: 602-840-0132   Fax: 602-277-9491

Books are available through retail book outlets,
online bookstores and our website:
www.niteowlbooks.com